BOY LIFE ON THE PRAIRIE

Frontispiece

BOY LIFE
ON THE PRAIRIE

by HAMLIN GARLAND, *1860–1940.*

Introduction by B. R. McELDERRY, JR.

University of Nebraska Press
Lincoln and London

The Introduction by B. R. McElderry, Jr., appeared in slightly different form as *"Boy Life on the Prairie*: Hamlin Garland's Best Reminiscence," in *The Educational Leader*, April, 1959 (XXII, 5-16). It is reprinted here with the kind permission of *The Educational Leader* (now *The Midwest Quarterly*).

The Bison Book edition of *Boy Life on the Prairie* reproduces in full the first edition published by Macmillan in 1899. It also includes an introduction addressed "To My Young Readers" and "Author's Notes" which appeared in the 1926 edition published by Allyn and Bacon.

Library of Congress Catalog Card Number 61–16185
International Standard Book Number 0–8032–5070–3

Most recent printing shown by first digit below:
7   8   9   10

INTRODUCTION

In 1917 Hamlin Garland published *A Son of the Middle Border,* the first of the four-volume Middle Border series. From the point of view of a man in his middle fifties he told the story of his life from 1860 to 1893: his birth among the coulees of southwest Wisconsin, the family removal to the prairies of northeast Iowa, the hardships and pleasures of country life, his schooling, his self-education in Boston, his early literary success with *Main-Travelled Roads* (1891). The chronicle closes with his purchase in 1893 of a home in West Salem, Wisconsin, his birthplace, to which he persuaded his elderly parents to move back from South Dakota. The broad scope of this book has overshadowed an earlier and better book of reminiscence dealing specifically with Garland's boyhood experiences on an Iowa farm from 1869 to about 1881. When he wrote *Boy Life on the Prairie* (1899) [1] Garland was much closer to the subject than he was in 1917, and he had the advantage of a more restricted aim: to tell directly and specifically what it was like to grow up in northeast Iowa in the years just after the Civil War. It may safely be said that no one else has given so clear and informative an account. When one considers other accounts of boyhood in nineteenth century America—those of Aldrich, Clemens, Warner, and Howells,[2] for example—one is impressed with the thoroughness and precision of Garland's book. Aside from *Main-Travelled Roads, Boy Life* is probably the best single book that Garland ever wrote.

In the original "Preface," reprinted without change as late as

1922, Garland stated that *Boy Life* grew out of a series of articles written in 1887, intended to record the way of life he had
known. *Boy Life*, however, is not an autobiography. It "is not
my intention to present in *Lincoln Stewart* the details of my
own life and character, though I lived substantially the life of
the boys herein depicted. I have used *Lincoln* merely as a connecting thread to bind the chapters together" (p. vi). The
"Preface" to a later school edition of *Boy Life* (1926) acknowledged the book as essentially autobiographical. "You may, if
you wish, substitute Richard Garland for 'Duncan Stewart'
[the father], Hamlin for 'Lincoln,' and Frank for 'Owen' [the
brother], for this book is substantially made up of the doings of
my own family. . . . All of the events, even those in fictional
form, are actual, although in some cases I have combined experiences of other boys with my own" (p. vii).

Despite the apparent discursiveness of the book, unity is
achieved by emphasis of the change in the prairie, which parallels
and intensifies the boy's growing up. Without the handicap of
artificial plot or a strictly chronological account of the fifteen
years which lie between the first chapter and the last, there is
a gradual shift of emphasis which implies the change of boy to
man. Another unifying factor is the effective development of
Lincoln Stewart as the central observer. The antics of Milton
Jennings in school, Rance Knapp's skill in riding and hunting,
Mr. Stewart's disciplined management of the farm work, the
Fourth of July in town, and the visit to a neighboring school,
are all sharply drawn, but they are seen consistently from Lincoln Stewart's point of view. They are part of the experience
that made him mature in the way he did. Though the book has
no plot in any formal sense, the effect is narrative rather than
expository. Dialogue is frequent, and uniformly natural. In
chapter one, "Hello! the house!"—a standard greeting for the

time and place—sets the tone. Throughout the book, the dialogue is a valid reminder of the way of life in the northeast Iowa of the eighteen-seventies and early eighties.

The dialogue remains incidental, however. The narrative effect is largely achieved by a selection of episodes which supply a normal suspense and an excitement which is convincing because of its moderation. The herd of wild horses seen at the end of Chapter one symbolizes the freedom of prairie life which, with certain limitations, is to be central in Lincoln's growing up. The great blizzard (Ch. IV) shows the harsher side of nature, the anxiety over the stock, the sense of relief when on the third day it is possible to feed and release the animals from the barn. (Whittier's "Snowbound" of 1866 presents a much more idealized picture of a similar experience, with almost no development of suspense.) "The Battle of the Bulls," and "Lincoln's First Stack," are little dramas of familiar life. In the second, Lincoln's father is injured while harvesting, and Lincoln, aged fourteen, takes over the difficult task of stacking bundles of grain. Part of the stack falls away and has to be done over. There is fear of rain before the job is done. And there is a mild country teasing which makes the boy all the more determined to prove himself a man. His success gives a genuine sense of climax. Several chapters derive a certain rise and fall of action from being formulated as typical days. "A Fourth of July Celebration," "The Coming of the Circus," "Owen Rides at the County Fair," are examples of special events thus treated. "The Old-fashioned Threshing" and "The Corn Husking" represent routine activities in a similar way.

Two features of the volume add a kind of third-dimensional charm to the account of Lincoln's boyhood: thirty-two of Garland's descriptive and lyrical poems, and fifty-three illustrations supplied by E. W. Deming, then a well-known artist. Almost

all of the poems had previously appeared in *Prairie Songs*
(1893), but they are more effective as occasional interpolations
in his prose text than they are in a collection, or read as isolated
poems. It cannot be claimed that Garland had great talent for
verse, but he had a genuine feeling for nature and some capacity
to express that feeling in simple, appropriate language. Garland's illustrator, born in 1860 at Ashland, Ohio, was an exact
contemporary. His forty-seven line drawings became an in-
tegral part of the text, skillfully visualizing the characteristic
activities of country life. The illustrations are not idealized, nor
is there any of the comic exaggeration which Kemble had given
to the original illustrations of *Huckleberry Finn* fifteen years
earlier (1884). The illustrations effectively re-enforce the impression of authenticity created by the text. This is the way
men farmed. These are the ways the boys helped with the work.
These are the recreations they had. In Henry James's phrase,
both writer and illustrator have caught the color of life. *Boy
Life on the Prairie* is thus not only valuable as a vivid record,
but as an attractive example of late nineteenth century book-
making.

Before comparing *Boy Life* with *A Son of the Middle Border*
(1917), let us first review the early articles which were Garland's first effort at reminiscence. Very early in Garland's career
as a writer came the desire to record and preserve the way of
life he had known, a way of life rapidly fading from memory, as
Garland was quick to realize.

All my life I had read of New England husking bees, apple parings, barn-
raisings, and the like, finding in them the charm of my ancestral life; but no
writer, so far as I knew, had ever put the farm life of the West into literature,
either as poem, essay, or novel. With no confidence in my ability to write a
story, I believed I could set down in plain words the life I had known and
shared. With a resolution to maintain the proper balance of rain and sun,

dust and mud, toil and play, I began an article descriptive of an Iowa corn husking, faintly hoping it might please some editor. *(Boy Life,* 1926, p. vi.)

This was in the fall of 1887. In *A Son of the Middle Border* (p. 351), Garland describes the scrape of the coal shovel in the Boston alley, which reminded him of the noise made by scooping corn from the wagon box into the crib. Later that year Garland was to return to Osage, go on to Dakota to visit his parents, and hear from his mother the story he entitled "Mrs. Ripley's Trip," his first real piece of fiction.

The article on corn husking (later Ch. XVI of *Boy Life*) was promptly accepted by William Wyckoff, editor of *The American Magazine,*[3] in which it appeared in January, 1888. Encouraged by Wyckoff, Garland wrote and published in this magazine five other articles in the same year: "The Thrashin'," (Ch. XIV and XV); "The Voice of Spring" (Ch. V); "Between Hay an' Grass" (Ch. VII, VIII, and IX); "Meadow Memories" (Ch. X); and "Melons and the Early Frost" (Ch. XIII and XIV). At this time Garland seems to have had no plans for a longer work, but simply wrote recollections that seemed sharpest in his memory. In reworking the material he made numerous changes and additions, and the parallels to chapters in *Boy Life* are only approximate. In these articles Garland speaks in his own person, addressing Eastern readers and explaining to them the peculiarities of Western farm methods. In "The Huskin'," for example, Garland begins by explaining that corn in the West is husked in the field instead of in the barn simply because the farms are larger. The corn is left in the field, and when it "no longer creaks if wrung" it is ready to be husked. The latter part of the sketch tells the story of finishing the husking on a Thanksgiving Day, when the pleasures of a turkey dinner were overshadowed by bitter cold winds, chapped hands, and aching bodies. In *Boy Life* the same material is used, but the focus is

steadily on the boy's experience, and the story of the Thanksgiving Day toil is a natural climax rather than a digression.
The conception of Lincoln Stewart as a center of interest was
not introduced until the material was put into book form.

By 1898 Garland had published *Main-Travelled Roads* (1891),
Prairie Songs (1893), *Crumbling Idols* (1894), *Rose of
Dutcher's Coolly* (1895), and several other lesser volumes. He
had nearly completed the manuscript of his *Life of Grant,* published later in 1898, and he had formed a plan to go to the
Yukon in search of literary material as well as gold. It was at
this time, he says,

> that I felt free to begin a work I had long meditated. I began to dictate to my
> stenographer a rough outline of the life I had led as a boy in Wisconsin and
> Iowa. "If I should happen not to return from this long trip into the British
> Northwest," I said to some of my friends, "I want to leave a fairly full and ac-
> curate chronicle of my youth."
>
> Each morning was spent on this task. In my walks about the suburbs of
> Washington or in the parks, I was constantly reminded of scenes of long ago.
> The keen harsh wind; sheep feeding on sunny slopes; the frogs beginning to
> croak—all had spiritual refreshment clearing my brain of library dust and
> drowning out the rumors of war. The manuscript I thus produced was rough
> and shapeless but it contained many of the essentials of our pioneer life, and
> I pushed ahead as rapidly as possible.[4]

To this page from his notebook, Garland added in 1929 the
statement: "This was the beginning of *A Son of the Middle
Border*. March, 1898." The statement is perhaps misleading,
since as we have seen, Garland gave much attention to the
theme of his boyhood from 1887 on. But no doubt it was in
1898 that he set about rearranging and expanding the material
into book form. Elsewhere Garland says that George Brett of
Macmillan, in taking over from Stone and Kimball the copyright of *Main-Travelled Roads, Prairie Folks,* and *Rose of*

Dutcher's Coolly, suggested that Garland write a book describing his life as a boy.[5]

After the publication of *Boy Life* in 1899, Garland gave his principal attention to the life of the Far West. Repeated trips to Colorado, Wyoming, and Oklahoma made him familiar with Indians, cowboys, soldiers, forest rangers, and miners. *The Eagle's Heart* (1900), *Her Mountain Lover* (1901), *The Captain of the Gray Horse Troop* (1902), *Hesper* (1903), *The Moccasin Ranch* (1909), *Cavanagh, the Forest Ranger* (1910), and *The Forester's Daughter* (1914) were only moderately successful efforts to treat this material. Garland had a serious and intelligent interest in labor problems in the mining towns, in the new conservation policies, and in the treatment of the Indian, but to the authentic observation of many descriptive passages he attempted to join conventional romance in the hope of greater popularity and financial reward. His relative failure left him depressed. Meanwhile he had written one additional sketch of his boyhood, "My First Christmas Tree," for the December, 1911, *Ladies Home Journal*.[6] This sketch, though Garland never reprinted it, has some excellent touches, especially the fifteen-year-old boy's astonishment at the unprecedented beauty of the tree at the country schoolhouse, and his embarrassment at receiving a present. No doubt Garland's friends saw in this sketch something of his older manner and material. Whether they did or not, the sketch shows that the reminiscent strain persisted.

At any rate, the early months of 1914 saw the appearance of five reminiscent sketches in *Collier's*[7], whose editor, Mark Sullivan, Garland knew well. Under the title of *A Son of the Middle Border*, they purport to be based on an abandoned autobiographical manuscript by Lincoln Stewart. The first two give the story of the move to Iowa (essentially the first chapter of *Boy*

Life), with additional material on ploughing, horseback riding, and early reading. The next two installments go back in time to the life in Wisconsin, including the private's return (Garland's father, of course, whose story had been included in *Main-Travelled Roads*). The fifth installment goes forward in time to the period when Garland (or Lincoln Stewart) was about fifteen, and includes several episodes of town life, concluding with a visit to the Seminary. An editorial note at the end stated that "Golden Days at the Seminary" would appear "in an early issue." But the following week saw the beginning of the European War, and the series was interrupted. In none of these 1914 sketches is there any mention of the previously published *Boy Life on the Prairie*.

Early in 1917 "Golden Days at Cedar Valley Seminary"[8] did in fact appear, but Lincoln Stewart had silently dropped from the scene. The sketch was straight autobiography, and was accompanied by a tribute from Theodore Roosevelt. There is a contrast between the delights of the Seminary and the burdensome farm work which had to be done between terms. There is an account of Garland's discovery of Poe, and of his commencement oration, "Going West." This installment closes with an account of South Dakota, where the family moved in 1881. The second sketch, "New England Rediscovered," recounts a trip which Garland and his brother Frank made in 1882 (treated in *A Son of the Middle Border*, Chapters XXII to XXIV). The third article of the series, "A Prairie Outpost," told of Garland's teaching in Illinois, his proving up a claim in Dakota, and his decision to go east. As in 1914, an editorial note promised a further installment, but the United States was now at war, and editorial plans changed. In September, the autobiography came out in book form.

Comparison of *A Son of the Middle Border* with the earlier

Boy Life on the Prairie soon establishes the superiority of the earlier book for the period that it covers.

Chapters eight through sixteen (pp. 79-188) of *A Son of the Middle Border* retell with variations the story of *Boy Life on the Prairie*. In general, the later account is more circumstantial about the Garland family, less specific about the typical experiences of country life. Earlier chapters of *A Son* describe the elder Garland's return from the Civil War, the McClintock family (Mrs. Garland's relatives), the difficulties of farming in southwest Wisconsin, and the decision to move west. Several pages are devoted to the first Iowa home near Hesper in Winneshiek County. Though interesting as a record, and frequently attractive in detail, there is no steady unity. There is little dialogue, although occasional remarks are recalled and set down. Dramatic scene thus almost disappears, and narrative grays out into exposition and digression. A few events are added to the experiences of *Boy Life*. There is a moving account of the loss of seventy acres of newly planted wheat in a windstorm (p. 128). Another episode tells of the boy's lonely night ride for the doctor, when the father became suddenly ill (pp. 139-143). Again, the boy in burning some field stubble accidentally set fire to four stacks of wheat, a serious loss for the family (pp. 157-158). The father's discovery of the boys playing cards in the cold granary surprised them by leading only to a mild invitation to move into the house to play (pp. 153-154). An amusing declaration of independence occurs when young Garland, now doing a man's work, insists on the right to choose his own hat (pp. 177-178). Another experience of young manhood was watching at a dance a determined girl stop a fight between two of her admirers. All of these episodes are of interest, and any or all of them might have been worked into *Boy Life*. As they stand in *A Son,* however, they seem isolated and directionless.

On the other hand, many of the best passages in *Boy Life* were condensed or omitted entirely from *A Son of the Middle Border*. The boy's experience on the prairie, instead of being important in itself, is now told as prelude to the later life of the author, and there is an inevitable tendency to consider the boy less interesting than the man. A characteristic condensation occurs in the first episode. Chapter eight of *A Son of the Middle Border* tells with little change the nighttime arrival in the new home, and the thrilling sight of wild horses on the prairie the next morning. The solitary herder who tries and fails to catch the horse remains unidentified. In *Boy Life* the herder rides up to the fence and the new boy, in very natural dialogue, meets his first neighbor, a boy about his own age. From the point of view of the boy this was suitable and important. From the point of view of Garland's development into well-known author, it could be omitted. Similarly, *Boy Life* records how "Lincoln" is sent to another neighbor's a few days later, to borrow a sand sieve. Near the neighbor's barn he discovers a pond boiling with fish. Excitedly he announces this important news. To this the neighbor boy replies:

"Think you're awful smart, don't you! S'pose I didn't see them fish."
"Well, if you did, why didn't you catch 'em?"
" 'Cause they're all *diseased*." He gave a dreadful emphasis to the word.
. . . (p. 15.)

The accent is exactly right, as is the subsequent conversation about the opening of school. This little episode does not appear in *A Son*. Another telling little scene, Lincoln's examination in reading on his first day at school, disappears from *A Son*.

After the opening six chapters of *Boy Life*, little of the material was directly transferred to *A Son of the Middle Border*. Such typical occupations as seeding, herding, haying, threshing, corn husking, and harvest, to which *Boy Life* gives full chapters, receive in the later book only brief and general treatment. Threshing, for example, which occupies over thirty pages in *Boy Life,* is reduced to a paragraph (pp. 156-157). "Lincoln's First Stack" (Ch. XIII) drops out, as do the lively interludes about the Fourth of July, the county fair, camping, and the battle of the bulls. The circus, a twenty-page chapter in *Boy Life,* is reduced to a paragraph in *A Son* (pp. 136-137). The chapter on hired men is likewise reduced to incidental mention (pp. 174-175). Prairie wild life, the subject of four chapters in *Boy Life,* also becomes incidental. The concluding chapters of *Boy Life* mark an end to boyhood by telling how Lincoln returns to Wisconsin to go to school, returning a few years later to find the prairie virtually gone. Though not strictly autobiographical, of course, this turn of events is an effective conclusion. *A Son of the Middle Border,* literally accurate, merges the end of the prairie period with the stimulus of Cedar Valley Seminary and youthful ambition. The prairie period is subordinated and allowed to fade out instead of being emphatically concluded.

The most important result of comparing Garland's sketches of 1888, *Boy Life on the Prairie,* and *A Son of the Middle Border* is to reclaim a forgotten book as a minor classic of nineteenth century boyhood, admirable in its faithful detail and its natural, unstrained formulation. Beyond that, we gain perspective on Garland's career, its mixture of success and failure, its strange anticlimax despite boundless energy and no small talent. The early sketches are pure journalism, vigorous reporting of fresh material. *Main-Travelled Roads,* three years later, achieved a concentration of sympathy and protest against the grim frustration of western farm life, that has made this his best-known volume. Yet there are in the stories of *Main-Travelled Roads* notes of melodrama, sentimentality, and propaganda. Garland is too personally involved. In *Boy Life* there is more balance, more restraint. Ploughing, harvesting, and husking corn could be bitter toil for a boy, and this he makes us see. But this was not the whole of a boy's life. The coming of spring, the games at school, and the Fourth of July were islands of delight. Taken by itself, boy life on the prairie was not a bad experience, and there was a wholeness about it. By 1917, when Garland began a full-scale autobiography, the boyhood experience was only prelude to a life so full of activity, so full of writing, so full of people that it had lost its wholeness. Digression sets in, and incidents come upon the page not because they are needed but because they are remembered. The autobiographical volumes, beginning with *A Son of the Middle Border,* speak chiefly to those already interested in Garland, or in the times which he describes. *Boy Life on the Prairie,* like any work of art, can stand apart from its author as the well-shaped record of a way of life.[9]

B. R. McElderry, Jr.
University of Southern California

NOTES

1. Macmillan brought out the first edition, which was reprinted in 1900, 1906, 1907 and 1908, though the 1908 edition is misleadingly labeled "revised." Full-page illustrations were omitted, but the text remained the same. The copyright then passed to Harper and Brothers, who included *Boy Life* in the Sunset Edition (1909) and in the Border Edition (1922). In 1926 Allyn and Bacon brought out a revised school edition, edited by Stella S. Center. The 1926 edition dropped four chapters from the original text (XI, XII, XXI, XXV), and rearranged other material. Chapters in the 1926 edition numbered X, XV, and XXVI are largely additions, explaining how the self-binding harvesters changed farm work, and what an impact the lyceums had on the rural community. For much of the bibliographical detail in this study, and for many clues, I am indebted to Mr. Lloyd A. Arvidson's "Bibliography of the Published Writings of Hamlin Garland," a master's thesis at the University of

Southern California (1952). To it some additions have been made by Donald Pizer, "Hamlin Garland: A Bibliography of Newspaper and Periodical Publications (1885-1895) ," *Bulletin of Bibliography,* XXII (1957) , 41-44.

2. Thomas Bailey Aldrich, *The Story of a Bad Boy* (1870) ; Samuel L. Clemens, *The Adventures of Tom Sawyer* (1876) and *The Adventures of Huckleberry Finn* (1884) ; Charles Dudley Warner, *On Being a Boy* (1878) ; William Dean Howells, *A Boy's Town* (1890) .

3. This is *The American Magazine* published in Brooklyn. The articles appeared in January, March, April, June, July, and October of 1888. See VII, 299-303, 570-577, 684-690; and VIII, 148-155, 296-302, 712-717.

The six sketches in *The American Magazine* seem to have been reprinted and expanded in some unidentified magazine or newspaper. A bound undated notebook among Garland's papers at the University of Southern California Library (Box 26) contains pasted clippings numbered I through XIV (IV and VIII are missing). Number II gives "American Magazine" as the source. These clippings are similar in content, and no mention of Lincoln Stewart is made. In a penciled page of the notebook entitled "Into the Winter Woods," however, there is a reference to "Lincoln." The notebook has a title page which reads as follows: "Boy Life on the Prairie/A Series of Impressionistic/Sketches of Western Life/by/Hamlin Garland." Following is this note: "These reminiscent pictures appeared first in the American Monthly Magazine during 87-8. Others of the series are to be published in the Youth's Companion, and elsewhere." Only one contribution to the *Youth's Companion* has been identified. (See paragraph 4 of this note.) Page 3 of the notebook contains a tentative outline in terms of the seasons.

Other manuscripts throw little light on *Boy Life.* There is an undated typescript of "The Coming of the Circus," and one of "A Night Ride in a Prairie Schooner," with minor penciled changes which do not correspond to either the 1899 or 1926 editions of the book. Garland's earliest diaries (1875 and 1877) have brief entries with little more than notes on the weather, chores, and visits to the neighbors. The diaries of later years do not mention his work on the articles or book dealing with his boyhood.

Three scattered articles of 1891-93 are boyhood reminiscences. "Going for the Doctor," an episode used in *A Son of the Middle Border,* but omitted from *Boy Life,* appeared in the *Youth's Companion,* March 12, 1891. "A Pioneer Christmas," a very good sketch unaccountably omitted from both volumes of reminiscences, appeared in the *Ladies Home Journal* for December, 1893 (XI, 11) . And in the February, 1894, *Midland* (published in Des Moines, Iowa), appeared "Boy Life in the West," chiefly recollections of games played at school, and similar to chapter III of *Boy Life*. "Saturday Night on the Farm," a chapter in *Prairie Folks* (Chicago, 1893), pp. 143-166, corresponds to pp. 158-177 of *Boy Life*. This section was omitted in the 1926 school edition.

4. Josephine K. Piercy, ed., *Modern Writers at Work* (New York, 1930), p. 239.

5. *A Daughter of the Middle Border* (New York, 1921), p. 79. Despite the merit of *Boy Life*, letters from publishers indicate that it was never widely popular. From 1899 to 1908 Macmillan reports a sale of "under 5,000 copies." From then until 1952, when the title went out of print, Harper and Brothers report a sale of 22,500 copies, many of these presumably in the sets called Sunset Edition and Border Edition. The Allyn and Bacon school edition of 1926 had "very meager" sales.

6. P. xvii. Reprinted by Edward Wagenknecht in *The Fireside Book of Christmas Stories* (New York, 1945), pp. 539-543; and, by the same editor in *A Child—An Anthology* (New York, 1946), pp. 337-341.

7. March 28, pp. 5-7; April 18, pp. 11-12; May 9, pp. 15-16; June 27, pp. 13-14; August 8, pp. 20-22.

8. March 31, pp. 9-10; April 21, pp. 8-9; May 26, pp. 13-14.

9. In Osage, Iowa, there are still reminders of that way of life. The old Seminary closed in 1922, but the building remains, near the center of town. The Garland farmhouse, remodeled, is two miles east and three miles north of Osage. The centennial edition of the Osage *Press-News*, June 21, 1956, carried (section B) a picture and brief story of Garland's life in Mitchell County, and much material on the early days of the region.

PREFACE

THIS book is the outgrowth of a series of articles begun as far back as 1887. It was my intention, at the time, to delineate the work and plans of a boy on a prairie farm from season to season, beginning with seeding and ending with threshing, and I wrote some six or eight chapters in conformity with this plan. It occurred to me then that twenty-seven was too young to begin to write reminiscences, and I put the book aside until such time as it might be seemly for me to say, " I remember." I was resting easy in this attitude when a friend startled me by saying, "Yes, that's right, put it off till you have forgotten all about it!"

There was enough disturbing force in this remark to set me at work. The life I intended to depict was passing. The machinery of that day is already gone. The methods of haying, harvesting, threshing, are quite changed, and the boys of my generation are already middle-aged men with poor memories; therefore I have taken a slice out of the year 1899 in order to put into shape my recollection of the life we led in northern Iowa thirty years ago. I trust the reader will permit my assumption of the airs of an old man for a single volume.

At the same time let me say, " Boy Life on the Prairie " is not an autobiography. It is not my intention to present in *Lincoln Stewart* the details of my own life and character, though I lived substantially the life of the boys herein depicted. I have used *Lincoln* merely as a connecting life-thread to bind the chapters together. *Rance* is the hero of the book, so far as any character can by courtesy be so called.

I ploughed and sowed, bound grain on a station, herded cattle, speared fish, hunted prairie chickens, and killed rattlesnakes quite in the manner here set down, but I have been limited neither by the actualities of my own life, nor those of any other personality. All of the incidents happened neither to me nor to *Rance*, but they were the experiences of other boys, and might have been mine. They are all typical of the time and place.

In short, I have aimed to depict boy life, not boys; the characterization is incidental. *Lincoln* and *Rance* and *Milton* and *Owen* are to be taken as types rather than as individuals. The book is as faithful and as accurate as my memory and literary skill can make it. I hope it may prove sufficiently appealing to the men of my generation to enable them to relive with me the splendid days of the unbroken prairie-lands of northern Iowa.

PROLOGUE

THE ancient minstrel when time befit
   And his song outran his laggard pen,
Went forth on the mart and chanted it
   In the noisy street to the busy men,
Who found full leisure to listen and long
For the far-off land of the singer's song.

Let me play minstrel, and chant the lines
   Which rise in my heart in praise of the plain;
I'll lead you where the wild-oat shines,
   And swift clouds dapple the wheat with rain.
If you'll listen, you'll hear the songs of birds,
And the shuddering roar of trampling herds.

The brave brown lark from the russet sod
   Will pipe as clear as a cunning flute,
Though sky and cloud are stern as God,
   And all things else are hot and mute —
Though the gulls complain of the blazing air
And the grass is brown and crisp as hair.

CONTENTS

Part II

Appendix

BOY LIFE ON THE PRAIRIE

CHAPTER I

A NIGHT RIDE IN A PRAIRIE SCHOONER

ONE afternoon in the autumn of 1868 Duncan Stewart, leading his little fleet of " prairie schooners," entered upon " The Big Prairie " of northern Iowa, and pushed resolutely on into the west. His four-horse canvas-covered wagon was followed by two other lighter vehicles, one of which was driven by his wife, and the other by a hired freighter. At the rear of all the wagons, and urging forward a dozen or sixteen cattle, trotted a gaunt youth and a small boy.

The boy had tears upon his face, and was limping with a stone-bruise. He could hardly look over the wild oats, which tossed their gleaming bayonets in the wind, and when he dashed out into the blue joint and wild sunflowers, to bring the cattle into the road, he could be traced only by the ripple he made, like a trout in a pool. He was a small edition of his father. He wore the same color and check in his hickory shirt and his long pantaloons of blue denim, had suspenders precisely like those of the men. Indeed, he considered himself a man, notwithstanding the tear-stains on his brown cheeks.

B   I

It seemed a long time since leaving his native Wisconsin coolly behind, with only a momentary sadness, but now, after nearly a week of travel, it seemed his father must be leading them all to the edge of the world, and Lincoln was very sad and weary.

"Company, halt!" called the Captain.

One by one the teams stopped, and the cattle began to feed (they were always ready to eat), and Mr. Stewart, coming back where his wife sat, said cheerily: —

"Well, Kate, here's the big prairie I told you of, and beyond that blue line of timber you see is Sun Prairie, and home."

Mrs. Stewart did not smile. She was too weary, and the wailing of little Mary in her arms was dispiriting.

"Come here, Lincoln," said Mr. Stewart. "Here we are, out of sight of the works of man. Not a house in sight — climb up here and see."

Lincoln rustled along through the tall grass, and, clambering up the wagon wheel, stood silently beside his mother. Tired as he was, the scene made an indelible impression on him. It was as though he had suddenly been transported into another world, a world where time did not exist; where snow never fell, and the grass waved forever under a cloudless sky. A great awe fell upon him as he looked, and he could not utter a word.

At last Mr. Stewart cheerily called: "Attention, battalion! We must reach Sun Prairie to-night. *Forward, march!*"

Again the little wagon train took up its slow way

through the tall ranks of the wild oats, and the drooping, flaming sunflowers. Slowly the sun sank. The crickets began to cry, the night-hawks whizzed and boomed, and long before the prairie was crossed the night had come.

Being too tired to foot it any longer behind the cracking heels of the cows, Lincoln climbed into the wagon beside his little brother, who was already asleep, and, resting his head against his mother's knee, lay for a long time, listening to the *chuck-chuckle* of the wheels, watching the light go out of the sky, and counting the stars as they appeared.

At last they entered the wood, which seemed a very threatening place indeed, and his alert ears caught every sound, — the hoot of owls, the quavering cry of coons, the twitter of night birds. But at last his weariness overcame him, and he dozed off, hearing the clank of the whippletrees, the creak of the horses' harness, the vibrant voice of his father, and the occasional cry of the hired hand, urging the cattle forward through the dark.

He was roused once by the ripple of a stream, wherein the horses thrust their hot nozzles, he heard the grind of wheels on the pebbly bottom, and the wild shouts of the resolute men as they scrambled up the opposite bank, and entered once more the dark aisles of the forest. Here the road was smoother, and to the soft rumble of the wheels the boy slept.

At last, deep in the night, so it seemed to Lincoln, his father shouted: "Wake up, everybody. We're almost home." Then, facing the darkness, he cried, in western fashion, "Hello! the house!"

Dazed and stupid, Lincoln stepped down the wheel to the ground, his legs numb with sleep. Owen followed, querulous as a sick puppy, and together they stood in the darkness, waiting further command.

From a small frame house, near by, a man with a lantern appeared.

" Hello! " he said, yawning with sleep. " Is that you, Stewart? I'd jest about give you up."

While the men unhitched the teams, Stewart helped his wife and children to the house, where Mrs. Hutchinson, a tall, thin woman, with a pleasant smile, made them welcome. She helped Mrs. Stewart remove her things, and then set out some bread and milk for the boys, which they ate in silence, their heavy eyelids drooping.

When Mr. Stewart came in, he said : " Now, Lincoln, you and Will are to sleep in the other shack. Run right along, before you go to sleep. Owen will stay here."

Without in the least knowing the why or wherefore, Lincoln set forth beside the hired man, out into the unknown. They walked rapidly for a long time, and, as his blood began to stir again, Lincoln awoke to the wonder and mystery of the hour. The strange grasses under his feet, the unknown stars over his head, the dim objects on the horizon, were all the fashioning of a mind in the world of dreams. His soul ached with the passion of his remembered visions and his forebodings.

At last they came to a small cabin on the banks of a deep ravine. Opening the door, the men lit a candle, and spread their burden of blankets on the floor. Lincoln crept between them like a sleepy puppy, and in a few minutes this unknown actual world merged itself in the mystery of dreams.

When he woke, the sun was shining, hot and red, through the open windows, and the men were smoking their pipes by the rough fence before the door. Lincoln hurried out to see what kind of a world this was to which his night's journey had hurried him. It was, for the most part, a level land, covered with short grass intermixed with tall weeds, and with many purple and yellow flowers. A little way off, to the right, stood a small house, and about as far to the right was another, before which stood the wagons belonging to his father. Directly in front was a wide expanse of rolling prairie, cut by a deep ravine, while to the north, beyond the small farm which was fenced, a still wider region rolled away into unexplored and marvellous distance. Altogether it was a land to exalt a boy who had lived all his life in a thickly settled Wisconsin coolly, where the horizon line was high and small of circuit.

In less than two hours the wagons were unloaded, the stove was set up in the kitchen, the family clock was ticking on its shelf, and the bureau set against the wall. It was amazing to see how these familiar things and his mother's bustling presence changed the looks of the cabin. Little Mary was quite happy crawling about the floor, and Owen, who had explored the barn and found a lizard to play with, was entirely at home. Lincoln had climbed to the roof of the house, and was still trying to comprehend this mighty stretch of grasses. Sitting astride the roof board, he gazed away into the north-west, where no house broke the horizon line, wondering what lay beyond that high ridge.

While seated thus, he heard a distant roar and trample, and saw a cloud of dust rising along the fence which bounded the farm to the west. It was like the rush of a whirlwind, and, before he could call to his father, out on the smooth sod to the south burst a platoon of wild horses, led by a beautiful roan mare. The boy's heart leaped with excitement as the shaggy colts swept round to the east, racing like wolves at play. Their long tails and abundant manes streamed in the wind like banners, and their imperious bugling voiced their contempt for man.

Lincoln clapped his hands with joy, and all of the family ran to the fence to enjoy the sight. A boy, splendidly mounted on a fleet roan, the mate of the leader, was riding at a slashing pace, with intent to turn the troop to the south. He was a superb rider, and the little Morgan strove gallantly without need of whip or spur. He laid out like a hare. He seemed to float like a hawk, skimming the weeds, and her rider sat him like one born to the saddle, erect and supple, and of little hindrance to the beast.

On swept the herd, circling to the left, heading for the wild lands to the east. Gallantly strove the roan with his resolute rider, disdaining to be beaten by his own mate, his breath roaring like a furnace, his nostrils blown like trumpets, his hoofs pounding the resounding sod.

All in vain; even with the inside track he was no match for his wild, free mate. The herd drew ahead, and, plunging through a short lane, vanished over a big swell to the east, and their drumming rush died rapidly away into silence.

This was a glorious introduction to the life of the prairies, and Lincoln's heart filled with boundless joy, and longing to know it — all of it, east, west, north, and south. He had no further wish to return to his coolly home. The horseman had become his ideal, the prairie his domain.

CHAPTER II

THE FALL'S PLOUGHING

BEFORE he could get down from the roof the boy rider turned and rode up to the fence, and Lincoln went out to meet him.

"Hello. Didn't ketch 'em, did ye?"

The rider smiled. "Lodrone made a good try."

"Is that the name of your horse?"

"Yup. What's your name?"

"Lincoln Stewart. What's yours?"

"Rance Knapp."

"Where do you live?"

The boy pointed away to a big frame house which lifted over the tops of some small trees. "Right over there. Can you ride a horse?"

"You bet I can!" said Lincoln.

"Well, then, you come over and see me sometime."

"All right; I will. You come see me."

"All right," Rance replied and dashed away.

He was a fine-looking boy, and Lincoln and Owen liked him. He was about twelve years old and tall and slender, with brown eyes and light yellow hair. He sat high in his saddle like a man, and his manners were not at all boyish. It was plain he considered

himself very nearly grown up. Lincoln made him his boy hero at once.

For a few days Lincoln and Owen had nothing to do but to keep the cattle from straying, and they seized the chance to become acquainted with the country round about. It burned deep into Lincoln's brain, this wide, sunny, windy country, — the sky was so big and the horizon line so low and so far away. The grasses and flowers were nearly all new to him. On the uplands the herbage was short and dry and the plants stiff and woody, but in the swales the wild oat shook its quivers of barbed and twisted arrows, and the crow's-foot, tall and willowy, bowed softly under the feet of the wind, while everywhere in the lowlands, as well as on the sedges, the bleaching white antlers of monstrous elk lay scattered to testify of the swarming millions of wild cattle which once fed there.

To the south the settlement thickened, for in that direction lay the country town, but to the north and west the unclaimed prairie rolled, the feeding ground of the cattle, but the boys had little opportunity to explore that far.

One day his father said : —

"Well, Lincoln, I guess you'll have to run the plough-team this fall. I've got so much to do around the house, and we can't afford to hire."

This seemed a very fine and manly commission, and the boy drove his team out into the field one morning with vast pride, there to crawl round and round his first "back furrow," which stretched from one side of the quarter section to another.

But the pride and elation did not last. The task soon became exceedingly tiresome and the field lonely. It meant moving toward and fro, hour after hour, with no one to talk to and nothing to break the monotony. It meant walking eight or nine miles in the forenoon and as many more in the afternoon, with less than an hour off at dinner. It meant care of the share, — holding it steadily and properly. It meant dragging the heavy implement around the corners, and it meant also many mishaps where thick stubble or wild buckwheat rolled up around the standard and threw the share completely out of the ground.

Lincoln, although strong and active, was rather short, and to reach the plough handles he was obliged to lift his hands above his shoulders. He made, indeed, a comical but rather pathetic figure, with the guiding lines crossed over his small back, plodding along the furrows, his worn straw hat bobbing just above the cross-brace. Nothing like him had been seen in the neighborhood; and the people on the roadway, looking across the field, laughed and said, " That's a little too young a boy to do work like that."

He was cheered and aided by his little brother Owen, who ran out occasionally to meet him as he turned the nearest corner. Sometimes he even went all the way around, chatting breathlessly as he trotted after. At other times he was prevailed upon to bring out a cooky and a glass of milk from the house. Notwithstanding all this, ploughing was lonesome, tiresome work.

The flies were savage, and the horses suffered from their attacks, especially in the middle of the day. They drove badly because of their suffering, their tails continually got over the lines, and in stopping to kick the flies off they got astride the traces, and in other ways were troublesome. Only in early morning or when the sun sank low at night, were the loyal brutes able to move quietly in their ways.

The soil was a smooth, dark, sandy loam, which made it possible for Lincoln to do the work expected of him. Often the plough went the entire mile " round " without striking a root or a pebble as big as a walnut, running steadily with a crisp, craunching, shearing sound, which was pleasant to hear. The work would have been thoroughly enjoyable to Lincoln had it not been so incessant.

He cheered himself in every imaginable way; he whistled, he sang, and he studied the clouds. He ate the beautiful red seed vessels upon the wild-rose bushes, and watched the prairie chickens as they came together in great swarms, running about in the stubble field seeking food. He stopped a moment to study the lizards he upturned. He observed the little granaries of wheat which the mice and gophers had deposited in the ground and which the plough threw out. His eye dwelt lovingly on the sailing hawk, on the passing of wild geese, and on the occasional shadowy presence of a prairie wolf.

There were days, however, when nothing could cheer him, when the wind blew cold from the north, when the sky was full of great, swiftly hurrying, ragged clouds, and the whole world was gloomy and dark; when the horses' tails streamed in the wind, and his own ragged coat flapped round his little legs and wearied him. There were worse mornings, when a coating of snow covered the earth, and yet the ploughing went on. These were the most distressing of all days, for as the sun rose the mud softened and "gummed" his boots and trouser legs, clogging his steps and making him weep and swear with discomfort and despair. He lost the sense of being a boy, and yet he was unable to prove himself a man by quietly quitting work.

Day after day, through the month of September and deep into October, Lincoln followed his team in the field, turning over two acres of stubble each day. At last it began to grow cold, so cold that in the early morning he was obliged to put one hand in his pocket to keep it warm, while holding the plough with the other. His hands grew red and chapped and sore by reason of the constant keen nipping of the air. His heart was sometimes very bitter and rebellious, because of the relentless drag of his daily toil. It seemed that the stubble land miraculously restored itself each night. His father did not intend to be cruel, but he was himself a hard-working man, an early riser, and a swift workman, and it seemed a natural and necessary thing to have his sons work. He himself had been bound out at nine years of age, and had never known a week's release from toil.

As it grew colder morning by morning, Lincoln

observed that the ground broke into little flakes before
the standing coulter. This gave him joy, for soon it
would be frozen too hard to plough. At last there came
a morning, when by striking his heel upon the ground,
he convinced his father that it was too hard to break,
and he was allowed to remain in the house. These
were beautiful hours of respite. He had time to play
about the barn or to read. He usually read, devouring
anything he could lay his hands upon, newspapers,
whether old or new, or pasted on the wall or piled up
in the garret. His mother declared he would stand
on his head to read a paper pasted on the wall. Books
were scarce, but he borrowed remorselessly and so read
" Franklin's Autobiography," " Life of P. T. Barnum,"
Scott's " Ivanhoe," and " The Female Spy."

But unfortunately the sun came out warm and bright,
after these frosty nights, the ground softened up, and his
father's imperious voice rang out, " Come, Lincoln,
time to hitch up," and once more the boy returned to
the toil of the field.

But at last there came a day when Lincoln shouted
with joy as he stepped out of the house. The ground
was frozen hard and rung under the feet of the horses
like iron, and the bitter wind, raw and gusty, swept out
of the northwest, with spiteful spitting of snowflakes.
Winter had come, and ploughing was over at last. The
plough was brought in, cleaned and greased to prevent
its rusting, and upturned in the tool-shed, and Lincoln
began to look forward to the opening day of school.

PLOUGHING

A LONELY task it is to plough!
  All day the black and clinging soil
Rolls like a ribbon from the mould-board's
  Glistening curve. All day the horses toil
Battling with the flies — and strain
  Their creaking collars. All day
The crickets jeer from wind-blown shocks of grain.

October brings the frosty dawn,
  The still, warm noon, the cold, clear night,
When torpid crickets make no sound,
  And wild-fowl in their southward flight
    Go by in hosts — and still the boy
And tired team gnaw round by round,
At weather-beaten stubble, band by band,
    Until at last, to their great joy,
The winter's snow seals up the unploughed land.

One day he was sent to borrow a sand-sieve of neighbor Jennings, and on his way he crossed a big pond in the creek. The ice, newly formed, was clear as glass, and looking down he saw hundreds of fish, pickerel, muskelunge, suckers, red-horse, mud-cats, sunfish — the water was boiling with them! Instantly the boy became greatly excited. Never had he seen so many fish, and he looked round to see the cause of it. The creek had fallen to a thin stream, over which these large fish could not move, and they were caught in a trap.

Hurrying on down to the Jennings place, he put his news into the most exciting words he could find. But Mr. Jennings, a large, jolly old fellow, only sucked his pipe and said, " They're no account, I guess, on account of the stagnant water."

Lincoln's face fell, and hearing a snicker behind him, he turned and saw Milton Jennings for the first time, and at the moment disliked him. He had a thin, fair, smiling, handsome face, and his curly, taffy-colored hair curled at the ends. His blue-gray eyes were full of mischievous lights, and his head was tipped on one side like a chicken's.

" You're the new boy, ain't ye ? "

" Well, s'pose I be ! "

" Think you're awful smart, don't you! S'pose I didn't see them fish ? "

" Well, if you did, why didn't you catch 'em ? "

" 'Cause they're all *diseased*." He gave a dreadful emphasis to the word, and Lincoln knew he got it from his father.

In the silence that followed Lincoln remembered his errand. "Father wants to borrow your sand-sieve."

"All right. Go get it for him, Milton."

The two boys walked off, shoulder to shoulder. Milton was about a year older than Lincoln, and readier of speech. His profile was as fine as the image on a coin, but he was not so handsome and strong as Rance Knapp. He wore a suit of store clothes; true, they were old, but the fit of the coat and trousers made a deep impression upon Lincoln. He had heard that Mr. Jennings was one of the well-to-do farmers of the prairie, and the gleaming white paint on their house seemed to verify the rumor.

With the sieve on his head, he lingered to say good-by, for he was beginning to like the smiling boy.

"Come over and see me," said Milton.

"All right; you come over and see me."

"I've got a gun."

"So've I — anyhow, father lets me fire it off. I hunt gophers with it."

"So do I, and ducks. Say, s'pose we set together at school."

"All right. I'd like to."

"Begins a week from Monday. Well, good-by."

"Good-by."

Lincoln went away feeling very light-hearted, for the last words of the boy were cordial and hearty. He loved to joke, but he was, after all, a good boy.

That night as they were all sitting round the lamp reading, Mr. Stewart said, "Well, wife, I suppose we've

got to take these boys to town and fit 'em out ready
for school."

" Oh, goody ! " cried Owen.   " Now I can spend
my six centses."

He danced with joy all the evening and could hardly
compose himself to sleep.   At breakfast neither of them
had any appetite, and their willingness to do chores
would have amazed Mr. Stewart, only he had known
such " spells " before.

As they rattled off down the road in the cold, clear
morning, the boys were round-eyed with excitement,
and studied every house and barn with such prolonged
interest that their heads revolved on their necks like
young owls.   It was a plain prairie road which ran part
of the way through lanes of rail fences, and part of
the way diagonally across vacant quarter-sections, but
it lead toward timber land and the county town !   It
was all wonderful country to the boys.

Rock River had only one street of stores and blacksmith shops and taverns, but it was an imposing place
to Lincoln, and Owen clung close to his father's legs
like a scared puppy.   Both stumbled over nail-kegs
and grub-hoes, while their eyes devoured people, and
jars of candy, and mittens hanging on a string.   When
they spoke they whispered, as if in church, pointing
with stubby finger, " See there ! " what time some new
wonder broke on their sight.

Each had a few pennies to spend, and they were
soon sucking sticks of candy, while they listened to the
talk of the grocer.   Owen's mouth was filled with

c

a big striped "marble" while his father was putting caps on his head as if he were a hitching-post, and his hands were so sticky he could scarcely try on his new mittens.

The buying of boots was the crowning joy of the day, or would have been, if Mr. Stewart had not insisted on their taking those which were a size too large for them. No one wore shoes in those days. The war still dominated, and a sort of cavalry boot was the model. Lincoln's had red tops with a golden moon in the centre, while Owen's were blue, with a flag. They had a delicious smell, too, and the hearts of the youngsters glowed every time they looked at them. Lincoln was delighted to find that his did not have copper toes. He considered copper-toed shoes fit only for babies. A youth who had ploughed seventy acres of land couldn't reasonably be expected to wear copper-toed boots.

Then there were new books to be bought, also. A new geography, a new "Ray's Arithmetic," and a slate. These new books had a nice smell, also, and there was charm in the smooth surface of the unmarked slates. At last, with all their treasures under the seat, where they could look at them or feel of them, with their slates clutched in their hands, the boys jolted home in silence, dreaming of the new boots and mittens and scarfs which they would put on when the next snow-storm came. Lincoln was pensive and silent all the evening, for he was digesting the mass of new sights, sounds, and sensations which the day's outing had thrust upon him.

Meanwhile, he had made but few acquaintances, and

looked forward to his first day at school with nervous
dread. He knew something of the torment to which
big boys subject little ones, and he felt very weak
and diminutive as he thought of leading Owen up the
the road that first morning, when every face was strange.
He knew but two boys, Milton Jennings and Rance
Knapp. Rance was not easy to become acquainted with,
but Lincoln felt a confidence in him which Milton did
not inspire. He had seen but little of either of them,
and had no feeling of comradeship with them. His battles, and those of Owen also, must be fought out alone.

As the cold winds arose, and the leaves of the popple
trees and hazel bushes were stripped away, the prairie
took on a wilder, fiercer look. The prairie chickens, in
immense flocks, gathered in the corn-fields to feed, and
the boys were fired with evil desires. They built a trap,
and caught several, and when they were killed and
dressed and fried they ate them with relish born of a
salt pork diet. Aside from these splendid birds, innumerable chickadees, and a few owls, there was no other bird
life. The prairies became silent, lone, wind-swept, and
the cattle drew close around the snow-piles, and the people crowded into their small shacks, and waited for
winter.

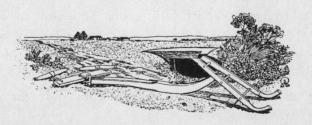

CHAPTER III

THE school-house stood a mile away on the prairie, with not even a fence to shield it from the blast. There had been a good deal of talk about setting out a wind-break, Mr. Jennings said, but nothing had yet been done. It was merely a square, box-like structure, with three windows on a side and two in front. It was painted a glaring white.on the outside and a drab within; at least that was the original color, but the benches were greasy and hacked until all first intentions were obscured.

A big box-stove, sitting in a square puddle of bricks, a wooden chair, and a table completed the furniture. The walls, where not converted into black-boards, were merely plastered over, and the windows had no shades. Altogether it was not inviting, even to the residents of Sun Prairie; and Lincoln, who stole across one Sunday morning to look in, came away much depressed. He was fond of school. It was a chance to get clear of farm work and also an opportunity to meet his fellows, — he never missed a day if he could help it, — but the old school-house in Wisconsin had stood in a lovely spot under some big burr oaks, with a meadow and trout brook not far away,

20

and this bare building on the naked prairie seemed a poor place indeed.

In this small room, whose windows rattled in the wind, in this little coop which congealed like an egg in the winds of winter and baked like a potato in the remorseless suns of summer, some thirty boys and girls met to study, and therein some of them received all the education in books they ever got. The fact that they endured it without complaint is a suggestive commentary on the homes from which they came.

Nearly every family lived in two or three rooms. The Stewarts had three rooms in winter. In one they lived and cooked and sat. The husband and wife occupied a bedroom below, and the children slept above in the garret, close to the stovepipe. In summer the small house mattered less, for the children had all outdoors to spread over; but in winter they were unwholesomely crowded, and Mrs. Stewart carried on her work at great disadvantage. It was terribly cold in the garret, and the boys usually made a dash for it when going to bed, and on very cold mornings ran down to dress beside the kitchen stove.

Their clothing was largely cotton and ill-fitting. Their underclothing was "cotton-flannel," made by their overworked mother. Over this they generally wore an old pair of trousers, and denim overalls went outside "to break the cold winds." Each boy had a sort of visored cap, with a gorget which fell down over his ears and neck in stormy weather, and which could be rolled up on sunny days. They also wore long mufflers of gay-colored wool, which they wound round their heads and over their ears when the wind was keen. It was common for the big girls to "work" these scarfs for their sweethearts. The boys' boots were always a size too large, in order to admit of shrinking in wet weather, and also to make the wearing of thick socks possible during midwinter. They looked exactly like diminutive men, with their long trousers, boots, gloves, and caps, and it took a savage wind to scare them.

It was a cold, bleak morning with much snow when Lincoln set out with his books under his arm and a little tin pail (filled with his lunch) dangling from his mittened hand, — a comical, squat, little figure. He trudged along alone, for Owen did not venture out. On the road he could see other children assembling, and upon nearing the school-house he found a dozen boys engaged in a game called "dog and deer," and too much occupied to pay any attention to him.

He had seen the game played before. It consisted of a series of loops through which the "dogs" were forced to run, while the "deer" were allowed to leap across the narrow necks where the loops approached each other. Two of the players having been selected to act as "dogs," all the others became "deer" and fled off into the loops, which were drawn in the deep snow by the entire band of players moving in single file, scuffling out the paths.

It was an exceedingly exciting and interesting game, and Lincoln forgot that he was a stranger. He was

brought to a sense of his weakness when Rangely Moss
ran up and threw him down and put snow in his
neck to see if he would cry. He did not. He swore
softly, for he had learned that to show fear or anger
would only bring other persecutions. He merely said
in his heart, " When I grow up, I'll kill you."

Upon the ringing of the bell, every boy made a
rush for a seat on the south side, while the girls
quietly took position opposite. Why this should be
Lincoln never understood, because it was exceedingly
cold and windy by the north windows. But as it gave
him a sunny seat, he had no mind to complain. There
was some squabbling and disputing, but in a short time
all were seated. Lincoln found himself sitting with
Milton Jennings, and was well pleased.

" Hello ! Got here, did you ? " said Milton.

The teacher turned out to be a slender, scholarly
young man, who seemed very timid and gentle to the
strong, rude boys. He toed in a little, and Rangely
Moss winked in derision of him and in promise of
mischief.

Lincoln was amazed to see so many pupils and
wondered where they all came from. There were
three or four " big girls," women they seemed to him,
and as many boys who were grown-up young men.
When the teacher came to his desk to look at his
books, he appeared to be a little surprised to find the
Fifth Reader in his hands.

" Is this your book ? " he asked.

" Yes, sir," replied Lincoln.

" Do you read this ? "

" Yes, sir." Lincoln was suffering agonies of bashfulness at being thus singled out for questioning before the school.

" Let me hear you. Read this." He opened the book at one of Wendell Phillips's orations.

The boy knew it by heart, and it was well he did, for his eyes were dim with confusion as he gabbled off the first paragraph.

" That'll do," said the teacher. " You may go on with the class."

The relief was so sudden that Lincoln could not thank him. His throat was " lumpy and sticky " for a few minutes.

This drew attention to him at once, and smoothed the way for him, too. He had no further rough usage by the boys. They had a certain respect for the shockheaded boy of ten, who could read " Webster's Reply to Hayne " or " Lochiel's Warning." He was found to be a good speller, also, and that was in his favor, and counterbalanced his slowness as a " dog."

At recess, when Rangely assaulted him, Rance ran up behind, and pushed the bully sprawling. Rangely was furious with rage, and chased Rance for five minutes, with intent to do him harm; but Rance was swift as a coyote, and eluded the big fellow with ease. When Rangely gave it up, Rance came close to Lincoln, and said, " When I'm fourteen I'm going to lick that fool like hell." And it was plain he meant it.

After winter fairly set in it was a long, hard walk to

school, but these little men prided themselves on not missing a day. They were almost the youngest pupils in school, but, led by Lincoln, Owen turned up every morning, puffing and wheezing like a small porpoise, his cheeks red as apples, and his boots frozen hard as rocks. He had the spirit of the old vikings in his soul, and laughed in the teeth of a gale which would have made a grown-up city-dweller shiver with dismay.

Sometimes the thermometer fell thirty degrees below zero, and the snow, mixed with dust from the ploughed land, swept like water across the road, confusing and blinding the lads, moving like fine sand under their feet. Many, many days, when flying snow hid the world, these minute insects set forth merrily as larks in springtime. The winter was an exceedingly severe one, and some of the children came to school with ears and noses badly frosted. Lincoln and Owen were quite generally in a state of skin-renewing, but these were battle scars, and not a subject of jest.

The boys always went early, in order to have an hour at " dog and deer," or " dare-goal," or " pom-pom pullaway." It seemed they could not get enough of play. Every moment of " ree-cess " (as they called it) was made use of. With a mad rush they left the room, and returned to it only at the last tap of the bell. They were all hardy as Indians, and cared nothing for the cold as they ran, chasing each other like wolves. But when they came in, they barked like husky dogs, and puffed and wheezed so loudly that all study was for a time suspended. They caught their colds in the house, and not in the open air; for when the " north end of a south wind " beat and clamored round the building, its ill-fitting windows rattled, and the cold streamed in like water. Many a girl caught her death-cold in that miserable shack, and went to her grave a gentle martyr to shiftless management.

Every one necessarily had chilblains, and on warm days the boys pounded their heels and kicked their toes against the seats, to allay the intolerable burning and itching. Lincoln suffered worse than Owen, and often pulled his left foot half-way out of its boot to find relief. The kicking, banging, and scuffling of feet became so loud and so incessant at times that the recitations were interrupted, but the teacher had known chilblains himself, and made as little complaint as possible.

" Dog and deer," or " fox and geese," could be played only when the snow was new-fallen and undisturbed, which was seldom, for the wind, that uneasy spirit of the sky, builder of scarp and battlement, scooper of vaults and carver of plinths, — tireless, treacherous tracker of the plains, — stripped the ground bare in one place, to build some fantastic structure in another, until the snow lay heaped and piled in long lines and waves and pikes behind every bush and post and rock, and the games of loops and circles were over.

Often Lincoln sat by the window, with a forgotten book in his hand, watching the snow as it rustled up against the leeward window, seeing it slide up some fantastic heap, a miniature Pike's Peak, or Shasta-like dome, only to swirl softly around the summit, and fall away in a wreath of misty white, apparently without accomplishing anything. But it did, for the heap grew larger and sharper, just as the peaks of frost grew higher on the window pane. Outside the shelter, the other snows went sweeping, streaming by, like the swash of swift foam-white water, misty for very speed. He used to wonder where a particular cloud or wave of snow came from and where it would stop. What was the mysterious force which hurried it on ?

There was little intercourse between the boys and girls in the school, mainly because the sports were austere and of a sort in which the girls took little interest. They (poor things) could only sit in the bare and chalky little room and make tattin' or some useless thing like that.

At twelve o'clock they all ate dinner; that is, such of them as had not eaten it at recess. This dinner was usually made up of long slices of white bread buttered prodigiously in lumps, and frozen as hard as "linkum vity." Dessert was a piece of mince pie, which being hastily warmed was hot on one side and like chopped ice on the other, and made many an aching tooth. Doughnuts, "fried-cakes" as they were called, were general favorites. They did not freeze so hard, were portable, and could be eaten "on the sly" during school hours, in order that no time should be wasted in eating at noon.

It will be admitted that these were grim experiences, and there will be little wonder that Lincoln's memories of those days are not unmixed with the stern and loveless. Most of the pupils went to school only from December to March, and the winter sky, dazzling with its southern sun, or dark with its stormy clouds, and the flutter and roar of the wind and the snow, runs through their recollection of the time. Sufferings and strife abounded, but these bold hearts fought the bitter and relentless cold and gloom with uncomplaining resolution.

The big girls and boys went miles away to dances in some small cabin and came yawningly to school next day, but the small boys had little recreation beyond occasional games of " hi spy " or " dare-gool."

As there were no hills on which to coast, they were forced to be content with " dare-gool," " snap the whip," and " pom-pom pullaway." Success in these sports depended upon swiftness in turning and dodging, and Lincoln was only moderately successful therein; but Rance, young as he was, held his own against the biggest and swiftest boys. He had the lightness and lithe grace of a young Cheyenne.

Milton preferred to stand in the lee of the building and make comical remarks about everybody else, and the big boys all had a healthy respect for his sharp wit.

The coolly boys adapted themselves to the level country at once, and really did not miss the hills and trees of their birthplace so much as one might imagine, but sometimes when the first soft flakes of a gentle snow-storm came whirling down, Lincoln remembered indefinably the pleasure he once took in seeing through the woodland the slant lines of the driving storm, and a feeling of sadness swept over him. When the icy crust sparkled under the vivid light of the moon, he recalled the long hill, down which he used to whizz on his red sled — down past the well, through the gate, and on over the meadow bog, — but which grew more and more remote as new interests and new friends and the pressure of other circumstances came on to make his memories of the Coolly very dim and insubstantial and far off. A house set close under a hill became now a picture in his mind — with the quality of a poem.

Milton was a source of trouble to Lincoln and others who possessed a keen sense of the ludicrous and small powers of self-restraint, for he was able to provoke them to spasmodic snorts of laughter in school hours, for which they were promptly punished, while the real culprit went free. He had a way of putting his little fingers in his mouth and his index fingers in the corners of his eyes, thus turning his long face into the most grotesque and mirth-provoking mask. Naturally, as he could not see how ludicrous he himself was, and as he had the power to laugh heartily without uttering a sound, and the ability also to instantly return to a very serious and absorbed expression, everybody suffered but himself. His scalp seemed made of gutta-percha, for he was able to corrugate it in most unexpected ways. He could wag his ears like a horse when drinking, and lift one eyebrow while the other sadly drooped; and, worse than all, he could look like old man Brown, who had sore eyes and no teeth, or like Elder Bliss, who was fat as a porker and had red cheeks and severe, small eyes.

Hardly a day passed that some boy did not explode in a wild whoop of irresistible laughter, to receive swift punishment from the master, who had no way of discovering the real disturber. Circumstantial evidence was always taken as conclusive proof of guilt, and Milton himself had an almost unimpeachable character in the eyes of his teacher; he was so bright and handsome and respectful, quite a prize scholar in fact. "A modil boy," old Mrs. Brown said in speaking of him.

Rance was a good student, but never showy even in mathematics, in which he was exceedingly apt. Lincoln soon took rank as one of the best spellers in school, and his memory was good in geography and history, but he was easily "stumped" in figures. He knew his old McGuffy Readers almost by heart, and loved the wild song which ran through "Lochiel's Warning" and "The Battle of Waterloo." "Webster's Reply to Hayne" thrilled him with its majestic rolling thunder of words, and he liked Whittier's "Prisoner of Debt," especially that verse which called on somebody to —

> "ring the bells and fire the guns,
> And fling the starry banner out."

He liked the vivid contrast of the next stanza : —

> "Think ye yon prisoner's aged ear
> Rejoices in your general cheer ?
> Think you his dim and failing eye
> Is kindled at your pageantry ?"

" Marco Bozzaris " and " Rienzi's Address to the Romans " and " Regulus before the Carthaginians " — dozens of other bombastic and flamboyant and mouth-filling poems and speeches — he knew by heart and often repeated in the silence of the fields or on the road to school. In the class he was always pleased (and scared) when the passionate verses came to him, — the verses with the " long primer caps," like : —

" STRIKE for your altars and your fires ! "
and
" ROUSE, YE ROMANS ! Rouse, ye slaves ! "

He generally came out very well, if his breath did not fail on the most important word, as it sometimes did when visitors were present.

Most of the scholars hated those dramatic passages, and slid over them in rattling haste with most prosaic intonation, but Lincoln had a notion that the author's intention should be carried out if possible. Sometimes swept away by some power within, he struck exactly the right note, and the scholars responded with a sudden thrill, and he felt his own hair stir. Altogether he had a modest estimate of his powers and a profound admiration for those who were able to see meaning in $x + y = z$.

The winter days were very well filled with work or study or pastimes. Every morning before it was light, his father called in exactly the same way : " Lincoln, Owen ! Come — your chores." Their chores consisted of cleaning out behind the horses, milking the

cows, and currying the horses. They disliked milking cordially, even in pleasant summer weather, when
the cows were clean and standing in the open air, but
they went to this task in winter with a bitter hatred,
for the cattle stood in narrow, ill-smelling stalls, close
and filthy, especially of a morning. Taking care of
the horses was less repulsive, but that had its discom-
forts. The scurf and hair got into their mouths and
ears, and currying was hard work besides. They always
smelled of the barn, and " Clean y'r boots " was a regular outcry from their watchful mother.

Having finished these tasks, they ate breakfast, which
was often made up of buckwheat cakes, sausage (of
home-made flavor), and molasses, — good, strong food
and fairly wholesome. After breakfast all the cattle
were turned into the yard and watered at the well.
This meant a half-an-hour of hard pumping, but ended
the morning duties. They then put on their clean
brown blouses and went away to school.

School closed at four, and they hurried home to do
the evening chores. The stalls were spread with fresh
straw, the cattle again watered, and the cows brought
into their places and again milked. This usually kept
them busy till dark. Supper was eaten by lamplight,
and ended the day's duties, and from seven to nine they
were free to go visiting, to play " hi spy," or pop corn,
or play dominoes or " authors," or read. With a book
or a paper Lincoln had little thought of playing any game.
Sometimes, with Owen, he set forth to find Rance and
play a game of " hi spy," or he went across the wide

and solemn prairie to some entertainment in a neighboring school-house. Generally, if anything special were going on, the family drove over in the big bob sleigh, the box filled with fresh straw and buffalo robes, which were cheap in those days.

There was a boy in most families just the right age to bring in the wood and the kindling, which he considered a mighty task. Lincoln did this until old enough to milk, when he moved up to give place to Owen. Owen puffed and wheezed and complained and shed bitter tears for a couple of years or so, and then began to train Tommy to the task. Mary, at eight years of age, began to help her mother about the dishes and in dusting things, which she detested quite as bitterly as Owen disliked milking, but was willing to take care of the horses.

Lincoln objected to work very largely because it took up time which might otherwise have been employed in reading. He was swift and strong in action, and hustled through his chores like a sturdy young cyclone, in order to get at some story. Owen objected to work, purely because it was work and interfered with some queer project of his own. He never read, but was always pottering about himself, busy at some mechanical thing, talking to himself like a bumblebee, and producing no results whatever.

D

LOST IN A NORTHER

There are voices of pain
In the autumn rain.
There are pipings drear in the grassy waste,
There are lonely swells whose summits rise
Till they touch and blend with the sombre skies,
Where massed clouds wildly haste.

I sit on my horse in boot and spur
As the night falls drear
On the lonely plain.   Afar I hear
The honk of goose and swift wing's whir
Through the graying deeps of the upper air —
Like weary great birds the clouds sail low —
The winds now wail like women in woe,
Now mutter and growl like lions in lair.

Lost on the prairie!   All day alone
With my faithful horse, my swift Ladrone.
And the shapes on the shadow my scared soul cast.
Which way is north?   Which way is west?
I ask Ladrone, for he knows best,
And he turns his head to the blast.
He whinnies and turns at my voice's sound,
And then impatiently paws the ground.

The night's gray turns to a starless black,
And the drifting drizzle and flying wrack
Have melted away into rayless night.
The wind like an actor, childish with age,
Plays all his characters — now sobs with rage,
Now flees like a girl in fright.

I turn from the wind, a treacherous guide,
And touch my knee to the glossy side
Of my ready horse, and the prairie wide
Slips by like a sea under bounding keel:
As I pat his neck and feel the swell
Of his mighty chest and swift limbs' play,
The sorrowful wind-voice dies away.

The coyote starts from a shivering sleep
On the grassy edge of a gully's steep,
And silently slips through wind-blown weeds.
The prairie hen from before my feet
Springs up in haste with swift wings' beat,
And into the dark like a bullet speeds.

Which way is east? Which way is south?
Is not to be answered when dark as the mouth
Of a red-lipped wolf the night shuts down.
I look in vain for a star or light;
Ladrone speeds on in steady flight,
His ears laid back in an anxious frown.

The long grass breaks on his steaming breast
As foam is dashed from the billow's crest

By a keen-prowed ship.
I see it not, but I hear it whip
On my stirrup-shield, and feel the rush
And spiteful lash of the hazel brush.

The night grows colder — the wind again —
Ah! What is that?   I pull at the rein
And turn my face to the blast.
It was sleet on my cheek.   Ay — thick and fast
The startled snow through the darkness leaps,
As massed in the mighty north wind's wing
Like an air-borne army's rushing swing,
The dreaded norther upon me sweeps.

I bowed my head till the streaming mane
Of my panting horse warmed cheek again
And plunged straight into the night amain.
    *   *   *   *   *   *
Day came and found me slowly riding on
With senses bound as in a chain.
Through drifting deeps of snow, Ladrone
Dumbly, faithful plodded on, the rein
Flung low upon his weary neck.
I long had ceased to fear or reck
Of death by cold or wolf or snow,
Bent grimly on my saddle-bow.
    *   *   *   *   *   *
My limbs were numb; I seemed to ride
Upon some viewless, rushing tide —
My hands hung helpless at my side.

The multitudinous, trampling snows,
With solemn, ceaseless, rushing din,
Swept round and over me : far and wide
A *roaring silence* shut the senses in.
Above me through the hurtling shrouds
The far sky, red with morning glows,
Looked down at times
And then was lost in clouds.

But were my tongue with poet's spell
Aflame, I could not tell
The tale of biting hunger — cold — the hell
Of fear that age-long night!
How life seemed only in my brain; the wind,
The foam-white breeze of wintry seas
That roared in wrath from left to right,
Striking the helpless deaf and blind.

     *   *   *   *   *   *

The third morn broke upon my sight,
Streamed through the window of the room
In which I woke, I know not how —
Broke radiant in a golden bloom
As though God smiled away the night.
Like an eternal, changeless sea
Of marble lay the plain
In dazzling, moveless, soundless waste,
Horizon-girt, without a stain.

The air was still; no breath or sound
Came from the white expanse —

The whole earth seemed to wait in trance,
In hushed expectant silence bound.
And oh the beauty of the eastern sky,
Where glowed the herald banners of the King —
And as I looked with famished eye,
Lo, day came on me with a spring!

Along the iridescent billows of the snow
The sun-god shot his golden beams,
Like flaming arrows from the bow.
He broke on every crest, and gleams
        Of radiant fire
        Alit on every spire,
Along the great sun's pathway as he came,
And cloudless, soft, serene as May,
Opened the jocund day.

CHAPTER IV

THE GREAT BLIZZARD

A BLIZZARD on the prairie corresponds to a storm at sea; it never affects the traveller twice alike. Each norther seems to have a manner of attack all its own. One storm may be short, sharp, high-keyed, and malevolent, while another approaches slowly, relentlessly, wearing out the souls of its victims by its inexorable and long-continued cold and gloom. One threatens for hours before it comes, the other leaps like a tiger upon the defenceless settlement, catching the children unhoused, the men unprepared; of this character was the first blizzard Lincoln ever saw.

The day was warm and sunny. The eaves dripped musically, and the icicles dropping from the roof fell occasionally with pleasant crash. The snow grew slushy, and the bells of wood teams jingled merrily all the forenoon, as the farmers drove to their timber-lands five or six miles away. The room was uncomfortably warm at times, and the master opened the outside door. It was the eighth day of January. One afternoon recess, as the boys were playing in their shirt-sleeves, Lincoln called Milton's attention to a great cloud rising in the west and north. A vast, slaty-blue, seamless dome, silent, portentous, with edges of silvery frosty light.

"It's going to storm," said Milton. "It always does when we have a south wind and a cloud like that in the west."

When Lincoln set out for home, the sun was still shining, but the edge of the cloud had crept, or more properly slid, across the sun's disk, and its light was growing cold and pale. In fifteen minutes more the wind from the south ceased — there was a moment of breathless pause, and then, borne on the wings of the north wind, the streaming clouds of soft, large flakes of snow drove in a level line over the homeward-bound scholars, sticking to their clothing and faces and melting rapidly. It was not yet cold enough to freeze, though the wind was colder. The growing darkness troubled Lincoln most.

By the time he reached home, the wind was a gale, the snow a vast blinding cloud, filling the air and hiding the road. Darkness came on instantly, and the wind increased in power, as though with the momentum of the snow. Mr. Stewart came home early, yet the breasts of his horses were already sheathed in snow. Other teamsters passed, breasting the storm, and calling cheerily to their horses. One team, containing a woman and two men, neighbors living seven miles north, gave up the contest, and turned in at the gate for shelter, confident that they would be able to go on in the morning. In the barn, while rubbing the ice from the horses, the men joked and told stories in a jovial spirit, with the feeling generally that all would be well by daylight. The boys made merry also, singing songs, popping corn, playing games, in defiance of the storm.

But when they went to bed, at ten o'clock, Lincoln felt some vague premonition of a dread disturbance of nature, far beyond any other experience in his short life. The wind howled like ten thousand tigers, and the cold grew more and more intense. The wind seemed to drive in and through the frail tenement; water and food began to freeze within ten feet of the fire.

Lincoln thought the wind at that hour had attained its utmost fury, but when he awoke in the morning, he saw how mistaken he had been. He crept to the fire, appalled by the steady, solemn, implacable clamor of the storm. It was like the roarings of all the lions of Africa, the hissing of a wilderness of serpents, the lashing of great trees. It benumbed his thinking, it appalled his heart, beyond any other force he had ever known.

The house shook and snapped, the snow beat in muffled, rhythmic pulsations against the walls, or swirled and lashed upon the roof, giving rise to strange, multitudinous, anomalous sounds; now dim and far, now near and all-surrounding; producing an effect of mystery and infinite reach, as though the cabin were a helpless boat, tossing on an angry, limitless sea.

Looking out, there was nothing to be seen but the lashing of the wind and snow. When the men attempted to face it, to go to the rescue of the cattle, they found the air impenetrably filled with fine, powdery snow, mixed with the dirt caught up from the ploughed fields by a terrific blast, moving ninety miles an hour. It was impossible to see twenty feet, except at long intervals. Lincoln could not see at all when facing the storm. When he stepped into the wind, his face was coated with ice and dirt, as by a dash of mud — a mask which blinded the eyes, and instantly froze to his cheeks. Such was the power of the wind that he could not breathe an instant unprotected. His mouth being once open, it was impossible to draw breath again without turning from the wind.

The day was spent in keeping warm and in feeding the stock at the barn, which Mr. Stewart reached by desperate dashes, during the momentary clearing of the air following some more than usually strong gust. Lincoln attempted to water the horses from the pump, but the wind blew the water out of the pail. So cold had the wind become that a dipperful, thrown into the air, fell as ice. In the house it became more and more difficult to remain cheerful, notwithstanding the family had fuel and food in abundance.

Oh, that terrible day! Hour after hour they listened to that prodigious, appalling, ferocious uproar. All day Lincoln and Owen moved restlessly to and fro, asking each other, "Won't it ever stop?" To them the storm now seemed too vast, too ungovernable, to ever again be spoken to a calm, even by God Himself. It seemed to Lincoln that no power whatever could control such fury; his imagination was unable to conceive of a force greater than this war of wind or snow.

On the third day the family rose with weariness, and looked into each other's faces with a sort of horrified surprise. Not even the invincible heart of Duncan Stewart, nor the cheery good nature of his wife, could keep a gloomy silence from settling down upon the house. Conversation was scanty; nobody laughed that day, but all listened anxiously to the invisible tearing at the shingles, beating against the door, and shrieking around the eaves. The frost upon the windows, nearly half an inch thick in the morning, kept thickening into ice, and the light was dim at midday. The fire melted the snow on the window-panes and upon the door, and ran along the floor, while around the key-hole and along every crack, frost formed. The men's faces began to wear a grim, set look, and the women sat with awed faces and downcast eyes full of unshed tears, their sympathies going out to the poor travellers, lost and freezing.

The men got to the poor dumb animals that day to feed them; to water them was impossible. Mr. Stewart went down through the roof of the shed, the door being completely sealed up with solid banks of snow and dirt. One of the guests had a wife and two children left alone in a small cottage six miles farther on, and physical force was necessary to keep him from setting out in face of the deadly tempest. To him the nights seemed weeks, and the days interminable, as they did to the rest, but it would have been death to venture out.

That night, so disturbed had all become, they lay awake listening, waiting, hoping for a change. About midnight Lincoln noticed that the roar was no longer so steady, so relentless, and so high-keyed as before. It began to lull at times, and though it came back to the attack with all its former ferocity, still there was a perceptible weakening. Its fury was becoming spasmodic. One of the men shouted down to Mr. Stewart, " The storm is over," and when the host called back a ringing word of cheer, Lincoln sank into deep sleep in sheer relief.

Oh, the joy with which the children melted the ice on the window-panes, and peered out on the familiar landscape, dazzling, peaceful, under the brilliant sun and wide blue sky. Lincoln looked out over the wide plain, ridged with vast drifts; on the far blue line of timber, on the near-by cottages sending up cheerful columns of smoke (as if to tell him the neighbors were alive), and his heart seemed to fill his throat. But the wind was with him still, for so long and continuous had its voice sounded in his ears, that even in the perfect calm his imagination supplied its loss with fainter, fancied roarings.

Out in the barn the horses and cattle, hungry and cold, kicked and bellowed in pain, and when the men dug them out, they ran and raced like mad creatures, to start the blood circulating in their numbed and stiffened limbs. Mr. Stewart was forced to tunnel to the barn door, cutting through the hard snow as if it were clay. The drifts were solid, and the dirt mixed with the snow was disposed on the surface in beautiful wavelets, like the sands at the bottom of a lake. The drifts would bear a horse. The guests were able to go home by noon, climbing above the fences, and rattling across the ploughed ground.

And then in the days which followed, came grim· tales of suffering and heroism. Tales of the finding of stage-coaches with the driver frozen on his seat and all his passengers within ; tales of travellers striving to reach home and families. Cattle had starved and frozen in their stalls, and sheep lay buried in heaps beside the fences where they had clustered together to keep warm. These days gave Lincoln a new conception of the prairie. It taught him that however bright and beautiful they might be in summer under skies of June, they could be terrible when the Norther was abroad in his wrath. They seemed now as pitiless and destructive as the polar ocean. It seemed as if nothing could live there unhoused. All was at the mercy of that power, the north wind, whom only the Lord Sun could tame.

This was the worst storm of the winter, though the wind seemed never to sleep. To and fro, from north to south, and south to north, the dry snow sifted till it was like fine sand that rolled under the heel with a ringing sound on cold days. After each storm the restless wind got to work to pile the new-fallen flakes into ridges behind every fence or bush, filling every ravine and forcing the teamsters into the fields and out onto the open prairie. It was a savage and gloomy time for Lincoln, with only the pleasure of his school to break the monotony of cold.

SPRING RAINS

WHEN the snow is sunk
And the fields are bare
And the rising sun has a golden glare
Through the window pane;
And the crow flies over
The smooth, low hills,
And all the air with his calling thrills,—
All hearts leap up in joy again
To welcome spring and the springtime rain.

THEN IT'S SPRING

WHEN the hens begin
   A squawkin'
An' a-rollin' in the dust;
When the rooster takes
   To talkin'
An' a-crowin' fit to bust;
When the crows are cawin', flockin',
An' the chickens boom an' sing, —
   Then it's spring!
When the roads are jest one mud-hole
And the waters tricklin' round
Makes the barn-yard like a puddle,

An' softens up the ground,
Till y'r ankle-deep in worter,
Sayin' words ye' hadn't orter;
When the jay-birds swear an' sing, —
    Then it's spring!

PRAIRIE CHICKENS

FROM brown ploughed hillocks
In early red morning,
They wake the tardy sower with their cheerful cry.
    A mellow boom and whoop
    That held a warning,
A song that brought the seed-time very nigh,
The circling, splendid anthem of their greeting,
Ran like the morning beating
Of a hundred mellow drums —
    Boom, boom, boom!
    Each hillock's top repeating
Like cannon answering cannon
When the golden sunset comes.

They drum no more,
Those splendid springtime pickets,
The sweep of share and sickle
Has thrust them from the hills;
They have vanished from the prairie
Like the partridge from the thickets,
They have perished from the sportsman,
Who kills, and kills, and kills!

CHAPTER V

THE COMING OF SPRING

SPRING came to the settlers on Sun Prairie with a wonderful message, like a pardon to imprisoned people. For five months they had been shut closely within their cabins. Nothing could be sweeter than the joy they felt when the mild south wind began to blow and the snow began to sink away, leaving warm brown patches of earth in the snowy fields. It seemed that the sun-god had not forsaken them, after all.

The first island to appear in the midst of the ocean of slush and mud around the Stewart house, was the chip-pile, and there the spring's work began. As soon as the slush began to gather, Jack, the hired man, was set to work each morning, digging ditches and chopping canals in the ice, so that the barn would not be inundated by the spring rains. During the middle of the day he busied himself at sawing and splitting the pile of logs which Mr. Stewart had been hauling during the open days of winter.

Jack came from far lands, and possessed, as Lincoln soon discovered, unusual powers of dancing and playing the fiddle. He brought, also, stirring stories of distant forests and strange people and many battles, and Lincoln, who had an eye for character, set himself to work to distinguish between what the hired man knew, what he thought he knew, and what he merely lied about.

There was plenty of work for the boys. They had cows to milk and the drains to keep open. It was their business also to pile the wood behind the men as they sawed and split the large logs into short lengths. They used a cross-cut saw, which made pleasant music in the still, warm air of springtime. Afterwards these pieces, split into small sticks ready for the stove, were thrown into a conical heap, which it was Lincoln's business to repile in shapely ricks.

Boys always insist upon having entertainment even in their work, and Lincoln found amusement in planning a new ditch and in seeing it remove the puddle before the barn-door. There was a certain pleasure, also, in piling wood neatly and rapidly, and in watching the deft and powerful swing of the shining axes, as they lifted and fell, and rose again in the hands of the strong men.

The chip-pile, where the hired hand was busy, was warm and sunny by mid-forenoon, and the hens loved to burrow there, lying on their sides and blinking at the sun. The kitchen was near, too, and the boys knew whenever their mother was making cookies or fried-cakes, and could secure some while they were hot and fresh. Around the bright straw-piles the long-haired colts frisked, and the young steers fought and bellowed, as glad of spring as the boys.

Then, too, the sap began to flow out of the maple logs, and Lincoln and Owen wore their tongues to the quick, licking the trickle from the rough wood. They also stripped out the inner bark of the elm logs and chewed it. It had a sweet nut-like flavor, and was considered most excellent forage; moreover, the residue made a sticky pellet, which could be thrown across the room in school and slap against some boy's ear, when the teacher was not looking. The ceilings were, in fact, covered with these pellets, but their presence over a boy's desk was not considered evidence that he had thrown them there.

It was back-breaking work, piling wood, and the boys could not have endured it, had it not been for the companionship of the men, and the hope they had of going skating at night.

The skates which the boys used were usually a rude sort of wooden contraption with a cheap steel runner, which went on with straps. Lincoln and Owen had one pair between them, and one was always forced to slide while the other used the skates. This led to frequent altercations and pleading cries of " Let me take 'em now."

To this day Lincoln can remember with what ecstasy, intermingled with rage, he sprawled about on the pond below the school-house, his skate-straps continually getting loose and tripping him, while his poor ankles, turning inward till the wooden top of the skates touched the ice, brought certain disaster. The edges of the outer counters of his hard boots gouged his feet, producing sores, which embittered his existence during the skating season, notwithstanding all devices for making

the skate stay in the middle of his sole, where it belonged. Even when doing his best, he leaned perilously
forward, swinging his arms, and toiling hard.

Rance had a fine pair of brass-mounted skates, with
beautifully curving toes, which terminated in brass swan-
heads. They had heel-sockets, also, and stayed where
they were put, and it was very discouraging to see him
as he skimmed over the ice almost without effort, now
standing erect, now "rolling" from one foot to the

other, in ease which
seemed impossible
for any human being to attain, though part of it was due,
even in Lincoln's worshipful thinking, to the skates.

These were days of trouble for foot wear. The boys
were in the water nearly all day while the snow was
melting, and their cowhide boots shrank distressfully
each night, causing their owners to weep, and kick the
mopboard, and say, "Goldarn these dam old boots —
I wish they was in hell," as they tried to put them on
in the early light. They suffered at this time, more

poignantly than ever, from chilblains, and to crowd their swollen feet into their angular cowhide prisons was too grievous to be gently borne. Mrs. Stewart mildly protested against their swearing, but she sympathized, in spite of all. After an hour or two the leather softened, and the boy forgot his rage and the agony of the morning, till the time to kick the mopboard came round again.

Every hour of free time was improved by Lincoln and Rance and Milton, for they knew by experience how transitory the skating season was. Early in the crisp spring air, when the trees hung thick with frost, transforming the earth into fairyland, and the cloudless sky was blue as a ploughshare, they clattered away over the frozen hubbles, to the nearest pond, where the jay and the snowbird dashed amid the glorified willow trees, and the ice outspread like a burnished share. On such mornings the air was so crisp and still, it seemed the whole earth waited for the sun.

There were no lakes or rivers near the Stewart farm, and the ponds were only small and temporary, formed by the melting snow in the wide, flat fields. The water, moving slowly down the hollows, or ravines, was stopped at the fences by huge banks of intermingled slush and ice, strong, hard, and thick, along some hedge or corn row. And there, on some evenings in March (as mysteriously as in the wonder tale by Hawthorne), a lake suddenly lay rippling, where the day before solid land was. And upon the very ground where he had ploughed but a few months before, Lincoln skated in riotous glee with his playmates.

At night, during the full moon, nearly all the boys and girls of the neighborhood met, to rove up and down the long swales, and to play "gool" or "pom-pom pullaway" upon the frozen ponds. These games could be played with skates, quite as well as in any other way. There was a singular charm in these excursions at night, across the plain, or winding up the swales filled with imprisoned and ice-bound water. Lincoln and Rance often skated off alone and in silence, far away from the others, and the majesty of the night fell upon them with a light which silenced and made them afraid.

Sometimes they built bonfires on the ice, both to keep them warm and to add the mystery and splendor of flame to the gray night. Around the crackling logs the girls hovered, coquetting with the older boys. Lincoln and Rance were usually in the thick of the games, or exploring new ponds far away.

The fields and meadows retained these ponds only for a few days. That part of the water which could not mine through the frozen ground went rushing into the next field with such power that nothing could withstand it. Then again, the sun was getting higher and warmer, and the ice thinner. By ten o'clock of a morning the boys were forced to end their sport, by reason of the growing danger of breaking, and also because of the water flowing over its surface. They returned sadly to work at the woodpile.

Sometimes Lincoln lingered long, studying the wonderful things which were taking place under the warm rays of the sun. As the water began to ebb, it left upon the grass of the meadow strange formations between the ground and the ice, which a boy's imagination could easily turn into towns and forests, and crowds of animals and men — tiny cathedrals with spires, horsemen with spears, riding through crystal arches, and labyrinths of shining pillars through which the water gurgled and tinkled with most entrancing music.

Often, with his ear pressed to the ice, Lincoln laid long listening to the faint, fairy-like melodies rung, as if upon tiny bells far down, mingled with splashing of infinitesimal waterfalls, and of rhythmical, far-away lapping of tiny wavelets, ebbing and flowing somewhere in crystal channels toward the sun.

Then there were ice bubbles, which lay just under the surface of the ice like pellucid palettes. These were called " money " by the boys, and Lincoln sometimes dug holes through the ice with his penknife, to let them escape, as if he intended to discover the mystery of their iridescence. As the dams broke, one by one, they left great crystal terraces at the banks, exposing a whole fairy world of architecture to the boy's inquisitive eyes, and when the sun struck in, and lighted up the arches, pillars, and colonnades of this frost world, his heart ached with the beauty of it.

There was a singular charm about this time of the year. Travel was quite impossible, for the frost had left the roads bottomless, and so upon the chip-pile the boys sat to watch the snow disappear from the fields, and draw sullenly away from the russet grass, to take a final stand at the fence corners and in the hedges. They watched the ducks as they came straggling back in long flocks, lighting in the corn-fields to find food. They came in enormous numbers, sometimes so great the sky seemed darkened with them, and when they alighted on the fields, they covered the ground like some strange down-dropping storm from the sky, and when alarmed they rose with a sound like the rumbling of thunder. At times the lines were so long that those in the front rank were lost in the northern sky, while those in the rear were dim clouds beneath the southern sun. Many brant and geese also passed, and it was always a great pleasure to Lincoln to see these noble birds pushing their way boldly into the north. He could imitate their cries, and often caused them to turn and waver in their flight, by uttering their resounding cries.

One day in late March, at the close of a warm sunny day (just as the red disk of the sun was going down in a cloudless sky in the west), down from a low hilltop, and thrilling through the misty, wavering atmosphere, came a singular soft, joyous " *boom, boom, boom, cutta, cutta, war-whoop !* "

" Hooray ! " shouted Lincoln.   " Spring is here."

" What was that ? " asked the hired man.

" That ?   Why, that's the prairie chicken.   It means it is spring ! "

There is no sweeter sound in the ears of a prairie-born man than the splendid morning chorus of these noble birds, for it is an infallible sign that winter has broken at last.   The drum of the prairie cock carries with it a thousand associations of warm sun and springing grass, which thrill the heart with massive joy of living. It is almost worth while to live through a long unbroken Western winter, just for the exquisite delight which comes with this first exultant phrase of the vernal symphony.

Day by day this note is taken by others, until the whole horizon rings with the jocund call of hundreds of cocks, and the whooping cries of thousands of hens, as they flock and dance about on the bare earth of the ridges. Here they battle for their mates, and strut about till the ground is beaten hard and smooth with their little feet.

About this time the banking was taken away from the house, and the windows, which had been sealed up for five months, were opened. It was a beautiful moment to Lincoln, when they sat at dinner in the kitchen, with the windows and doors wide open to the warm wind, and the sunshine floating in upon the floor. The hens, *caw*, *cawing*, in a mounting ecstasy of greeting to the spring, voiced something he had never felt before.

As the woodpile took shape, Mr. Stewart called upon Lincoln and the hired man to help fan up the seed wheat. This the boys hated because it was a dusty and monotonous job. It was of no use to cry out; the work had to be done, and so, on a bright afternoon, while Jack turned the crank of the mill, Lincoln dipped wheat from the bin into the hopper, or held the sacks for his father to fill. It seemed particularly hard to be confined there in the dust and noise while out in the splendid sunlight the ducks were flying, the prairie chickens calling, and the ice was cracking and booming under the ring of the skaters' steel.

It was about this time, also, that Lincoln became concerned in a series of informal cock-fights. It is difficult to tell how this came about. Probably because the roosters fought more readily than at any other season of the year. Anyhow, the boys were

savage enough to enjoy each battle that broke out in their barn-yard.

Lincoln yielded readily to Milton's banter, and, with a rooster in a bag under his arm, trotted off one Sunday to Neighbor Jennings's barn-yard, there to arrange a bout between his rooster and a chosen warrior of Milton's flock.

The actions of the roosters were amazingly human. The boys understood every note and gesture, and could tell what each bird was thinking about by the slant of his head, and by the way he lifted and put down his feet, as well as by the tones of his voice. Sometimes the strange bird would be so disheartened by his surroundings and by the savage aspect of his challenger, that he would drop his tail in dismay and run under the barn. This was considered a disgrace, and brought shame upon the owner of the fowl, which he must forthwith return to its own yard, and bring a better and more valiant warrior.

In this case, however, the long confinement in the darkness of the sack had made Lincoln's bird extremely belligerent, and, upon being released, he walked forth into the open arena with imperious strides, and blew his bugle in contempt of the world. This delighted his master and made him regret that he had agreed to trade him away.

Both birds were magnificent fellows, lofty of step, imperious of voice, with plumage of green and orange and purple, which shone in the sunlight like burnished brass. They were shapely, sinewy game-birds, quite unlike the ugly squat "Plymouth Rocks." They had the pride of Indian chiefs in their step, and the splendor of the rainbow in their curving tails.

As the combatants approached each other, the boys clapped hands in joy of the coming fray. Suddenly the roosters' heads lowered and out-thrust. The shining ruff around each neck bristled with anger and resolution. For a moment, with eyes seemingly bound together by some invisible thread, they moved their heads up and down, so silently it seemed that one was only the shadow of the other.

Suddenly with a rush Milton's bird flung himself upon his foe, striking with his spurs at the heart of his foe. For a time neither rested. The fight was hot. At times they seized each other by the bill, and rung and twisted like turkey-cocks, or flung themselves against each other with flutter of wings, in a cloud of feathers and dust, rushing again and again, until too tired to do more than brush against each other. Then began their most bloody execution, for they laid hands upon each other at short range. They seized each other by the comb, and chewed and tore like bulldogs.

At last Milton's bird gave way and started on a feeble run to escape his pursuer, who kept on with his fighting as if he were a clockwork mechanism and had not yet run down. And when at last the vanquished one had crawled under the barn, the conqueror lifted his head in perfectly human exultation and sent forth such a crow — so filled with scorn and pride — that Milton was a little nettled, and said, "Wait till old Hancock gets after you."

It then remained for Lincoln to take his choice from among the flock in Milton's yard, and the two boys returned home to witness another battle. Mrs. Stewart mildly reproved them for their brutality, but they argued with her that there was no help for it. If a new strain of blood was to be brought into the barn-yard, a fight must take place, and so long as it *must* take place there was no good reason why it should not be witnessed. To this she could not make convincing reply.

Another, and less savage diversion of the boys at this season of the year, was the hiding of Easter eggs.

There was no special reason for it, and yet as a custom
it was quite common among the children of the settlers
from New York and the Middle States. The avowed
purpose was to lay up a supply of eggs for Easter Sunday. But as they were always extremely plenty at this
season of the year, and almost worthless, the motive
must be sought deeper down. Perhaps it was a survival
of some old-world superstitions. Anyhow, Lincoln and
his brother Owen began to hide eggs in all sorts of out of
the way places for full three weeks before Easter Sunday.

It was understood by Mr. Stewart that if he could
discover their hiding-places, the eggs might be confis-
cated, and he made elaborate pretence of searching for
them. One of the shrewd ways in which the boys
made concealment, was by lifting a flake of hay from
the stack, and making a hole beneath it. Upon letting
the flake of weather-beaten thatch fall back into place,
all signs of the nest disappeared. As the hens were laying a great many eggs each day, it was very difficult for
Mrs. Stewart to tell how many the boys were hiding —
she did not greatly care.

In his meetings with Milton and Rance, Lincoln
compared notes, as to numbers, and together the four
boys planned their Easter outing. Day after day, Mr.
Stewart, to the great dread of the boys, went poking
about close to the very spot where the eggs were hidden,
and twice he found a small "nest." But this only
added to the value of those remaining and stimulated
the boys to yet other and more skilful devices in
concealment.

They were able, in spite of his search, to save up several dozens of eggs, which they triumphantly brought to light on Easter morning, with gusty shouts of laughter over the pretended dismay of their parents.

With these eggs packed in a pail, with a few biscuits, some salt and pepper, Lincoln and Owen started out to meet their companions, Rance and Milton, and together they all set forth toward a distant belt of forest in which Burr Oak Creek ran.

There, in the warm spring sun, on the grassy bank beside the stream, they built their fire and cooked their eggs for their midday meal. Some they boiled, others they roasted in the ashes. Rance caught a chub or two from the brook, which added a wild savor to the meal, but eggs were considered a necessary order of the day; all else was by the way.

Something primeval and splendid clustered about this unusual camp-fire. Around them were bare trees, with buds just beginning to swell. The grass was green only in the sunny nooks, but the sky was filled with soft white clouds. For guests they had the squirrels and the blue jays. It was a celebration of their escape from the bonds of winter, and a greeting to spring. There was no conscious feeling in this feast, as far as the boys were concerned. But the deep-down explanation was this, they had gone back to the worship of *Oestre*, the Anglo-Saxon divinity of Spring. They had returned to the primitive, to the freedom of the savage, not knowing that the egg was the symbol of regenerate nature.

As a matter of fact, the flavor of these eggs was not good; the burned shells had a disagreeable odor, and the boys would have been very sorry if Mrs. Stewart had served up for them anything so disagreeable of flavor. But the curl of smoke from the grass with which they started the fire, the scream of the jay, the hawk sweeping by overhead, the touch of ashes on their tongues, the smell of the growing grass, and the sky above, made it all wonderful and wild and very sweet. When at night they returned, tired and sleepy, to the warmly lighted kitchen and to mother, they considered the day well spent, uniting as it did the pleasures of both civilization and barbarism.

During these spring days the sunny side of the straw-stacks had a vivid charm. There the hens sat to dream in the sun, and the cows lay there chewing their cuds. The boys spent many of their leisure hours scuffling on the straw or lying dormant as the pigs, absorbing the heat and light. Next to the chip-pile it was the most comfortable resting-place about the farm, between the melting of the snow and the coming on of spring.

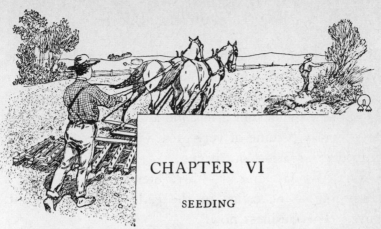

CHAPTER VI

SEEDING

AT last one morning Mr. Stewart said : —
" Well, boys, now we'll get out the drags." And a
most interesting day followed. The hired man jointed
the harrows, and Mr. Stewart put the seeder teeth on,
and scoured up the plough, and made every preparation
for the spring campaign.

A few days later, he said : " Well, Lincoln, get out
into the field to-day, and try it."

It was still freezing of nights, but by ten o'clock Lincoln was upon the land with the harrow. He found
the field dry on the swells, but still wet and cold in the
ravines. He kept at work all the afternoon, in a tentative way, retaining the delicious feeling that he could
really quit at any time, if he wished to do so. This
thought made the work seem almost like play. He
unhitched early for supper, and did not go out again.
The next day it was frozen in the morning, and the
man finished up the woodpile and raked away the
refuse in the front yard. In the afternoon Lincoln got
out the drag again, as before. On Saturday he worked
leisurely, nearly all day. Sunday he went to church

over at the Grove School-house, and met Rance and Milton and Ben, and they stood around on the sunny side of the building and talked of seeding, and boasted about how much they had done already. This meeting of a Sunday became of very great value after school was out, and the farm work begun.

On Monday morning Mr. Stewart's voice had a stern ring as he called in the early dawn: "All out, boys. It is business now."

No more dallying was allowed, no more tentative assaults — the seeding was begun. Mr. Stewart drove a load of wheat into the field and dispersed the white sacks across the land, like fence posts. The hired man followed with the broadcast seeder, while Lincoln moved into the "south forty" behind the fifty-tooth harrow, with mingled feelings of exultation and dismay.

Around him prairie chickens were whooping, and files of geese, with slow, steady flight, swept by at great height, wary and weary. Meadow-larks piped pleasantly. Ground sparrows arose from the soil in myriads, and flung themselves upward into the sky like grains of wheat from a sower's hand. Their chatter came out of the air like the voices of spirits invisible and multitudinous. Prairie pigeons on sounding wing swooped over the swells so close to the ground they seemed like monstrous serpents. As he struck across the field, the sun not far up in the sky was warm and red, but the wind was keen. He looked about to see if any of his neighbors had beaten him into action. There were no signs of Rance on his right, or Ben on his left. He heard the first bang of the seedbox, clear and sharp as a morning gun, as the hired man flung the cover shut and called "*Glang there, boys.*"

Back and forth across the wide field Lincoln moved, while the sun crawled up high and higher in the sky. It was viciously hard work. His heels sank in the soft earth, making the tendons of his heels creak and strain. The mud loaded itself upon his boots, till he seemed a convict with ball and chain, but he dragged himself along doggedly mechanical, like a fly stuck in molasses. He was hungry by half-past nine, and famished at eleven o'clock. Thereafter the sun appeared to stand still. His stomach caved in and his knees trembled with weakness, before the white flag fluttered from the chamber window, announcing dinner. However, he found strength to shout to the hired hand, and unhitching with great haste, climbed upon his nigh horse, and rode to the barn.

It was good to go into the kitchen, smelling sweet and fine with fresh biscuit and hot coffee. The men

F

all ate like dragons, devouring potatoes and salt pork, without end, but Mrs. Stewart only mildly remarked, " For the land's sake, don't bust yourselves."

After such a dinner, Lincoln despaired of being able to move again. Luckily he had half-an-hour in which to get his courage back, and besides, there was the stirring power of his father's clarion call. Mr. Stewart appeared superhuman to his son. He saw everything, seemed never to sleep, and never hesitated. Long before the nooning was up, so it seemed, he began to shout : —

" Roll out, boys, roll out ! Business on hand ! "

Lincoln hobbled to the barn, lame, stiff, and sore. The sinews of his legs had shortened and his knees were bent like an old man's. Once into the field he perceived a subtle change, a mellower charm; the ground was warmer, the sky more genial, and the wind more amiable, and before he had made his first round his legs were limbered up once more.

The tendency to sit and dream the hours away was very great, and he laid his tired body down in the tawny sunlit grass at the back of the field, behind a hedge of hazel bushes, and gazed up at the beautiful clouds sailing by, wishing he had nothing else to do in the world. He saw cranes sailing at immense heights, so far aloft their cries could be heard only when he held his breath. Oh, the beauty and majesty of their life !

The wind whispered in the tall weeds, and sighed to the hazel bushes. The grass blades touched each other in the passing winds, and the gophers, glad of escape from their dark, underground prisons, whistled their cheery greetings to the sun.

But the far-off voice of his father aroused the boy, and taking up the lines again, he returned to his toil, like some small insect, crawling across the wide brown field. His team was made up of two big, powerful colts, and he was forced to cross the reins over his back, in order to hold them down. He grew weak and lame as the sun went behind a cloud and the wind became chill, yet he dared not rest.

The hired man never halted, except to put in seed. Lincoln could hear his sharp commands to the team, and the noise of the seeder, as he pushed his way from one side of the farm to the other. Beyond the fence, too far away for even a signal to pass between them, he could see Rance hard at it, like himself, and that comforted him a little.

By five o'clock he was hungry, and not merely tired — he was exhausted. The sun was setting dimly at the west. The prairie chickens were again in evening chorus. The gophers had gone back to their burrows. The geese and ducks were flying low, seeking resting-places, and the wind was bitter — the piercing chill of coming night was in it. The going of the sun seemed to put the springtime farther off. Again he unhitched his tired horses, and moved slowly toward the house, where Owen was pumping water for the cattle, and bringing in wood for the kitchen fire. The kitchen fire seemed a good thing again and the supper of salt pork, mashed potatoes, and tea tasted very good indeed after five hours in the field.   He could not bring himself to go out after supper so painful were the tendons on his heels, but in a few days this soreness passed away.

Some of Mr. Stewart's fields were two miles away, and the men did not go home at noon, but ate their cold lunch in a clump of hazel bushes, or on the sunny side of a "sink-hole," which offered shelter.   There was a sense of strangeness and wildness in all this to Lincoln, as he lay in the tall, dead grass, hearing the gusty winds sweep by like vultures, whose wings wallowed the wild oats at furious speed.   Sometimes the blast was cold and swift and bleak, chilling them all to the marrow, making the tender cheeks of the boys red and painful.   Sometimes the snow came, spiteful and stinging, and the soil grew wet and sticky again.   But the clouds were fleeting, for the most part the sun shone, and the wind was soft and warm.

And so, day by day, the boys walked their monotonous rounds upon the ever mellowing soil.   They saw the geese pass on to the north, and the green grass come into the sunny slopes.   They answered the splendid challenge of the solitary crane, and watched the ground sparrow build her lowly nest.   Their muscles grew firm and their toil tired them less.   Each day the earth grew warmer, and the great clouds more summer-like; the wild chickens began to mate and seek solitary homes in the grassy swales.   The pocket gopher commenced to throw up his fresh purple-brown mounds.   Larks, blue-birds, and king-birds followed the robins, and at last the

full tide of spring was sweeping northward over the
prairie, and the final cross-dragging of the well-mellowed
soil had a charm which almost counterbalanced the
weary tramp, tramp behind the uncomplaining team.
Long before the last field was finished, the dust began
to move on the southern breeze, and the boy, who began by wading in the mud, ended by being blackened by
the dust as he rode the "smoocher."

During these busy weeks, the boys met each other
only on Sunday, when Milton and Rance or Ben came
to see Lincoln and Owen, or Milton and Ben "called
round" for Lincoln and stayed for dinner or supper.
These were pleasant days. Their playing was zestful.
As soon as the ground would allow it, they took off their
boots, and the delightful sense of lightness and deftness
thus gained, led them to turn handsprings and run races,
clean forgetting their week-day toil in the field.

At this time some heavy rains came on, and the " runs "

or ravines filled with rushing torrents of water, which added dignity and strangeness to the quiet prairie, and the boys spent a day wandering up and down the banks of Prairie Run, studying the wreckage in the boiling water, and listening to its roar. The current was so swift it swept away bridges, and cattle and pigs, whose bodies, floating in the eddies, added a sinister quality to the flood.

After a Sunday of riding about on their ponies, with their friends, the boys found it very hard to return to the stern toil of Monday morning. The world always seemed a little darker at sunset on Sunday night than on Saturday night. The week ahead of them seemed hopelessly long and profitless, and when they answered the imperious " revellie " of their father's " Roll out, boys, roll out ! " it was but feebly and gloomily.

On the new land it was no light job to run the harrow. The roots of the hazel brush clogged the teeth, and it was necessary to lift it often, and this was hard work for boys of ten and twelve. . It was necessary, also, to guide the horses constantly, to see that they " lapped half," and sometimes the dust blew so thickly that not only were the boys coated with it, but their eyes were blinded by it, and the tears of rage and rebellion they shed stained their cheeks with comic lines. At such times it seemed hard to be a prairie farmer's son.

Once Lincoln was tempted into giving chase to a big gray gopher, and the sound of his whip startled the spirited team, and they ran away across the field, each moment wilder, till at last one horse fell, and the other flung the overturned harrow upon his mate mangling him so that it was necessary to kill him. This was the most tragic event of Lincoln's life up to this time, and fairly stunned him with remorse, for he loved the colt and considered him one of the most wonderful creatures in the world.

He helped the hired man bury him, and when he threw the first shovelful of earth on the grand body, his throat ached and tears streamed down his cheeks. The hired man respected the boy's grief, and did not joke. Mr. Stewart remained stern and accusing for many days, but did not refer to the tragedy, which darkened the boy's life for many days.

One day as he went to the field he scared a great black bird from the spot where the colt was buried. It was the prairie vulture or "turkey-buzzard." With three flaps of his enormous wings he mounted the air, and then without an observable flutter of a feather he looped and circled and rose, calmly, easefully, until he mingled with the clouds and passed from sight. Not even his grewsome reputation could lessen the majesty of his flight, and Lincoln stood long wondering how he could make the wind his servant and the cloud his brother. Not even the crane could overtop this demon of the air.

THE VULTURE OF THE PLAINS

HE wings a slow and watchful flight,
His neck is bare, his eyes are bright,
His plumage fits the starless night.

He sits at feast where cattle lie
Withering in ashen alkali,
And gorges till he scarce can fly.

But he is kingly on the breeze!
On rigid wing in royal ease
A soundless bark on viewless seas,
Piercing the purple storm-cloud — he makes
The sun his neighbor, and shakes
His wrinkled neck in mock dismay,
Swinging his slow contemptuous way
Above the hot red lightning's play : —

Monarch of cloudland — yet a ghoul at prey.

THE HERALD CRANE

AH! Say you so, bold sailor,
In the sunlit deeps of sky,
Dost thou so soon the seed-time tell
In thy imperial cry,
As circling in yon shoreless sea
Thine unseen form goes drifting by?

I cannot trace in the noonday glare
Thy regal flight, O Crane;
From the leaping might of the fiery light
Mine eyes recoil in pain.
But on mine ear thine echoing cry
Falls like a bugle strain.

The mellow soil glows beneath my feet,
Where lies the buried grain;
The warm light floods the length and breadth
Of the vast, dim, shimmering plain,
Throbbing with heat and the nameless thrill
Of the birth time's restless pain.

On weary wing plebeian geese
Push on their arrowy line
Straight into the north, and snowy brant,
In dazzling sunlight, gloom, and shine.

But thou, O Crane, at thy far height,
On proud extended wings sweepst on
In silent, easeful flight.

Then cry, thou martial-throated herald!
Cry to the sun, and sweep
And swing along thy mateless course
Above the clouds that sleep
On lazy wind — cry on! Send down
Thy trumpet note; it seems
The voice of hope and dauntless will,
And breaks the spell of dreams.

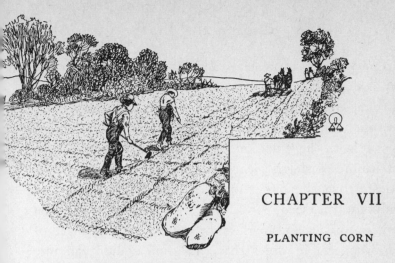

CHAPTER VII

PLANTING CORN

THE preparation for the corn planting followed immediately upon the cross-dragging of the wheat-field. The ground set apart for this crop had been ploughed in the fall, but it was necessary to cultivate it with the seeder and harrow, till it became smooth and tillable as a garden-patch.

At this time the earliest sown wheat-field was a lovely green, tender and translucent. The meadows rang with melody. The geese and loons had all passed over to the lakes of the north, but the crane still made the sky ring with his majestic note. Hardly a day passed but one of these inspiring birds called from the fathomless depths of the sky. The morning symphony of prairie chickens had begun to die away. The popple groves were deliciously green, and their round leaves were beginning to quiver in the wind. The oak's brown branches had taken on delicate pinks and browns, as the tender buds slowly unfolded, and though not yet quite as " large as a squirrel's ear," Farmer Stewart considered it quite time to plant his corn.

This was the 3d of May, and formed one of the most joyous experiences of the year. The field's broad acres lay out beautifully smooth and brown and warm after the final crossing of the harrow. Mr. Stewart rode cross it with the " marker " (a contrivance resembling a four-runnered sleigh), leaving the mellow soil lined with little furrows about four feet apart. The earth was now ready for the seed, for it was the custom of the best farmers to wait and mark it the other way, just ahead of the droppers, in order that the grain should fall into moist earth.

In those days the corn was still planted by hand and covered with a hoe. Lincoln, who had been helping to make the garden, to rake up the yard, to clip vines, and to set onions, was tired of " puttering," and eager to drop corn. " You'll have enough of it before Saturday night," said his father. Mr. Stewart was a lover of corn, and had set aside a larger field than any of his neighbors.

Early on a fine May morning, Lincoln made one of a crew, starting for the field. He was accompanied by Milton, Owen, Mr. Stewart, Neighbor Jennings, and Jack, the hired man. Mr. Jennings was " changing works " ; that is, he was helping Mr. Stewart, with the understanding that he would be paid in kind. His soil was a little " colder " and was not quite ready.

Mr. Stewart drove the " marker," followed by Milton and Lincoln, who dropped the seed, while Mr. Jennings and Jack, with light, shapely, flashing, steel hoes, followed, to cover it. Owen was commissioned to plant pumpkin-seeds, which he considered a high honor for the first half-hour, and a burden, grievous to be borne, there-after.

The " marker," as it passed over the field, crossed the lines running the other way, thus producing checks or squares about three feet and nine inches each way. At the intersection of these markings the seeds were dropped and covered. The field, mellow as a garden, lay palpitating under the sun ; the air was so still that the voices of the girls on the Hutchison farm could be heard in laughter. Ben's sisters were dropping corn over there, and Jack said, " By Mighty ! for a cent I'd quit and go work over there m'self."

The first thing Lincoln did was to pull off his boots, in order not to miss the delicious feeling of the warm soil, as the tender soles of his feet sank into it, burrowing like some wild thing lately returned to its native element. He wore one of his mother's old calico aprons tied round his waist, with a big knot in the slack of it, to make a pouch capable of carrying several quarts of corn. Having filled this with seed, he was ready to take his place in one of the rows.

Now, the rule was to drop three or four kernels (no more and no less) in each intersection of the grooves. The sharp eyes of those who followed were certain to detect any mistake, though if you were a pretty girl, the men with the hoes would say nothing about your blunders. After Lincoln got the swing of it, he planted his left foot each time close to the crossing, and dropped the seeds just before his toes, fearing not the swift, steady stroke of the hoes behind. The soil was so friable, and the hoes so light and keen, a single clip covered each hill, and the skilful hoemen pressed the droppers hard. The gait was a steady walk, and the dull ring of the steel at each boy's naked heel was like the tick of a clock, and an ever present incentive to speed and regularity. In a short time Lincoln became so skilful he could not only keep up his own row, but help Milton occasionally when he fell behind.

It was hard work; on this the boys were agreed. It made their necks ache, and stiffened their backs, especially as the day grew windy, and they were obliged to stoop to the hills. By the time they had gone the whole way across the wide field they were very glad to take a look at the sky, and at the end of each round they consumed a great deal of time in filling their pouches. As the forenoon wore away, the sun grew warmer, and Mr. Stewart, looking out over the fine, level wheat-field, getting greener each hour, said, in a voice solemn with veneration, "I just believe I can hear that wheat grow."

Notwithstanding, the work, these days of planting corn, had a distinct and mellow charm, filled as they were with superb dawns and warm, sensuous, slumbrous noons. Night came after most gorgeously colored and silent sunsets, when the orange light flamed across a sea of tender, springing wheat, and a rising mist was in the air. The diminishing chorus of the prairie chickens rang, in mournful, quavering chorus, through the haze, the joy of spring quite lost out of it, but the frogs in the marsh took up and carried forward the theme, as night slowly fell and the bird-voices slowly died away. Spring was merging into sultry summer.

Corn-planting practically finished the spring work, and there came a welcome breathing-spell for the boys and the teams. The horses, so shining and plump a few weeks before, were gaunt and worn. The men, also, felt a vast relief; for all through April, from early morning till late at night, they had tramped ceaselessly to and fro across the field. They were glad of the chance to break the wild sod and to build fences.

In a few days, with four horses hitched to a sixteen-inch breaking-plough, the hired man went forth to slit the smooth green sod into strips.

Lincoln sadly watched the tender grass and the springing flowers as they rolled beneath the remorseless mould-board, but there was also a deep pleasure in seeing the smooth, shining, almost unbroken ribbon of black soil tuck itself into the furrow, behind the growling share. Around them, on the swells, gophers whistled, and the nesting plover quaveringly called. The blackbirds clucked in the furrow, and gray-bearded badgers watched, with jealous eye, the ploughman's steady progress toward his knoll. The weather was perfect May. Big fleecy clouds sailed from west to east, and the wind was soft and kind.

It required a man to hold the big breaking-plough, as it went ripping and tearing through the groves of hazel brush, and sometimes Mr. Stewart was called to sit on the plough-beam, to hold it to its work, while Jack braced himself to the handles. And so, one by one, the "tow-heads" yielded to the axe and the plough. The boys helped to pile and burn the brush, which the men cut with a short, heavy scythe. This was pleasant business for a little while, but came at last to be a punishment and imprisonment, like all other toil. Every change of work brought joy, like a release from prison. From the seeding, corn-planting seemed very desirable; but when the hoes had clicked behind their heels for a couple of days the boys longed for breaking or fence-building. Burning brush seemed glorious sport until they had tried it, and found it very hot and disagreeable, after all. The fact is, they considered any continuous labor an infringement of their right to liberty and the pursuit of knowledge.

Fence-building suited Lincoln very well. Mr. Stewart went ahead, starting the holes with a crowbar. After him Lincoln drove a team containing sharpened posts and a barrel of water. The holes were filled with water to soften the ground, and then, the post being dropped therein and properly lined up, David McTurg swung the great iron beetle high in the air and brought it down upon the squared timber with a loud "hoh!" which the boys considered indispensable to powerful effort. There was something large and fine in his wide swing of the maul, and Lincoln looked forward eagerly to the time when he should be able to set a post three inches into the ground with every clip. As it was, he had nothing to do but drive the team, which pleased him very well.

But this, after all, was only a diversion. The work

of clearing and breaking the sod on the new land, and the daily care of the springing corn, were of first importance. They all returned to breaking sod and clearing away brush after a few days of fence-building.

One day as he was helping his father pile brush, Lincoln stopped to examine a blossoming strawberry vine. His fingers were almost touching it when he caught the glitter of a small, metallic eye, and discovered the severed head of a rattlesnake lying just under the white flower. He sprang back with a sudden cry of fear, which brought his father to the spot. Together they examined the reptile.

It was a " Massasauga " or meadow rattlesnake. The scythe had clipped his head and about four inches of neck from his body, and he lay sullenly quiet, with his little black, forked tongue playing in and out of his mouth. As Mr. Stewart presented a piece of popple bark, the head opened its mouth wide and flat and struck its fine, curving fangs into it. Immediately a light-green liquid collected and began to creep up the inner side of the bark, and Lincoln shuddered to think how powerful that minute drop of poison was.

He had been accustomed to rattlesnakes all his life. On the wooded hills of Wisconsin, in the limestone country, the big black-and-yellow *Crotalus horridus* was common. In the spring, when the suns of early April began to warm the rocks on southward-sloping bluffs, they came out to lie in the sun and breed before starting downward into the fields and meadows below. Nothing can be more sinister than a knot of these

G

terrible creatures, — a mass of twisting, shining bodies, from which the flat heads protrude like tassels, instinct with hatred and defiance, deadly as lightning and as swift. In autumn they returned to their dens in the seams of the cliffs.

Lincoln, when not more than eight years of age, used to go with his uncles hunting these breeding-places; and he had often seen them whip with long poles these masses of rattling monsters into bloody shreds, and he had seen the more agile of them slide away beneath the rocks silent as golden oil. He had happened upon them beside his path; his ear was acquainted with their ringing, rattling, buzzing, singing menace. Once a great, thick, sullen fellow was killed in his father's barn-yard, after he had scared the chickens into a frenzy by his mere presence. One of the men put the wounded snake near a hen with chickens, and it seemed she would go crazy with fear. She seemed to know by instinct his dread power.

The boys had often seen them cut in pieces by the mowing-machine, and in the harvest-field once a big one dropped from the sheaf David McTurg was binding. The boys knew them well and did not greatly fear them. In fact, Lincoln used to hunt the cows on the hills in Wisconsin barefooted and alone with less fear of the snakes than of purely imaginary bears and wolves. When he first heard of the " Massasaugas " in Rock County, therefore, he was curious rather than alarmed, and his parents were correspondingly undisturbed. These small gray fellows had the effect of being mild imitations after a long experience with the yellow monsters of the lichen-spotted limestone cliffs of their old home. They were smaller, more sluggish, and presumably less poisonous, though every herd of cattle had one or more invalids with jaw swollen to enormous size to testify to the terrible power of the virus even of these prairie cousins of the *Horridus* family.

Moreover, there was less liability of ambush in the prairie country, and the breaking ploughs were a remorseless agency in destroying the gray pests. Hardly a day passed without Jack's triumphant exhibition of several new bunches of rattles, and the men used to compare notes on Sunday as they sat around the horse-block at church, and boast of the number they had killed.

One of the neighbors who took dinner with Mr. Stewart about this time horrified the mother by declaring that he had killed three hundred Massasaugas on his place alone. " We don't mind 'em," said he, " any more'n so many garter-snakes. You jest want to mind where you step, and where you put your bare hand ; that's all."

Nevertheless the boys never came upon that cold gray coil and lifted, steady, poised triangular head and blurring tail, without feeling that a deadly weapon was aimed and remorselessly ready to take a life.

THE STRIPED GOPHER

HE is a roguish little wag;
He sits like priest with folded hands;
The farm-boy stops his dusty drag,
And mocks his whistle where he stands.

The crane in deeps of sunlit sky
Proclaims the spring with bugle-note—
Not less the prophecies which lie
Within the gopher's cheery note.

From radiant slopes of pink and green,
From warm brown fields, his greetings fret;
The eye of hawk is not more keen
Than his when danger seems to threat.

He is a cunning little wag;
He sits and jeers with folded hands;
The farm-boy stoops behind his drag,
And flings a missile where he stands.

CHAPTER VIII

SNARING GOPHERS

AFTER the corn was planted, the younger lads were set to work snaring and shooting the gophers from the corn-fields. The prairie abounded at this time with two sorts of ground squirrel, which the settlers called " the striped gopher " and " the gray gopher." The striped gopher resembled a large chipmunk, and the gray gopher was apparently a squirrel that had taken to the fields. The " pocket gopher " was considered a sort of mole or rat and not really a gopher.

The survival of the fittest had brought about a beautiful adaptation to environment in both cases. The small one had become so delicately striped in brown and yellow, as to be well-nigh invisible in the short grass of the upland, while the gray gopher, living in and about the nooks and corners of the fields, which held over from year to year long tufts of gray and weather-beaten grass, fitted quite as closely to his background, his yellow-gray coat aiding him in his efforts to escape the eyes of the hawk and the wolf.

The little striped rogues absolutely swarmed in the wild sod immediately adjoining the new-broken fields, and were a great pest, for they developed a most annoying cleverness in finding and digging up the newly planted corn. In some subtle way they had learned that wherever two deep paths crossed, with a little mound of dirt in the centre, there sweet food was to be had, and it was no uncommon thing to find a long row of sprouting kernels dug up in this manner, with most unerring precision.

It was clearly a case of inherited aptitude, for their cousins, far out on the prairie, were by no means so shrewd. Dwelling within the neighborhood of man for a few generations had been valuable. Inherited aptitude was plainly superimposed upon native shrewdness. They were a positive plague, and it became painfully necessary to wipe them out or give up the corn. It was the business of every boy in the neighborhood to wage remorseless war upon them each day in the week, from the time the corn was planted until it had grown too big to be uprooted.

So Lincoln carried a shot-gun about the field with which to slay these graceful little creatures, while Owen followed behind to cut off their tails as trophies. They were allowed two cents bounty (from their father) for every striped gopher, and three cents apiece for every gray gopher they killed. They generally made two rounds each day. They soon discovered that the little rascals were most likely to be out at about ten o'clock of each warm forenoon, and once again between four and five.

The boys went to this task with pleasure, but there was something æsthetic mingled with the delight of successful shooting. Like the angler or hunter, they enjoyed the vivid sunlight, the fresh winds, the warm earth, and especially the freedom of the hunter. Occasionally as Lincoln looked down at a poor bleeding little gopher at the door of his house, he suffered a keen twinge of remorse, and reproved himself for cruelty. However, it seemed the only way out, so he hardened himself and went on with his desolating work. He was too small to hold the gun at arm's length, but rested it on his knee or on a small stick which Owen consented to carry.

It was, after all, sad business, and often the tender, springing grass, the far-away faint and changing purple of the woods, the shimmer of the swelling prairie, leaping toward the flaming sun — all the inexpressible glow and pulse of blooming spring — witched him from his warfare. He lay prone on his back while the gophers whistled and dashed about in play, watching the hawks dipping and wheeling in the shimmering air, and listening to the quavering, wailing cry of the plovers as they settled to the earth with uplifted pointed wings. The twitter of innumerable ground sparrows passing overhead united with the sweet and thrilling signals of the meadow-lark, to complete the wondrous charm of the morning air.

Killing gophers was like fishing, — an excuse for enjoying the prairie. Often on Sunday mornings, together with Milton and Rance, Owen and Lincoln sallied forth, armed with long pieces of stout twine to snare the little pests, for they were not allowed to fire a gun on Sunday. They became very expert in this business.

Having driven a gopher to his burrow, they took a little turn on the sod, in order to drag their strings taut. Then, slipping the noose well down into the hole, they retired to the end of the string to wait for the little fellow to pop his head through the noose, which he usually did after some moments of perfect silence. It is their habit to come suddenly and silently to the top of their burrows, and to cautiously and slowly lift their heads until they can fix an eye on you. You must be keen-eyed, or you will fail to observe the small head, which is almost exactly the color of the surrounding grass. If you glance away from the burrow even for a moment, you may fail to find it when you look back.

For they are not only exceedingly shrewd, but they are rare ventriloquists. After sitting a couple of minutes and seeing nothing, you may hear a low, sweet trill, like that of a sleepy bird. You cannot place it — it seems to be in the air one moment and behind you the next moment. The crafty rascal has come up at some other hole and is laughing at you.

You turn your head, "*cheep-eep*" — a slight movement and he is gone. You adjust your snare at the new burrow and again sit patiently and as still as stone for four or five minutes, perhaps ten, before you hear again that sly, sleepy trill. It sounds back of you, at first, then in front, and at last, by studying every inch of the ground before you, you detect a bright eye gleaming upon you from the burrow where your snare had been set at first. You now understand that you are dealing with " an old residenter," not a young and foolish child.

Owen often struggled for hours to snare one of these cunning old tricksters. He was accustomed to lie flat on his belly, with his feet waving in the air like small banners, his eyes fixed upon the hole, with fingers ready to twitch the string, but he generally grew impatient and looked away or moved, and so lost his chance. It required even greater patience and skill to succeed in snaring the gray gopher, who was capable of breaking the string when caught.

However, snaring was only part of the fun. When they grew tired of killing things, they could lay out full length on the warm, bright green sod, and listen to the softened sounds of the prairie, seeing the girls picking "goslins" on the sunny slopes, enjoying in sensuous drowse the clouds, the sun, and the earth, content, like the lambs or like Rover, to be left in peace in the downpour of spring sunshine. There was no grass for the wandering wind to wave, no trees to rustle, nothing to break the infinite peace which brooded over the wide prairie.

They felt, at such moments, some such pleasure as that the fisherman knows, when dropping his rod among the ferns he watches the soaring eagle high in the air, or listens to the ripple of the restless stream.

But neither the snare nor the shot-gun sufficed to keep these bright-eyed little people from eating up the seed, and Mr. Stewart went to the great length of scattering poisoned grains of corn about the field. This seemed to Lincoln a repulsive and terrible thing to do, but the father argued, " The poor beasties must give way, or you'll have no Johnny cake for your milk."

The boys soon had a box partly filled with gray gophers, which they tried hard to tame. It was supposed that the gray gopher, like the squirrel, could be made a household pet, but as a matter of fact they were particularly savage and untamable. They not only fought their captors, but they fought each other with unrelenting ferocity. There was something hard and stern, something pitiless and threatening, in their eyes. They invariably gnawed a hole through the box and escaped long before they showed the slightest affection for the boys, though they fed them on bread and milk and the choicest grains of corn.

One day Jack brought home a half-grown badger, and the boys were at once wildly excited by his snarling and hissing. He was ready to do battle at any moment; and though Owen put him in a box and fed him fat gophers and milk, and all kinds of good things, he never grew much tamer. Lincoln, as a piece of daring, sometimes stroked his flat, pointed head, but always at risk of having his fingers snapped off. He had a bad smell, also, and at last they grew tired of him, and turned him out again, on the sod. He waddled away flat in the grass, eagerly, swiftly. They followed him until he burrowed into a ridge and hid himself from sight, and never again attempted to tame one of his kind.

It was impossible not to have business with skunks, for they were thick. They were a greater terror to the boys than rattlesnakes; for aside from their nauseating odor, they were said to destroy the eyes of men by means of their terrible discharge. Nearly every dog of the neighborhood smelled of them, and they often got under the houses and barns, and rioted on good things, for no one cared to kill them there.

Lincoln, being instructed by Rance, set traps with long ropes attached, and by gently hauling them at long range, was able to get them far out on the prairie without disaster. Their discharge was clearly only a last resort, and so long as they were unharmed they were themselves harmless. They were really pretty creatures, especially the young ones, and Lincoln considered it a pity that they should smell so horribly strong.

THE MEADOW–LARK

A BRAVE little bird that fears not God,
A voice that breaks from a snow-wet clod,
With prophecy of sunny sod
Set thick with wind-waved goldenrod.

From the first bare earth in the raw, cold spring,
From the grim, gray turf when fall-winds sting,
The ploughboy hears his clear song ring,
And work for the time is a pleasant thing.

PRAIRIE FIRES

A CURVING, leaping line of light,
A crackling roar from lurid lungs,
A wild flush on the skies of night —
A force that gnaws with hot red tongues
And leaves a blackened, smoking sod,
A fiery furnace where the cattle trod.

CHAPTER IX

SUMMER-TIME. — HERDING THE CATTLE

AT the time Duncan Stewart moved out upon Sun Prairie, wide tracts of unbroken sod still lay open for common grazing-ground, and every farmer kept from twenty-five to a hundred head of cattle and horses. As soon as the grass began to spring from the fire-blackened sod in April, the cattle left the straw-piles (under whose lee they had fed during the winter), and crawled out to forage on the open. They were still "free commoners" in the eyes of the law.

The colts were a fuzzy, ugly-looking lot at this time; even those who were well fed had long hair, and their manes were dirty and tangled, but as the grazing improved, and the warmth and plenty of spring filled them with new blood, they sloughed off their mangy coats of hair, and lifted their wide-blown nostrils to the western wind in glorious freedom. Many of them had never felt the weight of a man's hand, and even those that had wintered in and around the barn-yard lost all trace of domesticity after a few days' life on the springing grass. It was not unusual to find that the wildest and wariest of all the herd bore a collar mark or some other ineffaceable badge of previous servitude.

They were for the most part Morgan grades or "Canuck," with a strain of broncho to give them fire. It was curious, it was splendid, to see how the old, deep-buried instincts broke out in these halterless herds. In a few days, after many trials of speed and power, the bands of all the region united into one drove, and a leader, the swiftest and most tireless of them all, appeared from the ranks and led them at will. Often without apparent cause, merely for the joy of it, they left their feeding-grounds to wheel and charge and race for hours over the swells, across the creeks, and through the hazel thickets. Sometimes their movements arose from the stinging of gadflies, sometimes from a battle between two jealous leaders, sometimes from the passing of a wolf — often from no cause at all other than bounding vitality.

In much the same way, but less rapidly, the cattle went forth upon the plain. Each family herd not only contained the growing steers, but the family cows, and it was the duty of one boy from each family to mount a horse every afternoon and "hunt the cattle," a task he seldom shirked. Lincoln and Owen took turn and turn about at this, and they soon knew the sound of every bell. They seldom failed of discovering the herd at once. The cows were then cut out and driven back to the farm-yard to be milked. In this way every lad in the neighborhood could ride like a Comanche. Mr. Stewart turned over to Lincoln a little Morgan horse called "Ivanhoe," and cattle-herding became part of his business during the summer. Owen soon had a pony of his own. They lived in the saddle when no other duties called them. Rance and Lincoln met almost every day on the feeding-grounds, and the world seemed a very good place for a boy, as they galloped along together.

In this way Lincoln came to know the prairies, which was then very beautiful, and all its life. On the uplands a short, light-green, hair-like grass grew, intermixed with various resinous weeds, while the lowlands produced a luxuriant growth of bluejoint, wild oats, and other large grasses. Along the streams and in the "sloos," cattails rose from thick mats of wide-bladed marsh-grass. Almost without realizing it, the boys came to know every weed, every curious flower, every living thing big enough to be seen from the back of a horse. They enjoyed it all, too, without so much as calling it beautiful.

Nothing could be more generous, more joyous, than these natural meadows in June. The flash and ripple and glimmer of the tall, wide-bodied grass, the myriad voices of ecstatic bobolinks, the chirp and whistle of red-winged blackbirds swaying on the reeds or in the willows, the meadow-larks piping from grassy bogs, and the swift snipe and wailing plover adding their voices as they rose and fell on the flowery green slopes of the uplands. It was a big land, and a big, big sky to Lincoln, who had been born in a coolly home, and he had withal a sense of the still wilder country to the west.

Sometimes of a Sunday afternoon, as he wandered deep in these meadows with Bettie and Milton and Cora, gathering bouquets of pinks, sweet-williams, tiger-lilies, and lady-slippers, he had a vague perception of another and sweeter side of this landscape, though it did not remain with him long. The sun flamed across the splendid, moving, flashing deeps of the grasses, the perfumes of a thousand nameless plants rose in the warm midday air, and the mere joy of living filled his heart to the exclusion of any other desire.

Nor was the upland less interesting as they roamed over it, far and wide, on their horses. In the spring the huge antlers, bleached white and bare, in countless numbers, on the bare-burnt sod, told of the millions of elk and bison that had once roamed on these splendid pastures, in the days when the tall Sioux were the only hunters.

The gray hermit, the badger, made his home in deep dens on the long ridges, and on sunny April days the mother fox lay out with her young, on southward-sloping swells. The swift prairie wolf slunk, with backward-glancing eyes, from copse to copse, and many a mad race the boys had at the tail of this swift and tireless "spectre of the plains." They seldom did him any harm, but it brought out the speed of their ponies and broke the monotony of the herding. Antelope and deer were still occasionally seen, and to Lincoln it seemed that just over the next ridge toward the sunset, the shaggy brown bulls still fed in thousands, and in his heart he vowed sometime to ride away over there and see. All the boys he knew — all the young men talked of "the west," never of the east; always of the plains, of the mountains and cattle-raising and mining and Indians, and Lincoln could not but be influenced by this spirit.

Scattered over the clay lands were small groves or clumps of popple trees, called "tow-heads" by the settlers. They were commonly only two or three hundred feet in diameter, though in some cases they grow along a ridge many acres in extent. Around these islands, seas of hazel brush rolled, interspersed with lagoons of bluejoint-grass, that most beautiful and stately product of prairie soil. On the Maple River there were plum trees and crab-apples and haws and many good things, while the prairie produced immense crops of hazelnuts and strawberries.

Over these uplands, through these lakes of hazel brush, and round these coverts of popple, Lincoln and Rance, Owen and Milton and Ben and Bert, careered, chasing the rabbits, hunting the cows, killing rattlesnakes, racing the half-wild colts and the prowling wolves. It was an

H

alluring life for a boy.   Rance, tall, reliant, graceful, and
strong almost as a man, was a product of this life.   He
had a magnificent colt named " Ladrone," and rode him
as no other boy in the whole country could do.   He
used the cowboy saddle, with a high pommel, while
Lincoln and Milton rode army saddles without pommels.
They all carried short-handled drover's whips, which required considerable skill to manage, for the lash was long
and heavy and sure to wind around the neck of an

awkward lad.   Lincoln was soon exceedingly expert
with this whip, but Rance remained the best rider.

Rance was in the saddle most of the time, but Lincoln
continued to take a man's place with a team in times
when work pressed.   Captain Knapp was one of the
" best fixed " of all the farmers near.   He had a frame
barn and a house with a parlor.   He had also two grown-
up daughters, of whom Lincoln stood very much in awe.
They were the belles of the country, tall pale girls with
velvet-black eyes, very graceful of manner, and always
neat and pretty, even on wash days.

Rance was the only son and was the pride of his father,

a reticent and singular man, who had more books and newspapers than any other farmer in Sun Prairie. He was tall and a little bent, with a long brown beard; it was plain that Rance took his reticence and his black eyes from his father. Mrs. Knapp had been dead several years when Lincoln came to know the family, but everybody said Rance had the fair skin of his mother. He was not a notably studious boy. He loved the prairies and his horse " Ladrone " too much to remain in the house reading. He was a good scholar, always near the head of his class, but he had a contempt for those who could not leap, ride a horse, swing a cattle whip, and play ball. With heel behind the cantle of his saddle, and right hand sweeping the grass, he could pick up his hat or whip as his horse galloped past. Captain Knapp had been to California in the days of gold, and from him Rance had acquired a knowledge of the wonderful horsemanship of the Mexican vaqueros. He could throw a lasso, and ride backward on his horse, or standing in the saddle. Captain Knapp had been a cavalryman under Kilpatrick, and also taught his son to ride in army fashion. As a result he and Lincoln carried themselves half in the cowboy manner and half as the cavalryman sits.

They held the reins in the left hand, guiding their horse by the pressure of the rein on his neck, rather than by pulling at the bit. The right hand carried the whip; when not in use it dropped to the thigh, cavalry fashion. They rode with knees straight — sitting low in their saddles. Their horses were never allowed to trot, but were taught a gait which they called the "lope," which was a canter in front and a trot behind, a very good gait for long distances, and each horse was taught to keep it without the pressure of the rein, and to fall at the word into a swift walk.

For the first year Lincoln was Rance's pupil. Everything his hero did was fine and noble, and in truth Rance was a good boy. Though passionate and wilful, he was clean-spoken and naturally high-minded and honorable. He seldom joked (he left all that to Milton), and he was exceedingly sensitive to ridicule. He never quarrelled, never abused smaller boys, and yet he seldom showed a favor. Young as he was, the big boys were afraid to press him too far.

Milton could ride fairly well, but could not play ball and did not enjoy any game with running in it. The truth was, Milton was lazy. More than this, he had a sneaking fondness for girls, and Lincoln once caught him knitting. Only his love of horses and his fairly good horsemanship saved Milton from being called "a girl-boy."

All the boys but Rance had to milk cows, which was a peculiarly hateful task in summer, when the flies were bad, and worse in autumn, when the cold rains came on. It made their hands ache, and the cows' steaming hot sides were unpleasant to the touch, and they were liable at any moment to kick into the pail, in their efforts to drive off the flies. The boys had a trick of driving their heads hard in the cow's flank, so she could not bring forward her leg at all. The heavy tail was also a nuisance, and was tied by the long hairs around the cow's own leg. Humbolt Bunn tied it to the strap of his boot — and regretted it very much afterwards.

As the weather grew cold, the boys had a trick of urging the sleeping cows to their hoofs very gently, in order that their own bare feet might rest on the ground which the cows had warmed during the night. Lin-

coln often went out to milk barefooted when the ground was white with frost.

In midsummer they wore no shoes at all, except when they went to Sunday-school or to town. Their feet resembled "toad backs," their mother often said, and when ordered to wash their feet, they ran out into the tall grass, cleansed them in the dew, running backward in order to wash their heels. They were generally limping from a bruise or a brier or some other cause, but accepted each wound as one of the unavoidable things of human life.

There were always a lot of calves to be fed, and they

did not like that very well, either, for they were noisy and unruly little brutes. They were sure to blow a blast of milk upon you if you did not watch out, and each one tried hard to steal the other's portion, and often ended by spilling it all. The pigs were less trouble. They had but to empty the pail into a long trough and let them race for it. The boys taught the calves to drink by letting them suck their fingers beneath the surface of the milk, and Lincoln nailed a rag to the bottom of the pail, and it answered admirably.

As soon as the grain was threshed, the herd was brought in and turned on the stubble, and then it was Owen's business to keep them out of the corn. This was called "watching the cows," and it became very tiresome indeed after a few hours. After the cows had enjoyed a taste of the juicy young corn they became excessively eager to return to it, and the boy was forced to eye them closely. If he turned his back to get a melon or to visit with Lincoln, one of the rangy steers was certain to set forth in a bee-line for the corn, trailing all the herd behind him. Once within the shelter of the tall stalks, it required loud hallooing, and the best work of Rover to get them out, and even then they managed to get away with a nice taste of the succulent leaves. They loved it as Owen loved ice-cream.

So it was that the boys were in attendance on cattle from year end to year end, and they didn't like it. In fact, they didn't like any kind of work very well, at least not as a steady business. They liked riding and fishing and swimming and playing ball and lassoing the colts and training yearlings to the yoke, and breaking colts, and going to school, because at school there were no cows to milk or horses to curry, and yet in spite of all this they did an amazing amount of work. They grumbled and rubbed their eyes, but they got up early, and they were busy all day long either on the farm with the men or on the plains with the cattle.

MEADOW MEMORIES

O MEMORY, what conjury is thine?
　　Once more the sun shines on the wheat —
Once more I drink the wind like wine
　　When bursts the lark's song wildly sweet
From out the rain-wet new-mown grass.
　　I hear the sickle's clattering sweep,
And far-hallooings fleetly pass
　　From field to field.　Again I heap
The odorous windrows rank on rank —
　　Far from the tumult of the street,
From granite pavements' ceaseless clank,
　　From grinding grooves and jar of car,
I flee and lave my boyish feet
　　Where bee-lodged clover-blossoms are.

104

CHAPTER X

THE WILD MEADOWS. — HAYING TIME

HAYING was the one season of farm work which the boys thoroughly enjoyed. It usually began on the tame meadows about the twenty-fifth of June, and lasted a week or so. It had always appealed to Lincoln, in a distinctly beautiful and poetic sense, which was not true of the main business of farming. Most of the duties through which he passed needed the lapse of years to seem beautiful in his eyes, but haying had a charm and significance quite out of the common.

At this time the summer was at its most exuberant stage of vitality, and it was not strange that even the faculties of toiling old men, dulled and deadened with never ending drudgery, caught something of exultation from the superabundant glow and throb of Nature's life. The corn-field, dark green and sweet-smelling, rippled like a sea with a multitudinous stir and sheen and swirl. Waves of dusk and green and yellow circled across the level fields, while long leaves upthrust at intervals like spears or shook like guidons. The trees were in heavy leaf, insect life was at its height, and the air was filled with buzzing, dancing forms and with the sheen of innumerable gauzy wings.

The air was shaken by most ecstatic voices. The

bobolinks sailed and sang in the sensuous air, now sinking, now rising, their exquisite notes ringing, filling the air like the chimes of tiny silver bells. The king-bird, ever alert and aggressive, cried out sharply as he launched from the top of a poplar tree upon some buzzing insect, and the plover made the prairie sad with his wailing call. Vast purple-and-white clouds moved like bellying sails before the lazy wind, dark with rain, which they dropped momentarily like trailing garments upon the earth, and so passed on in stately measure with a roll of thunder.

The grasshoppers moved in clouds with snap and buzz, and out of the luxurious stagnant marshes came the ever thickening chorus of the toads and the frogs, while above them the killdees and snipe shuttled to and fro in sounding flight, and the blackbirds on the cattails and willows swayed with lifted throats, uttering their subtle liquid notes, made mad with delight of the sun and their own music. And over all and through all moved the slow, soft west wind, laden with the breath of the far-off prairie lands of the west, soothing and hushing and filling the world with a slumbrous haze.

It was time for vacation, and as a matter of fact the boys on the farm found a little leisure between corn-ploughing and haying for base-ball, swimming, fishing, and berrying, and they declined .to exchange places with the cowboys under these circumstances. They knew from dear experience that from the time the sickle set into the timothy there was no vacation till the snow fell.

In the ever changing West, " haying " covers a multitude of diverse experiences. Those whose recollections

extend over a term of twenty years, have seen many
changes in the implements of haying; from the old-
fashioned scythe and rake to the patent-geared-self-lift-
ing-adjustable-front-cut-yellow-King Mowing-machine,
and the self-dumping, spring-tooth horse-rake, not to
speak of the patent-loader harpoon-fork, and baling-
press.

Lincoln's earliest recollections of the haying-field
were of going into the field with an older boy, to take
a large white jug of " switchel" to the men. (The
jug was swung on a pole, and each accused the other
of trying to get the long end.) The men were bent
above the scythe, and cruel work it was — though Lincoln remembered only the glorious strawberries, which
the toilers tossed up on the green billows of damp
grass; and also with what awe he gazed at the great
green frogs, sitting motionless near by, and his horror
of the black snakes which ran with heads above the
timothy. The frogs always looked so mossy and in-
animate, it was a surprise to see them move. At this
time he was too small to have a set task, and was put to
look for berries and tumble down the " doodles."

But a year or two later, when his freedom to come
and go was ended, Lincoln began work in the field by
" raking after." Every middle-aged man in the West
will know what that subtends. It brings to mind a
gloomy urchin, with a long-handled rake, following a
huge, half-loaded wagon. He is treading gingerly the
" stubble-speared, new-mown sward," sliding his bare
feet close to the ground to avoid being spiked, or set-

ting foot carefully in the track of the "bull-wheel" for the same good reason. What a blessed relief it was when the boy found the slant of the stubble going his way! Scatterings — always the command, "Lincoln, hurry up with them scatterings."

All through June, before the haying came on, Lincoln and Owen kept track of the cattle on the wide prairies, or rode the horse in ploughing corn, and helped to build fence, and cut hazel brush before the breaking-plough. There was always something to do, even in "slack times." But the days grew hotter, the grass thicker and taller, and finally, on a bright, cloudless morning in June, the mowing-machine buzzed merrily around the grass-lot.

It had always been a joyous sound to Lincoln, this whizzing clatter of the mower. It was a pleasure to watch the sickle as it melted into the grasses stately and fragrant. They seemed to bow to the sweep of the shining bar. The timothy heads, sinking, shook out a fragrant, purple dust, and the clover blooms and fallen roses mingled their expiring breaths as they withered beneath the sun. The hay was even more fragrant than the grass. All day under the sun, all night under the dew, it lay, changing from green to gray; and the next afternoon it was ready to be raked into windrows and bunched, ready for stacking.

Raking, in the olden times, was a long and hard task. I can just remember seeing a row of men using hand-rakes as they gathered the hay on a valley farm in Wisconsin, but at the same time, on the Iowan prairies they

were using a revolving rake drawn by a horse and oper-
ated by a man walking behind. A year or two later
came the riding horse-rake; and by the time Lincoln
was able to take an important part in the haying-field,
the rake had been improved so that a boy could run it,
and it became his duty from his eleventh year forward.

It was with great joy and pride that he rode for the
first time into the field atop this new tool. He kept

his feet stoutly braced to the trip-lever until a big roll
of gathered hay bulged beneath him, then, with a
mighty pull, raised the teeth and dropped his load at
the " win'row." Three times round the piece, and the
" doodling " began. Owen now " raked after," a task
which he hated with cordial intensity. White, the
hired man, and Mr. Stewart put the hay into conical
heaps, their light and graceful forks flashing in the
vivid sunlight. There was very little drudgery connected with this harvest.

Each morning Mr. Stewart drove the mowing-machine, its clatter and buzz pulsing through the air like

the cheerful drone of a gigantic insect, while the boys and the hired men set up that already cured. The work was clean, not severe, and though the weather was warm, it was almost always enjoyable. Sometimes Mr. Stewart changed work with some of his neighbors, and so David McTurg and Rance or Milton came to help, and the work was almost like a picnic party.

Costumes were simple. A big, oat-straw hat, a hickory shirt, and a pair of denim trousers outfitted a boy, though Rance never went barefoot. The men wore boots (or a sort of army " brogan " shoe) in addition. If the sun were especially warm, they all filled their hats with cool, green cottonwood leaves, and " bore down " on the handle of their forks, which were three-tined, with smooth, curved handles, quite unlike the clumsy, two-tined things which Lincoln had often seen in pictures. The companionship, the merry voices of the men, the song of the machine, made haying very pleasant to all hands, although Lincoln's back sometimes ached with lifting the rake teeth, and the old mare grew stubborn and stupid as the day wore on.

Dinner came, bringing joy. Oh, the cool water at the well! And the fried pork, and the volcano of mashed potatoes, with a lump of butter in the crater! The salt pork, when dipped in bread-crumbs, tasted so good that the boys nearly " foundered themselves," as Jennings used to say. There was very little ceremony at these meals. Man and boy went to the table as they came from the field, wet with sweat and sprinkled with timothy bloom. Napkins were " against the law," and

To face page 111

steel knives were used to help out the three-tined forks. There were no courses, and no waiting on the table. The host merely said : "Now, boys, help yourselves. What you can't reach, yell for."

The weather was glorious, with only occasional showers to accentuate the splendid sunlight. There were no old men and no women in these fields. The men were young and vigorous, and their action was swift and supple. Sometimes it was hot to the danger point, especially on the windless side of the stack (no one had hay barns in those days), and sometimes the pitcher complained of cold chills running up his back. Sometimes Jack flung a pailful of water over his head and shoulders before beginning to unload, and seemed the better for it. Mr. Stewart kept plenty of "switchel" (which is composed of ginger and water) for his hands to drink. He had a notion that it was less injurious than water or beer, and no sunstrokes occurred among his men.

The sun rose in cloudless splendor each day, though during the middle hours vast domes of dazzling white clouds, half-sunk in misty blue, appeared, encircling the horizon. The farmers kept an anxious eye on these "thunder-heads," regulating the amount of cutting by the signs of the sky. At times the thermometer rose to one hundred degrees in the shade, but work went on steadily.

Once, on a hot afternoon, the air took on an oppressive density ; the wind died away almost to a calm, blowing fitfully from the south, while in the far west a vast dome of inky clouds, silent and portentous, uplifted, filling the horizon, swelling like a great bubble, yet seeming to have the weight of a mountain range in its mass. The birds, bees, and all insects, hitherto vocal, suddenly sank into silence, as if awed by the first deep mutter of the storm. The mercury is touching one hundred degrees in the shade.

All hands hasten to get the hay in order, that it may shed rain. They hurry without haste, as only adept workmen can. They roll up the windrows by getting fork and shoulder under one end, tumbling it over and over endwise, till it is large enough; then go back for the scatterings, which are placed, with a deft turn of the fork, on the top to cap the pile. The boys laugh and shout as they race across the field. Every man is wet to the skin with sweat; hats are flung aside; Lincoln, on the rake, puts his horse to the trot. The feeling of struggle, of racing with the thunder, exalts him.

Nearer and nearer comes the storm, silent no longer. The clouds are breaking up. The boys stop to listen. Far away is heard a low, steady, crescendo, grim roar; intermixed with crashing thunderbolts, the rain streams aslant, but there is not yet a breath of air from the west; the storm-wind is still far away; the toads in the marsh, and the fearless king-bird, alone cry out in the ominous gloom cast by the rolling clouds of the tempest.

"Look out! here it comes!" The black cloud melts to form the gray veil of the falling rain, which blots out the plain as it sweeps on. Now it strikes the corn-field, sending a tidal wave rushing across it. Now it reaches the wind-break, and the spire-like poplars bow

humbly to it. Now it touches the hay-field, and the caps
of the cocks go flying; the long grass streams in the
wind like a woman's hair. In an instant the day's work
is undone, and the hay is opened to the drenching rain.

As all hands rush for the house, the roaring tempest
rides upon them like a regiment of demon cavalry. The
lightning breaks forth from the blinding gray clouds of
rain. As Lincoln looks up he sees the streams of fire
go rushing across the sky like the branching of great red
trees. A moment more, and the solid sheets of water
fall upon the landscape, shutting it from view, and the
thunder crashes out, sharp and splitting, in the near dis-

tance, to go deepening and bellowing off down the
illimitable spaces of the sky and plain, enlarging, as it
goes, like the rumor of war.

In the east is still to be seen a faint crescent of the
sunny sky, rapidly being closed in as the rain sweeps
eastward; but as that diminishes to a gleam, a similar
window, faint, watery, and gray, appears in the west, as
the clouds break away. It widens, grows yellow, and
then red; and at last blazes out into an inexpressible
glory of purple and crimson and gold, as the storm

moves swiftly over. The thunder grows deeper, — dies to a retreating mutter, and is lost. The cloud's dark presence passes away. The trees flame with light, the robins take up their songs again, the air is deliciously cool. The corn stands bent, as if still acknowledging the majesty of the wind. Everything is new-washed, clean of dust, and a faint, moist odor of green things is everywhere.

Lincoln seizes the opportunity to take Owen's place in bringing the cattle, and mounting his horse gallops away. The road is wet and muddy, but the prairie is firm, and the pony is full of power. In full flower, fragrant with green grass and radiant with wild roses, sweet-williams, lilies, pinks, and pea-vines, the sward lies new washed by the rain, while over it runs a strong, cool wind from the clearing west. The boy's heart swells with unutterable joy of life. The world is exaltingly beautiful. It is good to be alone — good to be a boy and to be mounted on a swift horse.

O WIDE, cloud-peopled,
    summer sky,
Sea-drifting grasses, rust-
    ling reeds
Where young grouse to
    their mothers cry
And locusts buzz from
    whistling weeds;
O meadows lying like lagoons
Of sun-smit water — on whose swells
Float nodding blooms to tinkling bells
Of bob-o-linkums' wildest tunes —
My western land I love you yet!
In dreams I ride my horse again
And breast the breezes blowing fleet
From out the sunset cool and wet
From fields of flowers blowing sweet
With honey for the droning bees.
The wild oats swirl like ripened grain;
I feel their dash against my knees
Like rapid plash of running seas.

I pass by islands, dark and tall,
Of painted aspen thick with leaves,
The grass in rustling ripple cleaves
To left and right as waters flow,
And as I listen, riding slow,
Out breaks the robin's jocund call.
O shining suns of boyhood's time,
O winds that from the mythic west
Sang lures to Eldorado's quest,
O swaying thrushes' sunset chime,
When the loud city's ceaseless roar
Enfolds my soul as if in shrouds,
I hear your sounds and songs once more
And dream of western wind-swept clouds !

The farmers depended very largely upon the wild meadows for most of their hay, raising only enough timothy to feed their milch-cows. The near meadow being claimed, Mr. Stewart was obliged to go some miles away to find a midsummer cutting. The boys found these wild meadows of infinite interest. The tame meadows were prose, the upland meadows poetry, the sloughs mystery, filled as they were with flowers, weeds, aromatic plants, insects, and reptiles. Wild strawberries furnished sauce for the dinner, eaten beside the wagon, with the odor of the popple trees in the air, and the bob-o-linkums gave orchestral accompaniment. The trail of the sluggish gray rattlesnake added a touch of malignant menace. He was always near on these grasslands.

Once the boys secured permission to camp all night beside the wagon, and after the men drove away homeward, they busied themselves with eating their supper and making up their beds on piles of hay, with the delicious feeling of being real campers on the plains. This feeling of exaltation died out as the light paled in the western sky. The wind grew suddenly cold, and the sky threatened a storm. The world became each moment more menacing. Out of the darkness came obscure noises. Now it seemed like the slow, sinister movement of a rattlesnake — now it was the hopping, intermittent movement of a polecat.

Lincoln was secretly appalled by these sinister changes, but the feeling that he was shielding weakness made him strong, and he kept a cheerful voice. He lay awake long after Owen fell asleep, with eyes strained toward every moving shadow, his ears intent for every movement in the grass. He had the primitive man's sense of warfare against nature, recalled his bed in the garret with fervent longing, and resolved never again to tempt the dangers of the night. He fell asleep only when the moon rose and morning seemed near.

The coming of the sun rendered the landscape good and cheerful and friendly again, and he was ashamed to acknowledge how nervous he had been. When his father returned, and asked with a smile, "Well, boys, how did you enjoy it?" Lincoln replied, "O bully. It was lots of fun."

That night when they rode home, high on a fragrant load of hay, it seemed as though they had been away for a month. Mrs. Stewart had warm biscuits for supper, and the hearts of her sons overflowed with gratitude and love. "Campin' is all right for a day or two, but for a stiddy business give me mother's cookin'," said Lincoln.

HOME FROM WILD MEADOWS

Through cool dry dust the wagons chuckle,
Their talk subdued and grave and low,
The horses walk with heads low-swinging,
Their footfalls muffled, rhythmical, and slow.
Upon the weedy load of autumn grasses
I lie at ease and watch the daylight wane,
Hearing the hum of distant thresher,
And cowbells down the dusty lane.

The darkness deepens, and the stars appearing,
Line out the march of coming night,
And now I catch the farm-yard's calling,
And cross the kitchen's band of friendly light.
Familiar laughter wakes — the falling neck-yokes rattle,
The pump gives out a welcome squeal,
The barn's gloom swallows men and cattle,
And mother's call to supper rings like a bugle's peal.

119

During the hot days of summer the river came to be of greater and greater value to the older boys toiling in the hot corn rows, and trips for bathing and fishing were looked forward to with keenest longing, and remembered with deepest delight. Many of Lincoln's sweetest recollections of nature are associated with these swimming excursions. To go from the dusty field of the prairie farms to the wood shadows and to the cool murmuring of water, to strip stark to the caressing winds, and to plunge in the deeps of the dappled pools, was like being born again.

THE RIVER

It comes from the meadow
Where cool and deep,
In the elm's dark shadow,
In murmur of dream and of sleep,
It drowsily eddied and swirled
And softly crept and curled
Round the out-thrust knees
Of the basswood trees

And lifted the rustling, dripping sedge
In rhythmic sweep at the outer edge.

It was then the water-snake rippled across,
Through the shimmering supple the leaves cast down,
While the swamp-bird perched on the spongy moss
In the shadow-side looked gravely on.
'Twas there the kingfishers swiftly flew,
In the cool, sweet silence from tree to tree —
All silence, save when the vagabond jay
Flashed swiftly by with sharp "Te-chee,"
Swaggering by in his elfish way —

And I, a bare-legged boy again,
Can hear the low, sweet laugh of the river —
See on the water the dapples aquiver,
Feel on my knees the lipping lap
Of the sunny ripples, and see the snake
Slip silently into the sedgy brake,
And hear the rising pickerel slap
In a rushing leap
Where the lilies sleep.

The Maple River was about four miles away, a bright, sparkling stream, with occasional pools, overhung by great elm and basswood trees, and bordered with drooping water-grasses and delicate ferns. The road to these swimming-places led away through beautiful wild meadows, rich with waving crow's-foot, lit as with flame by pinks, lilies, roses, and sweet-williams. Young prairie chickens rose before each galloping horse with a sudden buzz, and the smell of roses burdened the slow wind. A mile of burr-oak openings followed, and then came the dip into the wooded bottom where the river ran.

The boys usually went in parties of five or six. Sometimes they started late on Saturday afternoon, more often on Sunday; for many of the parents took the view that cleanliness was next to godliness, and made no objection to such Sabbath excursions. Lincoln usually rode over after Milton, and together they picked up Rance on the way. Sometimes one of the herdmen took a team and gathered up a load of young men and boys.

When the river came in sight, a race began, to see who should first throw off his clothing and be as the frogs are.

Shadows seemed to beckon, the kingfishers called, and the water laughed up at the exultant fugitives from the burning dust of the fields, with delicious promise of coolness and vigor.

After they had taken their fill of swimming and plunging, and spattering each other with water, the boys returned to their hickory shirts and brown denim overalls, and wandered up and down the river, seeking the new and interesting things which the wood and the river offered to them. They dug clams out of the sand, and caught and killed the great spotted water-snakes that ventured out of the sedges along the river. They mocked the kingfishers, and the giant " thunder pumpers " in the reeds, and gathered the strange plants and

flowers which grew in the cool dusk under the shadow of the basswood trees.

All things not positively poisonous were eaten, or at least tasted. The roots of ferns, black haws, choke-berries, sheep-sorrel, Indian tobacco, clams, dewberries, May-apples — anything at all that happened to be in season or handy. Sometimes they fished, and usually with ill success — they were too impatient of silence, and too eager to enjoy to the full the cool paths and the pools. And when it was all over, they mounted their horses and rode reluctantly back into the heat and burning sunlight of the farm lanes — back to milk the cows and feed the pigs, and begin again their six days of toil.

Of course the lucky boys of Owen's age were able to reach the woodland oftener, but once a week was as often as Lincoln and Milton could get away during the corn-growing season. They had to ride horse to the single-shovel plough or to pull weeds with their brown and warty hands. A freshet in June brought large numbers of fish up the rivers from the Mississippi, and one day the boys organized a night expedition for spearing pickerel. After a day or two of toil making kerosene torches, while the blacksmith forged a spear out of a broken fork, Lincoln and Rance and Jack, the hired man, joined with several other sportsmen of the neighborhood, in a visit to the river. They arrived just at dark, and leaving a man in the wagon with orders to meet them at the bridge, the spearmen entered the shallows, and began to wade slowly upward, with torches held high, to light the fish as they swam slowly away.

Lincoln was torch-bearer, and counted it an honor. His torch lit the rushing waters and the deep pools, but threw into impenetrable darkness the farther landscape. After an hour of wading behind the men, the universe seemed reduced to a chill stream, rushing between snake-haunted jungles of grass beneath a feeble flare of light into endless night. The mere fact of being there in the cold water at midnight, rather than in his snug warm

bed, made the expedition heroic, and Lincoln again felt
the savage arms of nature close round him.

At first there was much outcry : —

" There goes one ! "

" I've got him ! "

" Here, Link, bring your light ! " and much exultation over captures. As the night wore on, — toward
twelve, — however, there was a steady decrease of talk
and corresponding increase of silence, wherein the lapping rush or soft purling ripple of the river could be
heard. The water chilled Lincoln's feet, and sharp
pebbles got into his old boots, until at last the fun was
quite lost out of carrying torch, and he was heartily glad
of a chance to climb into the wagon which was waiting
for them at " the big bend." And when he threw off
his wet clothing and tumbled into bed, the river and the
fish were of small account. In the days which followed,
this glimpse of nature from the night river came to pos-
sess singular charm, and though he never went again, he
often talked of it to Rance.

Nearly every farm-house on Sun Prairie sorely needed
protection from the winter winds, and the thriftiest of
the farmers set about planting trees at once. Naturally
they selected those which grew most rapidly, either
willows, cottonwoods, soft maples, or Lombardy poplars, which were being introduced by nurserymen. All
of these except the maples were planted by means of
cuttings from the branches, and Lincoln and Owen
spent a day pushing " slips " of willow and cottonwood into the soft, moist earth. They were delegated

also to report when the maple seeds were ripe and falling.

The Stewarts and the Knapps made up a picnic party, one day in June, to go to the river and gather tree seeds. This made another red-letter day in the calendar. It offered the small boys another chance to go in swimming, to climb trees, and to dig clams out of the sandbars; and it afforded the grown-up boys and girls an excuse for putting on their good clothes and riding in a buggy. It was at such times that the cowboys considered the business of cattle-herding an overrated amusement, and looked upon the passing wagons laden with joyous young folks, with dim and sullen eyes. They forgot how many weary days of corn-ploughing they had escaped. The seeds were soon gathered, and nothing remained but to lie under the trees and wait for dinner.

Here the big girls proved of some use. They set out large segments of pie and cold chicken and jelly cake for their sweethearts, and a boy could manage to fill his stomach while Jennie and Mace were passing compliments. It made no difference which came first, pie or chicken, each arrived at the same station in the end; so Lincoln and his comrades seized on any attractive victual at hand, and having filled up, returned to the river to swim in defiance of the well-known law of health, which says one should not bathe till three hours after eating. However, they kept on bathing the entire three hours and so came within the scope of the rule, after all. After swimming till they were tired, they painted them-

selves with mud and pretended to be Indians and hunted
each other in the alder thickets. It was very exciting,
and the afternoon slipped away with mournful swiftness.

Lincoln enjoyed the tree-planting. Bryant's " Planting of the Apple Tree " had made a mystical impression
on his mind, and to bring any kind of tree into being
seemed noble and fine. It was a great pleasure to see
them grow during the summer days. They shot up
like corn, by the second winter forming a considerable

check to the fierce winds, and yet, fast as they grew,
they were too slow for the settler. It seemed as though
they would never grow tall enough to shade him.
(They stand there now with bodies big as his own —
reaching out their arms like yawning young giants.)

Lincoln and Owen soon discovered that the prairies
were populous with a sort of wolf, half-way between
the coyote of the plains and the gray wolf of the timber land. They were called simply " prairie wolves."
Nothing else, save an occasional deer or antelope, remained of the splendid game animals which had once
covered these flowery and sunlit savannahs. Of the
elk, nothing remained but his great bleached antlers,

gleaming white in the grass, and only deep-worn trails in the swales of the unbroken prairie marked the places where the mighty bison had trod. But the wolf, more adaptable, remained to prey, like the fox, on the small cattle of the incoming settler.

Mr. Stewart, during the second season, planted a field of corn just back of his barn, nearly half a mile in length, and a quarter of a mile in breadth, which made a magnificent ambush for wolves and foxes and skunks, and as the spring chickens grew nice and fat, and the corn dark and tall as a forest, these marauders began to make their attacks upon the barn-yard. The corn, stretching away in sombre, dark-green, thick-standing rows, joined the tall grass and hazel thickets of the prairie to the north, and the wolves came easily to the very edge of the chicken range, even in broad daylight. Each day a wild commotion broke out in the edge of the corn-field near the barn, followed by screams of terror from the young chickens, a flutter and a squawk, and Mrs. Stewart only found a handful of feathers, and another fat broiler gone.

In vain Lincoln laid in wait with shot-gun, his heart beating wildly. In vain he set traps and put out poison. The wolves had eyes and ears all too keen for him. Each day the flock grew less, and the wolves fatter. Mr. Stewart considered chicken-raising too small business for men anyway, and was not particularly stirred up about it.

In this urgency the boys mysteriously acquired a defender of the farm-yard flock. A woebegone looking dog came to them one day out of his distress and stayed

with them because of their need of him. He was a mixture of liver-and-white pointer and foxhound, with a tail
like a broomstick, and ears that hung down like broken
hinges. His big eyes were meek and sorrowful, almost
to tears, his ribs stood out like hoops, and his neck was
covered with minute brown specks like flecks of blood.

The boys fed him, which was no light task, for his
capacity was enormous. "He don't stop to taste it,"
cried Owen, ruefully. He assumed an air of being at
home at once, and it became necessary to name him.
For some reason the boys imagined his home to be on
the Wapsypinnicon River, and Lincoln called him
"Wapsy," for short. This he accepted with a slow
wag of his tail, as if to say, "I am very grateful for so
nice a name."

He was a wonderful creature to the boys. There was
something forlorn and mysterious in his silent presence,
and when he gave voice, his bay was like the mournful
echoes of a battered bugle. "He'll keep the wolves
away," said Lincoln, and they all waited with eagerness
for the next commotion among the hens, and when it
came, Lincoln ran out among the pumpkin vines, calling
to Wapsy, "Sic 'em, boy! sic 'em!"

All to no purpose. He lumbered along, looking at
his master with dim, pathetic eyes, as if to say, "I am a
stranger, and I don't know what you want of me." All
this amused Mr. Stewart very much. "'Bout the only
thing he's good for is to keep bread from spoiling."

After trying this a number of times to no effect, it
occurred to Lincoln that Wapsy's eyes were of no use

K

to him, for he could never be induced to look in the
direction in which his master pointed. Lincoln therefore called his attention to the ground, and by moving
in a circle at last came upon the trail of the wolf. Then
old Wapsy awoke. With sudden bell-like outcry he
dashed away into the corn-field, straight on the trail, certain and swift, his tail lifted, decision in every movement.
The boys raced after him, wild with excitement. They
had discovered his peculiar powers. He was a " smeller,"
not a " looker."

They came to the edge of the corn-field just in time
to see him overtake a wolf on a little ridge some forty
rods in the open. The robber was a little nettled by his
failure to get a chicken, and not at all disposed to run ;
on the contrary, he seemed willing to try conclusions with
this new foe. As the hound pounced upon him, he
curled up like a cat, and reaching back snapped at Wapsy's
throat, then leaped away just out of the dog's reach.
Again giving tongue, the old hound struck after his
enemy, only to receive each time that wicked, clipping
snap ; so fighting and running they passed out of sight.

When Wapsy returned, the brown flecks on his neck
were reddened with the blood which his keen-fanged
antagonist had drawn from him, but he had won the
respect even of Mr. Stewart.

Having discovered his peculiar powers, the boys
amused themselves by setting him subtle tasks. Somebody said to Lincoln, " If you want a dog to be always
able to foller you, you jest rub a piece of meat or bread
on the sole of your shoe, and give it to him. He'll track

you anywhere after that." This was sufficiently mysterious to attract Lincoln, and as he wore no shoes at all, he rubbed the bread on the sole of his bare foot, instead. This the dog swallowed at a gulp as usual, and the boys set forth to experiment. While Owen held Wapsy near the house, Lincoln ran out on the prairie, doubling in every conceivable way, and at last hid in a deep hollow. Upon being released, the old dog started forth upon his search.

It was a little uncanny to Owen to see how accurately the hound traced his master's footsteps, gliding in and out, curving, circling, looping, with a certainty which became almost appalling to Lincoln as he listened to the old dog's deep baying. It was easy to imagine himself a fugitive, and Wapsy a ferocious bloodhound on his trail. And then, his tongue lolling out, and his long ears waving and flapping, he peered up with his dim eyes, that seemed, somehow, as pathetic as those of an old man; the old dog seemed to say, "Did I do it well?"

In a little time they could tell by the minute differences in his baying whether he was on the trail of a rabbit, a skunk, a fox, or a wolf. He was a faithful soul and of great value. Night after night he battled with his savage enemies, returning to the house each morning wet with his own blood.

He remained only one summer. He disappeared early in September, as silently and as mysteriously as he came. Perhaps his work was done. Perhaps the wolves united to kill him, or he may have eaten some poison. Mrs. Lincoln was not inconsolable, for he was an enormous eater, and smelled of polecats, while Mr. Stewart considered him the " measliest critter that ever punished a hunk o' meat." To the boys he was a visitor from the great world which lay just over the big ridge to the east.

CORN SHADOWS

WITH heart grown weary of the heat
And hungry for the breath
Of field and farm, with eager feet
I trod the pavement dry as death
Through city streets where crime is born,
And sudden — lo, a ridge of corn!

Above the dingy roofs it stood
A dome of tossing, tangled spears,
Dark, cool, and sweet as any wood
Its silken, green, and pluméd ears
Laughed on me through the haze of morn —
The tranquil presence of the corn!

Upon the salt weed from the sea
Borne westward swift as dreams
Of boyhood are, I seemed to be
Once more a part of sounds and gleams
Thrown on me by the winds of morn
Amid the rustling rows of corn.

I bared my head, and on me fell
The old-time wizardry again
Of leaf and sky, the mystic spell
Of boyhood's easy joy or pain,
When pumpkin trump was Siegfried's horn
Echoing down the walls of corn.

I saw the field (as trackless then
As wood to Daniel Boone)
Wherein we hunted wolves as men,
And camped and twanged the green bassoon;
Not blither Robin Hood's merry horn
Than pumpkin pipe amid the corn.

In central deeps the melons lay,
Slow swelling in the August sun.
I traced again the narrow way,
And joined again the stealthy run —
The jack-o'-lantern's wraith was born
Within the shadows of the corn.

O wide, sweet wilderness of leaves!
O playmates far away!   Over thee
The slow wind like a mourner grieves,
And stirs the plumed ears fitfully.
Would we could sound the signal horn
And meet once more in walls of corn!

CHAPTER XI

A FOURTH OF JULY CELEBRATION

MONEY in those days was less easily obtained than now, especially on the border, and Lincoln had never had fifty cents to spend on a Fourth of July. Once he had thirty cents, and it seemed that he was as rich as any boy could reasonably hope to be. For several years he had only fifteen cents, a dime of which went for a bunch of firecrackers; with the remaining five cents he bought an orange (which he carried in the hollow of his brown little paw, smelling of it from time to time, reluctant to break its skin) or some peanuts. But the year he was fourteen years of age he had a big silver dollar, and Owen had one just like it. For weeks they planned how to use these immense sums. One thing they decided upon early — they would have three bunches of firecrackers.

It had been their habit, for some years, to stealthily rise in the early morning, and fire the heavily charged shot-gun from the chamber window, and to wake the household with furious cheers. Once they tried to make a cannon out of an old mowing-machine wheel, but failed, and fell back on the shot-gun. On this particular morning the sound of the firearm was to be a signal to Rance and Milton, who were to meet them at the school-house, and go to Rock River, the county town, for a riotous day.

As Lincoln crept from his bed, and pushed the gun out through the open window, he was awed, for the moment, by the silence and beauty of the morning. It was scarcely dawn, and all over the grass, heavy with dew, lay a wavering, thin mist, which was like visible silence. For a moment the boy hesitated to break this solemn hush, but, remembering "the great day," he pulled both triggers at once, and the sound of the discharge rolled away over the prairie with the grandeur (it seemed to him) of a cannon-shot. Then he shouted "HURRAH FOR THE FOURTH OF JULY!" and Owen, struggling to his feet, his eyes heavy with sleep, joined in shrilly. Having succeeded in thoroughly disturbing the comfortable rest of their hard-working parents, the boys felt quite happy and well repaid for their trouble.

Too much excited to eat any breakfast, and too impatient to wait for it anyhow, they saddled their horses and rode away, a small haversack full of bread and butter dangling at their saddles, and their money pushed far down into the lowest corner of their trousers pockets. Their comrades were late, and it was full sunrise before they arrived.

"How much money you got?" asked Rance at once.

"A dollar. How much *you* got?"

He held up a bill. "Five dollars."

Lincoln stared in silent amazement, his big dollar

shrinking each minute.   Milton had only seventy-five
cents, however, and the other boys were partly consoled.

Taking the lead, Rance and Milton cantered away,
Owen and Lincoln close behind.   It was always an exciting experience to go to Rock River, but to go on horseback was glorious.   Lincoln soon forgot the difference
between his funds and those of his hero.   As they
passed other farm-houses, they saw men and boys going
out to milk the cows and feed the horses, and felt sorry
for them.   To all who were hitching up they uttered
exultant cheers.   No one else was moving along the
road but themselves, and as they entered the main
street of the town, they found it quite empty, except for
the grocers and notion-sellers, who were erecting bowers
of green trees before their shops, and setting out lemonade glasses, and heaps of rockets, firecrackers, and
candy.

Rance was acquainted in town, and found a yard in
which they were permitted to leave their horses.   As
soon as possible they returned to the street, in order to
miss nothing of the preparation.   They each bought an
orange, and stood about, sucking at it gently, in order to
make it last a long time.   They each bought a package
of " assorted candies."   Whatever one did, the others
did also, as a matter of course, though Milton was at a
disadvantage.   There came a time when Rance naturally
branched out and " went it alone," but at the start they
kept together.   Ultimately they fell under the fascination
of the prize candy package, and each paid five cents for
one of those deceitful boxes.   Lincoln drew a little gilt

pin, in shape like a locomotive, Rance a big yellow fly, and Owen and Milton some rings that shone like gold, but were not. However, they did not complain. It was all in the game.

Meanwhile the streets began to ring with the cries of the lemonade-dealers, who used their best wit to make people laugh. They amused the boys from Sun Prairie, at least.

"Roll up, tumble up, any way to get up. Here's your ice-cold lemonade, made in the shade, stirred with a spade, by an old maid. Here it is cool and sweet."

"Right HERE you'll find your Eyetallion oranges," called forth another, "five cents each. They weigh a pound and are sweet as sugar."

"Ice-cream! I scream, I scream!" bawled his neighbor, with his eyes on every pair of sweethearts who came his way. Wagons laden with whole families clattered in, raising a long cloud of dust, which settled over the bowers, and into the ice-cream which the boys were eating. But dust was a small affair. Men on horseback, brown, keen-eyed young fellows, pulled up and tied before the doors of the saloons. The farmers' wives and daughters sat in the grocery stores and gossiped for a time, in order to gain courage to go forth into the street, which was getting crowded with people, moving aimlessly back and forth along the walk.

To Lincoln the throng was enormous. It seemed as if the whole country must be in town, and he felt a pang of regret when he remembered his mother toiling at home.

Meanwhile, around in a side street the "Ragamuffins" were forming, and occasionally one of them irregularly galloped down the main street, to the immense amusement of the boys. Whatever this parade had originally been, it had degenerated into a rude caricature of political parties or persons, and was amusing only to simple minds. It always contained a negro preacher, a couple of grotesque sweethearts, and old Uncle Sam. It was considerably greater in the prologue than in the enactment. It was all over in a few moments after it started. With drumming pans and tooting of tin horns and the blare of a designedly cacophonous band it passed away, and the people were able to give attention to something better worth while.

Most of the forenoon was passed (and it seemed profitably spent by the Sun Prairie boys) in just looking at strange things and in devouring a mixture of nuts, candies, figs, and oranges. Little was necessary to amuse and interest them. A new sort of dog, an unusual carriage, a boy playing on a mouth-organ, — anything at all diverted them. Time did not exist. They knew nothing of clocks till the middle of the day drew near, and even then they felt no pang of hunger — they knew the middle of the day had come when, upon call of the marshal of the day, the elderly people " retired to the Court-house yard " to listen while " the stars and stripes were planted on the cloud-capped summit of the peaks of liberty," after which all took dinner. Even the boys from Sun Prairie began to feel that they ought to eat something besides candy and peanuts, and upon

Rance's suggestion they returned by the alley, and ex-
humed some bread and butter from their haversacks,
which they ate with ginger ale for drink. Lincoln was
already beginning to feel ill, and so was Rance. Milton
and Owen professed to be " all right."

" Let's go and see the games and races at the Fair
grounds," said Rance. Lincoln in secret wished to
remain on the streets, for he forecast battle among the
men, and did not want to miss it, but agreed. As they
were about finishing their lunch, a town boy came
along — a stalwart, freckle-faced youth of sixteen, who
looked them over closely. Having sized up the group,
he·made insolent demand.

"Gimme a drink of your pop."

" Go buy your own," replied Owen, promptly.

" You shut up, or I'll break your jaw, you little
country snipe."

Rance was moderate of speech, but he instantly said :
" You run along.   You ain't wanted here."

The town boy doubled his fists, " Mebbe you want
to fight me."

" I don't want to, but I will if you don't stir your
stumps out o' here."

" Oh, you will, will you ! " sneered the stranger.

Rance grew white.   " You go about your business."

The insolent one started to say something, but Rance
hurled himself against him like a bulldog, and both
went down in the dust, Rance on top spread out
" like a letter X."   The bully tried to rise ; he wriggled
and twisted and kicked and offered to bite, but Rance

held him flat on his back, a grim smile on his pale face. Lincoln's heart beat fast as he looked about, expecting each minute the rush of other foes.   He dreaded a fight, but was willing to do his best if it came.

"Good for you, Rance.   Hold him!" shouted Milton, his eyes shining with laughter.

At length the town boy ceased to struggle, and panting for breath, began to cry.

"Let me up!   I'm choking!   Let me up!"

"Got enough?" asked Rance sternly, but relaxing his hold a little.

"You better let me up, now."

There was a threat still in his voice, and Rance laid his strong hard wrist across his enemy's throat and again said: —

"Got enough?"

"Yes, yes.   Let me up!"

Rance let him up.   "Now you let us alone," he said, "and git out o' here."

The boy at a safe distance said: "I'll fix you.   I'll bring Shorty Sykes — he'll beat you black and blue."

Rance made a dash at him and he fled.   "Guess we better move," said Lincoln.   "He'll come back with his gang in a few minutes.   They're down on us country boys, anyway."

The street was swarming with people now, but four lads had eyes only for the freckle-faced boy, who pointed them out to his friends.   Trouble was brewing.   Meanwhile Lincoln was feeling sick, very sick. Starting the day without any breakfast, he had eaten all the morning, and his stomach was filled with candy, lemonade, oranges, peanuts, ginger-pop, and soda crackers. Besides, he was sick by reason of his over-wrought nerves. He was like a rabbit that has strayed into the city streets, and fears every moving thing.

It was plain the freckle-faced youth was urging his clan to action. They could see him talking excitedly, and making savage gestures in their direction.

Rance was grimly silent. "Not much," he said in answer to Lincoln, who wished to go home. "I'm not goin' to be run out o' town by these runts."

Lincoln was no fighter under the best circumstances, and with a splitting headache he was seeking a place to lie down and groan and sleep. The holiday street had become a field of warfare, and the surroundings were all alien to the country boys.

At last the redoubtable Sykes seemed to take command, and began to lead his forces in casual yet sinister fashion toward the little knot of Sun Prairie boys. Sykes was a sturdy chap, as his torn trouser legs too plainly showed. He was the town tatterdemalion, the yellow cur who delights to growl and yelp and roll in the dust with his betters. He had taken up the quarrel with ready joy, and only wanted an opportunity to leap upon Rance, whom he had plainly marked as "my meat." Freckle-face as obviously singled out Lincoln, while two or three others were detailed to bother at Owen and Milton.

At this critical moment Lincoln spied Ben Hutchison and called to him. Ben came up smiling, his long upper lip twitching like a colt's. He was stained with orange juice and candy, but ready for any sort of fun.

" Hello," he said. " Where you been keepin' yourselves ? "

" Say, Ben," replied Lincoln, " we've got business for you. See them fellers ? " He pointed to the enemy.

" Aha. What about 'em ? "

" Why, they're plannin' to lick us like shucks, that's all."

" Oh, they be ? I want to know. What for ? "

" 'Cause we wouldn't let 'em have part of our ginger-pop."

This aroused Ben thoroughly. " If they want fight, they can have a bellyful."

The confident strength of this reënforcement did not escape the attention of the enemy, and a council of war was held in the alleyway between the meat shop and the livery stable. At last a small aid was sent to secure new troops. His legs fluttered like those of a partridge as he sped away.

By this time the celebration and the crowd were entirely secondary matters. The people, indeed, seemed merely a wilderness of trees walking, a jungle wherein the coming battle must take place. The two hostile armies reconnoitered for position while seeking reënforcements. Rance and Ben did most of the talking. Milton and Lincoln were dumb from nausea, and Owen, too, began to suffer from internal wars among the nuts and candies he had munched, and the plans of the enemy did not profoundly interest him. Ben realized the weakness of his rank and file, and kept an eye out for wandering bands of guerillas. The best he could find and draw to his aid was Humboldt Bunn, whom everybody called " Hum-Bunn," unless they wished to pester him; then he naturally became " hum-*bug*." He was a lathy, loose-jointed youth, of slender physical prowess, but full of grit. He was always willing to try, and came into the war with joy.

" Show me 'um! " he cried, licking his lips as if in preparation for a pudding. " Show me to 'um! " and he doubled his rope-like arms and kicked up his heels so comically that even the sick ones laughed. Hum put humor into the war, anyway.

Meanwhile the enemy had been reënforced by a fat boy, who wore a small cap over his ear and looked wicked, very wicked indeed. His bulk was imposing, but Hum took a satirical view of him.

" I'll take that sack o' bran," said he. " I'll punch the wind out o' that bladder. Lem me put the kibosh on that puffball."

The fat boy began to roll up his sleeves to show his big arms. He seemed to supersede Sykes and the freckle-faced one, too. With imperious voice he ordered all hands to follow him, and marched straight toward Ben and his little army.

As he threaded his way through encumbering men and women, and carriages and babies and lemonade stands, his stride became wonderful. He absorbed all attention, completely overshadowing Sykes and Freckle-face.

With insolent visage and turbulent action, he stepped before Rance. " Want to fight, do ye ? Well, come on. I'll lick you into strips."

Rance was silent with rage, but Ben twisted his upper lip into a comical leer, and said : —

" What'll we be doin' ? "

" You dassent fight."

" We dassent ? "

" No."

" We'll show you in about a minute whether we dast or not."

" I *dare* ye to come back into the alley."

" Go on," said Rance, and at the tone of his voice the fat boy paled a little. Rance was white-hot with anger, and his eyes burned with dangerous intensity.

" Come on, fellers," commanded the fat general, and led the way back of the post-office, upon a vacant lot, where a number of horses were eating hay out of wagons. To Lincoln this had all the solemnity of war to the death. It was the country against the town. His headache was swallowed up in a sort of blurring numbness. He had forgotten who they were or what they came for, except that now battle was impending and that they must sell their lives as dearly as possible. That was the phrase always used by the scouts in Boodle's dime novels. Remembering that, he took a last look at the sun and faced the enemy. He kept a watchful eye on Freckles, for since the coming of the fat boy, Sykes had shifted his calculating eyes to Rance.

L

At last, just beside a barn, and hedged in by a fence on two sides, the armies took position. The rank and file of both sides were dolefully silent. The challenges were uttered by the commanders, and for a few moments words flew like brickbats.

The fat boy was game for war. He put a piece of shingle on his shoulder at last and said, " I dare ye ! "

Ben knocked it off with his left hand, and swatted the general's insolent cheek with his right, and in a moment the two were rolling in the dust, and Sykes and Rance were at it, hammer and tongs. Freckles charged savagely upon Lincoln, and with that, all the forces became engaged. In the first rush Freckles carried Lincoln to the ground, but could not hold him there. The first blow in his face seemed to transform the world. Thereafter he saw nothing but the strange, savage face of his assailant, though he leaped again and again, striking at it blindly. Sometimes he hit, and at last a stream of blood trickled down the freckled face. Then he rushed, and Lincoln went to the ground again, and there writhed, choking, gasping, till a cry from Owen pierced the blur of his senses.

" Link, Link, help ! He's chokin' me."

With a sudden surge of strength Lincoln rose, and flinging his assailant away, with a cry of rage leaped upon and tore the assailant off his brother, who was weeping and gasping for breath. As he fought the murderer with foot and hand, he heard a loud cry of pain, and looking up, saw Rance with a long sliver of board in his hand, battling back the redoubtable Sykes and Freckles. His face was set in a dangerous smile, and every sweep of his weapon brought forth a yell of pain. Sticks, stones, pieces of bricks, began to fly, and the country troops were just getting warmed to the work, when the town-dwellers suddenly scattered like a covey of prairie chickens, leaving the Sun Prairie forces amazed and inert. What was the cause of their sudden flight? It was deeply suspicious.

Around the end of the barn appeared a small man with a star on his coat, and all was explained. It was the City Marshal.

Walking up to Ben, he wound his hand in his collar, and said, " See here, what's all this row about ? "

Lincoln's blood was hot, and his heart big with a sort of desperate courage.

" Oh yes, that's right. Jump on *us* and let the town boys go."

The Marshal looked up at him. " Oh, you're from the country, are you ? What's your name ? "

" Lincoln Stewart. Them boys pitched into us, an' you arrest *us*. If my folks was here, you wouldn't do it."

" Shut up," said the Marshal. " What's your name ? " he said to Ben.

" Ben Hutchison."

" And yours ? "

" Milton Jennings, and that's Rance Knapp. If you want the votes of Sun Prairie, you better let us alone," replied Milton, who was a good deal of a politician, and knew the Marshal's tender spot.

The Marshal released Ben. He was a candidate for

party nomination as sheriff, and besides, he knew the families very well.

" What was it all about ? " he asked in a more reasonable way.   Lincoln told him.

He smiled.   " I'm from the country myself.   You flailed 'em out, didn't you ? " he said to Rance.

" I tried to."

" Did you know the boys ? "

" Yes."

" Who were they ? "

Ben started to reply.

" Keep quiet," commanded Rance.   " We're satisfied as long as you don't arrest us.   If you're going to arrest anybody, you've got to take us all."

Owen began to cry, and Humboldt looked very much alarmed.

" Well, now I'll tell you, boys.   Seein's you are all from the country, and seein's them ragamuffins set upon ye, I'll let ye go.   But I can't have any more rowin' here.   You better put out for home and get washed up. You look like you'd been run through a separator. Now, hyper," he added, with the air of being very gracious.

The boys stood in a knot, waiting until the officer reëntered the saloon from which he had emerged; then Ben said : —

" I move we stay to the fireworks, and show 'em we're not afraid."

But Lincoln, whose headache was returning, said, " I'm going home."

"So am I," said Milton, who was pale with a headache.

Under the circumstances it was unsafe for the remnant of the army to remain, and so they, too, went away, claiming a victory.

The glory of the day had departed for Lincoln. The noise and excitement had produced a blinding pain just back of his left eye, and the poisonous mixture of sweets and drinks had given him a sickness at his stomach, which was torture. Every leap of his horse seemed likely to split his poor head. Owen and Milton were almost as badly off, and Rance looked rather morose.

There was little talk on the way home. They rode rapidly, alternating the fox canter with the walk. As they journeyed, the sun sank behind a big bank of clouds. Teams clattered along, raising prodigious clouds of dust; the wagon-boxes filled with fretful, wailing children — they, too, were suffering from unaccustomed noise and soda-water and candy.

At the corner by the school-house, Rance and Milton turned off, and Lincoln and Owen rode on. They were so sick they could hardly put their horses in the barn, and when they crawled into the house, Mr. Stewart said: "Sick, are you?" and added disgustedly, "If you'd eat a little decent food and let 'truck' alone, you'd come home able to walk."

"Let 'em alone, father," said Mrs. Stewart. "They know that as well as anybody. Now, for land sakes! what marked you all up like that? And look at your clothes! Well, you *are* in nice shape."

"We licked 'em, anyway," chirped Owen.

"Licked 'em? Licked who?"

"The town boys. And the Sheriff was going to arrest us, an' Milton scared him off."

Mrs. Stewart looked helplessly at her husband.

"Well, now, Duncan, what do you 'spose the young 'uns have been into?"

"Send 'em to bed. We'll hear all about it in the morning," he replied, resuming his newspaper.

Weak, dizzy, groaning with pain, Lincoln and Owen crawled up the stairs to their beds. The Glorious Fourth, their outing, was over, and their dollars were gone to the purchase of a dreadful headache, but of such were the ways of boys.

CHAPTER XII

HIRED MEN

THE " hands " of Sun Prairie, even those hired by the
month, were a source of great
interest to Lincoln and Owen. Each March brought
a new personality into the home — sometimes a disagreeable and dangerous one, occasionally a fairly interesting one. Some of them could play the violin or
sing, and so brought new music into the family. Others
were famous dancers. Too often they were coarse and
vicious and given to low amusements, especially those
who came to help in haying and harvest.

However, a very distinct line was drawn between the
day-hand and the hired man. The hired man entered
the family, and his character was a consideration at the
start. Mr. Stewart always got at the antecedents of
his help if possible. With a fair chance, Lincoln was
disposed to make a hero of each new-comer, and brag
about him to the other boys of the neighborhood,

who had their own accomplished hired men to cele-
brate.

Jack, the first hired man, was a most amazing dancer
of negro breakdowns, and the boys delighted to get him
at it of an evening in the kitchen, and patted "juber"
for him, while he shuffled and double-shuffled and hoed-
down and side-stepped, and drummed with heel and toe
on the floor till Mrs. Stewart cried out, "For Peter's
sake! stop that racket."

He was a small man, hardy and willing, comically
ignorant, but a handy man to spear fish, a famous swim-
mer, and always good-tempered and ready for fun. The
boys liked him very well indeed, but ignored his advice.
They bragged of his dancing, not of his beauty. He
stayed till snow fell, then went away to the pinery, and
was seen no more.

The next one came from Tama County, and was
called "Tama Bill." He was a comical fellow, who
spoke with a drawl, and became famous for his boastful
references to "Tamy Caounty." "Why, talk about
soil," said he, "the black soil of Tamy beats the world.
Leave a crowbar in the ground over night, and ye can
pick a handful of tenpenny nails off of it in the morning." He was a perpetual circus, — at least the clown
part of it, — but he was slack and slow, and left just
before harvest.

One curious type was an old Cornishman, whom
the boys could hardly understand, so uncouth was his
pronunciation of the simplest words. He always seemed
a pathetic figure to Lincoln — to be so old, and lonely,

and far from home! Another, equally curious, was a near-sighted old German, who read everything, — Scott, Dickens, dime novels, weekly story-papers, — anything that contained a tale. He claimed a university education, and in truth his diction was always good, and his manner grave and sedate. He was not handsome to look at, but he was of much finer type than some of the drunken young daredevils who made sport of him. He knew the plots of all the stories of Scott and Dumas, and Lincoln and Rance delighted to get him spinning them out in his broken English. They also read his story-papers, and the gayly colored dime novels, which dealt mainly with Indians and scouts, and filled them with longing to be as these heroes in fringed buckskin jackets — but they were far too cautious of temperament to run away, as several boys in Rock River did.

Old Jacob read bushels of these tales, holding the page so near his eyes it seemed his eyelash must touch. His end was tragic. He became blind and helpless, and was taken care of by the town, and died far away from kith and kin. Others followed him on the farm; brisk, hardy young fellows, who bought teams, and began business for themselves. They made less impression on Lincoln, but they were better hired men. They were made to seem commonplace, also, by the troops of nomads from the south who swept over the country, like a visitation of locusts, in harvest, reckless young fellows, handsome, profane, licentious, given to drink, powerful but inconstant workmen, quarrelsome and difficult to manage at all times. They came in the season when work was plenty and wages high, and were very independent of bearing. They dressed well, in their own peculiar fashion, and on Saturday night and Sunday spent their wages in mad revels in the country along the river, where a couple of road-houses furnished harbor and amusement for their like. "We take no orders from any man," they often said, and made much of their freedom to come and go.

Each had a small hand-bag, which contained a change of clothing and a few personal knickknacks. Many of them bought the *Police Recorder*, and carried pictures of variety actresses, which pleased their coarse tastes. When dressed in their best they were dashing fellows. They wore close-fitting, high-heeled boots of calfskin, dark trousers, with a silk handkerchief in the hip pocket, a colored shirt with gay armlets, and a vest, genteelly left unbuttoned. A showy watch-chain, a big signet-ring (useful in fighting), and a soft black hat completed a costume easy and not without grace. They generally hunted in couples, helping each other out at work and in scrimmages on Sunday. The fights were furious and noisy, but not deadly. The revolver was not in common use on the prairie. The traditions were against it. "Tussling" and biting were common.

There were those, even of this nomadic army, of a different class, — men of good bringing up, who were working to get a start, and it often happened that such men remained as hired men, or paid court to some girl, became a farmer's son-in-law, rented a quarter-section, and settled down. But for the most part the harvest

hands passed on to the north, mysterious as the flight of
locusts, leaving the people of Sun Prairie quite as ignorant of their real names and characters as upon the
first day of their coming.

To Lincoln there was immense fascination in these
men. They came from distant lands. They told of
the city, and sinister and poisonous jungles all cities
seemed, in their stories. They were scarred with
battles. Some of them openly joked of " boarding at
the State's expense." They came from the far-away and
unknown, and planned journeys to other States, the
very names of which were poems to Lincoln, and then
they passed without so much as a courteous good-by
to the boy who admired, and sometimes loved them.
Sometimes a broken-hearted girl wept in secret over
their going, for they appealed with even greater power
to the farmers' daughters.

Among them each season were men of great physical
beauty and strength; men who carelessly asked, " Who
is your best man?" and then straightway challenged
him to combat. They were generally accommodated,
for the country held some half dozen men who considered themselves invincible, and who welcomed ambitious
strangers with closed fists. One of these was Steve
Nagle, a magnificently proportioned young fellow, but
pock-marked of face, with a shapeless and cruel mouth.
When sober he was likely to take offence, but when in
liquor he dreamed of dominion over the world. Stories
of his exploits abounded among the boys, who admired,
and feared, and hated him.

His favorite amusement, when inflamed with whiskey, was to enter a saloon suddenly, and snarl : —

" Git out o' here.   Every blank blank *blank !* "

And they got! They crawled on the floor, they jumped through the windows, anyway to get out, while Steve walked the floor, and laughed like a hyena in enjoyment of his joke.

If any of the harvest hands desired trouble, they could always get it, by merely crossing Steve's path, and to refuse to move at his bidding. Not a Saturday night passed without some self-confident person contributing another good story of Steve's method of entertainment. Monday morning was usually filled with half-told stories of Saturday night's debaucheries.

There were but three men in the country whom the boys believed to be Steve's equal. They were Jim Moriarty, the sheriff who whipped the counterfeiter; Dan, his brother, whom nobody but Jim dared to face; and Lime Gilman, a big, good-natured, golden-haired, slope-shouldered giant, who came along the road one spring day and hired out to old man Bacon, and married his daughter, Marietta, in less than a month. Bacon was tremendously incensed at first, but became reconciled, and put the young couple on his lower eighty, which diamond-cornered with the Stewart farm.

The boys loved Lime and made him their hero at once. His face was almost always shining with a smile, and his blue eyes gleamed good-naturedly on man and beast. His voice was so soft and low it expressed weakness, or at least laziness, but it was in truth a very deceptive peculiarity. He loved horses and dogs and children, and they all obeyed him instantly. He knew no poetry or history, could barely cipher out the price of a load of barley, and had not travelled much, and yet he never uttered a word that was not, somehow, interesting to his hearers. Part of this was due to his natural reticence, and part to his manner of speech, which made even a statement of fact worth listening to.

It was six months before the men even suspected his enormous strength. Lincoln and Owen knew it first, for he occasionally did wonderful things to please them, such as tossing a two-bushel sack of wheat over the wheel of the wagon, or slyly lifting one wheel of the threshing-machine, or holding an iron sledge at arm's-length. These things he did with a smile of amusement at the round-eyed admiration of the boys, saying, "When you can do this, boys, demand full pay."

These things the boys promptly related to their father and the other hired men, in order to get a comparison of strength. The other young fellows strained at bags of shot and the sledge, and professed to believe Lincoln was mistaken. In one sly way and another, the boys got Lime to widen his fame, till his giant strength became known. Clothing concealed his muscles. When stripped for swimming he seemed twenty pounds heavier, so enormous were his arms and shoulders. The calves of his legs would not go into the tops of his boots, and he always looked untidy, because his boot-legs were wrinkled or slit, to admit his vast muscles. He could split the sleeve of a new coat by doubling up his arm.

At last all the young men of the neighborhood acknowledged his superiority. He could outjump and outlift them all. He could set a bear-trap with his hands, and hold a boy on a chair at arm's-length. He could throw the maul ten feet beyond the best man, and turn headsprings with his arms folded. Only for his friends, and after much urging, would he put himself on display, and a year went by before his fame reached the bar-rooms, for he very seldom so much as entered a saloon. He had never met "Big Ole" or the "Yancy boys" or Steve Nagle, when hot with liquor, and in cool blood not one of these redoubtables cared to measure forearms with him. His calm blue eye was a powerful check to indiscriminate assault.

Steve Nagle had at times uttered a desire to meet him, but only when excited with drink among his cronies, and when his challenge was conveyed to the big fellow, Lime merely laughed, and said, " He knows where I live."

Steve was one of a group of men gathered in Councill's barn one rainy day in September; the rain had stopped the stacking, and the men were amusing themselves with feats of skill and strength. Steve was easily champion, no matter what came up; whether shouldering a sack of wheat, or raising weights, or suspending himself with one hand, he left the others out of the game.

" Aw! it's no good foolun' with such puny little men as you," he swaggered at last, throwing himself down upon a pile of sacks.

" If Lime Gilman was here, I bet he'd beat you all holler," piped Owen from the doorway.

Steve raised himself up and glared.

"What's that thing talkun'?"

Owen held his ground. "You can brag when he ain't around, but I bet he can lick you with one hand tied behind him; don't you, Link?"

Lincoln was doubtful, and kept a little out of sight. He was afraid of Steve. Owen went on about his hero : —

"Why, he can take a sack of wheat by the corners and snap every kernel of it clean out; he can lift a separator just as easy! You'd better not brag when he's around."

Steve's anger rose, for the others were laughing; he glared around at them all like a wolf. "Bring on your wonder; let's see how he looks."

"Pa says if Lime went to a saloon where you'd meet him once, you wouldn't clean out that saloon," Owen went on calmly, with a distinct undercurrent of glee in his voice.

"Bring on this feller; I'll knock the everlasting spots offen 'im f'r two cents."

"I'll tell 'im that."

"Tell him and be damned," roared Steve, with a wolfish gleam in his eyes that drove the boys away whooping with mingled terror and delight.

Steve well understood that the men about him held Owen's opinion of Lime, and it made him furious. His undisputed sovereignty over the saloons of Rock County was in doubt.

Lime was out mending fence when Owen came

along to tell him what Steve had said. The boy was anxious to have his faith in his hero justified, and watched Lime carefully as he pounded away without looking up. His dress had an easy slouch about his vast limbs, and his pantaloons were tucked into his boot-tops, his vest swinging unbuttoned, his hat carelessly awry.

"He says he can knock the spots off of you," Owen said, in conclusion, watching Lime roguishly.

The giant finished nailing up the fence, and at last said, "Now run along, sonny, and git the cows." There was a laugh in his voice that showed his amusement at Owen's disappointment. "I ain't got any spots."

On the following Saturday night, at dusk, as Lime was smoking his pipe out on the horse-block, and telling stories to Lincoln and Owen, a swiftly driven wagon came rattling down the road, filled with a noisy load of men. The driver pulled up at the gate, with a prodigious shouting.

"Hello, Lime!"

"Hello, the house!"

"Hurrah for the show!"

"It's Al Crandall," cried Owen, running down to the gate. Lime followed slowly, and asked, "What's up, boys?"

"All goin' down to the show; climb in!"

"All right; wait till I git my coat."

"Oh, can't we go, Lime?" pleaded Owen.

"If your dad'll let you; I'll pay for the tickets."

The boys rushed wildly home and as wildly back

again, and the team resumed its swift course, for it was getting late. It was a beautiful autumn night; the full moon poured down a cataract of silent white light like spray, and the dew (almost frost) lay on the grass and reflected the glory of the sky; the air was still and had that peculiar property, common to the prairie air, of carrying sound to a great distance.

The road was hard and smooth, and the spirited little team bowled the heavy wagon along at a swift pace. "We're late," Crandall said, as he snapped his long whip over the heads of his horses, "and we've got to make it in twenty-five minutes or miss part of the show." This caused Lincoln great anxiety. He had never seen a play and wanted to see it all. He looked at the flying legs of the horses and pushed on the dashboard, chirping at them slyly.

To go to town was an event, but to go with the men at night, and to a show, was something to remember a lifetime.

There was little talk as they rushed along, only some singing of a dubious sort by Bill Young, on the back seat. At intervals Bill stopped singing and leaned over to say, in exactly the same tone of voice each time, "Al, I hope t' God we won't be late." Then resumed his monotonous singing, or said something coarse to Rice, who laughed immoderately.

The play had begun when they climbed the narrow, precarious stairway which led to the door of the hall. Every seat of the room was filled; but as for the boys, after getting their eyes upon the players, they did not

M

think of sitting, or of moving, for that matter; they were literally all eyes and ears.

The hall seated about three hundred persons, and the stage added considerably to the fun of the evening by the squeaks it gave out as the heavy man walked across, as well as by the falling down of the calico wings at inopportune moments. At the back of the room the benches rose one above the other until those who occupied the rear seats almost touched the grimy ceiling. These benches were occupied by the toughs of the town, who treated each other to peanuts and slapped each other over the head with their soft, shapeless hats, and laughed inordinately when some other fellow's cap was thrown out of his reach into the crowd.

The play was Wilkie Collins's "New Magdalen," and the part of "Mercy" was taken by a large and magnificently proportioned woman, a blonde, and in Lincoln's eyes she was queenly in grace and majesty of motion. He took a personal pride in her at once and wanted her to come out triumphant in the end, regardless of any conventional morality.

True, his admiration for the dark little woman's tragic utterance at times drew him away from his breathless study of the queenly "Mercy," but such moments were few. Within a half-hour he was deeply in love with her and wondered how she could possibly endure the fat man who played the part of "Horace," and who pitched into the "practicable" supper of cold ham, biscuit, and currant wine with a gusto that suggested gluttony as the reason for his growing burden of flesh.

And so the play went on. The wonderful old lady in the cap and spectacles, the mysterious dark little woman who popped in at short intervals to say " Beware ! " in a very deep contralto voice, the tender and repentant " Mercy," all were new and wonderful and beautiful things to the boys, and though they stood up the whole evening through, it passed so swiftly that the curtain's fall drew from them long sighs of regret. From that time on Lincoln dreamed of that wonderful play and that beautiful, repentant woman. So securely was she enthroned in his regard that no rude and senseless jest could ever unseat her. Of course, the men, as they went out, laughed and joked in the manner of such men, and swore in their disappointment because it was a serious drama in place of a comedy and the farce which they had expected.

" It's a regular sell," Bill said. " I wanted to hear old Plunket 'stid of all that stuff about nothin'. That was a lunkin' good-lookin' woman though," he added, with a coarse suggestion in his voice, which exasperated Lincoln to the pitch of giving him a kick on the heel as he walked in front. " Hyare, young feller, look where you're puttin' your hoofs ! " Bill growled, looking about.

Lincoln was comforted by seeing in the face of his brother the same rapt expression which he felt was on his own. He walked along almost mechanically, scarcely feeling the sidewalk, his thoughts still dwelling on the lady and the play. It was after ten o'clock, and the stores were all shut, the frost lay thick and white on the plank walk, and the moon was shining as only a moon can shine through the rarefied air on the Western prairies, and overhead the stars in innumerable hosts swam in the absolutely cloudless sky.

Owen stumbled along, keeping hold of Lime's hand till they reached the team standing at the sidewalk, shivering with cold. The impatient horses stretched their stiffened limbs with pleasure and made off with a rearing plunge. The men were noisy. Bill sang another song at the top of his voice as they rattled by the sleeping houses, but as he came to an objectionable part of the song Lime turned suddenly and said, "Shut up on that, will you?" and he became silent.

Rock Rivers, after the most extraordinary agitation, had just prohibited the sale of liquor at any point within two miles of the school-house in the town. This, after strenuous opposition, was enforced; the immediate effect of the law was to establish saloons at the limit of the two miles and to throw a large increase of business into the hands of Hank Swartz in the retail part of his brewery, which was situated about two miles from the town, on the bank of the river. He had immediately built a bar-room and made himself ready for the increase of his trade, which had previously been confined to supplying picnic parties with half-kegs of beer or an occasional glass to teamsters passing by. Hank had an eye to the main chance and boasted, "If the public gits ahead of me, it's got to be up and a-comin'."

The road along which Crandall was driving did not lead to Hank's place, but the river road, which branched off a little farther on, went by the brewery, though it was a longer way around. The men grew silent at last, and the steady roll and rumble of the wagon over the smooth road was soothing, and Owen laid his head in Lime's lap and fell asleep while looking at the moon and wondering why it always seemed to go just as fast as the team.

He was awakened by a series of wild yells, the snapping of whips, and the furious rush of horses. Another team filled with harvesters was trying to pass, and not succeeding. The fellows in the other wagon hooted and howled. The driver cracked the whip, but Al's little bays kept them behind until Lime protested, "Oh, let 'em go, Al," and then with a shout of glee the team went by and left them in a cloud of dust.

"Say, boys," said Bill, "that was Pat Sheehan and the Nagle boys. They've turned off; they're goin' down to Hank's. Let's go, too. Come on, fellers, what d'you say? I'm all-fired dry. Ain't you?"

"I'm willun'," said Frank Rice; "what d'you say, Lime?" Lincoln looked up into Lime's face and said to him, in a low voice, "Let's go home; that was Steve a-drivin'." Lime nodded and made a sign of silence, but Lincoln saw his head lift. He had heard and recognized Steve's voice.

"It was Pat Sheehan, sure," repeated Bill, "an' I shouldn't wonder if the others was the Nagle boys and Eth Cole."

"Yes, it was Steve," said Al. "I saw his old hat as he went by."

It was perfectly intelligible to Lime that they were all

anxious to have a meeting between Steve and himself. Lincoln also understood that if Lime refused to go to the brewery he would be called a coward. Bill would tell it all over the neighborhood, and his hero would be shamed. At last Lime nodded his head in consent, and Al turned off into the river road.

When they drew up at the brewery by the river, the other fellows had all entered, and the door was shut. There were two or three other teams hitched about under the trees. The men sprang out, and Bill danced a jig in anticipation of the fun to follow. " If Steve starts to lam Lime, there'll be a circus."

As they stood for a moment before the door, Al spoke to Lime about Steve's probable attack. " I ain't goin' to hunt around for no row," replied Lime, placidly, " and I don't believe Steve is. You lads," he said to the boys, " watch the team for a little while; cuddle down under the blankets if you git cold. It ain't no place for you in the inside. We won't stop long," he ended cheerily.

The door opened and let out a dull red light, closed again, and all was still except an occasional burst of laughter and the noise of heavy feet within. The scene made an indelible impress upon Lincoln. Fifty feet away the river sang over its shallows, broad and whitened with foam which gleamed like frosted silver in the brilliant moonlight. The trees were dark and tall about him and loomed overhead against the starlit sky, and the broad, high moon threw a thick tracery of shadows on the dusty white road where the horses stood. Only the rhythmic flow of the broad, swift river, with the occasional uneasy movement of the horses under their creaking harnesses or the dull noise of the shouting men within the shanty, was to be heard.

Owen nestled down into the robes and took to dreaming of the lovely lady he had seen, and wondered if, when he became a man, he should have a wife like her. He was awakened by Lincoln, who was rousing him to serve a purpose of his own. He rubbed his sleepy eyes and rose under orders.

"Say, Owen, what d'yeh s'pose them fellers are doen' in there? You said Steve was goin' to lick Lime, you did. It don't sound much like it in there. Hear 'um laugh," he said viciously and regretfully. "Say, Owen, you sly along and peek in and see what they're up to, an' come an' tell me, while I hold the horses," he said, to hide the fact that Owen was doing a good deal for his benefit.

Owen got slowly off the wagon and hobbled on toward the saloon, stiff with cold. As he neared the door he could hear some one talking in a loud voice, while the rest laughed at intervals in the manner of those who are listening to the good points in a story. Not daring to open the door, Owen stood around the front, trying to find a crevice to look in at. The speaker inside had finished his joke, and some one had begun singing.

The building was a lean-to attached to the brewery, and was a rude and hastily constructed affair. It had only two windows: one was on the side and the other

on the back. The window on the side was out of
Owen's reach, so he went to the back of the shanty.
It was built partly into the hill, and the window was
at the top of the bank. Owen found that by lying
down on the ground on the outside he had a good
view of the interior. The window, while level with
the ground on the outside, was about as high as the
face of a man on the inside. The boy was extremely
wide-awake now and peered in at the scene with round,
unblinking eyes.

Steve was making sport for the rest and stood leaning his elbow on the bar. He was in rare good humor,
for him. His hat was lying beside him, and he was in
his shirt-sleeves, and his cruel gray eyes, pock-marked
face, and broken nose were lighted up with a frightful
smile. He was good-natured now, but the next drink
might set him wild. Hank stood behind the high pine
bar, a broad but nervous grin on his round, red face.
Two big kerosene lamps, through a couple of smoky
chimneys, sent a dull red glare upon the company,
which half filled the room.

If Steve's face was unpleasant to look upon, the
nonchalant, tiger-like poise and flex of his body was
not. He had been dancing, it seemed, and had thrown
off his coat, and as he talked he repeatedly rolled his
blue shirt-sleeves up and down as though the motion
were habitual with him. Most of the men were sitting
around the room, looking on and laughing at Steve's
antics and the antics of one or two others who were
just drunk enough to make fools of themselves. Two

or three sat on an old billiard table under the window
through which Owen was peering.

Lime sat in characteristic attitude, his elbows upon
his knees and his thumbs under his chin. His eyes
were lazily raised now and then with a lion-like action
of the muscles of his forehead. But he seemed to take
little interest in the ribaldry of the other fellows. Owen
measured both champions critically, and exulted in the
feeling that Steve was not so ready for the row with
Lime as he thought he was.

After Steve had finished his story there was a chorus
of roars : " Bully for you, Steve ! " " Give us another,"
etc. Steve, much flattered, nodded to the alert saloon-
keeper, and said, " Give us another, Hank." As the
rest all sprang up, he added : " Pull out that brandy
kaig this time, Hank. Trot her out, you white-livered
Dutchman ! " he roared, as Swartz hesitated.

The brewer fetched it up from beneath the bar, but
he did it reluctantly. In the midst of the hubbub thus
produced, an abnormally tall and lanky fellow known
as " High " Bedloe pushed up to the bar and made an
effort to speak, and finally did say, solemnly : —

" Gen'lmun, Steve, say, gen'lmun, do'n' less mix our
drinks ! "

This was received with boisterous laughter. Bedloe
could not see the joke, and looked feebly astonished.

Just at this point Owen received such a fright as
entirely took away his powers of moving or breathing,
for something laid hold of his heels with deadly grip.
He was getting his breath to yell when a familiar voice

at his ear said, in a tone somewhere between a whisper and a groan : —

"Say, what they up to all this while? I'm sick o' wait'n' out there."

Lincoln had become impatient; as for Owen, he had been so absorbed by the scenes within, he had not noticed that the frosty ground had stiffened his limbs and set his teeth chattering. Owen simply pointed with his mittened, stubby thumb toward the interior, and Lincoln crawled along to a place beside him.

Mixing the drinks had produced the disastrous effect which Hank and Bedloe had anticipated. The fun became uproarious. There were songs and dances by various members of the Nagle gang, but Lime's crowd, being in the minority, kept quiet, occasionally standing treat, as was the proper thing to do.

But Steve grew wilder and more irritable every moment. He seemed to have drunk just enough to let loose the terrible force that slept in his muscles. He tugged at his throat until the strings of his woollen shirt loosened, displaying the great, sloping muscles of his neck and shoulders, white as milk and hard as iron. His eyes rolled restlessly as he paced the floor. His panther-like step was full of a terrible suggestiveness. The breath of the boys at the window came quicker and quicker. Steve was working himself into a rage that threatened momentarily to break forth into a violence. He realized that this was a crisis in his career; his reputation was at stake.

Young as Owen was, he understood the whole mat-

ter as he studied the restless Steve, and compared him
with his impassive hero, sitting immovable.

" You see Lime can't go away," he explained breathlessly to Lincoln in a whisper, " 'cause they'd tell it
all over the country that he backed down for Steve.
He daresn't leave."

" Steve ain't no durn fool," replied Lincoln, with
superior wisdom. " See Lime there, cool as a cucum-
ber. He's from the pineries, he is." He ended in a
tone of voice intended to convey that fighting was the
principal study of the pineries, and that Lime had gradu-
ated with the highest honors. " Steve ain't a-go'n'
pitch into him yet awhile, you bet your bottom dollar;
he ain't drunk enough for that."

Each time the invitation for another drink was given,
they noticed that Lime kept on the outside of the crowd,
and some one helped him to his glass. " Don't you see
he ain't drinkin'. He's throwin' it away," said Lincoln;
" there, see! He ain't goin' to be drunk when Steve
tackles him. Oh, there'll be music in a minute or
two."

Steve now walked the floor, pouring forth a flood of
profanity and challenges against men who were not
present. He had not brought himself to the point of
attacking the unmoved and silent giant. Some of the
younger men, and especially the pleader against mixed
drinks, had succumbed, and were sleeping heavily on the
back end of the bar and on the billiard table. Hank
was getting anxious, and the forced smile on his face
was painful to see. Over the whole group there was a

singular air of waiting. No one was enjoying himself, and all wished that they were on the road home, but there was no way out of it now. It was evident that Lime purposed forcing the beginning of the battle on Steve. He sat in statuesque repose.

Steve had his hat in his hand and held it doubled up like a club, and every time he turned in his restless walk he struck the bar a resounding blow. His eyes seemed to see nothing, although they moved wildly from side to side.

He lifted up his voice in a snarl. " I'm the man that struck Billy Patterson ! I'm the man that bunted the bull off the bridge ! Anybody got anything to say, now's his time. I'm here. Bring on your champion. I'm the wildcat of the prairie."

Foam came into the corners of his mouth, and the veins stood out on his neck. His red face shone with its swollen veins. He smashed his fists together, threw his hat on the floor, tramped on it, snarling out curses. Nothing kept him in check save the imperturbability of the seated figure. Everybody expected him to clear the saloon to prove his power.

Bedloe, who was asleep on the table, precipitated matters by rolling off with a prodigious noise amid a pandemonium of howls and laughter. In his anxiety to see what was going on, Lincoln thrust his head violently against the window, and it crashed in, sending the glass rattling down on the table.

Steve looked up, a red sheen in his eyes like that of a wild beast. Instantly his fury burst out against this new object of attention — a wild, unreasoning rage.

"What you doen' there? Who air ye, ye mangy little dog?"

Both boys sank back in tumultuous, shuddering haste, and rolled down the embankment. They heard the voice of Steve thundering, "Fetch the little whelp here!"

There was a rush from the inside, a sudden outpouring, and the next moment Owen felt a hand touch his shoulder. Steve dragged him around to the front of the saloon before he could draw his breath or utter a sound. The rest crowded around.

"What are y' doen' there?" said Steve, shaking him with insane vindictiveness.

"Drop that boy!" said Lime. "Drop that boy!" he repeated, and his voice had a peculiar sound, as if it came through his teeth.

Steve dropped him, and turned with a grating snarl upon Lime, who opened his way through the excited crowd while Owen stumbled, leaped, and crawled out of the ring and joined Lincoln.

"Oh, it's you, is it? You white-livered — " He did not finish, for the arm of the blond giant shot out against his face like a beetle, and down he rolled on the grass. The sound of the blow made Owen utter an involuntary cry.

"No human bein' could have stood up agin that blow," Crandall said afterwards. "It was like a mule a-kickin'."

As Steve bounded to his feet, the silence was so great Owen could hear the thumping of his heart and the fierce, almost articulate breathing of Steve. The chatter and roar of the drunken crowd had been silenced by this encounter of the giants.　The open door, where Hank stood, sent a reddish bar of light upon the two men as they faced each other with a sort of terrific calm.　In his swift gaze in search of his brother, Lincoln noticed the dark wood, the river murmuring drowsily over its foam-wreathed pebbles, and saw his brother's face white with excitement, but not fear.

Lime's blow had dazed Steve for a moment, but at the same time it had sobered him.　He came to his feet with a curse which sounded like the swelling snarl of a tiger.　He had been taken by surprise before, and he now came forward with his hands in position, to vindicate his terrible reputation.　The two men met in a frightful struggle.　Blows that meant murder were dealt by each.　Each slapping thud seemed to carry the cracking of bones in it.　Steve was the more agile of the two and circled rapidly around, striking like a trained boxer.

Every time his face came into view, with set teeth and ferocious scowl, the boys' spirits fell.　But when they saw the calm, determined eyes of Lime, his watchful, confident look, they grew assured.　All depended upon him.　The Nagle gang were like wolves in their growing ferocity, and as they outnumbered the other party two to one, it was a critical quarter of an hour. In a swift retrospect Lincoln remembered the frightful tales told of this very spot — of the killing of Lars Petersen and his brother Nels, and the brutal hammering a crowd of drunken men had given to Big Ole, of the Wapsy.

The blood was trickling down Lime's face from a cut on his cheek, but Steve's face was swollen and ghastly from the three blows which he had received. Lime was saving himself for a supreme effort. The Nagle party, encouraged by the sound of the blows which Steve struck, began to yell and to show that they were ready to take a hand in the contest.

"Go it, Steve, we'll back yeh! Give it to 'im. We're with yeh! We'll tend to the rest."

Rice threw off his coat. "Never mind these chaps, Lime. Hold on! Fair play!" he yelled, as he saw young Nagle about to strike Lime from behind.

His cry startled Lime, and with a sudden leap he dealt Steve a terrible blow full in the face, and as he went reeling back made another leaping lunge and struck him to the ground — a motion that seemed impossible to one of his bulk. But as he did so, one of the crowd tripped him and sent him rolling upon the prostrate Steve, whose friends leaped like a pack of snarling wolves upon Lime's back. There came into the giant's heart a terrible, blind, desperate resolution. With a hoarse, inarticulate cry he gathered himself for one supreme effort and rose from the heap like a bear shaking off a pack of dogs; and holding the stunned and nerveless Steve in his great hands, with one swift, incredible effort literally swept his opponent's body in the faces of the infuriated men rushing down upon him.

"Come on, you red hellions!" he shouted, in a voice like a lion at bay. The light streamed on his bared head, his hands were clinched, his chest heaved in

great gasps. There was no movement. The crowd
waited with their hands lowered; before such a man
they could not stand for a moment. They could not
meet the blaze of his eyes. For a moment it seemed as
if no one breathed.

In the silence that followed, Bill, who had kept out
of sight up to this moment, piped out in a high, weak
falsetto, with a comically questioning accent, " All quiet
along the Potomac, boys ? "

Lime unbraced, wiped his face, and laughed. The
others joined in cautiously. " No, thank yez, none in
mine," said Sheehan, in answer to the challenge of
Lime. " Whan Oi take to fightin' stame-ingins Oi'll
lit you knaw."

" Well, I should say so," said another. " Lime,
you're the best man that walks this State."

" Git out of the way, you white-livered hound, or I'll
blow hell out o' yeh," said Steve, who had recovered
himself sufficiently to know what it all meant. He lay
upon the grass behind the rest and was weakly trying to
get his revolver sighted upon Lime. One of the men
caught him by the shoulder and the rest yelled : —

" Hyare, Steve, no shootin'. It was a fair go, and
you're whipped."

Steve only repeated his warnings to get out of the
way. Rice kicked the weapon from his outstretched
hand, and the bullet went flying harmlessly into the air.

Walking through the ring, Lime took Owen by the
hand and said : " Come, boy, this is no place for you.
Let's go home. Fellers," he drawled in his customary

lazy way, "when y' want me you know where to find me. Come, boys, the circus is over, the last dog is hung."

For the first mile or two there was a good deal of talk, and Bill said he knew that Lime could whip the whole crowd.

" But where was you, Bill, about the time they had me down ? I don't remember hearin' anything of you 'long about that time, Bill."

Bill had nothing to say.

" Made me think somehow of Daniel in the lions' den," said Owen.

" What do you mean by that, sonny ? " said Bill. " It made me think of a circus. The circus there'll be when Lime's woman finds out what he's been a-doin'."

" Great Scott, boys, you mustn't tell Merry Etty," said Lime, in genuine alarm.

As for Owen, he lay with his head in Lime's lap, looking up at the glory of the starlit night, and with a confused mingling of the play, of the voice of the lovely woman, of the shouts and blows at the brewery, in his mind, and with the murmur of the river and the roll and rumble of the wagon blending in his ears, he fell into a sleep which the rhythmic beat of the horses' hoofs did not interrupt.

N

AUGUST

From cottonwoods the locusts cry
In quavering ecstatic duo — a boy
Shouts a wild call — a mourning dove
In the blue distance sobs — the wind
Wanders by heavy with odors
Of corn and wheat and melon vines.
The trees tremble with delirious joy as the breeze
Greets them, one by one — now the oak,
Now the great sycamore, now the elm —
While the locusts, in brazen chorus, cry
Like stricken things, and the ringdove's note
Sobs on in the dim distance.

IN STACKING TIME

Within the shelter of a towering stack
I lie in shadow, blinking at the sky.
I hear the glorious southern wind
Sweep the sere stubble like a scythe.
The falling crickets patter like the rain
Shaken from wind-tossed yellow wheat.

O first ripe day of autumn!
O memory half of pain and half of joy!

As if the harsh fate of some dead girl
Haunted my heart, I dream and dream
With aching throat of dim but unforgotten days.
O wind, and light, and cool, high clouds,
O smell of corn leaves ripening!
It is so sweet to lie here, dumb and rapt
With wordless weight of ancient scenes and suns,
Of unremembered millions of autumn days,
Filled with the wonder of a million vanished years,
Wonder of winds and woods and waters,
The smell of ripening grain and nuts,
And the joy of sunset rest from toil
In rude, small fields in dim ancestral days.

As I muse, the shadows wheel and lengthen
Across the stubble-land, which glows,
A mat of gold inlaid with green.
The sun sinks.   Sighing, I rise to go —
The noise of near-by street-car breaks the spell
Of cloud and sun and rustling sheaves,
Drowning the call of the mystical wind —
And overhead I hear the jar and throb
Of giant presses; and the grinding roar
Of ceaseless tumult in the street below
Comes back and welters all my world
As the gray sea returns to sweep
In sullen surges where the roses bloomed.

CHAPTER XIII

LINCOLN'S FIRST STACK

FROM the time he had reached his eighth year, it had been Lincoln's business in stacking time to "turn bundles." That is, he stood in the middle of the stack, and receiving the sheaves from the pitcher on the wagon, turned them, and laid them butt-end foremost at the elbow of the stacker, while on the far side of the stack, as he came round on the side near the wagon, the pitcher could place them without aid.

The stacks were often six or eight yards in diameter, and as the stacker rose far above the wagon, he was quite out of sight of the pitcher while making his round. Turning the sheaves was not hard work, and Lincoln rather enjoyed it, for he had wheat to eat, and the talk of the men interested him, and besides, he was learning to be a stacker himself.

A boy wants to do everything, but he doesn't want to do anything long. No matter how enjoyable a job may be for a time, it soon grows old to him. He is an experimenter. That is his trade. To do one thing long cuts him off from acquiring a complete education. Moreover, he wants to do a man's work. Set him to turning bundles, he longs to pitch in the field, or some other job for which he is not fitted.

Lincoln enjoyed the close of each old job and the beginning of each new one. He was intensely pleased when harvest ended and stacking began. There was something fine in the coming of his uncles, the McTurgs, rattling up the road in the early dawn of late August. They changed work, thus making up a crew in order to get the services of Duncan Stewart, who was a skilful stacker. They often came with the avowed intention of catching the Stewarts at breakfast, but they never succeeded. Lincoln considered his father an owl, because of his early rising.

Often by half-past six in the morning the teams moved out into a field where the rising sun was flaming through a mist that clothed the world like a garment, and clung to the jewelled grass like a bridal veil.

The prairie at this time was quite silent. The young chickens had ceased to peep, the meadow-lark was heard only infrequently — the cricket and the katydid possessed the land. The corn rustled huskily now and then, as if in intermittent, meditative speech, brooding upon the decay which was falling upon the world. The pumpkins and melons were ripening in the deeps of the corn-forests, the waving fields of wheat had given place to wide reaches of cleanly shaven stubble, beautifully mottled in green and purple by smart-weed and mats of morning-glory vines, wherein the shocks, weather-beaten as granite, sat in sagging rows waiting the stacker, eaten into by pocket-gophers below and ravaged by swarms of blackbirds above. By contrast with the fierce heat and the unrelenting strain of the harvest-field, stacking time seemed leisurely and full of genial intercourse. The teams moved lazily at the most, and the men worked on quietly with the action of those who meditated. The crew was made up of "monthly hands" and neighbors; the wild and lawless element was pretty thoroughly eliminated. A single crew consisted of two teams with their drivers, one pitcher in the field, a stacker, and a boy to hand bundles. Sometimes Mr. Stewart ran a double crew and superintended the stacking, while Lincoln and Owen turned bundles and "raked down," keeping the stack clean of "scatterings."

It was pleasant business at first, to stand on the growing stack, facing the rushing breeze, counting the number of settings in sight, hearing the voices of the men, and tossing the sheaves into place. But before noon came the boy dropped with amazing readiness upon the stack, to shell wheat between his hands (out of which to make "gum") and to listen to the crickets, while the stacker was at work on the side

next to the pitcher. Each time he called " Come,
Lincoln," the boy rose with reluctant weariness. If
a boy could only toil when he felt like it, work
wouldn't be so bad, but to be interrupted in a day-
dream by a call to hand bundles was disagreeably like
being enslaved to a treadmill.

There were days when a powerful, persistent wind,
hot and dry, moved up from the south, making the
ripening corn hiss and flutter, a blast that swept the
sear stubble like a scythe invisible, but sounding with
swiftness, a wind that drove the loose wheat into the
boy's face like shot, and lifted the outside sheaves of
the stack in spite of all precaution, and laughed and
howled like an insane fury. It was the mighty equa-
torial wind, and Lincoln loved it. All day while the
sun shone and the prairie lay dim in its garment of mist,
that steady, relentless, furious, splendid breeze swept
from the burning south to the empty, mysterious north
like an invisible fleeing army of invisible harpies. Sometimes on such a day, fires broke out and raged, sweeping
from field to meadow and from stubble-land to pasture.
Fires were infrequent at this time in the settled places,
but when they came they worked woes. Sam Hutchison
lost all his horses on such a day by a spark from the
kitchen stovepipe, and Humboldt Bunn burned up two
enormous ricks of grain by setting fire to the stubble
which plagued him. For all these things Lincoln
always found something extremely worth while in the
sound of this wind.

It browned the men till they looked like Sioux, and

made the boys' lips chap. The hawks seemed to delight in it — tipping, wheeling, down-shooting, up-darting, apparently its toy, but in reality its master. The turkey-buzzards went abroad in it without hesitancy and their majestic flight always appeared to Lincoln as almost miraculous. They seemed to fling themselves into the air and ride above the storm at their own will without a particle of physical effort. They had the sovereign pride of eagles and the taste of carrion beetles.

For several years Lincoln had been instructed by his father in the rudiments of stacking, and had been allowed to "start the bottom," and even to lay a course or two of the "bulge." To stack well was considered a nice job, requiring skill and judgment, and the privilege of doing even an occasional "inside course" was of great value to ambitious boys.

The bundles are laid in rings, butt-ends out, each inner course lapping to the bands of the outer sheaves. Thus when a stack is started the courses form a series of circular terraces rising to a dome of crossed sheaves in the middle, the design being to keep the straw always slanting out, so that any rain sinking in must necessarily work its way outward of its own weight. In order to further insure their slant, skilful stackers like Duncan Stewart laid "bulges," so that when the stack was complete it was shaped like a gigantic egg; small on the bottom, swelling to a much larger diameter six or eight feet from the ground, and gradually tapering to a point at the top.

This was done by studying the slant of the sheaves.

After a shock has set for some time in the field, the ends of the outside bundles take on a " slanch" at the butt, and when the stacker wishes to "carry the stack up straight," he lays the sheaves sidewise. When he wishes to "lay out" his bulge, he turns the long point of the "slanch" upward. When he wishes to "draw in," he reverses them, putting the point down and the slant upward, — "and always keep your middle full," Duncan reiterated to his son. "Pack your middle hard, especially when you come to draw in. Tramp it down well, and you won't have any wet grain."

The year he was thirteen, Lincoln regularly laid the bottoms and brought the stacks to the bulge, but hardly dared go on through that ticklish spot. He came to "top out" for his father, being light and agile, and able to cling like a chicken to the high stack after it was far above the ladder, but he had never been able to put up a full stack. One day in Lincoln's thirteenth year, Mr. Stewart, while topping off a very high oat-stack, slipped and fell to the ground, spraining his arm and side so badly that he could not continue his work. For a few minutes he could not speak for his pain. As he grew easier, he reassumed his dauntless tone.

"Well, Lincoln," he said grimly, "I guess you are the boss stacker from this on." They laid him on a wagon and carried him to the house. "I'm all right now, — go back to work," he said.

Lincoln's heart swelled with pride. He was not quite fourteen, but his father's words made a man of him. He assumed command, and the work went on as before.

Owen passed bundles, and Lincoln began a new bottom in a sort of tremor, such as a young lieutenant feels when he assumes command for the first time. The hired men were curious to see how the boy would come out. The wind was against him, but the oats were long and not likely to slip, so Lincoln started boldly on a new stack, resolved to make it a big one. He moved swiftly round on his knees, catching the bundles with his left hand and drawing them under his right knee. The men did not spare him, and he did not ask mercy of them.

It was hard work. The knees of his trousers soon gave way, and the backs of his hands swelled from the exertion of grasping the heavy bundles, which often struck him in the face, filling his neck with chaff and beards. Briers got into his fingers, and his neck ached, but after all, it was a man's work, and he had no mind to complain.

By three o'clock he began to lay out his bulge, and then the hired hands began to bother him.

"Better not try to put on too much of a bulge, Link," said one.

"Ain't you layin' 'er out a little too much on one side?" asked David, with an air of great solicitude.

"I guess not," Lincoln replied. He had been taught to tell by the dip of the stack whether it was balancing properly or not; nevertheless he got down often to look at it. "I'll make her a twenty-five-footer," he said to Owen.

"It's time to eat our melons," replied Owen, who was already tired of handling bundles.

Lincoln, with the air of the boss, called on all hands for a rest and a hack at a big " mountain sweet " which had been picked in the early morning, and put under the edge of a stack to keep cool.

The boys considered it almost providential that melons should ripen just in time to relieve the drouth of stacking time.   And such melons!   They seemed to grow spontaneously from the new land.   Sometimes by merely scattering seeds as he broke the sod, a farmer would find thousands of splendid melons ready in August.   Everybody had a patch, generally in the middle of the corn-field, for safe keeping, and Lincoln and Owen took great pride in having the best seed known to them.   They were skilled in ways to tell when a melon was ripe, and in the darkest night made no mistakes.

In the shade of his stack, with the crickets chiming dully in the stubble, Lincoln and all hands drew around an immense green-striped globe, rich in the summer's sweetness, and laved in the cool dew of the night before.   There is no other place where a melon tastes so good (a table is no place for a melon).   The midday meal was just far enough away to make the red core delicious food, as well as cool drink.   When the men slit off great pink and green crescents, and, disdaining knives, " wallered into it," when nothing remained of it but the seed and green " rine," Lincoln rose and walked toward the ladder, and thus set the crew again in motion.

Round by round he pushed out his bulge, the pitch-

ers warning him, " Better look out, Link, you'll have a
' slide-out.' "

But he, with wilful pride, had determined to build a
monster, just to show his father he was really a boss
stacker. At last the huge, half-built stack stood like a
top poised on a twelve-foot bottom, and Lincoln, fairly
alarmed, crept round on the top of the outside course,
fearing disaster.

" Don't touch them outside bundles," he said sharply
to the pitcher. " Send 'em up to Owen. Owen, slide
'em down easy — don't jiggle me."

Another round bound the outside sheaves, but still
the stack was in danger. Not till the third round did
Lincoln's muscles relax. Even then he knew that the
first course of " drawing in " was almost as full of danger. His nerves were a little shaken, but his pride
would not let him show his doubt of the issue. Slowly
he " drew in," but when all danger of a " slide-out " was
over, a new problem presented itself. The stack was
growing out of reach of the pitcher. It bid fair to be
thirty feet high, and to finish it by night was impossible,
though a dark cloud rising in the west threatened rain.
It must be " topped out " somehow.

As they went up to supper at five o'clock, the men
were full of admiration of the stack.

" She's a linger, and no mistake."

" When ye goin' to top her out, Link ? "

" Who has the honors ? "   (The " honors " meant the
privilege of pitching the last sheaves to the top of the
stack, an ironical phrase.)

"Well, I'm not anxious," said David. "I guess I'll let Dan have it."

They found Mr. Stewart stretched out on two chairs, with his arm bandaged, but fairly comfortable.

"Well, my son, how do you come on?"

"Oh, all right, I guess."

"Leave everything snug — it looks like rain."

"You want to see that stack," said David. "We put ten loads into her, and she's only a little ways above the bulge."

Duncan looked at his son. "Ten loads?"

"Oh, I'll taper off — don't worry."

Dan took a hand. "He'll top 'er off if we can get the bundles to him. She's as big as a mountain."

Duncan smiled. "Trying to beat your old dad, are you?"

Lincoln felt hot. "I wanted to make it big enough to take all the afternoon," he said.

"You have," said David, "and part of the night."

"Put a man on the ladder," said Mr. Stewart, "and do the best you can."

Lincoln set his lips, and said no more in the house.

"I'll make you pay for this," he said to Dan, as he climbed to his place on the wagon. "Now hump yourselves." Slowly the top of the stack contracted, and the pitchers sank below. The shadows of the teams began to lengthen along the stubble, which the setting sun glorified. The crickets sang innumerably. The cloud in the west hung low down on the horizon, awaiting the coming of the night to advance. The wind had died away, as if "to give the boy a chance," as David said, and Lincoln's heart was resolute.

The "honors" fell on Dan, but David came in to stand on the ladder and pass the bundles up to the stacker, who looked like a child working all alone high up in the air. There was something fine and exalting in that last hour's work. To feel that his first stack was, after all, a success made the boy feel like a young soldier just promoted. He worked in his bare feet in order to cling better, — worked swiftly, and yet calmly.

David "gassed" Dan. "Come, bear down on your fork, there! Your hide's been crackin' with strength all day. Now here is your chance for exercise. A little more steam, Danny. I can't come down after 'em."

At last the boy, hardly larger than a sheaf, stood erect on the completed top of the stack, and called for the centre stake. He was so far above even the man on the ladder, that David grumbled in flinging the cap-sheaf to him, but at last the final bundle was broken and upturned upon the stake, and as the boy, sliding to the ground, agile as a squirrel, walked around the stack, which towered, big, and stately, and graceful, far above him, his heart was big with pride. He had demonstrated his skill, and was happy.

But all night long he crept round that wide, slippery bulge, the bundles sliding away from him again and again, till he was worn and brain-weary with the effect. It was always so with any new thing he did; he toiled over it all night, and rose in the morning limp and unrested.

The following day tried him sorely. He passed from oats to wheat, which is much more slippery and more difficult to handle in the bulge. He had a disastrous " slide out " in his forenoon's stack. The rain which threatened had not come, the air was hot and close, and he was lame and sore, his hands badly swollen, and his knees tender, and on all these accounts, when a third of his bulge fell out, he wept tears of mortification and rage. To crown his misfortunes, his father came out before he was able to straighten out the " mess."

But something rose in him which made him sullenly determined, and with only an hour's delay he was once more master of the situation. Mr. Stewart wisely said nothing — preferring to " let the boy wiggle." When he turned his back and started for the house, Lincoln's heart grew strong again. His father considered him quite equal even to a disaster, capable of taking care of himself and a crew. By nightfall he had repaired all mistakes ; thereafter, he was the stacker of the crew.

The finest part of all the stacking time lay in the " home setting " in the barn-yard, for the work lay near the house, the road, the well, and the berry patch. A part of the crop was always housed in and stacked around the barn, in order that the straw might be used for sheds, and as feed for the cattle in winter. Here Lincoln was forced to do his handsomest, for every passing team minutely studied the work of his hands.

By the time they reached this home setting, his father was able to supervise, and his warnings and advice enabled Lincoln to outdo himself. Hardly a neighbor passing by but had his remark about the boy stacker. Old man Bennett came along and stopped to drawl out : —

"Say, Link, your stack's tarvin' over."

"Oh, I guess not."

"I say 'tis.   You'll be off in a minute."

Jennings pulled up to say, "Get full pay ? "

"Yes, sir."

"Well, you d'oughto.   How do you build 'em on air, that way ? "

Lincoln enjoyed all this very much, and as a matter of fact, so did his father.   If a man seemed disposed to linger, Mr. Stewart went out to the fence to gossip about his injured arm, and to state the age of the boy. It was perfectly obvious vanity, but it led to no ill results.

The kitchen was handy, and Mary came out with a cooky and a cup of milk occasionally.   The turkeys and chickens fluttered about, picking up crickets and grass-hoppers, and singing harsh songs of joy, as if giving thanks for this unexpected feast.   David's wife came over once to spend the day, and Dan's sister came to tea at night.   Rance, on his way to town one afternoon with a drove of steers, made Lincoln discontented for a time.   "I wish I could go along," he shouted as Rance pulled up at the gate.

"I wish you could ; I'd treat you to ice-cream."

"Just my darn luck," said Lincoln, ruefully, and Rance rode on.

There was a peculiar charm in the work as night fell

and the lights flamed up in the kitchen. As the last load was finished, the crickets increased their shrill chorus; the rumble of wagons on the road grew more distinct, and the cattle came snuffing and lowing uneasily at the bars, surprised at being shut off from their accustomed quarters. Stiff and weary, but serenely well pleased, Lincoln slid down from his high place, and with the privilege of a boss stacker went directly to the house, with no chores to do — a very decided honor and high distinction indeed.

There was only one thing better — to go with Rance to market with the steers. It made his mouth water to think of the peaches and ice-cream he might have had with his chum after the " bunch " of steers at the cattle chutes had been safely corralled. But the good things of life never seemed to go in a " string," anyway. They came singly and far apart.

o

CHAPTER XIV

THE OLD-FASHIONED THRESHING

LIFE on an Iowa farm, even for the older lads, had its compensations. There were times when the daily routine of lonely and monotonous life gave place to an agreeable bustle for a few days, and human intercourse lightened the toil. In the midst of the dull, slow progress of the fall's ploughing, the gathering of the threshing crew was a most dramatic event.

There had been great changes in the methods of threshing since Mr. Stewart had begun to farm, but it had not yet reached the point where steam displaced the horse-power. In the old days in Wisconsin, the grain, after being stacked round the barn ready to be threshed, was allowed to remain until late in the fall before calling in the machine.

Of course, some farmers got at it earlier, for all could not thresh at the same time, and a good part of the fall's labor consisted in " changing works " with the neighbors, thus laying up a stock of unpaid labor ready for the home job. Day after day, therefore, Mr. Stewart and the hired man shouldered their forks in the crisp and early dawn and went to help their neighbors, while Lincoln ploughed the stubble-land.

All through the months of October and November,

the ceaseless ringing hum and the *bow-ouw, ouw-woo boo-oo-oom* of the great balance wheels of the threshing-machine and the deep bass hum of the whirling cylinder, as its motion rose and fell, could be heard on every side like the singing of some sullen and gigantic autumnal insect.

For weeks Lincoln had looked forward to the coming of the threshers with the greatest eagerness, and during the whole of the day appointed Owen and he hung on the gate and gazed down the road to see if the machine were not coming. It did not come during the afternoon — still they could not give it up, and at the falling of dusk still hoped to hear the rattle of its machinery.

They moved about restlessly in momentary expectation of a shout, notwithstanding the hired man said, " They're probably stuck in the mud." A score of times Owen ran to the window to see if he could not catch a glimpse of it or hear the shouts of the men to their horses.

It was not uncommon for the men who attended to these machines to work all day at one place and move to another "setting" at night. In that way, they might not arrive until nine o'clock at night, or they might come at four o'clock in the morning. And the children were about starting to "climb the wooden hill" when they heard the peculiar rattle of the cylinder and the voices of the McTurgs singing.

" There they are," said Mr. Stewart, getting the old square lantern and lighting the candle within. The air was sharp, and the boys having taken off their boots, could only stand at the window and watch the father as he went out to show the men where to set the "power," the dim light throwing fantastic shadows here and there, lighting up a face now and then, and bringing out the thresher, which seemed a silent monster to the children, who flattened their noses against the cold window-panes to be sure that nothing should escape them. The men's voices sounded cheerfully in the still night, and the roused turkeys in the oaks peered about on their perches, black silhouettes against the sky. The children would gladly have stayed up to greet the threshers, who were captains of industry in their eyes, but they were ordered off to bed by Mrs. Stewart, who said, " You must go to sleep in order to be up early in the morning." As they lay there in their beds under the sloping rafter roof, they heard the hand riding furiously away to tell some of the neighbors that the threshers had come. They could hear the cackle of the hens as Mr. Stewart assaulted them and wrung their innocent necks. The crash of the " sweeps " being unloaded sounded loud and clear in the night, and so watching the dance of the lights and shadows cast by the lantern on the plastered wall, they fell asleep.

They were awakened next morning by the ringing beat of the iron sledge as the men drove the stakes to hold the " power " to the ground. The rattle of chains, the clash of rods, the clang of iron bars, intermixed with laughter and snatches of song, came sharply through the frosty air. The smell of sausages being fried in the

kitchen, the rapid tread of their busy mother as she hurried the breakfast forward, warned the boys that it was
time to get up, although it was not yet dawn in the
east, and they had a sense of being awakened to a strange
new world. When they got down to breakfast, the men
had finished their coffee and were out in the stock-yard
completing preparations.

This morning experience was superb. Though shiv-
ery and cold in the faint frosty light of the day, the
children enjoyed every moment of it. The frost lay
white on every surface, the frozen ground rang like iron
under the steel-shod feet of the horses, the breath of the
men rose up in little white puffs while they sparred
playfully or rolled each other on the ground in jovial
clinches of legs and arms.

The young men were all anxiously waiting the first
sound which should rouse the countryside and proclaim
that theirs was the first machine to be at work. The
older men stood in groups, talking politics or speculating
on the price of wheat, pausing occasionally to slap
their hands about their breasts.

The pitchers were beginning to climb the stacks, and
belated neighbors could be seen coming across the fields.

Finally, just as the east began to bloom and long
streamers of red began to unroll along the vast gray
dome of sky, Joe Gilman — " Shouting Joe " as he was
called — mounted one of the stacks, and throwing down
the cap-sheaf lifted his voice in " a Chippewa war-
whoop." On a still morning like this his voice could
be heard three miles. Long drawn and musical, it sped

away over the fields, announcing to all the world that the McTurgs were ready for the race. Answers came back faintly from the frosty fields, where the dim figures of laggard hands could be seen hurrying over the plough-land; then David called "All right," and the machine began to hum.

In those days the machine was a "J. I. Case" or a "Buffalo Pits" separator, and was moved by five pairs of horses attached to a power staked to the ground, round which they travelled to the left, pulling at the ends of long levers or sweeps. The power was planted some rods away from the machine, to which the force was carried by means of "tumbling rods," with "knuckle joints." The driver stood upon a platform above the huge, savage, cog-wheels round which the horses moved, and he was a great figure in the eyes of the boys.

Driving looked like an easy job, but it was not. It was very tiresome to stand on that small platform all through the long day of the early fall, and on cold November mornings when the cutting wind roared over the plain, sweeping the dust and leaves along the road. It was far pleasanter to sit on the south side of the stack as Tommy did and watch the horses go round. It was necessary also for the driver to be a man of good judgment, for the power must be kept just to the right speed, and he should be able to gauge the motion of the cylinder by the pitch of its deep bass hum. There were always three men who went with the machine and were properly "the threshers." One acted as driver, the others were respectively "feeder" and "tender"; one of them fed the grain into the rolling cylinder, while the other, oil-can in hand, "tended" the separator. The feeder's position was the high place to which all boys aspired, and they used to stand in silent admiration watching the easy, powerful swing of David McTurg as he caught the bundles in the crook of his arm, and spread them out into a broad, smooth band upon which the cylinder caught and tore like some insatiate monster, and David was the ideal man in Lincoln's eyes, and to be able to feed a threshing-machine, the highest honor in the world. The boy who was chosen to cut bands went to his post like a soldier to dangerous picket duty.

Sometimes David would take one of the small boys upon his stand, where he could see the cylinder whiz while the flying wheat stung his face. Sometimes the driver would invite Tommy on the power to watch the horses go round, and when he became dizzy often took the youngster in his arms and running out along the moving sweep, threw him with a shout into David's arms.

Lincoln, who was just old enough to hold sacks for the measurer, did not enjoy threshing so well, but to Owen and his mates it was the keenest joy. They wished it would never end. The wind blew cold and the clouds were flying across the bright blue sky, the straw glistened in the sun, the machine howled, the dust flew, the whip cracked, and the men worked like beavers to get the sheaves to the feeder, and to keep the straw and wheat away from the tail-end of the machine.

These fellows, wallowing to their waists in the chaff, did so for the amusement of Owen and Mary, and for no other reason.

And the straw-pile — what delight they had in that! What fun it was to go up to the top where the four or five men were stationed, one behind the other. They tossed huge forkfuls of the light, fragrant stalks upon the boys, burying their light bulk, from which they came to the surface out of breath, and glad to see the light again.

They were always amused by the man who stood in the midst of the thick dust and flying chaff at the head of the stacker, who took and threw away the endless cataract of straw as if it were all play. His teeth shone like a negro's out of his dust-blackened face, and his shirt was wet with sweat, but he motioned for more straw, and the feeder, accepting the challenge, motioned for more speed, and so the driver swung his lash and yelled at the straining horses, the pitchers buckled to it, the sleepy growl of the cylinder rose to a howl, the wheat rushed out in a stream as "big as a stovepipe," and the carriers were forced to trot back and forth from the granary like mad, and to generally "hump themselves" in order to keep the wheat from piling up round the measurer where Lincoln stood disconsolately holding sacks for old man Smith.

When the children got tired with wallowing in the straw, and with turning somersaults therein, they could go down and help Rover catch the rats which were uncovered by the pitchers when they reached the

stack bottom. It was all drama to Owen, just as it
had once been to the others. The horses, with their
straining, outstretched necks, the loud and cheery
shouts, the whistling of the driver, the roar and hum
of the machine, the flourishing of the forks, the supple
movement of brawny arms, the shouts of the threshers
to each other, all blended with the wild sound of the
wind overhead in the creaking branches of the oaks,
formed a splendid drama for such as he.

But for Lincoln, who was forced to stand with old
Daddy Smith in the flying dust beside the machine, it
was a bad play. He had now become a part of the
machine — of the crew. His liberty to come and go
was gone. When Daddy was grinning at him out of
the gray dust and the swirling chaff, the wheat beards
were crawling down his back, scratching and rasping.
His ears were stunned by the noise of the cylinder and
the howl of the balance-wheel, and it did not help him
any to have the old man say in a rasping voice, " Never
mind the chaff, sonny — it ain't pizen."

Whirr — bang ! something had gone into the cylinder, making the feeder dodge to escape the flying teeth,
and the men seized the horses to stop the machine.
Lincoln hailed such accidents with delight, for it afforded
him a few minutes' rest while the men put some new
teeth in the "concave." He had time to unbutton his
shirt and get some of the beards out of his neck, to take
a drink of water, and to let the deafness go out of his
ears.

At such times also some of the young fellows were

sure to have a wrestling or a lifting match, and all kind of jokes flew about. The man at the straw-stack leaned indolently on his fork and asked the feeder sarcastically if that was the best he could do, and remarked, " It's gettin' chilly up here. Guess I'll haf to go home and get my kid gloves."

To this David laughingly responded, " I'll warm your carcass with a rope if you don't shut up," all of which gave the boys infinite delight.

There was not a little joking about the extraordinary number of times the oil-can had to be carried to the kitchen fire and warmed by Len Robbins, the driver. When David was tending and Len feeding, the can was all right, but the moment Len took it up it congealed. David said, " It always does that whenever there's a pretty girl in the house, even in the warmest days of September."

Len laughed and said, " Don't you wish you had as good a chance, boys ? " and triumphantly flourished a half-eaten doughnut on the tip of his forefinger.

But the work began again, and Lincoln was forced to take his place as regularly as the other men. As the sun neared the zenith, Lincoln looked often up at it — so often in fact that Daddy, observing it, cackled in great amusement, " Think you c'n hurry it along, sonny ? The watched pot never boils, remember ! " — which made the boy so angry he nearly kicked the old man on the shin.

But at last the call for dinner sounded, the driver began to shout, " Whoa there, boys," to the teams and to hold his long whip before their eyes in order to convince them that he really meant "Whoa." The pitchers stuck their forks down in the stack and leaped to the ground, Billy the band-cutter drew from his wrist the string of his big knife, the men slid down from the straw-pile, and a race began among the teamsters to see who should be first unhitched and at the watering trough and at the table.

It was always a splendid and dramatic moment to the boys as the men crowded round the well to wash, shouting, joking, cuffing each other, sloshing themselves with water, and accusing each other of having blackened the towel by using it to wash with rather than to wipe with.

Mrs. Stewart and the hired girl and generally some of the neighbors' wives (who had " changed works " also) stood ready to bring on the food as soon as the men were seated. The table had been lengthened to its utmost and pieced out with the kitchen table, which usually was not of the same height, and planks had been laid for seats on stout kitchen chairs at each side. The men came in with a noisy rush and took seats wherever they could find them, and their attack on the " biled 'taters and chicken " should have been appalling to the women, but it was not. They smiled to see them eat. One cut at a boiled potato followed by two motions and it disappeared. Grimy fingers lifted a leg of a chicken to a wide mouth, and two snaps at it laid it bare as a slate pencil. To the children standing in the corner waiting, it seemed that every smitch of the chicken was going and that nothing would remain when the men got through, but there was, for chickens were plentiful.

At last even the "gantest" of them filled up. Even Len had his limits, and something remained for the children and the women, who sat down at the second table, while David and William and Len returned to the machine to put everything in order, to sew the belts, or take a bent tooth out of the "concave." Len, however, managed to return two or three times in order to have his joke with the hired girl, who enjoyed it quite as much as he did.

In the short days of October only a brief nooning was possible, and as soon as the horses had finished their oats, the roar and hum of the machine began again and continued steadily all the afternoon. Owen and Rover continued their campaign upon the rats which inhabited the bottoms of the stacks, and great was their excitement as the men reached the last dozen sheaves. Rover barked and Owen screamed half in fear and half from a boy's savage delight in killing things, and very few rats escaped their combined efforts.

To Lincoln the afternoon seemed endless. His arms grew tired with holding the sacks against the lip of the half-bushel, and his fingers grew sore with the rasp of the rough canvas out of which the sacks were made. When he thought of the number of times he must repeat these actions, his heart was numb with weariness.

But all things have an end. By and by the sun grew big and red, the night began to fall and the wind to die out. Through the falling gloom the machine boomed steadily with a new sound, a sort of solemn roar, rising at intervals to a rattling yell as the cylinder ran empty. The men were working silently, sullenly, looming dim and strange; the pitchers on the stack, the feeder on the platform, and especially the workers on the high straw-pile, seemed afar off to Lincoln's eyes. The gray dust covered the faces of those near by, changing them into something mysterious and sad. At last he heard the welcome cry, "Turn out!" The men raised glad answer and threw aside their forks.

Again came the gradual slowing down of the motion, while the driver called in a gentle, soothing voice: "Whoa, lads! Steady, boys! Whoa, now!" But the horses had been going on so long and so steadily that they checked their speed with difficulty. The men slid from the stacks, and, seizing the ends of the sweeps, held them; but even after the power was still, the cylinder went on, until David, calling for a last sheaf, threw it in its open maw, choking it into silence.

Then came again the sound of dropping chains and iron rods, and the thud of hoofs as the horses walked with laggard gait and weary down-falling heads to the barn. The men, more subdued than at dinner, washed with greater care, brushing the dust from their beards and clothes. The air was still and cool, the wind was gone, the sky a deep, cloudless blue.

The evening meal was more attractive to the boys than dinner. The table was lighted with a kerosene lamp, and the clean white linen, the fragrant dishes, the women flying about with steaming platters, all seemed very dramatic and very cheery to Lincoln as well as to the men who came into the light and warmth with aching muscles and empty stomachs.

There was always a good deal of talk at supper, but it was more subdued than at the dinner hour. The younger fellows had their jokes of course, and watched the hired girl attentively, while the old fellows discussed the day's yield of grain or the matters of the township. Lincoln was now allowed a place at the first table like a first-class hand.

There was a brisk rattle of implements, and many time-worn jokes from the wags of the party — about "some people being better hands with the fork at the kitchen table," etc.

The pie and the doughnuts and the coffee disappeared as fast as they could be brought, which seemed to please Mrs. Stewart, who said, "Goodness sakes, yes; eat all you want. They was made to eat."

The men were all, or nearly all, neighbors' boys, or hands hired by the month, and were like members of the family. Mrs. Stewart treated them like visitors and not like hired help. No one feared a genuine rudeness from the other.

After supper Mr. Stewart and the men withdrew to milk the cows and to bed down the horses, and when they were gone, the women and the youngsters ate their supper while two or three of the young men who had no teams to take care of sat round the room and made the most interesting remarks they could think of to the girls.   Lincoln thought they were very stupid, but the girls seemed to enjoy it.

After they had eaten their supper it was a great pleasure to the boys to go out to the barn and shed (all wonderfully changed now to their minds by the great new stack of straw), there to listen to the stories or jolly remarks of the men as they curried their tired horses munching busily at their hay, too weary to move a muscle otherwise, but enjoying the rubbing down which the men gave them with wisps of straw held in each hand.   The lantern threw a dim red light on the harness and the rumps of the horses, and on the active figures of the men.

The boys could hear the mice rustling the straw of the roof, while from the farther end of the dimly lighted shed came the regular *strim — stram* of the streams of milk falling into the bottoms of the tin pails as Mr. Stewart and the hired hand milked the contented cows. They peered round occasionally from behind the legs of a cow to laugh at the fun of the threshers, or to put in a word or joke.

This was all very momentous to Lincoln and Owen as they sat on the oat box, shivering in the cold air, listening with all their ears.   When they all went toward the house, the stars were out, and the flame-colored crescent moon lay far down in the deep west.   The frost had already begun to glisten on the fences and well-curb.   High in the air, dark against the sky, the turkeys were roosting uneasily, as if feeling some premonition of their approaching fate.   Rover pattered along by

Lincoln's side on the crisp grass, and Owen wondered if his feet were not cold — his nose certainly was when he laid it in his hot palm.

The light from the kitchen was very welcome, and how bright and warm it was with the mother's merry voice and smiling face where the women were moving to and fro, and talking even more busily than they worked.

Sometimes in these old-fashioned threshing days, after the supper table was cleared out of the way, and the men returned to the house, there followed an hour or two of delicious merrymaking. Perhaps two or three of the sisters of the young men had dropped in, and the boys themselves were in no hurry to get home.

Around the fire the older men sat to tell stories while the girls trudged in and out, finishing up the day's work and getting the materials ready for breakfast. With speechless content Lincoln used to sit and listen to stories of bears and Indians and logging on the " Wisconsc," and other tales of frontier life, and then at last, after much beseeching, the violin was brought out and David played. Strange how those giant hands could supple to the strings and the bow — all day they had been handling the fierce straw or were covered with the grease and dirt of the machine, yet now they drew from the violin the wildest, weirdest strains (David did not know the names of these tunes), thrilling Norse folk songs, Swedish dances, and love ballads, mournful, sensuous, and seductive.

Lincoln could not understand why those tunes had

that sad, sweet quality, but he could listen and listen to them all night long.

At last came the inevitable call for the " Fisherman's Hornpipe," or the " Devil's Dream," to which Joe Gilman jigged with an energy and abandon only to be equalled by a genuine darky. Sometimes, if there were enough for a set, the young people pushed the table aside and took places for " The Fireman's Dance," or " Money Musk," and at the end the boys went home with the girls in the bright starlight, to rise next dawn for another day's work with the thresher. Such had been the old-time threshing in the coolly.

Oh, those rare days and rarer nights! How fine they were then — and how mellow they are growing now as the slow-paced years drop a golden mist upon them. From this distance they seemed too hearty and wholesome and care free to be lost out of the world.

P

CHAPTER XV

THRESHING IN THE FIELD

THE fields of grain were much larger on the prairie, and the work of taking care of the wheat was new to Mr. Stewart. The larger part of the wheat was "threshed from the shock" early in September, though the barn-yard settings of oats remained till October, or even November, as in Wisconsin.

As soon as the grain was hard enough, the machine was moved into the centre of the field and "set." Six teams with their drivers, three pitchers in the field, and two band-cutters, one on each side of the feeder, were necessary to supply the wants of the wide-throated monster. It was stacking and threshing combined. A wagon at each "table" kept the cylinder busy chewing away, while the other teams were loading. At the tail of the stacker, a boy with a pair of horses hitched to the ends of a long pole hauled away the straw and scattered it in shining yellow billows on the stubble, ready to be burned. Straw was not merely valueless,

it was a nuisance.   Burning was the quickest and
cheapest way of getting rid of it.

There was less of the old-time neighborliness and
charm in field threshing.   The days were hot and
long, and the hands nearly all nomadic workmen, who
had no intimate relation with the family.   They worked
like day-help, doing no chores, sleeping in the barn or
granary, taking little interest in anything beyond their
pay.   There was less chance to change works, and
often the whole of the early threshing was finished with
hired help, though the late threshing retained for several
years something of the quality of the old-time " bee."
Work was less rushing then, and the young men came
in to help, just as in the home coolly.

The first year Lincoln left the position of sack-holder
to Owen, and moved up to hauling away the straw.
The third season Owen took his place at the stacker,
and Lincoln became a band-cutter, while Tommy took
his turn at holding sacks for the measurer.   All other
work was necessarily suspended while the thresher was
in the field.   Work for the women was harder than
ever, for the crew was increased from twelve to twenty-
one and the threshing lasted longer.   The kitchen
was hotter, too, and the flies more pestiferous.

It was not long before the " mounted power " gave
way to the stationary engine, and the separator surren-
dered its " apron " and its bell-metal cog-wheels, its
superb voice diminished to a husky roar and loose rattle.
It was as if some splendid insect had become silent.
The engine made a stern master, and work around the

thresher became one steady, relentless drive from dawn to dusk; the black monster seemed always yelling for coal and water, and occasionally uttered cries of hate and anger.

How long those early autumn days did spin out! The steady swing of the feeder on the platform, the hurried puffing of the engine, the flapping of the great belt, made a series of related motions without thought of stopping.

On the far plain the tireless hawks wheeled and dipped through the dim splendor of the golden autumn days. They had no need to toil in the midst of stifling dust and deafening clatter; they had only to swim on the crisp, warm air, and scream at each other in freedom. It was at such moments that the boys recalled their own liberty as horsemen on the plains, and longed to be once more a-gallop behind the herd.

Lincoln, who served regularly as a band-cutter, held himself to his work, though his arms were aching with fatigue, toiling on and on until the sun went down, and the dusk and dust came to hide the look of pain on his face.　He did not dislike this work, but it overtaxed his strength.

There was great danger of fire from the engine on the hot, dry, September days, when the wind was strong and gusty, and all too frequently a separator burned before it could be drawn away from the blazing straw. The engine had a bad smell of mingled gas and steam, and sometimes when the wind was right for it, suffocation was added to the pain of aching muscles.　Lincoln

was sorely tempted at times to leap from his platform
and walk away, so intolerable did the smoke and gas
become — but he didn't.   A sort of stubborn pride or a
fear of ridicule held him to his place, and he swore
under his breath and kept his place.

All pain has an end.   At last the engine signalled
" stop ! "   The tender put his shoulder under the belt
and threw it from the pulley.   The feeder choked the
cylinder to a standstill.   The men leaped to the ground
stiffly and in silence, and with quiet haste melted away
in the dusk, leaving the hissing engine alone in the field.

Though very tired, the boys seldom failed to take a
hand in burning the straw.   After supper was eaten and
their chores finished they returned to the field where
the last setting had stood, and kneeling in some hollow
between the waves, Mr. Stewart set a match to the
straw, while the boys twisting big handfuls into torches,
ran swiftly over the stubble like bent gnomes of fire,
leaving a blazing trail which transformed the world.

The roaring flames threw a cataract of golden sparks
high in the air — the wind suddenly returned, and great
whisps rose like living things, with wings of flame, and
sailed away into the obscure night, to fall and die in the
black distance.   The smoke, forming a great inky roof,
shut out the light of the stars, and the gray night
instantly thickened to an impenetrable wall, closing in
around them, filling Lincoln's heart with a sudden awe
of the world of darkness.

The shadows of Owen and his father, in the dancing
light, twisting smoke, and wavering, heated air, seemed

wild and strange, enormous, deformed, menacing, and for a moment Lincoln imagined himself transported to some universe of intermingled flame and darkness, where men were formed in the image of wreathing mist.

Billows of glowing coals rolled away beneath the smoke, and it was easy to imagine himself looking down upon some volcanic valley, where the rocks were blazing. He was glad when his father's voice called him back to reality. As he turned his back on the flame and started homeward, he thrilled with surprise to find the stars calmly shining and the wide landscape serenely untroubled, with an atmosphere of sleep hovering over it, like mist. The barking of dogs at this moment was weirdly suggestive. Once he looked back and saw the distant horizon lit with other burnings, from which other columns of smoke, gloriously lighted, soared to the stars.

After the early threshing he returned to his ploughing, while Jack dug potatoes, cut corn, changed work with the neighbors, and at last, set to work husking. Late in October, or early in November, when the ploughing was nearly done, the settings at the barn were threshed, and the straw stacked around the stables, quite as in Wisconsin. The uncouth monster, the engine, was planted between the well and the corn-crib, looking savage and out of place; the grimy engineer, with folded arms, fixed his eyes on the indicator and waited for the hand to swing round to " eighty." Then a wild screech broke from the engine. " All ready, boys," called the feeder. The men scrambled to their places, and the hum of the cylinders began.

By this time most of the "tramp hands" had moved on. The crew was made up of regular hired men and neighbors. The wheat or oats was hauled away and emptied in the bins of the granary, the straw was carefully stacked by skilled men; given the purple hills, the wind in the oaks, and it would have seemed like the good old days in Boscobel.

No sooner was the home setting threshed than the boys made use of the straw-stack. Milton and Ben came over, and they all worked like moles to "tunnel" the rick while it was still permeable. They pierced it in every direction, with burrows big enough to allow a boy to creep through on his hands and knees, and constructed chutes which began high on the stack, and ended at the bottom, through which it was possible to descend like a buck-shot through a tin tube. They built caves deep in the heart of it, and constructed a sort of maze, so that only the well-instructed could find way thereto; so that when a game of "hi spy" was going on, the "blinder" could be properly surprised and outwitted.

A large part of the boys' fun, at night and on Sunday, went on around the straw-pile. With deadly weapons composed of corn-cobs, stuck on willow wands, and swords of lath, sharpened to savage keenness on the edges, they battled for hours. No actual danger could exceed the weakening spasms of fear which followed upon moments of imminent capture in these games. When Rance, with deadly corn-cob slug, stepped from ambush and made ready to slay, to Owen a blind

fear of death came, paralyzing his limbs, and his shriek
of terror was very real. Generally, however, they
played "hi spy," counting out in the good old way,
saying, "Intra, mentra, cutra, corn," etc.

As the nights grew colder, the boys met regularly,
now at Lincoln's, now at Rance's, to pop corn on the
kitchen stove, and to play in the vivid moonlight.
Cold made little difference to them. Many a night,
when the thermometer was ten degrees below zero,
Lincoln and Owen walked across to Milton's home,
there to play till nine o'clock, walking home thereafter
in the stinging frosty night, without so much as feeling
a fire the whole evening long. Their big boots, frozen
stiff, stumped and slid on the snowy road, but the boys
did not mind that. They were sleepy, but the serene
beauty of the winter world was not lost upon them.

It was cold in the garret, but in contrast to the outside air, it was very comfortable, and so they flung off
their outside garments (night-shirts were unknown to
them), and snuggled down into the middle of their
"straw-ticks," like a couple of Poland China shotes,
and were asleep in thirty seconds. Their slumber was
dreamless and unbroken during all these years.

As the winter came on, the straw-pile settled down
into a shapeless mass, weighted with snow. The cattle
ate irregular caves and tunnels into it, and at last it lost
its charm. The school entertainments, protracted meetings, or Lyceums claimed their interest and attention.
"Pom-pom pullaway" at the school-house replaced the
game of "hi spy" around the straw-stack.

* * * * * * *

The spirit which made the old-time threshing a festival, the circumstances which made of it a meeting together of neighbors, is now largely a memory. The passing of the wheat-field, the growth of stock-farms, the increase in machinery, have removed many of the old-time customs. Lincoln Stewart walks no more in the red dawn of October, his fork on his shoulder, while the landscape palpitates in ecstasy, waiting the coming of the sun. The frost gleams as of old on the sear grass at the roadside, the air is just as crisp and clear. The stars are out, Venus burns to her setting, and the crickets are sleepily crying in the mottled stubble, but Rance and Milton and Owen are not there to meet the majesty of the night.

THE AUTUMN GRASS

HAVE you ever lain low
In the deeps of the grass,
In the lee of a swell that uplifts,
Like a small brown island out of the sea —
When the bluejoint shakes
Like a forest of spears,
When each amber wave breaks
In bloom overhead,
And the wind in the doors of your ears
Is wailing a song of the dead?

If so, you have heard in the midst of the roar,
The note of a lone gray bird,
Blown slant-wise by overhead,
Like a fragment of sail
In the grasp of the gale,
Hastening home to his southland once more.

O the music abroad in the air,
With the autumn wind sweeping
His hand through the grass, where
Each tiniest blade is astir,
Keeping voice in the dim hid choir —
In the infinite song, the refrain,
The majestic wail of the plain!

To face page 219

CHAPTER XVI

THE CORN HUSKING

In the autumn of his eleventh year Lincoln again went into the stubble-field to plough, and for seventy days he journeyed to and fro behind his team, overturning nearly one hundred and fifty acres of stubble. When he began, the sun was warm and the flies pestiferous, the corn green, the melons ripe. As he followed the plough the corn grew sear, the melon leaves turned black under the heel of frost, the ducks flew south again, the grain-stacks disappeared before the thresher, and the huskers went forth to gather the ripened corn. All day, and every day but Sunday, he worked, seeing the black land grow steadily, while slowly but surely the stubble-land wasted away.

It was a harsh day indeed, when he did not work. Occasionally for an hour or two during a heavy shower he took shelter in the barn, but squalls of snow or rain he was not able to avoid without censure. Owen was a great comfort to him as before, but he had his own work to do in bringing the cattle and in pumping water at the well, picking up chips, and other chores. It was lonely business, and when at last he had laid aside the plough and joined the corn-huskers, Lincoln's heart was very light.

Already in Sun Prairie husking the corn or "shucking"

it, as people from the South called it, was a considerable part of the fall work. Each farmer had a field running from twenty to fifty acres, generally near the homestead. Along toward the first of October these fields got dry and yellow under the combined action of the heat and sun. All through the slumbrous days of September the tall soldiers of the corn dreamed in the mist of noon, and while the sun rolled red as blood to its setting, they whispered like sentries awed by the passing of their chief. Each day the mournful rustle of the leaves grew louder, and flights of noisy passing blackbirds tore at the helpless ears with their beaks. The leaves at last were dry as vellum. The stalk still held its sap, but the drooping ear revealed the nearness of the end. At last the owner, plucking an ear, wrung it to listen to its voice; if it creaked, it was not yet fit for the barn. It was solid as oak, and the next day the teams began the harvest.

In big fields like that of Mr. Stewart it was the custom to husk in the field, and from the standing stalk. No one but a stubborn Vermonter like Old Man Bunn thought of cutting it up to husk from the shock. With Jack, the hired man, Lincoln drove out with a big wagon capable of holding fifty bushels of ears. On one side was a high "banger board," which enabled the man working beside the wagon to throw the husked ears in without looking up. The horses walked astride one row — bending it beneath the axle; this was called the "down row," and was invariably set aside as "the boys' row." Lincoln took the down row while Jack husked two rows on the left of the wagon. The horses were started and stopped by the voice alone, and there was always a great deal of sound and fury in the process. The work was easy and a continual feast for the horses after their long, hard siege at ploughing, and right heartily they improved the shining days.

At first this work was not devoid of charm. The mornings were frosty but clear, and the sun soon warmed the world; but as the days passed, the boys' hands became chapped and sore. Great, painful seams developed between the thumb and forefinger, the nails wore to the quick, and the balls of each finger became tender as boils. The leaves of the corn, ceaselessly whipped by the powerful winds, grew ragged, and the stalks fell, increasing the number of ears for which the husker was forced to stoop. The sun rose later each day and took longer to warm the air. At times he failed to show his face all day, and the frost hung on till nearly noon.

Husking-gloves became a necessity, but this by no means preserved the hands. The rains came and flurries of snow; the gloves, wet and muddy, shrank at night and in the morning were hard as iron. They soon wore out at the ends where the fingers were sorest, and Mrs. Stewart was kept busy sewing on "cots" for Lincoln and her husband: even Jack came to the point of accepting her aid.

To husk eighty or a hundred bushels of corn during the short days of November means making every motion count. Every morning, long before daylight, Lincoln stumbled out of bed, and dressed with numb and swollen fingers, which almost refused to turn a button. Outside he could hear the roosters crowing far and near. The air was still, and the smoke ran into the sky straight as a Lombardy poplar tree. The frost was white on everything, and made the boy shiver as he thought of the thousands of icy ears he must husk during the day.

Sore as his hands were, he had his cows to milk before he could return to breakfast, which consisted of home-made sausages ("snassingers," the boys called them) and buckwheat pancakes.

"You won't get anything more until noon, boys," said Mr. Stewart, warningly; "so fill up."

Mrs. Stewart flopped the big, brown, steaming disks into their plates two or three at a time, and over them each man and boy poured some of the delicious fat from the sausages, cut them into strips, and having rolled the strips into wads, filled their stomachs as a hunter loads a gun.

Often they drove afield while the stars were still shining, the wagon clattering and booming over the frozen ground, the horses "humped" and full of "go." It was very hard for the boy to get limbered up on such mornings. The keen wind searched him through and through. His scarf chafed his chin, his gloves were harsh and unyielding, and the tips of his fingers were tender as "felons." The "down" ears were often covered with frost or dirt and sometimes with ice, and as the sun softened the ground, the mud and dead leaves clung to his feet like a ball and chain to a convict.

Owen shed some tears at times. Mr. Stewart was a rapid workman, and it was hard work for the boy to keep up the down rows, especially when he was blue with cold and in agony because of his mistreated hands. When the keen wind and the snow and mud conspired against him, it was hard indeed. Each morning was a dreaded enemy.

There were days when ragged gray masses of cloud swept down on the powerful northern wind, when there was a sorrowful, lonesome moan among the corn rows, when the cranes, no longer soaring at ease, drove straight into the south, sprawling low-hung in the blast, or lost to sight above the flying scud, their necks out-thrust, desperately eager to catch a glimpse of their shining Mexican seas.

On Thanksgiving Day, Mr. Stewart, being apprehensive of snow, hired some extra hands and got out into the field as soon as it was light enough to see the rows. "We must finish to-day, boys," he said. "We can't afford to lose an hour. We're in for a big snow-storm."

It was a bitter day. Snow and sleet fell at intervals, rattling in among the sear stalks with a dreary sound. The northeast wind mourned like a dying wolf, and the clouds seemed to leap across a sky torn and ragged, rolling and spreading as in summer tempests. The down ears were sealed up with ice and lumps of frozen earth, and the stalks, ice-armored on the northern side, creaked dismally in the blast. "We need a hammer to crack 'em open," said one of the men to Mr. Stewart.

With great-coats belted around them, with worn fingers covered with new cots, Lincoln and Owen went into the field. Thick muffled as they were, the cold found them. Slap and swing their hands as they might, their fingers and toes would get numb.

Oh, how they longed for noon! Though he could not afford a holiday, Mr. Stewart had provided turkey and cranberry sauce; and the men talked about it with increasing wistfulness as the day broadened.

"I hope it is a big turkey," said one.

"Say, I'll trade my cranberry sauce for your piece of turkey."

"Stewart don't know what he's in for."

It seemed as though the wagon box held a thousand bushels! And the hired man took a malicious delight in taunting the boys with lacking "sand." "Smooth down your vest and pull up your chin," he said to Owen. "Keep your eye on that turkey."

But the hour of release came at last, and the boys were free to "scud for the house." Once within, they yanked off their old rags, threw their wet mittens under the stove, washed their chafed hands and chapped fingers in warm water, and curled up beside the stove, with their mouths watering for turkey. "They were all eyes and stummick," as Jack said when he came in.

Once at the feast they ate until their father said, "Boys, you must 'a been holler clear to your heels."

Owen made no reply. He merely let out a reef in his waistband and took another leg of turkey.

But the food and the fire served to show how very cold they had been. A fit of shivering came on, which

the fire could not subdue. Lincoln's fingers, swollen
and painful, palpitated as if a little heart hot with fever
were in each one. His back was stiff as that of an old
man. His boots, which he had incautiously pulled off,
were too small for his swollen chilblain-heated feet, and
he could not get them on again.

He wept and shivered, saying, "Oh, I can't go out
again," but Mr. Stewart was a stern man, who admitted
no demurrer so far as Lincoln was concerned. Owen,
shielded by his mother, flatly rebelled. At last, by the
use of flour and soap, and the help of his mother, Lincoln forced his poor feet back into their prison cells,
belted on his coat, tied on his rags of mittens, and went
out, bent, awkward, like an old beggar, tears on his
cheeks, his teeth chattering. His heart was big with
indignation, but he dared not complain.

The horses shivered under their blankets that afternoon. The men yelled and jumped about, and slapped
their hands across their breasts to warm them, but the
work went on. By four o'clock only a few more rows
remained, and the cheery, ringing voice of his father
helped Lincoln to do his part, though the wind was roaring through the fields with ever increasing volume,
carrying flurries of feathery snow and shreds of corn
leaves.

Slowly the night came. It began to grow dark,
but the men worked on with desperate energy. They
were on the last rows, and Lincoln, exalted by the nearness of release, buckled to it with amazing energy, his
small figure lost in the dusk behind the wagon. Jack

Q

only knew he was there when he pounded on the end-gate to start the horses; the boy's own voice was gone. There was an excitement as of battle in the work now, and he almost forgot his bleeding hands and the ache in his back. The field grew mysterious, vast, and inhospitable as the wind. The touch of the falling snow to his cheek was like the caress of death's ghostly finger-tips.

Belated flocks of geese swept by at most furious speed, their voices sounding anxious, their talk hurried.

Suddenly a wild yell broke out. One of the teams had broken through the last rows. Jack and Lincoln answered it, being not far behind.

" Hurrah! Tell 'em we're comin'."

Five minutes later, and they, too, reached the last hill of corn. Night had come, but the field was finished. The extra help had proved sufficient. " Now let it snow," said Stewart.

It was good to see the lights shining in the kitchen, and, oh, it was delicious comfort to creep in behind the stove once more, and feel that husking was over. It was better than the supper, though the supper was good.

When quite filled with food, Lincoln crept back to the fire, and opening the oven door, laid a piece of wood thereon, upon which to set his heels, and there he sat till the convulsive tremor went out of his breast and his teeth ceased to chatter. His mother brought him some bran and water in which to soak his poor claws of fingers, and so he came at last to a measure of comfort. At nine o'clock the boys crept upstairs to bed.

BOYISH SLEEP

AND all night long they lie in sleep
  Too deep to sigh in or to dream,
Unmindful how the wild winds sweep
  Or snow-clouds through the darkness stream
Above the trees that moan and cry,
Clutching with naked hands the flying sky.
  Beneath their checkered counterpane
They rest the soundlier for the storm ;
  Its wrath is only lullaby,
  A dim, far-off, and vast refrain.

PART II

BOY LIFE ON THE PRAIRIE

CHAPTER XVII

THE COMING OF THE CIRCUS

THERE were always three great public holidays, — the Fourth of July, the circus, and the Fair, which was really an autumn festival. To these was added the Grange picnic, which came in about 1875 and took place on the 12th of June. Of all these, the circus was easily the first of importance; even the Fourth of July grew pale and of small account in the "glittering, gorgeous Panorama of Polychromatic Pictures," which once a year visited the county town, bringing the splendors of the great outside world in golden clouds, mystic as the sky at sunset. The boy whose father refused to take him wept with no loss of dignity in the eyes of his fellows. He could even swear in his disappointment and be excused for it.

The boys of Sun Prairie generally went. Nearly all of them had some understanding with their fathers, whereby they earned the half-dollars necessary for their tickets. This silver piece seemed big as the moon when it was being earned, but it was small and mean beside the dirty blue slip of cardboard which admitted "bearer" to the pleasures of the circus. Lincoln and Owen earned their money by killing gophers. Rance was paid for herding. Ben raised chickens.

June was usually the month for the circus. In those days, even the "colossal caravans" did not travel in special trains, but came across the country in the night and bloomed out in white canvas under the rising sun, like mysterious and splendid mushrooms, seemingly as permanent as granite to the awed country lads who came to gaze timidly from afar.

No one but a country boy can rightly measure the majesty and allurement of a circus. To go from the lonely prairie or the dusty corn-field and come face to face with the "amazing aggregation of world-wide wonders" was like enduring the visions of the Apocalypse. From the moment the advance man flung a handful of gorgeous bills over the corn-field fence, to the golden morning of the glorious day, the boys speculated and argued and dreamed of the glorious "pageant of knights and ladies, glittering chariots, stately elephants, and savage tigers," which wound its way down the long yellow posters, a glittering river of Elysian splendors, emptying itself into the tent, which housed the "World's Congress of Wonders."

The boys met in groups on Sunday and compared posters, while lying beneath the rustling branches of the cottonwood trees. Rance, who always had what he wanted and went where he pleased, was authority. He had seen three circuses before — Lincoln only one.

From the height of his great experience, Rance said: "No circus is ever as good as its bills. If it is half as good, we ought to be satisfied."

The important question was: "Shall we go in the afternoon or in the evening?" The evening was said by some to be much the best. Others stood out for the afternoon. Milton suggested going to both, but such extravagance was incredible, even to Rance. No banker was ever known to do such a preposterous thing.

"Well, then, let's go down to the parade in the morning, and hang round and see all the fun we can, and go to the circus in the evening."

To this Lincoln made objection. "We'd all be sick by that time."

The justice of this remark was at once acknowledged. Only one thing remained to do, — see the usual morning parade, then lunch, and go early to see the animals. They parted with this arrangement, but at the last moment their plans were overruled by their parents, who quietly made ready to go in the big wagons and family carriages; and the boys were bidden to accompany their mothers, who considered a circus much more dangerous than a Fourth of July.

So, early on the promiseful day, Lincoln and Owen, seated on a board placed across the wagon box behind the spring seat (on which the parents sat), jarred and bounced on their way to the county town, while Rance galloped along in gay freedom on his horse. Milton was another unwilling guest of his parents, and sat in the back seat of the old family carryall, with a sense of being thrust back into childhood.

Other teams were on the road: young men and their sweethearts in one-seated "covered buggies," while other parties of four and six rumbled along in big wagons trimmed with green branches. The Richardsons went by with the box of their lumber wagon quite overflowing with children and dogs; and Mr. Stewart remarked that "such men would pawn the cook-stove to go to the circus," but Lincoln did not share his father's disgust. It seemed to him that poor folks needed the circus just as much as any one — more, in fact.

Teams came streaming in over every road till the town was filled as if it were the Fourth of July. Accustomed to the silence of the fields, or the infrequent groups of families in the school-houses, the prairie boys bowed with awe before the coming together of two thousand people. It seemed as if Cedar County and part of Cerro Gordo had assembled. Neighbors greeted each other in the midst of the throng with such fervor as travellers show when they unexpectedly meet in far-off Asiatic cities.

Every child waited in nervous impatience for the parade, which was not a piece of shrewd advertising to them, but a solemn function. A circus without a parade was unthinkable. It began somewhere — the country boys scarcely knew where — far in the mystery of the East and passed before their faces, — the pageantry of "Ivanhoe" and the "Arabian Nights," and red Indians, and Mohammedanism and negro slavery, — in procession. It trailed a glorified dust, through which foolish and slobbering camels, and solemn and kingly lions, and mournful and sinister tigers, moved, preceded by the mountainous and slow-moving elephants, two and two, chained and sullen, while closely following, keeping step to the jar of great drums and the blaring voices of trumpets, ladies, beautiful and haughty of glance, with firmly-moulded busts, rode on parti-colored steeds with miraculous skill, their voices sounding small in the clangor of the streets. They were accompanied by knights corsletted in steel, with long plumes floating from their gleaming helmets. They, too, looked over the lowly people of the dusty plains with lofty and disdainful glance. Even the drivers on the chariots seemed weary and contemptuous as they swayed on their high seat, or cried in far-reaching voices to their leaders, who did not disdain to curvet for their rustic admirers.

The town boys, alert and self-sufficient, ran alongside the open chariot where the lion-tamer sat, surrounded by his savage pets, but the country boys could only stand and look, transfixed with pleasure and pain, — the pleasure of looking upon it, the pain of seeing it pass. They were wistful figures, standing there in dusty, ill-fitting garments, sensitive, subtle instruments on which the procession played, like a series of unrelated grandiose chords. As the lion passed, vague visions of vast deserts rose in their minds. Amid toppling towers these royal beasts prowled in the vivid moonlight. The camels came, reaching long necks athwart the shadows of distant, purple pyramids, and on hot sands at sunset, travellers, with garments outblown by the sirocco, passed near a crouching Arab. Mounted on elephants with uplifted trunks, tiger-hunters rode through long yellow grass. The feudal tournaments rolled back with the glittering knights. The wealth of the Indies shone in the golden chariots of the hippopotami. The jungles of Hindoostan were symbolized in the black and yellow bodies of the tigers, the heat of Africa shone from their terrible eyes. All that their readers, histories, and geographies had taught them seemed somehow illustrated, illuminated, irradiated, by this gorgeous pageantry.

When it passed, Lincoln found his legs stiffened and his hands numb. Owen's unresisting fingers, close clasped in his, testified to his absorbed interest. Upon this trance, this sleep of flesh and not of imagination, the voice of their father broke sharply.

"Well, boys. That's all of it. Now we'll go and get some dinner." In such wise does practical middle age justle the elbow of the dreaming boy.

Lincoln drew a deep sigh and turned away. He had no desire to follow the chariots, but he wished they would all come his way again.

Out on a vacant lot on a back street, in the shade of their wagon, Mrs. Stewart set out a lunch, and while the horses munched over the end-gate, the boys tried to eat, but with small success. The cold chicken was quite tasteless, the biscuits were like cotton-batting — only the jelly cake and the cold tea had power to interest them. Lincoln was eager to get to the grounds, and heartily wished his father would let him go alone. It was humiliating to be forced to tag along behind, leading Owen by the hand, but the time for rebellion had not yet come.

At last, after agonies of impatience, while the mother put things in order and brushed her own clothes as well as those of little Mary, the family set out, joining the streams of people converging upon the grounds. The country folk tramped heavily along the unaccustomed sidewalks, while the townspeople, lighter shod and defter moving, in groups, seemed like another race of beings. Their women were more graceful and gayer. The town boys, many of them, wore new suits that fit, with stylish straw hats, and they went unattended by elders, chattering like blackbirds. The bankers drove their families down in fine carriages, and the District Attorney, going by in a white "Manila" hat, with a wide black band, said, "Good afternoon, Neighbor Stewart," and Lincoln bobbed his head while his father saluted.

As they came out upon the green, the huge white tents, the fluttering flags, the crowds of people, the advertisements of the side-shows, the cries of the ticket-sellers and lemonade and candy men, appalled the country boys, and they were glad to keep in the protective shadow of their resolute and stalwart father. The tumult was benumbing. On the left of the path was a long line of side-shows, with enormous billowing canvas screens, on which were rudely painted the wonders

within,— a pig playing a violin, an armless man sewing
with his toes, a bearded lady, a fat boy, a man taking a
silk hat from a bottle, while on a stool before each door
stood alert and brazen-voiced young men, stern, contemptuous, and alien of face, declaring the virtues of
each show, and inviting the people to enter.   Lincoln
could have listened to these people all day, so fascinated
was he by their faces, so different from those he knew.
They were so wise and self-contained, and certain of
themselves, these men.   To them the noise, the crowd,
the confusion, were parts of ordinary, daily life.

"You have still a half an hour, ladies and gentlemen,
before the great show opens," one called with monotonous, penetrating, clanging utterances, like a rusty bell.
"Still a half an hour to see the wonders of the world,
Madame Ogoleda, the snake woman.   Walk in — walk
in; only a dime to see this wondrous woman and her
monstrous serpent.   The Bible story related.   The
woman and the snake.   Only a dime apiece."

"He *is!*   He *is!*" called another.   "The fattest
boy in the world.   He weighs four hundred and eighty
pounds.   See him eat his dinner.   Only a dime to see
the fat boy eat a whole ham!"

"Professor Henry, court wizard of Beelzebub himself.
Come in and see the great and marvellous man.   You
can see a glutton eat any day, but this is your only
chance to see the magician of Mahomet.   The Magi of
the East!   The King of Conjurors!" called a third.

At this moment, just as they were passing the door,
the sound of a blow was heard, and a stern voice cried,
"You come with me,"

Oaths and the sound of a struggle followed, and the canvas side of the tent waved to and fro violently. Then a voice rose in command, —

"Clear the way there," and others replied, —

"All right, Jim; hang to him."

As the spectators outside stopped, the man on the stool sprang down, crying, —

"What's the matter in there?"

At this precise moment, a powerfully built man, with a stern and handsome face, came from the tent, holding a revolver in his right hand, with his left fastened to the collar of a wiry, slick-looking fellow, who was bareheaded and foaming with rage.

"Drop that man!" yelled the ticket-seller.

"Get out of the way," said the heavy man, quietly.

The ticket-seller put his fingers in his mouth and blew a sharp whistle.

The man with the revolver swept his weapon around, and laid the ticket-seller flat on the ground by a blow on the temple.

The crowd cheered. "Good for you, Jim!"

"What's up, Jim?" cried a dozen others.

The immense throng lost all interest in the circus, and closed around the scene like a wall. The Stewarts found themselves fenced in and unable to escape, even had they desired it. Lincoln was quite in front now and knew that this was Jim Moriarty, Sheriff of the county. The crowd was wild with excitement. The criers had ceased their clatter, and men were approaching from every direction. Oaths, jeers, signals, could be heard; but Jim, with keen, round gray eyes, faced his new antagonists, with ready revolver.

The ticket-seller sprang to his feet, with the blood streaming from his wound.

"I'll kill you!" he hoarsely snarled.

"It's the Sheriff, you fool," said a companion.

"Sheriff, and the best man in the country, bar none," said a townsman.

Jim explained. "This is a thimble-rigger. He's wanted in Cerro Gordo for robbery — and he goes."

The crowd laughed. "You bet he goes. We know you, Jim. Go ahead."

Jim said: "And I want you, me friend, for inter-ferrin' with an officer in the discharge of his duty. Open a path, b'ys."

The crowd opened a lane, and Jim said, "Go before me, an' don't look back."

"If you weren't an officer and armed, you couldn't take me," replied the angry man.

Jim smiled grimly. "My friend, ye're too ambitious. Ye're a foine bit of a b'y, but too soft to talk loike that to a workin' man."

"For a copper I'd show you."

"Has anny one a copper?" asked Jim. "I'm an ac-commodatin' man."

The circus men pushed to the front, so far as possi-ble, but fell to sullen silence when told it was the Sheriff. The manager, red of face, and dripping per-spiration, his silk hat at an anxious angle, appeared at this moment.

"What's all this? Are you the Sheriff? What's wanted? Let that man go!"

Jim turned on him. "Kape a civil tongue in yer head, an' shove out yer sharpers, or it'll go hard with ye to get out o' the county."

"This is a straight show. I want you to understand nothing goes crooked around me. I won't have my men interfered with. I won't have no gay sheriff jumpin' —"

"Listen!" said Jim, swift and sharp. "Open yer jaw at me agin, and I'll break yer silk hat, and stuff yer t'roat with the pieces."

A man in the crowd yelled: "Lay a hand on our Sheriff, and, by God, we'll lynch every man o' ye," and the roar that followed made the manager's red face change to a ghastly white. He turned and walked away amid the laughter of the citizens.

The ticket-seller was pacing up and down: —

"Oh, if you weren't Sheriff! I'd learn you to strike me. I'd waller ye till your mother wouldn't know ye."

Jim winked at the crowd: "He has a consate of his powers that is commuck. Will somebody hold me thimble-rigger for a few seconds?"

A big man stepped out. "I'll take care of him."

"All right, Steve. It's a holiday. I've a little consate of meself, and it won't take long, annyway." He handed his revolver to his deputy, and took off his coat. "Now, me lad. I've laid down me authority wid me coat. I'm plain Jim Moriarity, from the Wapseypinnicon, wishin' to be instructed; but be quick, or you'll delay

R

the circus." The fellow hesitated a moment. Jim's brow darkened. "Come ahn, or I'll lift ye on the toe of me boot."

The ticket-seller squared off as Jim drew near, and began dancing around with his arms in fighting posture, but Jim only faced him with a smile on his handsome brown face, his hands carelessly hanging at his sides. At last the circus man struck out, but fell short, and Jim cuffed him on the cheek with the flat of his palm.

"Wake up, me lad," he called.

With a curse the ticket man leaped forward, striking out furiously. Jim stepped aside, and as the man went by, struck him behind the ear. He fell like a log, and Jim, taking him by the collar, set him on his feet. "Try it onct more, me bucco."

He did try again, wildly, blindly, and Jim cuffed him right and left, till he spun round dizzily on his feet; then taking him by the collar, kicked him in the rear till he sprawled on his hands and knees. Jim lifted him again, amid the laughter of the crowd. Every man, woman, and child knew his wonderful powers, and took personal pride therein. The second time he landed, the man did not rise, and Jim said, "Anny time when I'm not busy, I'll be glad to have fun with ye, or anny of yer mates."

He came back, and said: "We've still a few minutes to spare. Is there anny other gentleman would like to amuse the crowd? Me father was born in Donegal, and dearly loved a shindy." No one offered, and Jim put on his coat. "Now, me friend," he said, returning to

his professional tone, "we'll lave the people to enjoy
the show." He deftly snapped a handcuff to the prisoner's right arm, and put the other to his own wrist.
Steve handed over the revolver. Jim lifted his eyes:
"Go ahn to the show, b'ys. Come," he said to his
prisoner; "if ye break so much as the skin av me wrist,
I'll kill ye."

As they walked down the lane of grinning citizens,
the prisoner kept close, very close, to his captor's side.

Then the tide of sound swept back. The cries began
again. The pent-up excitement of the crowd broke
forth in a clatter of talk, as they moved away toward
the big tent, where a splendid band was playing furiously,
and the ticket-seller was crying in a monstrous voice:—

"*Right this way to the big show! The only entrance!
Have your tickets ready!*"

Carried along by the pressure of the crowd, the boys
neared the entrance, their blue tickets crushed to a
pulp in their sweaty hands. The stern and noisy gate-
keeper snatched at them, and a moment later they were
inside the animal tent, and the circus was just before
them. But somehow, the breathless interest of the
morning was gone. The human drama before the side-
show had put the wonders of the menagerie on a different plane. For a few moments all the talk was of the
Sheriff and his victim.

Slowly but surely the power of "the circus" reasserted its dominion over the boys, as they moved slowly
round the circle of the chariots, wherein the strange
animals from the ends of the earth were on view. The

squalling of parrakeets, the chatter and squawk of monkeys, the snorting of elephants, the deep, short, gusty elemental *ough* of the lions, the occasional snarl of the leopards, restlessly pacing, with yellow-green eyes glaring, the strange, odd, hot smells, — all these made the human fist very small and of no account. These beings whose footfalls were like velvet on velvet, whose bodies were swift as shadows and as terrible as catapults, whose eyes emitted the blaze of undying hate; these monstrous, watery, wide-mouthed, warty, uncouth creatures from rivers so remote that geographers had not reached them; these birds that outshone the prairie flowers in coloring; these serpents whose lazy, glittering coils concealed the strength of a hundred chains, — these forms too diverse to be the work of Nature, stupefied Lincoln, and he stumbled on, a mere brain insecurely toppling on a numb and awkward body. All the pictures of the school-books, all the chance drawings in the periodicals open to him, all the stories of the sea and far countries, were resurged and vivified in his brain, till it boiled like a kettle of soap; and then, on top of it all, came the men and women of the circus proper.

Stumbling along behind the broad shoulders of his father, hearing and not heeding the anxious words of his mother, " Keep close to us, boys," Lincoln passed from the pungent air of the animal tent out into the ring of the circus, which crackled with the cries of alert men selling fans, ice-cream, sticks of candy, and bags of peanuts. It was already packed with an innumerable throng of people, whose faces were as vague to the boys

as the fans they swung. Overhead the canvas lifted
and billowed, and the poles creaked and groaned, and
the rope snapped with the strain of the brisk outside
wind. To Lincoln it seemed nearly a quarter of a mile
across the ring, and he feared the performance might
begin before they got safely out of it and seated. The
feel of the sawdust under his feet was a thing long to be
remembered.

Jokes and rude cries passed between those already
seated and the families wandering along with faces upturned like weary chickens looking for a roost. Mr.
Stewart heard a familiar voice, and looking up, saw Mr.
Jennings, who was pointing to a vacant strip of plank
near him.

" There's our place, mother," said Mr. Stewart.

" Away up there? Good land! " exclaimed she, in
dismay.

" All a part of the show," replied her husband.

They climbed slowly up the terraced seats of thin
and narrow boards, and at last found themselves seated
not far from the Jennings family.

" Where do we put our feet ? " inquired Mrs. Stewart.

" Anywhere you can get 'em," replied Milton.

" They don't improve on their seats," said Mr. Jennings. " It seems to me the seats used to be a good
deal wider."

" You were young then, Neighbor Jennings."

" I guess that's the truth of it."

The boys did not think of making complaint. It
was enough for them that they were at last on a seat,

ready for the wonders of the performance. The band was already beating upon Lincoln's sensitive brain, with a swift and brazen clangor, and at a signal twelve uniformed attendants filed into the ring and the gates were closed. The band flared out into a strongly accentuated march, and forth from the mystic gateway came the knights and their ladies, riding two and two on splendid horses, and the boys thrilled with the joy of it. They were superb horsemen, these riders, and the prairie boys were able to understand and appreciate their skill. Nothing was lost on them; every turn of the knee, every supple twist of the waist was observed, never to be forgotten. The pride and joy of the action, the ringing cries, the exultant strength of the horses, who seemed to enjoy it quite as much as their riders, — these things went deep with Lincoln and his playmates.

The color, the glitter, the grace of gesture, the precision of movement, all so alien to the plains — so different from the slow movement of stiffened old farmers and faded and angular women, as well as from the shy and awkward manners of the beaux and belles of the country dances; the pliant joints and tireless limbs, the cool, calm judgment, the unerring eyes, the beautiful muscular bodies of the fearless women — a thousand impressions, new and deep-reaching, followed so swiftly that Lincoln had no time to even enjoy them. He could only receive and taste — he could not digest and feed.

Oh, to be one of those fine and splendid riders, with no more corn to plough, or hay to rake, or corn to husk.

To go forth into the great, mysterious world, in the company of those grand men and lovely women; to be always admired by thousands, to bow and graciously return thanks, to wear a star upon his breast, to be able to live under the shining canvas in the sound of music. In such course Lincoln's vague aspirations ran. He had no desire to serve as ring-master. To be the manager and wear a white vest and tall hat was of small account, but to be "an artist" was the finest career in the world.

One of the clowns was not a good clown, but he was a strong man. He formed the walking pedestal for the deft performance of two fine acrobats. He was a spotted clown, with an enormous, artificial belly, and was very loud and boisterous, but the audience did not like him so well as the little short, stout man, who sang "Little Brown Jug," "May slap-jacks hang an inch on me if ever I cease to love," and "Where was Moses when the Light went out?"

The spotted clown was following the singer about, imitating his walk, when a man in citizen's dress came quietly walking out of the inner entrance into the ring, and laid his hand on him. It was Jim, the Sheriff. A great shout went up from the crowd.

The clown wrenched himself loose, and running swiftly backward a few steps, threw a somersault, intending to strike the Sheriff in the breast with his feet. Jim evaded him with a lightning-swift movement, and struck him, just as he landed on the sand, and he went down with a heavy sound. He bounded to his feet, but

Jim was at his ear with his left, and he went to the earth again. Five or six attendants came running — the ring-master clubbed his whip to strike, but he did not. A roar went up, the like of which he had never heard before. And over the ropes, tumbling, shouting, cursing, the men of the benches broke, like a grisly, gray-black flood. The ropes were cut, the stakes pulled up for weapons, and in a breath a densely packed ring of angry men surrounded the indomitable Sheriff and his new antagonists.

For a few moments all was confusion and frenzy; nothing could be seen and heard. At last those in front turned and thrust their palms in the air, and hissed for silence, and almost immediately the penetrating, harmonious voice of the Sheriff could be heard.

" B'ys, ye can see better on yer seats. Go back; I'll attend to this small business. Go back, I say, and lave me to me work. This man is not a clown; he's a crook, and I need him to make a pair."

The crowd laughed and yelled, " You're all right, Jim."

" I *am*. You're all *wrong*. Go back, I say." The crowd laughed, and uttering exclamations of amusement and pride in Jim, clambered back to their seats.

When the ring cleared, Jim was seen standing with the clown handcuffed to his left wrist, a revolver in his right hand facing the ring-master, the manager, and a crowd of circus people.

" Be quiet ! " he was saying. " B'ys," — he turned to the acrobats and equestrians, — " I've nothin' agin ye.

I'm sorry to interrupt the fun, but no three-card monte man can play in this county while I'm Sheriff. And as to you, me beauty," he said, addressing the manager, " I am not so sure you don't stand in with these crooks. Me advice is, when ye come agin, lave the thieves behind. Come, me man."

The clown sullenly complied, and with his drawn revolver in his hand, Jim walked toward the exit, followed by hundreds of the men who wanted to see that no evil befell their hero.

This practically ended the circus. In vain the criers went over the audience, shouting : —

" Tickets for the Minstrel Show only a quarter of a dollar. Let no one miss the songs and dances to follow. A grand entertainment will follow the final act ! "

To the boys, the incident came as a disagreeable interruption. It was exciting, but was out of place. They grumbled at missing the lion-tamer's act and the dance of the elephants.

Both the Stewart and Jennings families had remained in their seats during the arrest of the clown, and at Mr. Jennings's suggestion they waited while the crowd rushed out.

"We'll take a little more time to see the animals," said Mr. Stewart. " Jim will take care of the man."

But the charm of the circus was broken, so far as Lincoln was concerned. The day had been too exciting. His head was throbbing with pain, and the smells of the animal tent were intolerable. Only the lions and tigers interested him, and when he came out into the clear, sweet air and felt the fresh wind in his face, he wished he were already at home. The end of all holidays were the same to him; sickness, weariness, pain, and aching muscles and a gorged brain, blotted out all the pleasures that had gone before.

As he pounded up and down on the board behind his father and mother, he had no words to say, no thoughts which were articulate. His brain was a whirling wheel, wherein all his impressions were blurred into bands of gray and brown and gold and scarlet. But in the days that followed, the splendid men and women reasserted themselves. His brain cleared, and as he lay with Rance under the rustling poplars on Sunday, he could pick out and dreamily define the events of the day. The Sheriff's dramatic actions came to be an entirely separate thing — a thing to be condemned, for it interrupted the circus, which they had all gone to see.

One by one the splendid acts, the specially beautiful women, and the most wonderful men were recalled and named and admired, and Rance compared them with the events of other circuses. But deeper down, more impalpable, more intangible, subtler, — so subtle they ran like aromatic wine throughout his very blood and bone, — were other impressions which threw the prairie into new relief and enhanced the significance of the growing corn as well as the splendor of the pageant which had come and gone like the gold and crimson clouds at sunset.

Lincoln had a dream now, that the world was wide, and filled with graceful men and wondrous women, as well as with innumerable monsters and glittering, harsh-throated birds and slumbrous serpents.   Some day, when he was a man, he would go forth and look upon the realities of his dream.

A SUMMER MOOD

O TO be lost in the wind and the sun,
　　To be one with the grass and the stream,
With never a care while the waters run,
　　With never a thought in my dream;
To be part of the robin's lilting call,
　　And part of the bobolink's chime,
Lying close to the shy thrush singing alone,
　　And lapped in the cricket's rhyme!

O to live with these care-free ones,
　　With the lust and the glory of man
Lost in the circuit of springtime suns —
　　Submissive as earth, and a part of her plan;
To lie as the snake lies, content in the grass;
　　To drift as the clouds drift—effortless, free,
Glad of the power that drives them on,
　　With never a question of wind or sea!

CHAPTER XVIII

A CAMPING TRIP

IT was the fifteenth of June, and the sun blazed down on the dry corn-field, as if it had a spite against Lincoln, who was riding a gayly-painted new sulky corn-plough, guiding the shovels with his feet. The corn was about knee-high, and rustled softly, almost as if whispering, not yet large enough to speak aloud.

Riding about all day, in such a level field, with the sun burning one's neck brown as a leather glove, is apt to make one dream of cool river pools, where the water-snakes wiggle across, and the kingfishers fly, or of bright ripples where the rock bass love to play.

It was about four o'clock, and Lincoln was tired. His neck ached; his feet were swollen, and his tongue calling out for a drink of water. He got off the plough, after turning the horses' heads to the faint western breeze, and took a seat on the fence in the shade of a small popple tree on which a king-bird had a nest.

Somebody was galloping up the road in a regular rise and fall, that showed the perfect horseman and easy rider. It was Milton.

" Hello, Lincoln ! " shouted Milton.

" Hello, Milt," Lincoln returned. " Why ain't you at home workin' like an honest man ? "

" Better business on hand. I've come clear over here to-day to see you — "

" Well, here I am."

" Let's go to Clear Lake."

Lincoln stared hard at him.

" D'ye mean it ? "

" You bet. I can put in a horse. Bert Jenks will lend us his boat — put it right on in place of the wagon box — we can borrow Captain Knapp's tent."

" I'm with you," yelled Lincoln, leaping down, his face aglow with the idea. " But say, won't you go up and break it gently to the boss. He's got his mind kind o' set on goin' through this corn again. When'll we start ? "

" Let's see — to-day is Wednesday. We ought to get off on Monday."

" Well, now, if you don't mind, Milt, I'd like to have you go up and see what father says."

" I'll fix him," said Milton. " Where is he ? "

" Right up the road, mending fence."

He was so tickled he not only leaped the fence, but sprang into the high seat from behind and started on another round, singing, showing how instantly hope of play can lighten a boy's task. But when he came back to the fence Milton was not in sight, and his heart fell a little — the outlook was not so assuring.

It was nearly an hour later when Milton came riding back and stood by the fence, waiting. Lincoln looked up and saw him wave his hand and heard his shout. The victory was won. Mr. Stewart had consented.

Lincoln whooped with such wild delight that the horses grew frightened, and swerving to the right, ploughed up two rows of corn for several rods before they could be brought back into place.

"It's all O. K.," Milton called. "But I've got to come over with my team and help you go through the corn the other way."

From that on, nothing else was thought of or talked of. Each night the four boys got together at Mr. Jennings's house, each time bringing things that they needed. In their dreams, the gleam of the lake drew nearer. They had never looked upon a sheet of water larger than the mill-pond on the Cedar River, and the cool wind of that beautiful lake of which they had heard so much seemed to beckon them. The boat was carefully mended, and Rance, who was a good deal of a sailor, naturally talked about making a sail for it.

Lists of articles were carefully drawn up thus : —

4 tin cups,	4 knives and forks,
1 spider,	1 kettle, etc.

Sunday afternoon, at Sunday-school, the campers became the centre of attraction for the other small boys, and quite a number went home with Lincoln to look over the preparations.

There stood the vehicle — a common lumber wagon, with a boat for the box, projecting dangerously near the horses' tails, and trailing far astern. From the edges of the boat arose a few hoops, making a kind of cover, like a prairie schooner. In the box were "traps" innumerable in charge of Bert, who was "chief cook and bottle-washer."

Each man's duty had been assigned. Lincoln was to take care of the horses, Milton was to look after the tent and places to sleep, Rance was treasurer, and Bert was the cook, with the treasurer to assist. All these preparations amused an old soldier like Captain Knapp.

"Are you going to get back this fall?" he asked slyly, as he stood about, enjoying the talk.

"We'll try to," replied Milton.

But there the thing stood, all ready to sail at day-break, with no wind or tide to prevent, and every boy who saw it said, —

"I wish I could go."

And the campers, not selfish in their fun, felt a pang of pity, and said, —

"We wish you could, boys."

It was arranged that they were all to sleep in the craft that night, and so as night fell, and the visitors drew off, the four navigators went into the kitchen, where Mrs. Jennings set out some bread and milk for them.

"Now, boys, d'ye suppose you got bread enough?"

"We've got twelve loaves."

"Well, of course you can buy bread and milk, so I guess you won't starve."

"I guess not — not with fish plenty," they assured her.

"Well, now, don't set up too late, *talkin'* about gettin' off."

"We're goin' to turn right in, ain't we, boys?"

"You bet. We're goin' to get out of here before sun-up to-morrow mornin'," replied Bert.

"Well, see't you do," said Mr. Jennings, who liked to see boys have a good time. "But I guess I'll be up long before you are."

"Don't be too sure o' that."

It was delicious going to bed in that curious place, with the stars shining in, and the katydids singing. It gave them all a new view of life.

"Now, the first feller that wakes up, yell," said Bert, as he crept under the blanket.

"First feller asleep, whistle," said Lincoln.

"That won't be you, that's sure," grumbled Rance, already dozing.

As a matter of fact, no one slept much. About two o'clock they began, first one, and then the other: —

"Say, boys, don't you think it's about time?"

"Boys, it's gettin' daylight in the east!"

"No, it ain't. That's the moon."

At last the first faint light of the sun appeared, and Lincoln arose and fed the team, and harnessed them while the other boys got everything in readiness.

Mr. Jennings came out soon, and Mrs. Jennings got some hot coffee for them, and before the sun was anywhere near the horizon, they said good-by and were off. Mr. Jennings shouted many directions about the road, while Mrs. Jennings told them again to be careful on the water.

To tell the truth, the boys were a little fagged at first, but at last the sun rose, the robins chattered, the

s

bobolinks began to ring their fairy bells, the larks whistled from the meadows, and the boys began to sing. For the first hour or two the road was familiar and excited no interest. But at last they began to come upon new roads, new fields, and new villages. Streams came down the slopes and ran musically across the wood, as if on purpose to water their horses. Wells beside the road, under silver-leaf maples, invited them to stop and drink and lunch. Boys they didn't know, going out to work, stopped and looked at them enviously. How glorious it all was!

The sun grew hot, and at eleven o'clock they drew up in a beautiful grove of oaks, beside a swift and sparkling little river, for dinner and to rest their sweaty team. They concluded to eat doughnuts and drink milk for dinner, and this gave them time to fish a little, and swim a good deal, while the horses munched hay under the trees.

After a good long rest, they hitched the team in again, and started on toward the west. They had still half-way (twenty-five miles) to go. The way grew stranger. The land, more broken and treeless, seemed very wonderful to them. They came into a region full of dry lake-beds, and Bert, who had a taste for geology, explained the cause of the valleys so level at the bottom, and pointed out the old-time limits of the water.

As they rode, the boys planned their week's stay, breaking out occasionally into song. As night began to fall, it seemed they had been a week on the way.

At last, just as the sun was setting, they saw a dark

belt of woods ahead of them, and came to a narrow river, which the farmers said was the outlet of the lake. They pushed on faster, for the roads were better, and just at dusk they drove into the little village street which led down to the lake, to which their hungry eyes went out first of all.

How glorious it looked, with its waves lapping the gravelly beach, and the dark groves of trees standing purple-black against the orange sky. They sat and gazed at it for several minutes, without saying a word. Finally Rance said, with a sigh, —

"Oh, wouldn't I like to jump into that water!"

"Well, this won't do. We must get a camp," said Milton; and they pulled the team into a road leading along the east shore of the lake.

"Where can a fellow camp?" Bert called to a young man who met them, with a pair of oars on his back.

"Anywhere down in the woods." He pointed to the south.

They soon reached a densely wooded shore where no one stood guard, and drove along an old wood road to a superb camping-place near the lake shore, under a fine oak grove.

"Whoa!" yelled Milton.

The boys leaped out. Milton and Lincoln took care of the horses. Bert seized an axe and chopped on one side of two saplings, bent them together and tied them, cleared away the brush around them, and with Rance's help drew the tent cloth over them, and there was the camp. While they dug up the bedding and put it in place, Rance built a fire and set some coffee boiling.

When they sat down to eat their bread and coffee and cold chicken, the grove was dark; the smoke rose up, lit by the fire, and then was lost in the dark, cool shadows of the oak above. Below them they could hear the lap of the waves on the boulders. A breeze was rising. It was all so fine, so enjoyable, that it seemed a dream from which they were in danger of waking. After eating they all took hold of the boat and eased it down the bank into the water.

" Now, who's goin' to catch the fish for breakfast ? " asked Bert.

" I will," replied Rance, who was a " lucky " fisherman. " I'll have some fish by sun-up — see if I don't."

Their beds were hay, with abundant quilts and blankets spread above, and as Lincoln lay looking out of the tent door at the smoke curling up, hearing the horses chewing and tramping and an owl hooting, it seemed gloriously like the stories he had read, and the dreams he had had of being free from care and free from toil, far in the wilderness.

" I wish I could do this all the time," he said to Milton, who was looking at the fire, his chin resting in his palms.

" I can tell better after a week of it," said Milton, with rare wisdom.

To a boy like Lincoln or Rance, that evening was worth the whole journey, that strange, delicious hour in the deepening darkness, when everything seemed of some sweet, remembered far-off world and time — they were living as their savage ancestry lived, they were getting close to nature's self.

The pensiveness did not prevent Milton from hitting Bert a tremendous slap with a boot-leg, saying, —

"Hello! that mosquito pretty near had you that time." And Bert, who knew Milton's pranks, turned upon him, and they had a rough and tumble tussle, till Rance cried out: —

"Look out there! You'll be tippin' over my butter!"

But at last the rustle of the leaves over their heads died out in dreams. The boys fell asleep, deliciously tired and full of plans for the next day.

Morning dawned, cool and bright, and Bert was stirring before sunrise. Rance was out in the boat with Milton before the pink had come upon the lake, while Milton was "skirmishing" for some milk.

How delicious that breakfast! Newly fried perch, new milk with bread and potatoes from home — but the freedom, the strange familiarity of it all! There in the dim, sweet woods, with the smoke curling up into the leafy masses above, the sunlight just dropping upon the lake, the killdee, the robin, and the blue jay crying in the still, cool morning air. This was indeed life. The hot corn-fields were far away.

Breakfast eaten to the last scrap of fish, they made a rush for the lake and the boat. There it lay, moving a little on the light waves, a frail little yellow craft, without keel or rudder, but something to float in, anyhow. And there rippled the lake miles long, cool and sparkling. Boats were getting out into the mid-water like huge " skimmer-bugs," carrying fishermen to their tasks.

While the other boys fished for perch and bass for dinner, Lincoln studied the lake and shore. The beach where they had their boat-landing was made up of fine varicolored boulders, many of them round as cannon-balls, and Lincoln thought of the thousands of years they had been rolling and grinding there, rounding each other and polishing each other till they glistened like garnets and rubies. And then the sand !

He waded out into the clear yellow waters and examined the bottom, which was yellow sand set in tiny waves beautifully regular, the miniature reflexes of the water in motion. It made him think of the little wind waves in the snow, which he had often wondered at in winter.

Growing tired of this, he went to the bank, and lying down on the grass gave himself up to the rest and freedom and beauty of the day. He no longer felt like " making the most of it." It seemed as if he were always to live like this.

The others came in, after awhile, with some bass and perch. The perch were beautifully marked in pearl and gray, to correspond with the sand bottom, though the boys didn't know that. There were no large fish so near shore, and they lacked the courage to go far out, for the whitecaps glittered now and then in mid-water.

They ate every " smidgin' " of the fish at dinner, and

things looked desperate. They went out into the deep water, all feeling a little timorous, as the little boat began to rock on the waves.

Lincoln was fascinated with the water. It was so clear that he could see fish swimming far below. The boat seemed floating in the air. At times they passed above strange and beautiful forests of weeds and grasses, deep down there. These scared him, for he remembered the story of a man who had been caught and drowned by just such clinging weeds, and besides, what monsters these mysterious places might conceal!

Other boats came round them. Sail-boats passed, and the little steamer, the pride of the lake, passed over to "the island." Yachts that seemed to the boys immense, went by, loaded with merrymakers. Everything was as strange, as exciting, as if they were in a new world.

Rance was much taken by the sail-boats, and when they went home to dinner he declared, —

" I'm going to rig a sail on our boat, or die tryin'."

He spent the whole afternoon at work while the other boys played ball and shot at a target. By night he was ready for a sail, though the others were sceptical of results.

That second night the mosquitoes bit and a loud thunder-storm passed over. As they heard the roar of the falling rain on the tent, and the wet spatter in their faces, and heard the water drip-drop on their bread-box, Milton and Lincoln wished themselves at home.

But it grew cooler, and the mosquitoes left, and they

all slept like bear cubs, and woke fresh as larks in the morning. It was a little discouraging at first. Everything was wet, the bread was inclined to be mouldy and tasted of the box, but the fish were fresh and sweet — the birds were singing and the sky was bright and cool, with a fresh western wind blowing.

Rance was eager to sail, and as soon as he had put away the breakfast, he shouldered his mast.

"Come on, boys, now for the boat."

"I guess not," said Milton.

The boat was soon rigged with a little triangular sail, with an oar to steer by, lashed in with wires. Lincoln, finally, had courage to get in, and with beating heart Rance pushed off.

The sail caught the wind, and the boat began to move.

"Hurrah! Whoop!" Rance threw water on the sail; where he learned *that* was a mystery. The effect was felt at once. The cloth swelled, became impervious to the wind, and the boat swept steadily forward.

Lincoln was cautious. "That is all right. The question is, can we get back?"

"You wait an' see me tack."

"All right. Tack or nail, only le's see you get back where we started from." Lincoln was sceptical of sailboats. He had heard about sailing "just where you wanted to go," but he had his doubts about it.

But the boat obeyed the rudder nicely, and came around slowly and started in smoothly and steadily. After this successful trip the boys did little else but sail, making longer voyages thereafter.

"I'm going up to town with it after dinner," Rance announced. But when he came out, after dinner, the sky was overcast and the breeze rising, blowing from the southwest, and Milton refused to experiment.

"I'd sooner walk than ride in your boat," he explained.

"All right; you pays your money — you takes your choice."

The boat drove out into the lake steadily and swiftly, making the water ripple at the stern delightfully; but when they got past a low-lying island where the waves ran free, the boat began to heave and slide wildly, and Lincoln grew a little pale and set in the face, which made Rance smile.

"This is something like it. I'm going to go out about half a mile, then strike straight for the town."

It was not long before he found the boat was getting unmanageable. The long oar crowded him nearly off the seat, as he tried to hold her straight out into mid-water. She was flat-bottomed, and as she got into the region of whitecaps, she began to be blown bodily with the wind.

Lincoln was excited, but not scared; he realized now that they were in great danger. Rance continued to smile, but it was evident that he, too, was thinking new thoughts. He held the sail with his right hand, easing it off and holding it tight, by looping the rope on a peg set in the gunwale. But it was impossible for Lincoln to help him. All depended upon him alone.

"Turn! — turn it!" shouted Lincoln. "Don't you see we can't get back?"

"I'm afraid of breakin' my rudder."

There lay the danger. The oar was merely lashed into a notch in the stern, with wire. The leverage was very great, but Rance brought the boat about and headed her for the town, nearly three miles away.

They both thrilled with a sort of pleasure to feel the boat leap under them as she caught the full force of the wind in her sail. If they could hold her in that line, they were all right. She careened once till she dipped water.

"Get on the edge!" commanded Rance, easing the sail off. Lincoln climbed upon the edge of the little pine shell, scarcely eighteen inches high, and the boat steadied.

Both looked relieved.

The water was getting a lead color, streaked with foam, and the hissing of the whitecaps had a curiously snaky sound, as they spit water into the boat. The rocking had opened a seam in the bottom, and Lincoln was forced to bail furiously.

Rance, though a boy of unusual strength, clear-headed and resolute in time of danger, began to feel that he was master only for a time.

"I don't suppose this is much of a blow," he yelled, "but I don't see any of the other boats out."

Lincoln glanced round him; all the boats, even the two-masters, were in or putting in. Lightning began to run down the clouds in the west in zigzag streams. The boat, from time to time, was swept sidewise out of its course, but Rance dared not ease the sail, for fear he could not steer her, and, besides, he was afraid of the rapidly approaching squall. If she turned sideways toward the wind, she would fill instantly.

He sat there, with the handle of the oar at his right hip, the rope in his hand, with one loop round the peg. Each time as the gust struck them, he was lifted from his seat by the crowding of the oar and the haul of the rope. His muscles swelled tense and rigid — the sweat poured from his face, but he laughed when Lincoln, with reckless drollery, began to shout a few nautical words.

" Luff, you lubber — why don't you luff? "

" Suppose you come help ! "

" I guess *not !* I'm only passenger. Hard-a-port, there, you'll have us playin' on the sand, yet. That's right. All we got to do is to hard-a-port when the wind blows."

The farther they went, the higher the waves rolled, till the boat creaked and gaped under its strain, and the water began to come in fast.

" Shut up, there, Link. Bail 'er out ! " the pilot cried. The thunder broke over their heads, and far away to the left they could see the rain on the lake, and the water white with foam, but they were nearing the beach at the foot of the street. A crowd was watching them with motionless intensity.

Soon they were in the midst of a fleet of anchored boats — the rain began to fall. The blast struck the sail, tearing it loose, and filling the boat with water, but Rance held to his rudder, and darting among the boats a moment later, the little craft ran half her length upon the sand.

As Rance leaped ashore, he staggered with weakness. Both took shelter in a near-by boat-house. The boat-keeper swore at them : —

" Don't you know any more'n to go out in such a *tub* as that on a day like this ? I expected every minute to see you go over."

"We didn't," said Rance. " I guess we made pretty good time."

" Time ! you'd better say time ! If you'd been five minutes later, you'd had *time* enough."

It was a foolhardy thing, — Rance could see it now, as he looked out on the mad water, and at the little flat, awkward boat on the sand.

An hour later, as they walked up the wood, they met the boys half-way on the road, badly scared.

" By golly ! We thought you were goners," said Milton. " Why, we couldn't see the boat, after you got out a little ways. Looked like you were both sittin' in the water."

They found the camp badly demoralized. The other boys had been too worried to put things snug before the squall, and their blankets were wet, and the tent blown out of plumb. But they set to work clearing things up. The rain passed away and the sun came out again, and when they sat down to their supper, the storm was far away.

It was glorious business to these prairie boys. Released from work in the hot corn-fields, they were in camp on the lovely lake, with nothing to do but swim or doze when they pleased. They had the delicious feeling of being travellers in a strange country, — explorers of desert wilds, hunters and fishers in the wildernesses of the mysterious West.

To Lincoln it was so fine it almost made him sad. When he should have enjoyed every moment he was saying to himself, " Day after to-morrow we must start for home,"—and the happy days passed so swiftly.

They went down and brought the boat home, and as the weather continued fine, they were able to sail about near the camp with comfort, and trail a line, and watch the fish swimming deep down in the clear, crystal water. Occasionally Milton said : —

" By golly ! I wish I had one o' mother's biscuits this morning," or some such remark. Some one usually shied a potato at him and shut him up. Such remarks were heretical.

They explored the woods south of the lake, a wild jungle, which it was easy to imagine quite unexplored. Some years before a set of horse thieves had lived there, and their grass-grown paths were of thrilling interest to the boys. They never quite dared to follow them to the house where the shooting of the leader had taken place.

Altogether it was a wonderful week, and when they loaded up their boat and piled their plunder in behind, it was with sad hearts, although it must be said the question of " grub " was giving Bert a good deal of trouble. At meal-time they thought of home — with their stomachs fairly filled they were pleased with the wilderness.

The journey homeward occupied parts of two days. They made camp by the roadside, and the next day being Saturday they were delayed by a game of base-ball in Taylor City. It was late Saturday night when they drew up in Mr. Jennings's yard, and to show that they were thoroughly hardened campers they slept in the wagon another night — at least three of them did. Milton shamelessly sneaked away to his bed, and they did not miss him until morning.

They upbraided him in severe terms, but he only laughed. When Mr. Jennings invited them all to breakfast, nobody refused.

"Land o' Goshen," said Mrs. Jennings, "you eat as if you were starved. What did you live on?"

"Fish," replied Bert.

"Sour bread," said treacherous Milton.

"Well, no wonder you look gaunt as weasels."

"Oh, but it was fun, wasn't it, boys?" cried Lincoln.

"You bet it was. Let's go again next year."

"All right," said Milton; "raise your weapons and swear to be true to the 'poet.'"

They all lifted their knives in solemn consent, while Mrs. Jennings laughed till the tears came to her eyes.

But they never did. Of such stuff are the plans of youth.

To face page 271

COLOR IN THE WHEAT

LIKE liquid gold the wheat-field lies,
   A marvel of yellow and green,
That ripples and runs, that floats and flies,
   With the subtle shadows, the change, the sheen
That plays in the golden hair of a girl.
      A cloud flies there —
      A ripple of amber — a flare
Of light follows after.   A swirl
In the hollows like the twinkling feet
   Of a fairy waltzer; the colors run
   To the westward sun,
Through the deeps of the ripening wheat.

I hear the reapers' far-off hum,
   So faint and far it seems the drone
Of bee or beetle, seems to come
   From far-off, fragrant, fruity zone,
      A land of plenty, where
      Toward the sun, as hasting there,
      The colors run
      Before the wind's feet
      In the wheat.

The wild hawk swoops
  To his prey in the deeps;
The sunflower droops
  To the lazy wave; the wind sleeps;
Then, moving in dazzling links and loops,
  A marvel of shadow and shine,
A glory of olive and amber and wine,
  Runs the color in the wheat.

CHAPTER XIX

A DAY IN THE OLD-TIME HARVEST FIELD

Who shall describe the glory of growing wheat? Deep as the breast of a man, wide as a sea, heavy-headed, supple-stalked, many-voiced, full of multitudinous, secretive, whispered colloquies, — a wilderness of wealth, a meeting-place of winds and of magic. Who shall sing the song of it, its gold and its grace?

See it when the storm-wind lays hard upon it! See it when the shadows drift over it! Go out into it at night when all is still — so still you seem to hear the passing of the transforming elixir as it creeps upward into the tiny globes of green, and you must cry, " Oh, the music and magic of growing wheat ! "

Stand before it at eve when the setting sun floods the world with crimson, and the bearded heads lazily swirl under the slow, warm wind, and the mousing hawk dips into the green deeps like the sea-gull into the ocean, and your eyes will ache with the light and the color of it.

The boy on the old-time wheat farm generally began his apprenticeship by carrying luncheon and fresh water to the men, or by riding the lead horse for the man who drove the reaper. This he enjoyed for an hour or two the first day. Thereafter it became wearisome and a burden of care. The sun beat down upon his shoulders, the salt sweat of the horse made his chafed legs smart, and the monotonous creak-creak of the harness became an intolerable nuisance. He was glad when his father set him to carrying bundles for the " shocker."

But this soon became worse than riding the lead horse, and the boy, seeing his younger brother riding along in the cool wind, with gloomy face, felt a keen pang of sorrow to think he had outgrown that without being able to " bind on a station."

Sometimes as the boy stopped to rest his worn and swollen hands and looked at the wilderness of sheaves already bound and scattered over the field, and considered the thousands which the sturdy arms of the men were constantly adding to those other myriads, his heart grew sick with despair. What to him were sailing hawk, piping chicken, and whistling bob-white? No sooner did he bring twelve bundles together than he was forced to move on to twelve other bundles, equally heavy and equally filled with briers; and there beyond waved a vast field not yet yielded to the reaper.

All these gloomy transitions had been the lot of Lincoln Stewart, and when he was set to " bind up the corners," out of the way of the horses, he felt a glow of exultation; he was nearing the time when he, too, should be considered a man and take his "station." He was very deft and powerful, and in the harvest of his fifteenth year, Mr. Stewart said: —

"Well, Lincoln, you've been aching to take your station for some years. Now you can show your mettle. I'll put you into the field this year as a full hand."

This was pretty nearly equivalent to being knighted, and the boy replied: —

"All right. I'm ready for it."

The coming on of harvest was always of great interest to the Western farmer boy. There was a certain excitement as of battle in it. It was the event waited for — the end and reward of all the ploughing and sowing of the year. There was a certain anxious solicitude in the eyes of the older men, as they watched the sky from day to day. Every cloud rising in the west was a menace, each thunder roll in the night a disquieting threat.

But day by day Lincoln watched with unusual interest the hot sun transforming the rain and soil into gold. His day of trial was coming swiftly. He went out into the wheat often, lying prone in its deeps, hearing the wind singing its whispered mystic song over his head. He watched the stalks as they turned yellow at the root and at the neck, though the middle height remained green and sappy, and the heads had a blue-green sheen. The leaves, no longer needed, were beginning to die at the bottom, and the stalk to stiffen as it bore the daily increasing weight of the milky berries. As he looked along the edge of the field, Lincoln felt the beauty of the broad ribbon of green and yellow, as it languidly waved in and out with every rush of the wind.

At last Mr. Stewart began to get out the reapers and put them in order. Provisions were bought in generous measure. The wheels and cogs were all cleaned and oiled, the hands assembled, and early on a hot morning in July, the boss mounted his self-rake reaper and drove into the field. Owen rode the lead horse, and Lincoln and four stalwart "hands" followed the machine to bind the grain. It was "work from the word go!"

Wheat harvest always came in the hottest and driest part of the summer, and was considered the hardest work of the year. It demanded early rising for both man and wife. It meant broiling all day over the hot stove in the kitchen for the women, and for the men it brought toil from dawn to sunset, each man working with bent back beneath the vivid sunlight. Some days the thermometer stood at a round hundred in the shade, but immense fields of wheat ripening at the same moment and threatening to "go back into the ground" made rest impossible.

There are no tasks on the farm which surpass the severity of binding on a station, as Lincoln well knew, but he was ready for the trial. Three of the hands were strange nomadic fellows, which the West had not yet learned to call tramps. One was called "Long John," a tall, lathy, freckle-faced man of twenty-five or thirty, while his "partner" was a small, dark, secretive middle-aged fellow whom Lincoln disliked. John called him " Little Bill." The fourth was a cousin named Luke McTurg. The fifth was Ben Hutchison, who had developed into a long-armed, stalwart youth.

The field had been trimmed by means of the old-fashioned cradle, and the boss swung into the field at the corner, without hitch. Giving a final touch of oil

to the sickle, he mounted the seat of the self-rake McCormick, and said : —

" Now, boys, it's going to be hot, and this being the first day, we'll take it tolerably slow and easy. I'd hate to have any of you ' peter out.' "

Long John sneered a little : " Oh, you needn't worry about us. If the boy goes through, I think we will."

Lincoln spoke up, " You follow the boy, and you'll earn your wages, and don't you forget it."

Mr. Stewart smiled. " When I was sixteen I could rake and bind with any man I ever saw. I guess Lincoln'll look after himself."

Under these conditions the work began. Long John " took in " immediately after the machine. Bill went on and set in at the second fifth, and Luke at the third, while Ben and Lincoln walked back the other way to meet the machine.

"That 'jacknape' thinks he is going to bind us off our legs," said Lincoln.

Ben put out his tongue. "Well, if he does, he'll earn his board. I'd break my back rather than get caught to-day."

As Lincoln stood at his station, looking across the level sweep of grain, he could see the flashing reels whirl, and see the heads of the two strangers bobbing up and down, as if they were binding in a race. The wind was light, and the sun was growing warmer each moment. The boy was dressed in brown ducking trousers, a plain hickory shirt, and stout shoes, while a wide straw hat shaded his face. His brown hands were bare.

As the purring sickle passed him, and the angry rake delivered his first bundle to him with a jerk, Lincoln's heart leaped. Right there he became a man. Running to the gavel, he scuffled it together with his feet, while he jerked a handful of the wheat from the sheaf with his left hand. A swift whirl of the band, a stooping clutch, and he rose with the bundle on his knee. A sudden pull, a twist, a twirl over his thumb, and the first bound sheaf dropped into the stubble. He scarcely halted in the work, for his deft action was like that of some cunning machinery. Swiftly the gavels turned to sheaves behind him, and before the reaper had turned the second corner his station was half finished. He did not allow himself to exult too much, for he knew the real struggle was yet to come. Behind him Ben came, stooping low.

Lincoln's heart was full of pride to feel he was part of the crew. As the morning wore on, the sun grew hotter, and a great void developed in Lincoln's chest. His breakfast had been ample, but no mere stomachful of food could carry a growing boy through such toil. Along about a quarter to ten he began to scan the field with anxious eye, to see if little Mary were not coming with the luncheon. He had less time to rest at the end of his station, and his arms began to ache with fatigue.

Just when it seemed as if he could stand no more, Mary came with a jug of cool milk, and some cheese and fried-cakes. Setting a couple of tall sheaves together like a tent, Lincoln flung himself down flat on his back in their shadow and devoured his lunch, while his aching muscles relaxed and his tired eyes closed. Weary as he was, his dim eyes apprehended something of the glory of the waving wheat and sailing clouds, and the boy's heart in him regretted at the moment the privileges of the man. He would gladly have lain there listening to the faint wailing of the wind, and seeing the great silent clouds sail by.

The delicious zephyrs kissed his face with lips as cool as the lofty clouds which rolled like storms of snow in the deep blue space of sky.

Lying silent as a clod, he could hear the *cheep* of the crickets, the buzzing wings of flies and grasshoppers, and the faint, fairy-like tread of unseen insects just under his ear in the stubble. Strange green worms, and staring flies, and shining beetles crept over him as

he listened, in dreamful doze, to the far-off, approaching purr of the sickle, flicked by the faint snap of the
driver's whip, while out of the low rustle of the ever
stirring wind amid the wheat came the wailing cry of a
lost little wild chicken, a falling, thrilling, piteous little
sob. This momentary communion with nature seemed
all the sweeter for the terrible toil which had preceded
it, and was to follow it. It took resolution to rise and
fall in behind the sickle.

But the dinner signal came at last in the shape of a
cloth hung from the chamber window, or a tin horn blown
by the stalwart hired girl, or through Gran'papa Stewart,
who had long ago given up his place in the fields, and
whose white hair, shining afar, was signal for release.

As they left their stations, Ben and Lincoln walked
to the house together. "Well, the boys didn't get
caught, after all."

"No," replied Ben. "I came mighty near it once.
I run a stubble under my nail, and had to get it out."

"The tug of war will come about four o'clock to-
day," answered Lincoln. "But I reckon I'm good for
it."

No one can know how beautiful water is, till they
have toiled thus in the harvest field, and have come at
last to the spring or well, to lave a burning face, and
worn, aching arms. Lincoln soused head and all into
the huge bucket again and again, dashing the cold water
upon his bared arms with a shout of pleasure. He
could not get enough of it.

And so, with their hair "smooched" back, all wet

with perspiration as they were, the hands surrounded
the table, and fell upon the boiled beef and potatoes with
unexampled ferocity, while the wind through the open
door brought the smell of corn in bloom, and the sound
of bees at the hives. The table, covered with homely
ware, had a sort of rude plenty, — raspberries, bread,
coffee, with pie for dessert. There was no ceremony,
and very little talking, till the wolf was somewhat satisfied. Then came a delicious hour of lying on the thick,
cool grass, under the shade of the trees, a doze sensuous
and dreamful as the siesta of a tropical monarch, cut
short all too soon by the implaca-
ble voice of the boss, —

" Roll out, boys, and stock y'r
jugs."

Again the big white
jugs were filled at the well
or spring. The horses,
" lazy " with food, led
the way back to the
field, and work be-
gan again. All na-
ture seemed to invite
to sleep, rather than
to work, and the boys longed, with a wordless longing,
for the woods and the river. The gentle wind hardly
moved the bended heads of grain ; hawks hung in the
air like trout sleeping in deep pools ; the sunlight seemed
a golden silence, — and yet men must strain their tired
muscles and bend their aching backs to the harvest.

At the starting-point, just to let the boys know that he was "all right," "Long John" put both heels behind his neck and walked about on his hands.

"Why, it's play," he said, "standing up against you boys."

Lincoln was nettled, and as Mr. Stewart passed him the next time, he said : —

"You never mind me, father.   Take the conceit out of that chap, or we can't live with him."

It was foolish, but Duncan had a pride in his boy, and swung the long whip above his team, settling the sickle full length into the heavy grain.

For a couple of hours Lincoln found time to rest after each station, and each time he felt his strength ebbing.   His fingers were wearing to the quick from raking the stubble, and his thumb was lame from tucking the band.   He no longer bound as he walked, for he had not the strength to draw the band without pressing the sheaf against the ground.   Twice he got his last bundle out of the way just in time to avoid the disgrace of being "doubled."   The sweat streamed into his eyes, blinding him, and a throbbing pain filled his temples, yet he toiled on with set teeth, determined not to be beaten.   At every opportunity he dropped flat on his back, like a prize-fighter at the end of his round, with every muscle limp as a rag.

"How're you standing it, Lincoln?" his father asked anxiously.

"Oh, I'm all right.   You catch and double that fellow. Don't worry about me.   How's Ben?"

" He's about ' bushed,' but I guess he'll hold out till supper."

" All right, we'll make that Jack-knife think he's in the harvest field."

The whip cracked and the flying sickle swept through the grain like a steel-blue ribbon. The clang of the rake was like the advancing footfalls of an angry giant. Ben bent almost double, his tongue licking his parched lips, came after Lincoln, holding his own by reason of his long arms and his low stature. Bill, hard as iron, silent and grave, worked away methodically, just keeping out of the reapers' way, and no more. Luke was always waiting when the driver came to him, and on his face was little sign of effort. Long John still sneered and asked : " Is that the best you can do ? How's the boy ? Had to give him a rest this round, didn't you ? "

As he passed his son the next time, Duncan said, " Look out for yourself, Lincoln. I'm going to double that bean-pole or heat a pinion."

The hour that followed tested the boy to his innermost fibre. The speed of the machine was almost doubled, and when he snatched his last sheaf from before the lead horse's feet, Owen piped out with glee, —

" We caught Little Bill and Ben this round, and Long John, pretty near."

Catching a handful of green weeds from the stubble, Lincoln dashed some water on them, crowded them in the crown of his hat, and set in after the machine, doggedly, blindly. There was no beauty now in the sky or grain. He saw only the interminable rows of sheaves, felt only the harsh stubble, heard only the sound of the sickle. He calculated every movement. While his left hand was selecting the band, his feet rolled the gavel together, and putting the band beneath was but a single motion. He allowed no stop, no hurry. He reduced himself to the precision and synchronism of a piece of machinery — all in vain; on the third round he had four gavels unbound. He was "doubled" at last. As he realized this, he straightened his aching back and looked at his father.

"Did you get him?"

"Not quite, but I will this time," he replied, cracking his whip. "Get out o' there, Dan."

Lincoln took up the next station with the feeling of having been beaten. His heart was gone and he was faint with hunger, but he worked on.

He heard Owen whoop, and his father laugh. Had they doubled the long man? He looked back toward the house and saw the supper signal fluttering from the window. It came just in time to save him from defeat.

As he came back slowly toward the oil-can corner, he joined Ben.

"Well, he got all of us but Luke and that long-legged kangaroo."

"Looks that way. He'll crow over us all the rest of the harvest, I suppose."

But he didn't. On the contrary, he looked rather crestfallen, and before they could put in a word, Mr. Stewart said : —

"I guess I don't want you round. He's been cheat-

THE COOL GRAY JUG

O COOL gray jug that touched the lips
In kiss that softly closed and clung,
No Spanish wine the tippler sips
Or port the poet's praise has sung,
Such pure untainted sweetness yields
As cool gray jug in harvest fields.

I see it now!   A clover leaf
Outspread upon its sweating side.
As from the standing sheaf
I pluck and swing it high, the wide
Field glows with noonday heat —
The winds are tangled in the wheat.

In myriads the crickets blithely *cheep*.
Across the swash of waving grain
I see the burnished reaper creep —
The lunch-boy comes! and once again
The jug its crystal coolness yields —
O cool gray jug in harvest fields!

ing for the last four rounds. See here." He led them all to the end of Long John's last station, and walking along, pulled the bands off the sheaves. They had not been tied at all.

"Now, what I don't understand," said the boss, " is this. How did you expect to do that without being found out?"

Long John sullenly replied, "Well, I made up my mind at noon I didn't want to work for a man who drives his hands as you do."

"But it was your own fault," said Lincoln. "Your bragging started the whole thing."

"Well, let's go to supper," said Ben. "I'm empty as a tin boiler."

Again a dash of cool water at the well, and then, weary and sore, the boys sat down to hot tea, salt pork, and berries, while the horses rested in the shed. It was a hasty meal, and in less than an hour they were all back in the field.

But the pace was leisurely then. There was a wondrous charm in this part of the day, when the shadows began to lengthen across the stubble, and the fiery sun, half veiled in thin gray clouds in the west, abated his fierceness, and the air began to grow cool and moist.

A few rounds, and then long-drawn and musical arose the driver's cry : —

"Turn out! All hands — *turn out!*" and slowly, with low-swinging heads, the horses moved toward the barn, followed by the men, who walked with lagging steps.

Lincoln and Ben walked side by side with swollen hands and aching arms, too tired to exult over their victory.   Around them the katydids and treetoads were singing, and down the lane Mary and Gran'pap were bringing the sober-gaited cows.

"To-morrow — that's where we catch goudy," said Ben.

"Oh, I don't know; it may rain," replied Lincoln. "Anyhow, we've got a good long night to rest in."

That night Mr. Stewart called Little Bill and Long John one side and handed them some bills. "Here's your 'walking papers,'" he said grimly. "I don't want a hand round me that I can't trust. I don't like your style. Good day."

II

The next year Mr. Stewart bought a "harvester," which was a reaper on which two men stood to bind the grain, which was carried over the bull-wheel by a sort of endless apron and dropped upon a table between the binders. This was considered a wonderful invention and a great improvement over the self-rake reaper, for two men could bind as much as four on the ground.

The boys were instantly ambitious to try their hands on this new machine. Lincoln was at once gratified. He took his place beside the hind man and bound his half of all the grain that rolled over the bull-wheel — no matter how heavy it was. In some ways the work was quite as hard as binding on a station, but the labor of walking and gathering the grain was saved, and besides, a canopy shut off the sun, while the motion of the machine helped to keep a breeze stirring.

It looked to be a very picturesque way of gathering the grain, and those who looked on considered that the machine was doing all the work — but it wasn't. To bind one-half of ten acres of wheat each day was work, incessant and severe. Every motion must count. No bands must break or slip, for at that precise moment a mountain of grain would be waiting for the band.

Each man drove the other, and the driver was master of both their fates. The motions of good binders were regular and graceful, and as certain as those of faultless machinery.

Lincoln, being the lighter, always bound on the front table, and his partner had no cause to complain of him. The "knack" which always came to help him out, served him particularly well on the harvester. He could tuck the knot with his right thumb while reaching for a band with his left hand, and the heap of grain was seldom too large for even his short arms. The hired man accused him of taking "light loads" each time, but to this Mr. Stewart merely said: "You know what you can do. Put your band around the straw a little quicker."

Sometimes the hired man tried this while Mr. Stewart laughed at them from his seat in the machine. It was of no avail; no matter how quickly he worked, Lincoln's deft fingers were a little nimbler, and he was forced to return to his usual pace. Part of the time Owen drove, and then the hired man was very quiet, for Owen had no scruples about crowding the sickle to its full length even when the wheat was full of thistles or wild sunflowers.

It was hard work. The briers got into Lincoln's arms and fingers. His shirt-sleeves wore out, and the rust from the oats stung like vitriol. His hands chapped, and the balls of his fingers became raw, so that when he returned to work after dinner or supper he groaned every time he drew a band. If the ground were rough, he was banged about till his knees were lame — and yet in spite of all these trials no one cared to return to binding on the ground. Harvesting was enormously facilitated by this reaper, but invention was already busy on something far more wonderful.

Already there were rumors that a machine had been invented which cut and bound the grain entirely of its own motion. This was incredible, a tale out of the "Wonder Book," and no one really believed it till Captain Knapp brought one home and set it to work on his own farm. The whole of Sun Prairie turned out to see it — Lincoln and Owen among the rest. It was like a harvester save that a heavy mass of machinery hung where the binders used to stand, and when these intricacies revolved, a long iron arm, which looked like the neck of a goose, rose and plunged down through the grain, pushing a wire tight around a sheaf, while some cunning little twisters and a knife tied and cut the wire, and a small foot came up from below and kicked the bundle clear. It had the weight of a thresh-ing-machine, but it did the work, and thereafter Cap-tain Knapp and Rance could cut, bind, and stack more grain than seven men in the old way. Soon every farmer had a self-binder. It was improved each year, and became less ponderous and cheaper. Then a sort of twine was invented which the crickets would not eat (they ate everything else, fork handles, vests, jack-knives, gloves), and the wire, which had become a great nuisance in the field, was laid by in favor of the string.

The excitement and bustle of the harvest passed with

the old-time reaper.   On many farms the regular hired man and the men of the family were able to take care of the grain, and the women hardly knew when reaping began or left off. The blinding toil of binding by hand was gone, and the work of shocking was greatly lightened by the bundle-carrier attachment, which dropped the sheaves in windrows. The iron arm did better work than even those of David McTurg, and never grew tired or careless.

But with all these gains there was a loss — the inexorable change from old to new forever drops and leaves behind pleasant associations of human emotion — the poetry of the familiar and the simpler forms of life. The self-rake reaper and binding on a station joined the "down-power," the tin lantern, the bell-metal cogwheels of the separator, and the tallow candle. The new had its poetry, too, but it was a little more difficult for the old folks to see it — even Lincoln and Rance did not recognize it as poetry, though they enjoyed the mystery and excitement of it as they looked across the bull-wheel and saw the faithful arm of insensate steel doing its glorious work, unwearied and uncomplaining.

In his home in the city the middle-aged man of country birth hears the wind blowing through the branches of a sparse elm, and instantly he is back on the prairies of Iowa, in the harvest field of twenty years ago, or in the hay-field where the larks and bobolinks are swaying and whistling. The king-bird chatters from the little popple tree by the fence under whose shade the toiler lies in momentary rest.

Oh, ineffaceable sunsets! Oh, mighty sweep of golden grain beneath a vaster, more glorious sea of clouds, your light and song and motion are ever with us. We hear the shrill, myriad-voiced choir of leaping insects whose wings flash fire amid the glorified stubble. The wind wanders by and lifts our torn hats. The locusts leap in clouds before our heedless feet, the prairie hen's brood rises out of the unreaped barley and drops into the sheltering deeps of the tangled oats, green as emerald. The lone quail pipes in the hazel thicket, and far up the road the cow-bell's steady clang tells of the homecoming of the herd.

Even in such hours of toil, and through the sultry skies, the sacred light of beauty broke; worn and grimed as we were, we still could fall a-dream before the marvel of golden earth and a crimson sky.

A WESTERN HARVEST
FIELD

On every side the golden stubble stretches,
Looped and laced with spiders' silvery maze.
From stalk to stalk the noisy insects leaping,
Add sparks of glittering fire to gold and purple haze,
　　Their clicking flight the only sound of living
　　In all the solemn plain
Of flooding, failing light through drooping, dreamy grain.

The warm sweet light grows every instant richer,
Ever more sonorous the night-hawk's sudden scream,
And now there comes the clatter of the sickle,
And loud and cheery urging of the reaper's tired team.
Around, unseen, the choir of evening crickets
Deepens and widens with the sunset's lessening heat,
And distant calls to supper pulse across the tangled wheat.

The overarching majesty of purple clouds grows brighter.
Soaring serene in seas of blue and green,
A tumbled mountain-land of cloud-crags fired and lighted
To glowing bronze with red and yellow sheen.
And through the grain the reaper still goes forward —
And still the insects leap and night-hawks play,
While overhead the glory of the sunset turns to gray.

COMING RAIN ON THE PRAIRIE

In sounding southern breeze
The spire-like poplar trees
Stream like vast plumes
  Against a seamless cloud — a high,
Dark mass, a dusty dome that looms
  A rushing shadow on the western sky.

The lightning falls in streams,
Sprangling in fiery seams,
Through which the bursting rain
  Trails in clouds of gray;
The cattle draw together on the plain,
  And drift like anchored boats upon a wind-swept bay.

THE HERDSMAN

A waste of grasses dry as hair;
Stillness; insects' buzz; and glare
Of white-hot sunshine everywhere!

The Herdsman like a statue sits
Upon his panting horse, while far below
  The herd moves soundlessly as a shadow flits,
The weak wind mumbles some mysterious word.

The word grows louder, and a thrill
Of action runs along the hot twin bands
   Of steel.   A low roar quivers in the ear, and still
No motion else in all the spotted sands.

The roar grows brazen, and a yell
Bursts from an unseen iron throat;
   The Herdsman's eyes rest on a distant swell,
Whence seems to pulse the savage welcome note.

Sudden it comes, a crawling, thunderous thing!
A monstrous serpent hot with haste,
   The cannon-ball express with rushing swing
Circles the butte and roars across the waste.

The embodied might of these our iron days,
The glittering moving city, rushes toward the east,
   Bringing for a single instant face to face
Barbaric loneliness and a flying feast.

A roguish maiden from an open window throws
(Or drops) her handkerchief among the cacti spears,
   The Herdsman plucks and wears it like a rose
Upon his breast, and laughs to hide his grateful tears.

    Again the waste of grasses crisp as hair;
    Stillness; crickets' chirp; and glare
    Of boundless sunshine everywhere!

To face page 296

CHAPTER XX

THE BATTLE OF THE BULLS

DURING the first three years of Lincoln's life on Sun Prairie, the cattle remained " free commoners," ranging at will on the unfenced land, but all this suddenly changed. The stockman was required to take care of his cattle, and fencing became optional with the owner of crops. This reversal of liability was due to an enactment called " The Herd Law," and was a great relief to farmers, to whom fencing was a very considerable burden.

As to the rights or wrongs of this change, the boys of Sun Prairie had no opinion, and the cause was only vaguely understood, but the change in their own lives was momentous. Up to this time their watch over the cattle had been easy and lax, now it became necessary to

know where the herd was every hour of the day and night. The herder must stay with his charges until relieved, like a sentinel. This led to an arrangement between the Stewarts, Knapps, and Jenningses by which the cattle were held in one drove, and the boys took turn and turn about in watching them.

Meanwhile a still greater change was taking place. As the settlers poured into the county in hundreds, the wild lands yielded to the breaking-plough, and the range disappeared with incredible swiftness, until at last only two great feeding-grounds existed. One to the west, a wet, cold tract covered with fine grass interspersed with patches of willow, the other the burr-oak opening on the Wapseypinnicon. To these ranges the cows had to be driven each morning, and brought home each night. This led to the next important step. A part of the home farm was "seeded down" to timothy grass, and the cows separated from the general herd, which could thus be driven farther away and held during the entire season.

So at last Milton and Owen or Lincoln and Rance kept watch every day over the combined flocks of the neighborhood, while the other boys worked at corn-planting or haying or harvest. As it happened, the farmers for a year or two kept up their fences, and the boys, after seeing the herd quieted for the night, were able to return home to sleep; but at last the range grew too small and the fences too poor (new-comers made none at all) to allow this, and then came the final change of all. One day, Captain Knapp called to ar-

range with Mr. Stewart about having the young cattle
and the steers driven over into the next county, in
search of wider range.

When the decision and date of the moving were announced, the boys were deeply excited.   Whoever herded
the cattle now would be a herder indeed.   He must not
expect to return to his mother at night.   He must sleep
in a tent and follow his cattle.   In imagination Lincoln
saw files of Indians moving over smooth ranges, out-
lined against the sky, or heard the thunderous trample
of migrating buffaloes.   On the night before they were
to start, the boys were all too excited to sleep.   Every
lad in Sun Prairie wanted to go, and most of them
did go, to spy out the land.

Lincoln, Rance, and Milton rounded up the herd and
kept it moving, while Mr. Stewart and Mr. Knapp and
several of the smaller boys followed in a wagon, in
which were tent and bedding for the herders.   Mr.
Stewart had said : " You don't want a tent.   We will
get a place for you at some settler's shanty."   But the
boys insisted, and so a little " dog tent " was purchased
by Lincoln and Rance, to be their very own, and they
were happy.

For a couple of hours the ground was familiar, but at
last they came to the Cedar River, beyond which all
was unknown.   They were deeply disappointed to find
houses there, but toward noon they came to a long, low
swell of wild land, reaching far to right and to left.   It
seemed to be the beginning of the wild country.   It
was a wet and swampy country ; for that reason it was

yet unclaimed, but there were herds of cattle already feeding there, and Mr. Stewart said, —

" Let 'em feed, boys, while we take a snack."

It was a glorious business! The grass was green and tender, the wind fresh, the sunlight vivid.

" I'd like to keep right on all summer, wouldn't you, Rance ? " said Lincoln.

" Yes," replied Rance, but his voice was not as fervid as Lincoln had expected.

They stopped for the night, about four o'clock. They were still in the wet country, but about twenty miles from home. It seemed a very long way indeed to Lincoln when Mr. Stewart said, " Well, boys, I guess we'll have to go into camp."

Captain Knapp being an old soldier and a plainsman took direction of affairs. He selected a place to camp on the east side of a popple grove, out of the wind, which grew cold as the night fell. He soon had a bright fire going in a trench, while Rance galloped away to a cabin near by to get some milk. Lincoln dismounted, but kept his horse in hand, in case the cattle should become restless, while Mr. Stewart erected the little tent and got out the bedding.

The scene filled Lincoln's heart with emotions and vaguely defined splendid pictures, which he could not utter. It was all so grand and true and primeval to him. He felt like singing — like chanting a great poem, but he only squatted on the ground and stared at the flaming fire.

The meal was eaten hunter-fashion, and its rudeness

was a merit. Home seemed very far away, and the prairie very wide and wild, as night fell. Owen snuggled close to his father's knee, listening in silence to Captain Knapp's stories of " the service." That was his way of alluding to his term of enlistment as a soldier in the Civil War. Rance and Lincoln were out keeping the herd close to the camp, with orders to stay with them till they began to lie down.

It was all very mysterious and solemn out there. Ducks were gabbling in the pools — frogs seemed singing out of the ground everywhere. Flights of prairie pigeons went by, with a whistling sound. The twitter of sparrows, the lonely piping of the plover, and the ceaseless boom and squawk of the prairie chickens, filled the air. Once a wolf barked from a ridge, and Rance said " Hark ! " in the tone of one who fears to be heard.

At last the cattle, tired and well filled, began to drop down on the sod, uttering loud sighs of contentment, and the boys returned to the camp fire, which beckoned from afar, like the signal fires of the Indians, in the novels the boys had read.

As they drew near, Captain Knapp said : " Leave the saddles on, boys, and put your bridles where you can find them. We may need to rout you out, any time."

This pleased the boys, also ; for they laid down before the fire, feeling like young soldiers doing picket duty. As a matter of fact, they were tired and needed a good bed, but would not complain.

Mr. Stewart and Owen, with the other boys, drove away to a neighboring house, leaving Captain Knapp and

Lincoln and Rance at the camp. And after an hour of talk around the fire, they all crawled into the little tent and slept soundly till sunrise. They rose stiff and lame from their hard beds, and Lincoln rode forth to turn the herd back toward the west, while Rance helped about the breakfast.

Lincoln considered himself a well-seasoned cowboy, as he galloped around the herd, and headed them back toward the camp. Breakfast was soon ready, and once more they took up their line of march toward the west. As they moved they passed another thin line of settlement, and came at last to the edge of a superb range, several miles in extent, and comparatively unspotted with cattle.

"Here's the pasture," said Captain Knapp.

It was a beautiful place. A great stretch of rolling prairie, with small ponds scattered about. It had beautiful stretches of upland, also, and Lincoln's imagination turned the cattle into bison, and his own party into redmen, and so felt the bigness and poetry of the scene.

Again they camped, and Captain Knapp selected their permanent camping-ground, and laid out a corral, into which the cattle were to be driven at night. Arrangements were made with the nearest settler to board the boys, and night fell with all arrangements made, except the building of the corral. That night only deepened the wonder and wild joy of the task.

The next morning, as they watched the men climb into the wagon, the cowboys began to realize that they were now to be actually responsible herders. Captain Knapp said : —

"Now, Rance, be careful. Put the cattle into the corral every night for a week; after that, if they are quiet, you won't need to. Watch 'em till they fill up, and then go to bed. But if it threatens rain, or if the flies are bad, you'd better bring 'em in. Good-by — take care o' yourselves."

"Look out for Sau-

gas," said Mr. Stewart.

"Go to your meals regular," was Mr. Jennings's jocose parting word.

As the wagon passed over a swell, out of sight, Milton cocked his head on one side and said, "Well, boys, we're in for it."

"I guess we weigh a hundred and enough," replied Lincoln.

The first thing necessary was to get the lay of the

land, so they galloped away to a swell, which ran against the sky to the west; from there they could see a large blue line of timber, and houses thickening to a settlement. To the north, the land seemed open and comparatively free of tillage — to the south, farms could be seen.

Below them, to the west, was a big drove of colts, and Rance said, —

"Milton, you watch the cattle, while Link and I go down and look at that herd of horses."

"All right," said Milton. "Don't be gone long."

There was mischief in Rance's eyes as he rode gently down toward the herd, which had finished its morning feeding and was standing almost motionless on the prairie. Some were feeding, others stood gnawing each other's withers in friendly civility, some were in a close knot to keep away from the flies, stamping uneasily or jostling together. Others, still, were lying flat on their sides, or rolling in a dusty spot. They were a very excellent grade of horses.

"I wonder which is the leader," said Lincoln.

"That black mare," replied Rance. "See her eyes. She's ready to stampede."

Gathering the reins well in hand, he rode slowly up to the herd. The colts and young stallions, never handled by man, approached with insolent curiosity. They had not the craft of the Morgan mare, who knew all too well what it meant to fall into the hands of men.

Lincoln's "Rob" began to breathe heavily, and to

dance in sidewise motion, as the restless ones began to swerve and circle around each other.

Rance raised a whoop. The black whirled on her feet agile as a cat, and away they all went, with thunder of hoofs, and bugling from wide-blown nostrils. The clumsy colts were transformed into something swift and splendid. Their lifted heads and streaming manes dignified and gave majesty, as they moved off awkwardly but swiftly, looking back at their pursuers with peculiar, insulting, cunning waving of the head from side to side, — the challenge of the horse, — their tails flung out like banners.

But Rance was a light weight, and his horse once the proud leader of a similar herd. He soon outstripped all but the savage little black mare, who was running easily. Side by side the two horses moved as if in harness, but Rance's Ladrone pulled hard at the bit, showing that he was capable of more speed. Lincoln was close behind. The herd dropped away and was lost. Rance, lifting his short-handled whip, and swirling the long lash round his head, brought it down across the mare's back, yelling like a Sioux.

The mare seemed to flatten out like a wolf, as she let out the last link of her speed. Lincoln could see the veins come out on her neck, and could hear the roaring breath of his own " Rob Roy." The muscles along the spine and over the hips of the mare heaved and swelled, as Rance again raised the whip in the air, and brought it down along the mare's glossy side. She did not respond. She had reached the limit of her stride.

To face page 304

Suddenly changing the pressure of his knees, the exultant lad let the rein fall, and leaning forward shouted into the ear of his roan, whose head, hitherto held high, straightened and seemed to reach beyond the flying mare — she fell behind and wheeled — she was beaten! And Lincoln joined in the exultant whoop of his hero.

But while the boys were glad to turn and recover their breath, the tireless mare lead the drove in wide evolutions, wheeling and charging, trotting and galloping, always on the outside track, as if to show that while Ladrone could beat her on a short run, she was fresh and strong while he was winded. The boys returned to Milton, who had watched the race from the ridge.

x

Such movements as this, common with colts, did not occur among the cattle. They never moved, except for a purpose. They did not seem to feel the same need nor to take the same joy in exercise. But they had their own tremendous dramas, for all that. They were almost incessantly battling among themselves, steer against steer, and herd against herd. In this the boys took immense delight. In comparison with the struggle of great steers, the cock-fighting in which they gloried in early spring became of small account. It was as if lions warred, when two herds met.

The boys understood the voices and gestures of cattle quite as well as those of roosters, and each had one particular animal in whose skill and prowess he had betting confidence, and during the long, monotonous days herds were often driven into contact. War always resulted, for these cattle were not meek " polled Angus " or Jerseys, but great rangy, piebald creatures with keen and cruel horns, to whom battle was as instinctive as in a wildcat.

As the boys returned to Milton, he said : —

" Say, boys, we'll have a dandy fight one o' these days. See them cattle ? "

Sure enough. Slowly rising from a ravine was a big herd of cattle, attended by a single horseman.

" Boys, you stay here," said Lincoln, " and I'll go over an' see that feller."

As he galloped up to the herd, he discovered the herder to be a boy a little younger than himself, a very blond boy, with a keen, shrewd face.

" Hello, where'd you come from ? " he asked.

" Cedar County.   Where do you live ? "

" 'Bout four miles west o' here.   What's your name ? "

" Lincoln Stewart.   What's yours ? "

" Cecil Johnson.   Say, you want to look out for our old bull; he's roamin' round somewhere.   He's a terrible fighter."

" What if he is ?   If he comes round our herd, old Spot'll 'tend to him."

" Mebbe he will and mebbe he won't.   Old Brin killed a steer last Sunday.   You want to keep on your horse when he comes round."

" We ain't afraid, but you want 'o head your herd south, o' there'll be war."

" I guess our cattle can take care o' their selves."

This was virtually a declaration of war, and when Lincoln reported to Rance and Milton, Rance ominously said, " Let 'em come; we're here first."

They were all deeply excited at the prospect of seeing the two strange herds come together.   No such battle had ever before been possible, and Milton said several times during the middle of the day, —

" Let's kinder aige 'em along toward each other, and have it over an' done with."

But Lincoln opposed this.   " Oh, gosh, no !   If we did, an' some of 'em got killed, we'd catch lightnin'; but if they come together themselves, we're not to blame."

The herds fed quietly on opposite sides of a timbered ridge, till about three o'clock, when a low, deep, sullen, far-off roaring was heard.

"That's the brindle bull. He's comin' this way, too," said Lincoln, who could see in imagination the solitary beast, pacing slowly along, uttering regular muttering growls, as if half-asleep, and yet angry.

Rance twisted his lip into a queer smile. "Well, let him come. Old Spot will meet him."

Old Spot was a big tiger-bodied beast, half Durham and half Texan ; a wild, swift, insolent, and savage steer, with keen, wide-spreading horns. He had whipped every animal on Sun Prairie, and considered himself the necessary guard of the flock. He was quarrelsome among the members of the flock, a danger to horses, and a menace to the boys, though they kept him half in awe by occasional severe hidings. He heard the distant sound, and lifting his head, listened, critically, while the boys quivered with delight.

Soon the solitary warrior topped the ridge, and looking over the prairie to the west, challenged the world. He tore at the sod with his flat, sharp horns, and threw showers of dust and pieces of sod high in the air, and threatened and exulted in his strength.

Then Old Spot commenced to brag in his turn. Drawing a little out of the herd, he, too, began to show what he could do with hoofs and horns, while the boys, wild with interest, cut in behind and urged him gently on.

It was worth while to see these resolute and defiant animals approach each other, challenging, studying each other, seeking battle of their own free will. With heads held low and rigid as oak, with tongues lolling from their red mouths, while the skin wrinkled on their curved and swollen necks, like the corrugations of a shield, they edged in sidelong caution, foot by foot, toward a common centre. They came on like skilled boxers, snuffing, uttering short and boastful roarings, their eyes protruding, their tails waving high, until, with sudden crash of skull and horns, they met in deadly grapple.

A moment's silence took place, as they measured strength, pushing and straining with sudden relaxations and twisting throats, impatient to secure advantages. The clash of their shaken, interlocked horns, their deep breathing, the terrible glare of their bloodshot eyes, became each moment more terrible. The sweat streamed from their heaving sides, their great hoofs clutched and tore the sod. The boys, tense with excitement, kept the herds away, and waited, almost breathlessly, the issue. At last Brindle, getting the upper hold, pressed the spotted steer's head to the ground, nearly shutting off his breath. Lincoln, who was betting on the bull, raised a cheer, but the steer was not defeated. From his great nostrils he blew the bloody foam, and gathered himself for one last desperate effort; with a sudden jerk he ran one long horn under the bull's neck, and with a mighty surge, rose under him, flinging him aside, and literally running away with him.

The Sun Prairie boys cheered, but the owner of the bull, who had joined them, calmly said, "Old Brin is still on deck; don't you forget it."

Once beaten is always beaten, as a rule, with a steer or cow. They seldom dispute the outcome of a first encounter, no matter how old or weak the victor becomes, but with the bull it is a different matter. A young bull will return to the battle twice, and even a third time. The brindle fled as long as he saw no chance to recover, but when the big steer paused, he turned, and the battle went on again. The two herds became aware of the struggle, and drew near, snuffing and pawing, circling restlessly, threatening to interfere, but the boys held them away with sudden dashes toward them, with their whips in hand.

Never had such a battle taken place on the prairie. Lincoln, skilled in the sign language of animals, understood that this was a fight to a finish, and a sort of awe fell on him. The brindle was heavier, but the steer had keener horns, and was quicker on his feet. His tiger-like body bent almost double under the bull's mighty rushes, but out-sprang again, like a splendid sword blade. Both were sensibly weaker at the end of ten minutes, but their ferocity continued unabated. They were fighting in silence now, wasting no breath in boasting.

Suddenly, with a dexterous fling, the steer tossed the bull aside, and followed with a swift rush for his heart, with his keen right horn. Out burst a thin stream of blood, and the boys looked at each other in alarm.

" He's killed him," said Milton. " Old Spot's killed him."

" Not much he hasn't," replied Cecil. " A bull never gives up. He's just beginning to get mad."

Whipping into line, the brindle again met his antagonist, and with another mad rush pinned Spot to the ground, as before, but his horns were too short to hold him. Again the steer rose.

The battle-ground shifted, the boys following, their muscles aching with the strain. At this moment arose a new sound, a wild and savage roar, a long-drawn, powerful, raucous note, ending in a singular upward squealing inflection, which was instantly followed by other similar outcries. The boys, pale with fear, turned to look. A big, line-back-steer stood above the pool of fresh blood, and with nose held to the ground, with open mouth and protruding tongue, was calling for vengeance. The herds, hitherto merely restless, woke to fury. They flung themselves upon that calling sentinel. From a herd of largely feeding, stupidly sleeping domestic animals, they woke to the fury of their mighty ancestors. They had the action of bison — the voices of lions.

In an instant the two gladiators were hidden by a swarm of bawling, rushing, crowding cattle, from which the herders fled in terror. Out of the mass of dusty, sweaty, bloody beasts, waving tails fluttered, and up-flung dust and sod arose; while above the mutter and roar and trample that thrilling, hair-uplifting, bawling roar, heard only when roused by the scent of blood, was emitted by old and young. It seemed as if the herds would annihilate each other, and the boys were pale with apprehension and a sense of guilt. Nothing could be done but wait. "They'll kill each other. There won't be a yearling left," said Lincoln.

For nearly thirty minutes the herds fought, then panting, wet with sweat, and covered with grass and dust, the two herds wore apart, and the boys, gaining courage, darted in and forced them in opposite directions. The brindle bull was then discovered still fighting, but weak and bloody. He had become separated from his chief antagonist. As his herd moved off, he sullenly, slowly followed, scorning to be hurried, and the boys called it a " draw game," and declared all bets off, glad to find that no dead animals remained on the field of battle.

As night drew on, the boys began to realize that they were alone with a restless herd. It was two miles to the shanty where they were to get their meals, and as Milton and Lincoln galloped away, leaving Rance to keep an eye on the cattle, Lincoln said, " I hope it won't rain to-night."

" I'm a little nervous myself."

They were very critical of the food at Mrs. Anderson's table. The butter didn't suit them, and the bread was sour. They returned to Rance in gloomy spirits. While he went to supper, they rounded up the cattle, and held them near the corral till he came back to help force the reluctant beasts in.

As they unsaddled their horses and picketed them out, the sky looked gray and lowering.

" It would be just our luck to have a three-days soaker," said Rance.

Just as they were going to sleep, a wolf set up a clamor, and a thrill of fear shot through Lincoln's heart. He knew the wolf was harmless, but in his voice was the loneliness and mystery of night, and the boy shivered. The cattle stirred uneasily, and the horses snorted; but Rance, who was the strong man of the party, rose and spoke to them and they became quiet.

The rain did not come, and they found the cattle safe when they awoke next morning, but their bones were sore on account of their hard beds, and it was a long way to breakfast and a mighty poor breakfast when they sat down to it. Herding seemed to have lost something of its glamour. However, as the sun rose and the blood of youth began to warm up, the charm of the wild life came back again.

The hard beds they soon got used to, but the bad bread was a trial which each day made more grievous. They were all accustomed to good cooking. Their food was monotonous, but it was always tastily prepared. Milton gave in first. "I'm going home to get a square meal," he said, as he swung into the saddle. Lincoln was homesick, too, but dared not show it in the presence of his commander.

Milton came back a week later with Owen, who brought word that Lincoln was wanted to work in the corn-field.

This laconic message brought back all the charm of the wild, free life on the prairie, which was growing more beautiful each day, and Lincoln rode away homeward joylessly. He knew all too well what it meant to run a wheeled plough through the dust and heat of a midsummer day.

To make matters worse, he was obliged to turn Rob Roy over to Owen and ride a plough-horse on the homeward journey. But it seemed good to get home, to get a good meal once more, and to hear the familiar voices. He had been three weeks with the herd, and this was a prodigious long time to an imaginative boy. It was good to sleep in a bed again without a hair's-weight of responsibility, with no thought of the darkness outside or the rising clouds in the west. Shingles had their uses, after all.

MASSASAUGA

A COLD, coiled line of mottled lead,
He wakes where grazing cattle tread
And lifts a fanged and spiteful head.
His touch is deadly, and his eyes
Are hot with hatred and surprise.
Death waits and watches where he lies.

His hate is turned toward everything;
He is the undisputed king
Of every path and meadow spring.
His venomed head is poised to smite
All passing feet — light
Is not swifter than his bite.

His touch is deadly, and his eyes
Are hot with hatred and surprise.
Death waits and watches where he lies.

CHAPTER XXI

THE TERROR OF THE RATTLESNAKE

THIS new pasture ground was filled with Massasaugas. Hardly a day passed that the boys did not kill one or more with their whips, and several of the cattle were badly bitten during the first week. The boys were heedful where they set their feet, and never lay down in the grass without a glance at the ground around them. They seemed to know almost by instinct the kind of herbage in which the reptiles were likely to be found.

Tales of their deadly fangs were not so common as one might suppose, but one or two had made a profound impression upon Lincoln. One was the minute account of a boy who had been bitten while out after the cows and who had run all the way home, heating his blood to boiling-point, and diffusing the virus through every vein. Before the doctor could be brought, the wounded one was delirious with pain and fear, and died as the sun went down.

Whiskey was supposed to be a sure cure if the victim could be made drunk at once, and there were a great many jokes current among the men about " an ounce of prevention," etc. Each accused the other of taking a drink every time a locust rattled, but it always seemed a grisly subject for joke to Lincoln, especially after Doudney's nephew, Will, died of a bite. He was riding home with his uncle one Saturday night, when they overtook a big " Sauga " crossing the road.

" Wait, see me snap his head off," said Will, leaping from the wagon.

" Don't do it. Let him alone, you fool," cried Doudney.

The man had been drinking and was reckless. " Oh! I've done it dozens of times," he called back, as he approached the serpent, which coiled and faced his enemy, ready for war.

The reckless young man waved his hat before the snake, and as he uncoiled and started to run, snatched him up, but flung him to the earth with a curse of pain and rage. The snake had sunk his fangs deep into his hand, between the forefinger and the thumb.

With snarling fury, the frenzied man flung himself on the snake, and literally tore him to pieces with his hands. He foamed at the mouth as he cursed: " Bite, will ye! God damn you, bite me! I'll show you." He ended by grinding the snake under his heel.

Doudney sprang out of the wagon, and rushing up to him, called out : —

" Stop, you fool. You'll die in thirty minutes if you keep that up. Keep quiet. Give me your arm."

He bared the bitten arm, and put a tourniquet about it, and opening his whiskey flask said, " Drink this, every drop of it, or you're a dead man."

The young man began to realize what he had done, and with a face made gray with fear, turned to Doudney and gasped : —

"I can't. Get me to a doctor, quick. I'm going to die."

"Drink! That'll keep you up till we can reach help."

The man was a coward, and the reaction was almost instantaneous. He was so weak he could hardly return to the wagon. Hastening his horses into a run, Doudney turned to the nearest house, and there put his nephew to bed and sent for the doctor. The whiskey did not avail. He died before the doctor arrived.

These two cases were known to all the boys in Sun Prairie, and they had been instructed not merely how to avoid the snake, but what to do in case they were bitten. Though Lincoln had no fear of them, they awed him. They appealed to his imagination. Often when he found them on the prairie (the horses always found them first — they seemed to smell them) he dismounted, and if the place were open, studied the fearsome creatures. There was dignity in their slow movement. They were not to be hurried, and there was power in the poise of their flat, triangular heads, and deep meaning in their jewel-bright eyes, and death was in the flicker of each forked, black tongue.

They seemed to say: "Let me alone, and I'm harmless. Touch me, and I kill."

So long as he could see them, Lincoln had no fear; but when they were hid in the deep grass, or when their rattle sounded from a tangle of weeds, his heart grew cold with the sense of being in the presence of death's ambuscade. Somewhere that poised head waited. In the shadow that mottled coil was slowly sliding.

Often, as the herd was feeding quietly through a meadow, a cow or a colt would suddenly leap aside in terror of some unseen form, and the boys knew the cold gray body of a "Sauga" had blocked the way. By riding carefully about the spot in a circle, they often found him curled and singing, and cut him to pieces with their whips, eager to destroy him before he could escape. These encounters always left them a little excited, and at night Lincoln sometimes dreamed of them, especially of those which escaped into the weeds.

As a matter of fact their habits and habitations were so well known, and so few cases of poisoning were authenticated, that no one paid very much heed to tales of horror — the case of Doudney's nephew was questioned by some, who said, "He had heart disease, anyway. He wouldn't have died if he had been a well man."

One hot June day, three boys came over the ridge with tin buckets in their hands, seeking strawberries. They were all barefoot and very noisy. They set to work in the edge of a patch of hazel, where the berries were especially large and fine.

Rance was lying on his back under a popple tree, resting, while Lincoln, sitting slaunch-wise in his saddle, was watching the movement of the herd.

Suddenly a cry of mortal terror broke from one of the berry-pickers. There was an instant pause, and then scream after scream in rapid succession, each moment weaker, till they died away in a whimper, like the cries of a wounded dog.

Rance leaped to his feet, just in time to see the other boys scatter wildly, calling frenziedly : —

"Rattlesnake ! Rattlesnake ! "

Rance dug his heels into his horse, and was instantly away, Lincoln following at once.

As he rode up, Rance saw a boy of about twelve years of age sitting on the ground with his bare foot in his hands, his face ghastly, his eyes stupid with fear, his lips dry and twitching, his voice sunk to a gasping moan. The snake was gone.

Leaping down, Rance examined the foot. On the instep were four small wounds, from which blood and a light green foam issued. The width of the jaw of the snake was indicated in the distance between the punctures. The reptile was large, and had bitten the boy twice.

"Shut up ! " said Rance. "Keep still. Crying only makes it worse. Link, give me a strap, quick," he called, as Lincoln came galloping up.

As he held the boy's ankle tightly gripped in both his hands, Rance thought rapidly. It was three miles to the nearest house, and eight miles to the nearest town. The boy could not be moved eight miles, and he would die before help could be brought, unless the poison could be stayed in its course through the blood. He took the strap, which Lincoln loosened from his bridle, and winding it round just below the knee, twisted it with a jack-knife till the lad cried out in pain.

"Set it up tight," said Lincoln. "It's the only chance."

"Say, you remember the story about putting the fellow in the mud?" Lincoln nodded.

"Well, you go for help. I'm going to put the boy into that puddle and hold him there. Here, you fellers. Come here." The other two boys came cautiously up. "Git, Link. Ride like hell!"

Lincoln leaped to the saddle, and was off before Rance had time to speak a second time.

"Come here!" commanded Rance. "What you 'fraid of? Grab a hold here. The snake is gone. We've got to get this boy into that puddle. One of you hold my horse. You take hold here."

Under his vigorous commands the larger of the two boys took hold under the stricken lad's shoulders, and they partially carried and partially dragged him to the edge of the little pool. With swift and resolute action, Rance scooped out a hollow in the mud and forced the boy's leg down into it, and began heaping the cool, ill-smelling muck over him.

"Lie still, now. I won't drown you. You'll die if you don't do as I say. Dig, dig!" he shouted to the other lad. "Sink him down. There, don't that feel good? That cool mud will draw the poison out. One o' you go cut a big hazel bush. I'm going to keep the 'turnkey' on him."

The touch of the cool mud, as well as Rance's encouraging words, quieted the boy, and he lay gasping pitifully, his big set and staring eyes like some poor dumb animal waiting the death stroke of his captors. The tourniquet made him cry out again, but Rance held it with all his force.

Y

"It won't do no good if it don't hurt," he said.

For half an hour he held this ligature in the mud and water, while the others were sinking their comrade deeper in the muck. Sitting so, Rance had a full realization of the desolating power which lay in the little, white, needle-pointed curved fangs of the Massasauga.

"He was in the path. I stepped on him," the boy gasped in answer to a question, and Rance could see the sullen reptile striking once, and shaking loose with a sinister curve of his neck, to strike again, and then, as if knowing his poison sacks were empty, slipping away into cover, leaving his victim to writhe and die.

Rance's muscles ached with the strain, but he held on grimly, changing hands as he grew numb. It seemed an hour before a man came galloping over the ridge. It was Anderson, the Norwegian, with whom they boarded.

"Hello!" he said, as he galloped up. "Hae baen bit by snake?"

"That's what," replied Rance. "Come here and take hold of this turnkey. I'm just about used up."

"Ae got al-co-hol. Yimmy, haer, yo' take good swig."

The boy took a mouthful of the burning stuff, but could not swallow it. He spit it out with a cry: "I can't. I can't!"

"Batter yo' try," persisted Anderson. "Hae baen gude."

"Why didn't you bring some water to mix with it?" said Rance. "Go get some quick. He can't drink that stuff."

By the time the alcohol was diluted, the boy was crazy with the pain of his wound and the cramp of his position in the water, and refused to drink.

Anderson was for forcing it down his throat, but Rance stopped him.

The boys set up a shout. " Here comes somebody."

Lincoln, followed by a wagon driven furiously, topped the swell. The driver was swinging the reins, beating the horses to still more furious pace. Link came floating down the ridge, sitting his horse gracefully, making the excitement seem only a part of a merry race.

As the wagon drew near, a shrill voice was heard in weeping. Two men were holding a woman from leaping out of the wagon. It was the mother of the boy crazed with maternal fear.

Lincoln called out : " He's all right. Don't worry."

" You hear. He's alive. Be quiet now," said one of the men, as he leaped to the ground. " Now come down."

In a moment the three men and the frenzied mother encircled the boy.

The father of the boy excitedly said : " What's he in the mud for ? Take him out."

"That's all right. Leave him alone," put in one of the other men, as he relieved Rance. " Good idea."

The mother, kneeling by the boy's head, said over and over, " Do you know me, Freddie ? "

Rance rose and fairly staggered to his horse. His responsibility ended when the parents came. He watched them while they dragged the boy out of the mud and examined his swollen leg. In truth, it all began to look like a foolish piece of business even to him. He looked round him at the horses nibbling grass, at the cattle peacefully grazing, at the shadow-dappled prairie, and it all seemed a mistake, a dream. It could not be that the boy was in the throes of dissolution. It could not be that death lurked in the sun-bright grass and the rustling hazel bushes. For a moment he felt hot with shame for having done such a foolish thing. But the moaning of the stricken boy helped him to remember the wound, the oozing froth, and the terror of the snake.

The mother climbed into the wagon, the boy was laid in her lap, the father, holding the ligature, knelt beside him, and so they drove away, leaving Rance and Lincoln standing beside the pool with the Norwegian.

"Well — bote tem to eat; ae tank ae go home. Batter yo go home too, Link."

"As soon as we kill the snake," replied Rance.

Beginning in a narrow circle, the boys rode slowly round and round, in a constantly widening course; but the bush was too thick; the snake had crawled away deep in the tangle to wait till his fangs should once more be charged with venom.

"They didn't thank you for putting that boy in the mud, did they?" remarked Lincoln, as they were riding away to supper. "It got his clothes dirty."

Rance did not reply. He felt foolish and a little hurt, also. Suppose it was not the very best thing to do, he deserved a good word for his intentions, anyway.

The next morning one of the men who had helped to carry the boy came riding over the prairie. As he drew near, he looked at Rance closely.

" Are you the chap that put Fred into the mud ? "

Rance hotly replied : " Yes, I am. What y' goin' to do about it ? "

" You needn't get huffy. I just came over to say that my sister, Mrs. Pease, wants to see you. The doctor says you saved the boy's life, and she'd kind o' like to do for you some way."

Rance was suspicious and angry. " Well, you go back and let me alone. The next time your darn boy gets bit, he can go to hell. I did the best I could, and I've been devilled about it ever since, and I'm sick of it. Think I'm a doctor out here herdin' cattle for my health ? " He turned his horse and galloped off, leaving the stranger stupefied.

" I didn't mean to devil him," he said to Lincoln, who was also turning away in sympathy. " The doctor said the boy done the best thing that could a' been done. Mrs. Pease did send me over here to get the boy."

" Well," said Lincoln, " you let him alone. He don't want a woman slobbering over him. He did the best he knew how, and that's all anybody can do."

When Rance and Lincoln went home to help harvest, the wounded boy had not yet risen from his bed. It was reported that his leg was spotted " just like a snake, and swelled so you can't see where his knee is." They never saw the boy or his mother again.

As the autumn came on, the herding became serious

business. Into beautiful gold and purple October, great slashes of gray rain swept. There were days when the wind was northeast and the drizzle steady and pitiless. It was damp and gloomy in the trail, the ground was soggy under foot. The bridles and saddles were slippery and the landscape sombre. On such days hours stretched out like rubber, and night came cheerlessly. The boys, unkempt and miserable, hovered around a small camp-fire, or sat by the kitchen stove in Anderson's shanty, thinking how nice it would seem to be at home.

These rains ended each time in weather partly clear and progressively colder. The sumach blazed forth in beauty. The popple trees dropped their leaves and stood bare in the whistling winds. The hazel thickets were also bare and brown, and on the ground the nuts lay thickly strewn. The barbs of the wild oats, twisted and harsh, fell to the earth, and the stalks of the crow's-foot stood slenderly upholding a frayed sprangle of empty seed-cells. The gophers were busy storing nuts and seeds, the badgers, heavy with fat, were seen waddling along the ridges on warm days, or sitting meditatively beside their dens, as if taking their last view of the landscape they loved.

The blackbirds, assembling in enormous flocks, loaded down the branches of the aspen groves, and chattered of the joys past as well as of the sunny days to come. Prairie pigeons whistled by on mysterious imperative errands, curving over the hills like an aerial serpent. The prairie chickens assembled in large flocks also, the young no longer distinguishable from their elders. The grasshoppers and crickets sang only during the warm hours of the day — and long intervals of silence fell upon the plain, when only the piping of the wind in the weeds could be heard. One by one all the hardy autumn plants ripened or were cut down by the frost until only stern grays and drabs and sombre yellows and browns remained upon the landscape.

There was something fine and prophetic in these days, for all that. The moaning of the wind, the hurry of the clouds, the blown birds hastening south, the harsh sky filled with torn gray clouds, forecasting winter, made the hearts of the herd-boys leap, for they anticipated release, and foretasted the pleasures of their winter games.

At last the order for return march came, and the four inseparable boys started eastward with the cattle fat and full of mischief. The beeves were cut out and sold at Taylor City, and the young cattle hurried homeward.

Captain Knapp sold all his young stock, and as no one else cared to engage the herd, neither Rance nor Lincoln returned to the range. Mr. Stewart set aside part of the farm for pasture, and the boys put away their cattle-whips and hung up their pouches. Each year the output of butter increased and the production of beef diminished. On every side the tame was driving out the wild. The sickle soon swept every acre of meadow, and the reign of the Massasauga was ended.

IN THE DAYS WHEN THE CATTLE RAN

IT was worth the while of a boy to live
In the days when the prairie lay wide to the herds,
When the sod had a hundred joys to give
And the wind had a thousand words.
        It was well to be led
        Where the wild horses fed
As free as the swarming birds.

Not yet had the plough and the sickle swept
The lily from meadow, the roses from hill,
Not yet had the horses been haltered and kept
In stalls and sties at a master's will.
        With eyes wild-blazing,
        Or drowsily grazing,
They wandered untouched by the thill.

And the boy! With torn hat flaring,
With sturdy red legs which the thick brambles tore,
As wild as the colts, he went faring and sharing
The grasses and fruits which the brown soil bore.
        Treading softly for fear
        Of the snake ever near,
Unawed by the lightning or black tempest's roar.

But out on the prairie the ploughs crept together,
The meadow turned black at stroke of the share,

The shaggy colts yielded to clutch of the tether,
The red lilies died, and the vines ceased to bear.
   And nothing was left to the boys
   But the dim remembrance of joys
   When the swift cattle ran,
   Unhindered of man,
And their herders were free as the clouds in the air.

CHAPTER XXII

OWEN RIDES AT THE COUNTY FAIR

THE one break in the monotony of the farm's fall work was the County Fair, which usually came about the 20th of September. Toward this, Lincoln and his mates looked longingly. By this time they were inexpressibly weary of the ploughing and cattle-tending, and longed for a visit to the town. There were always three days of the Fair, but only two were of any amusement to the boys. The first day was always taken up in preparation, getting the stock housed and the like; the fun came on the last day with the races, though Lincoln was always mildly interested in the speech-making on the second day.

The older boys planned to take their sweethearts, just as on the Fourth of July, and the wives and mothers baked up dozens of biscuits, and baked chicken, and made pies and cake for dinner on the grounds. The country was new, and the show was not great, but it called the people together, and that was something. So most of the threshing-machines fell silent for a single day, the ploughs rested in the furrow, and the men put on clean shirts. The women, however, kept on working up to the very hour of starting for the grounds. Their work was never done. After getting everything and everybody else ready they took scant time to get themselves ready — all the others clamoring to be off. The weather was usually clear and dry, cool of a morning, becoming hot and windless at noon, but on this particular day it was cold and cloudy, making overcoats necessary at the start.

The four inseparable boys rode away together, their horses shining with the extra brushing they had endured. Rance was mounted on "Ivanhoe," Lincoln rode "Rob Roy," Milton "Mark," while Owen rode a four year old colt which he called "Toot," for some curious reason, while the rest of the family generally spoke of her as "Kitty." She was almost pure blood Morgan, a bright bay, very intelligent, and for a short dash very swift. Owen was entered for "The Boys' Riding Contest"; the other three boys were all too old to come in, but were going down with him as body-guard. It was a goodly land to look at; trim stacks of wheat stood four and four about the fields. The corn was heavy with ears, and the sound of the threshing-machine came into hearing each mile or two. Only the homes showed poverty.

The boys did not stop in town — merely rode through the street and on down toward the Fair Grounds. At the gate, where two very important keepers stood at guard, the boys halted, and Rance, after collecting quarters from his fellows, bought the four tickets; the keepers fell back appeased, and the boys rode in, their fine horses causing people to remark, "There are some boys for the races, I guess."

The boys were all very proud of these remarks, and galloped around the track to show off their horses and to get the lay of the land.

"We mustn't wind our nags," said Rance, after making the circuit once or twice. "Let's tie up."

While the people were pouring in at the gates, the boys rode slowly round the grounds to see what was displayed; on past fat sheep and blooded stallions and prize cows and Poland-China pigs; on past new-fangled sulky ploughs, "Vibrator" threshing-machines, and so on. The stock didn't interest them so much as the whirligig and the candy-puller, and the man who twisted copper wire into "Mamie" and "Arthur" for "the small sum of twenty-five cents, or a quarter of a dollar."

One or two enormous Norman horses, being a new importation, commanded their attention, and they joined the crowd around them and listened to the comments with interest; but the crowd, after all, was the wonder. The swarming of so many people, all strangers, was sufficient, of its own motion, to keep the open-eyed boys busy. They were there, not to see hogs and cattle, but the strange fakirs and the curious machines, and the alien industries. A deft and glib seller of collar-buttons and lamp-chimney wipers enthralled them, and a girl, playing a piano in "Horticultural Hall," entranced them; at least, she so appealed to Lincoln and to Rance — her playing had the vim and steady clatter of a barrel piano, but it stood for music in absence of anything better.

Hitching their horses to the family wagons, which had by this time arrived, the boys wandered about afoot.

Lincoln and Owen had on new suits. The Fair was the time set apart for the one suit they were able to afford each year. Sometimes it was bought on Fair day, but usually a little before, so that the great day should be free for other pleasures. Their suits never fitted, of course, and Owen's was always of the same goods precisely as Lincoln's, differing in size merely. They were of thick woollen goods of strange checks and stripes, the shoddy refuse of city shops which the local dealers bought cheap and sold dear — being good enough for country folks. As they were intended for all the year round, they were naturally uncomfortable in the middle of September and intolerable in July. Even on this windy day, the boys sweated their paper collars into pulp before they concluded to lay off their coats and go about in their shirt-sleeves. As it was one of the few occasions when they could reasonably be dressed up, they were willing to suffer a little martyrdom for pride's sake.

Lincoln's heart was full of bitterness as he saw the town boys go by in well-fitting garments, looking comfortable even while in dressed-up conditions. His hat troubled him also, for it was of a shape entirely unlike anything else on the grounds. The other boys were almost all wearing a hat with a tall crown and a narrow rim, but his hat, and Owen's as well, was a flat-crowned structure, heavy and thick, and to make matters worse, it was too large, and Owen's, especially, came down and rested against his ears.

Another cause of shame to Lincoln was the cut on

his hair.   Up to this time he had never enjoyed a " real
barber cut."   Mr. Stewart generally detailed one of the
hired men to the duty, and the boys were, in very truth,
" shingled."   Both had heavy heads of brown hair, and
after Jim Beane got done with them they had ruffles like
a pineapple, or a girl's nightgown.   Rance and Milton
had long ago rebelled against this kind of torture, and
employed the barber at least twice each year.   Milton
declared on his thirteenth birthday, " No hired man shall
chaw my hair off again, and don't you forget it."

This Fair day marked another great advance in Lincoln's life.   He ate no candy or peanuts, and by his advice
Owen limited himself to " home-made candy " and a
banana, which he allowed Lincoln to taste.   Neither
of them had ever seen one before.   " If you want to
scoop in that saddle, Owen, you keep well," Lincoln
said, every time Owen suggested trying some new drink
or confection.

Rance was bitterly disappointed when he found himself shut out of the contest for the saddle, and was very
glum all the forenoon.   Lincoln shared his disappointment, although he cared very little about his own part
in it.   He believed Rance to be the best rider in the
county, but did not expect to win a prize himself.

One by one they met all their friends from Sun
Prairie and Burr Oak, and once they met " Freckles,"
the town bully, face to face.   He made furious signs of
battle, and dared them to go over to the back fence with
him, to which Owen replied by putting his thumb to his
nose, and waving his fingers like a flag.   " Freckles " was

visibly enraged by this, but as the Sun Prairie boys were in full force, and confident, he withdrew, uttering threats.

Wonderful to say, the boys were able to share in the jolly dinner which their mothers arranged on the grass between the wagons, over on the south side of the grounds. The wagon-seats were taken off to serve as chairs: a snowy-white cloth was spread as neatly as on a table, and the entire Jennings family joined in the feast of cold chicken, jelly, pickles, " riz " biscuits, dried beef, apple pie, cake, and cheese. Lincoln had never felt so well on a holiday, and his spirits rose instead of sinking as the day wore on. Owen was fed with anxious care by his mother. He was even allowed to drink a cup of coffee as a special tonic.

Mr. Stewart declined to take the contest seriously, but Mr. Jennings agreed that some provision should be made for the older boys.

" I'll see the President of the Day," he said, " and see if a special contest can't be arranged to follow the boys' race."

The idea pleased everybody, and spread from lip to lip, till it became a definite announcement.

Meanwhile various unimportant matters, like displaying sheep and cattle, and beets and honey, for prizes, were going on, when Mr. Stewart came back where Lincoln was observing the candy-puller for the twentieth time. He said, " Lincoln, go get the team; I've entered you for the pulling match."

Lincoln's heart suddenly failed him, " Oh, I can't do that before all those people."

"Yes, you can. Go hitch up."

As he drove his team through the crowd, with alternate traces unhooked to drag the double tree, Lincoln felt just as he used to feel when rising to recite a piece in school on a holiday. He was queer and sick at his heart, but something nerved him to the trial.

The crowd opened, and he swung the horses to the stone-boat walled in by spectators. Dan and Jule were not large, but they were broad in the chest, and loyal to the centre of each brown eye, and they knew him. He had the opinion that they could pull anything they set their shoulders to, and as he gathered up the reins his eyes cleared. He climbed upon the load. The Judge said : —

"Keep quiet, everybody. All ready, my boy."

Lincoln's voice was calm as he said : "Steady now, Jule. Chk-chk, Dan, steady now." The noble animals settled to the load, obeying every word. Dan was a little in advance, a few inches, with his legs set. "Get down there, Jule," called the boy. The old mare squatted, set her shoulders to the collar, lifting like a trained athlete, and the stone-boat slid half its length. The crowd applauded. "Bully boy !"

"All right," said the Judge, "take 'em off for a minute. Anderson, it's your turn again."

Anderson, a Norwegian, with a fine showy team, hitched on, but could not move it; not because his horses were not strong enough, but because they were nervous and tricky. The audience jeered at him —
"Take 'em off; they're no good."

Lime Gilman came next, and Lincoln lost his exultation as the big fellow winked at him. His team were brown Morgan grades, as responsive to his voice as dogs. They were the lightest of all the teams, but they were beautiful to see as they swung to place. Their harnesses were covered with costly ivory rings, and as they wore no blinders, they eyed their master in love, not fear. The crowd uttered a cheer of genuine admiration as Lime heaved two extra rocks upon the load.

As he took the reins in one hand Lime began uttering a pleasant, bird-like, chirping sound. Slowly, softly, the superbly intelligent creatures squared and squatted together, setting their feet fairly, flatly, and carefully on the sod.

" Dexter, boy ! " said Lime, and at the soft word the load slid nearly a yard.

" Ho ! that'll do, boys," called Lime, and said with a smile, as he turned to Lincoln, " Try again, Link."

" It's yours," shouted the crowd.

" Oh, no it isn't," said Lime. " I know this boy and his team ! "

A big, long-legged gray team took a second trial, but though they tugged furiously, could not move the extra weight. " They're up too high upon legs," said the Judge, critically.

Anderson was out of the contest, so that Lincoln was Lime's only rival. The boy had forgotten all his shyness. He threw off his coat and hat, and said to the Judge, —

" Pile on two more stones."

z

" Good for you, sonny ! " some one said as Lime
threw on one of the big flat limestone slabs. Again
Lincoln swung his faithful team in and hooked the
traces. As he climbed on the load and took the reins
in hand, he was tense with excitement ; he saw only
Lime's pleasant face and his father's anxious smile.

" Stiddy, Dan. Take hold of it ; w-o-oo-p, stiddy ! "
Again they settled to the task, their great muscles rolling, their ears pointing, their eyes quiet. For a few
moments they hung poised —

" *Now, Jule !* " shouted Lincoln, and the mare lifted,
strained to her almost best, but the load did not
move.

" Ho ! " shouted Lincoln, checking them so that they
would not become discouraged.

" Give it up. Take off a stone," cried a friendly
voice.

" Not much," said Lincoln.

Springing from the load, he drew the reins over Jule's
back, and again called on Dan to take his position, and
just as they settled to their work, Lincoln brought his
hand with a sharp slap under Jule's belly.

" *Jule !* "

With a tremendous effort the grand brute lifted the
boat six good inches, and the crowd clapped hands
heartily.

" That's enough. Unhitch," called the Judge.

It was now Lime's turn to swing into place.

" Good boy, Link," he said as he passed.

Once more he swung his horses to the load, but this

time he looped the reins over Dexter's brass-bound harness, and took his place nearer his side.

Chirp, chirp, chirp!

Again the brown team settled into place.

" Easy now, Dexter. Easy, Dave. Now then, boys, all together. *Get down, hoy!*" With the simultaneous action of shadows, the beautiful horses squatted and lifted, guided only by their master's words. For nearly half a minute they held to the work, their necks outthrust, their feet clutching the earth, steady, loyal, bright-eyed, unwavering, pulling every pound that was in them. Such action had never been seen on the Fair Grounds, but they were defeated, — they had not the weight necessary ; the task was too great.

They released their hold only when Lime spoke the word, and the crowd was vociferous with admiration.

" That's what ye might call pullin'."

" Call it a draw, Judge."

" I'm willing," said Lincoln, who had expected the browns to move the load, for he knew Lime's wonderful horsemanship.

Mr. Stewart came forward, " We'll divide the honors, Lime."

And the Judge so decided, while the spectators pressed close around the brown horses, to feel of their sleek coats and to look at their sturdy legs. In looks and character no team on the grounds approached them.

As Lincoln rejoined the boys, they received him with a touch of awe, because of his honorable public exhibition of skill and the prize he had won.

" I knew old Jule would lift it," said Lincoln.　" But Lime's team scared me.　I knew they could pull.　I've seen 'em dig down on a load while Lime lit his pipe."

The ringing of the signal bell broke in upon the talk, and a crier galloped through the grounds shouting, " Get ready for ' the Boys' Contest.' "

" That's you, Owen," said Lincoln.

Owen stripped as for battle.　He could not ride in his lumpy, heavy coat, and his hat was also an incumbrance.　With hands trembling with excitement, Lincoln helped him set the saddle on Kitty, and wipe from her limbs all dust and sweat.　She shone like a red bottle when the youngster clambered to his seat.

" Don't touch her with the whip," said Lincoln.

" Look out for the crowd at the home-stretch," said Rance ; but Owen was as calm as a clam, and rode forth in silence, accompanied by his body-guard.　Kitty danced and flung her head, as though she knew some test of her quality was about to be made.　At the entrance to the track Lincoln and Rance halted, and Owen rode into the track alone, his head bare, his shirt-sleeves gleaming.

Five or six boys, on all kinds of ponies, were already riding aimlessly up and down before the judges' stand.　Four of them were town boys, who wore white-visored caps and well-fitting jackets.　The fifth was a tall, sandy-haired lad in brown overalls and a checked shirt.　He rode a " gauming " sorrel colt, with a bewildering series of gaits, and he was followed up and down the track by a tall, roughly dressed man and a slatternly girl of thirteen or fourteen, who repeated each of the old man's orders.

"HOLD HIM UP A LITTLE!" shouted the father.

"*Hold him up a little,*" repeated the girl.

"LET HIM OUT A GRAIN!"

"*Let him out a grain.*"

"SET UP A LITTLE."

"*Set up a little.*"

This was immensely entertaining to the crowd, but interfered with the race, so the Marshal was forced to come down and order them both from the track. This was a grateful relief to the boy, who was already hot with rebellion.

The bell's clangor called all the boys before the grand stand, and the Judge said : —

"Now, boys, we want you to ride up and down past us, for a few turns. Don't crowd each other, and don't hurry, and do your prettiest."

A single tap of the bell, and the boys were off at a gallop. The town boys, on their fat little ponies, cantered along smoothly, but Kitty, excited by the noise and the people, forced Owen to lay his weight against the bit, which didn't look well. Sandy was all over the track with his colt, pounding up and down like a dollar's worth of tenpenny nails in a wheelbarrow. He could ride, all the same, and his face was resolute and alert.

As they turned to come back, Kitty took the bit in her teeth and went round the other horses with a wild dash, and the swing of Owen's body at this moment betrayed the natural rider; but he was only a bareheaded farmer's son, and the judges were looking at Frank Simpson, the banker's boy, and Ned Baker, Dr. Baker's handsome nephew. Their ponies were accustomed to crowds and to the track and to each other, while everything was strange to Sandy's colt and to fiery little Kitty.

Owen did not see his father and mother, but Lincoln and Rance kept near the entrance, and each time he came to the turn they had a word of encouragement.

As the boys came under the wire the third time, the Judge said : —

"When you turn again, go round the track — and don't race," he said as an afterthought.

At every turn Kitty whirled in ahead as if rounding a herd, swift as a wolf, a bright gleam in her eye, her ears pointing. What all this see-sawing back and forth meant, she could not tell, but she was ready for anything whatever.

The town boys came about in a bunch, with Owen close behind and Sandy over at one side, sawing at his colt's open jaw, while his father yelled instructions over the fence.

"Let him go, son!"

"*Let him go, son*," repeated the girl.

As they passed under the wire, some wag on the stand tapped the bell, and hundreds of voices yelled, —

"Go!"

The boys forgot previous warnings. Plying whip and spur, they swept down the track, all in a bunch, except Sandy, who was a length behind.

"Where's Owen?" asked Rance.

"Wait a minute," replied Lincoln. "He'll show up soon." As he spoke, the white sleeves of Owen's shirt flashed into sight ahead of the crowd. The bay mare was a beautiful sight then. She ran low like a wolf. Her long tail streamed in the air, and her abundant mane, rising in waves, almost hid the boy's face. He no longer leaned ungracefully. Erect and at his ease, he seemed to float on the air, and when at intervals he looked back to see where his rivals were, Lincoln laughed.

"Oh, catch him, will you? Let's see you do it. *Now* where are your fancy riders?"

The slick ponies fell behind, and Sandy, yelling and plying the "bud," came on, the only possible competitor. He gained on Kitty, for Owen had not yet urged her to her best. As he rounded the turn and saw that the colt was gaining, he brought the flat of his hand down on Kitty's shoulder with a shrill whoop, — and the colt gained no more! As he swept under the wire at full speed, the boy had on his face the look of a Cheyenne lad, a look of calm exultation, and his seat in the saddle was that of the born horseman. Lincoln's heart was big with pride.

"He's won it! He's won it sure!"

When the red ribbon was put to Simpson's bridle, a groan went up from hundreds of spectators.

"Aw, no. The other one — the bare-headed boy!"

"Stewart!"

"Sandy!"

A crowd gathered around the Judges, and Mr. Stewart and Mr. Jennings joined it. Talk was plainly in Owen's favor.

"This is favoritism," protested Mr. Jennings. "Anybody can ride those trained town ponies. The decision lies between MacElroy's son and Owen Stewart. Put your slick little gentlemen on those two horses, and see how they will go through."

The crowd grew denser each moment, and Kitty was led through up to the Judges as they stood arguing. Owen did not know what it was all about, except that he had not won the prize.

The Judge argued: "We were not deciding a race. The specifications were 'displaying most grace and skill at horsemanship.'"

"How you going to decide? You can't do it without a change of horses. Owen will ride any horse you bring him. Will your natty little men ride the bay mare and the sorrel colt?"

MacElroy and his daughter, by this time, had fought their way through the crowd.

"This ain't no fair shake. I wouldn't a minded your givin' it to the feller on the bay mare, but them little rockin'-horse ponies — why, a suckin' goose can ride one of them."

"Now this is my opinion," said one of the Judges. "I voted for the first prize to go to Stewart, the second prize to MacElroy, and let 'em change horses and see what they can do."

"That's fair. That's right," said several bystanders.

The third Judge went on : " *But*, I was out-voted. Mine is a minority report, and can't stand."

The Chairman remained firm, notwithstanding all protests, but the second Judge, who was a candidate for election to the position of County Treasurer, became alarmed. He called Beeman aside, and after a moment's talk the Chairman said : —

" Mr. Middleton, having decided to vote with Mr. Scott, we have to announce that the first prize will go as before to Master Simpson, the second to Master Stewart, and the third to Master MacElroy, and this is final."

Returning to his stand, he rang the bell sharply, and again announced the decision, which was cheered in a mild sort of way.

" Clear the track for the Free-for-all running race — best two in three."

Lincoln helped Owen put the fine new bridle on Kitty without joy, for young Simpson was riding about the grounds on the saddle which almost every one said should be Owen's.

Sandy rode up, the white ribbon tied to his sorrel's bridle, a friendly grin on his face.

" I say, your horse can run five or six a minute, can't she ? "

And Owen, who counted the bridle clear gain, and held no malice, said : —

" I was scared one while, when I saw your old Sorrel a-comin'. I'm dry. Le's go have some lemonade. Link, hold our horses."

And they drank, Owen standing treat with all the airs of a successful candidate for senatorial honors.

"Get out your horses for the four-year-old sweep-stakes," shouted the Marshal as he rode down the track. "Bring out your horses."

The boys put down their glasses hastily. "Oh, let's see that," said Owen.

"Let's climb the fence," suggested Rance, indicating the high board fence which enclosed the ground, on whose perilous edge rows of boys were already sitting like blackbirds. From this coign of vantage they could "sass" anybody going, even the Marshal, for at last extremity it was possible to fall off the fence on the outside and escape. Here all the loud-voiced wags were stationed, and their comical phrases called forth hearty laughter from time to time, though they became a nuisance before the races were over. They reached the top of the fence by two convenient knot-holes, which formed toe-holes, and the big fellows then pulled the smaller ones after them.

It was a hard seat, but the race-course was entirely under the eye, and no one grumbled.

The boys were no sooner perched in readiness for the race than the Marshal came riding down the track, shouting. As he drew near, Owen heard his name called.

"Is Owen Stewart here?"

"Yes!" shouted Lincoln, for Owen was too much astonished to reply.

"Here he is," called a dozen voices.

The Marshal rode up : " You're wanted at the Judges' Stand," he said.   " Come along."

" Go ahead," said Lincoln, and as Owen hesitated, he climbed down himself.   " Come on, I'll go with you. It's something more about the prize."

Owen sprang from the fence like a cat, at the thought that perhaps the Judges had reconsidered their verdict, and were going to give him the saddle, after all.

The other boys, seeing Owen going up the track beside the Marshal, also became excited, and a comical craning of necks took place all along the fence.

" Here's your boy," said the Marshal, as he reached the Judges' Stand.

" Come up here, son," called the Judge, and Owen climbed up readily, for he saw his father up there beside the Judge.

A tall and much excited man took him by the shoulders and hustled him before a long-whiskered man, who seemed to be boss of the whole Fair.

" Will this boy answer ? "

The Judge looked Owen over slowly, and finally lifted him by putting his hands under his arms, then he asked his weight of Mr. Stewart.   The answer was satisfactory.

" Now, my boy, you are to ride this man's horse in the race, because his own boy is too light.   Do you think you can handle a race-horse ? "

" Yes, sir," replied Owen, sturdily.

" All right, sir, if his father is willing, I can mount your horse."

As they went down the stairs, Mr. Mills, the owner

of the running horse "Gypsy," said : " You needn't be afraid.   When once she's off, ' Gyp ' is perfectly safe."

" I don't think he's afraid," remarked Mr. Stewart, quietly.   " You tell him what you want him to do, and he'll do it."

" Now there are two horses," Mills explained as he got opportunity.   " The bald-faced sorrel don't cut any figger — but the black, the Ansgor horse, is sure to get away first — for Gypsy is freaky at the wire.   You will get away a couple of lengths behind, but don't worry about that — don't force the mare till you come around the last turn."

At the barn Owen took off his coat and hat while they led out the horse, a beautiful little bay mare, with delicate, slender legs, and a brown eye full of fire.   The saddle was a low racing pad, and as they swung the boy to his seat, the mare began to rear and dance, as if she were a piece of watch-spring.

A thrill of joy and of mastery swept over the boy as he grasped the reins in his strong brown hands.   It was worth while to feel such a horse under him.

" Let down my stirrups," he commanded.   " I can't ride with my knees up there."

They let down his stirrups, and then with Mills holding the excited colt by the bit, he rode down the wire.

Gypsy's peculiarity was that she could be started at the wire only by facing her the other way, and it took both Mills and the hostler to hold her.   At the tap of the bell, each time, the mare reared and whirled like a mad horse, and Mrs. Stewart trembled with fear of her son's life. Lincoln was near her, and said, "Don't worry, mother; he's all right."

Twice a false start was made, and the horses were called back. The third time they were off, the black in the lead, the sorrel next, the bay last. As Gypsy settled smoothly to her work, Owen had time to think of his instructions. Just before him was the black, running swiftly and easily, and he felt that Gypsy could pass him. At the turn he loosened the reins and leaned to the outside, intending to pass, but the jockey on the black pulled in front of him. He then swung the bay to the left to pass on the inside of the track, but again the jockey cut in ahead, and looking back with a vicious smile said, "No, you don't!" It was "Freckles," and the recognition took the resolution out of Owen, and before he could devise a plan to pass they rushed under the wire, Gypsy a length behind.

Mills was much excited and threatened to break the jockey's head, — and asked that he be taken off the track, — but the Judges decided that Gypsy had not been fouled. Mills then filled Owen's ears with advice, but all the boy said was: "He won't do that again. Don't you worry." He was angry, too.

At the second start they got away as before, except the sorrel ran for a long time side by side with Gypsy. The two boys could talk quite easily as the horses ran smoothly, steadily, and the jockey on the sorrel said: —

"Don't let him jockey you. Pass him on the back stretch, when he ain't lookin'."

Owen again loosened the rein, and the bay mare shot by the sorrel and abreast of the black. Again the jockey cut him off, but Owen pulled sharply to the left, intending to pass next the pole. For the first time he struck the mare, and she leaped like a wolf to a position at the flank of the black. Freckles pulled viciously in crowding his horse against the mare, intending to force Owen against the fence and throw him; but the boy held his mare strongly by the right rein, and threw himself over on his saddle with his right knee on the horse's back, uttering a shrill cry as he did so. In first leap the mare was clear of the black, and went sailing down the track, an easy winner — without another stroke of the whip.

He now had a clear idea of his horse's powers, and though he got away last, as before, he put Gypsy to her best and passed the black at once, and taking the pole, he held it without striking a blow or uttering a word, though the black tried twice to pass. The spectators roared with delight, to see the round-faced boy sitting erect, with the reins in his left hand, his shirt-sleeves fluttering, come sweeping down the inside course, the black far behind and laboring hard.

There was something distinctly comic in Owen's way of looking behind him to see where his rival was.

Mills pulled him from the horse in his delight, and put an extra five dollars in his hand. "I'll give you ten dollars to ride Gypsy at Independence," he said.

"All right," said Owen.

But his parents firmly said, " No, this ends it. We don't want him to do any more of this kind of work."

Swiftly the sun fell to the west, and while the dealers and showmen redoubled their outcries in hopes to close out their stocks, the boys began to think of going home. Out along the fences where the men were hitching up the farm-teams, the women stood in groups for a last exchange of greetings. The children, tired, dusty, sticky with candies, pulled at their skirts. The horses, eager to be off, pranced under the tightening reins. The dust rose under their hoofs, whips cracked, good-bys passed from lip to lip, and so, in a continuous stream the farm-wagons passed out of the gate, to diverge like the lines of a spider's web, rolling on in the cool, red sunset, on through the dusk, on under the luminous half-moon, till silent houses in every part of the country bloomed with light and stirred with the bustle of home-comers from a day's vacation at the Fair.

Lincoln and Owen slipped off their new suits and resumed their hickory shirts and overalls and went out to milk the cows and feed the pigs, while Mrs. Stewart skimmed the milk and made tea for supper. The boys had no holiday to look forward to till Thanksgiving came, and that was not really a holiday, for it came after the beginning of school.

Next morning, long before light, they rose to milk cows and curry horses again, and at sunrise the boys went forth upon the land to plough.

CHAPTER XXIII

A CHAPTER ON PRAIRIE GAME

LINCOLN STEWART, like other boys in Sun Prairie, had the ambition to be a successful hunter and early became a very good wing-shot. As the harvest drew to a close, and even while it was going on, he brought many prairie chickens to the house. The broods at this time were about two-thirds grown and made very tempting dishes. Rance Knapp never hunted them. He had a queer notion that they were too innocent and helpless to shoot. He never would kill a tame chicken for his sisters, and refused to have any hand in the cock-fighting which Milton and the other boys arranged for.

It is not easy to kill prairie chickens if you are a boy of twelve and have no dog to find them for you. Lincoln kept his gun handy in the field during harvesting and stocking, and whenever a covey was accidentally put up he marked the place where they settled, in order to return to them with his gun. He could seldom get more than two shots, for his gun was a muzzle-loader, and besides, a covey put up by the hunter is apt to move all at once, whereas with a good dog they can be put up singly or in twos and threes.

For the first year or two Lincoln was obliged to trust to luck or to his skill in calling them. He could not lift the heavy gun quick enough to shoot on the wing, and so having scattered a covey he crouched in ambush and waited.

The little ones have vanished like a handful of sand. One after the other they have dropped into the deeps of the tangled oats. Lincoln lies in the edge of corn, watching, listening. The smell of ripe grain is in the air, the beards of the uncut barley shine like burnished gold. The corn speaks huskily now and then as if in warning to the helpless birds. The sun is sinking redly to the west. All is peaceful, fruitful, serene.

Now faint and far away comes a little wailing whistle, a pathetic, sweet, down-falling cry, lonely, full of tears. Nothing could be more helpless, more pleading, than this sob of the baby grouse far away in the gloomy oat-forest.

Lincoln repeats the note: *Pee-ee-oo-on! phee-oo-ow!*

One by one, near and far, the note is taken up, and the brood begins to return to the place from which it flew, and out of the edge of the corn, not far away, the mother-bird steps, and, standing there for a moment listening, begins to utter a low, clucking call: " *Come, my dears, come, come, come! All is well-ll-ll — very well — verrrry well — now — now — now — come to me — come to me, come!* "

It is evidence of the terrible power of the instinct to kill, that Lincoln's fingers tingle with the desire to pull the trigger, but he waits while the little ones assemble,

2 A

in order to be the more murderous. In his heart a struggle is going on. He feels that this faithful and gentle mother should go free — and yet the primitive hunter in him cries out for game. One by one the pleading voices fall silent as they see the mother, and at last only one is left wandering in the jungle.

Lincoln lifts the muzzle of his gun, and takes aim — the watchful mother sees it, and with loud flutter flies away; the little ones squat in the stubble, duck low, and scatter again, and the boy finds a certain element of relief mingled with his disappointment. Next time he will be quicker on the trigger.

By the time he was thirteen he became able to shoot on the wing. He missed a great many, but managed, after all, to bring down a bird now and then. He never had a dog of his own, but occasionally he went out with Sam Hutchison, who had a big liver-and-white pointer named Growler. It was a great pleasure to see the work of this well-trained animal. With nose in the wind he lopes over the stubble or along the edge of a swale, swift and certain. Suddenly he stops short, with his head at right angles with his body, and feels the air. Then, turning on his hind feet as on a pivot, with tail levelled, he follows the scent as a sailor takes in a rope. His feet rise and fall like the cranks on a machine, his head is held to the wind, poised, horizontal, without motion. His master knows every sign of his dog. He can tell by the way he puts down his feet how far away the game is, whether it is a covey or only a single bird.

Now the dog stops, rigid as bronze, one hind foot lifted and held.   He is upon them.

" Down, Growler," calls Sam.

The noble fellow sinks into the grass softly as melting wax.   If need be, he will hold the birds for an hour without moving.

The hunters approach rapidly till within shooting distance, and then, with weapons ready, move alertly forward.

" Put 'em up, boy — steady, now ! " calls Sam.

The dog rises as slowly as he sank.   He lifts one forefoot and puts it before him, pushing himself, inch by inch, upon the birds.

Whirr-rr — bang !

The first bird falls, and the dog waits for orders. Sam reloads, while Growler waits immovably.

" Go on, boy ! "

Another rises and falls, then two who escape, then six, and two fall.   The faithful dog again waits while his master reloads.   He seems to know precisely what is wanted of him.   When all are ready, he begins again to move, and, nosing the warm nests where the birds were squatted, begins to search for scattered ones, while the hunters follow within shooting distance.   At last he points out the ones that have fallen, and begins once more to range the field.

Lincoln always liked the pointer best, he was so much nobler in his action than the setter, who wiggled and wormed among the weeds and grasses with great pains and little dignity.   The pointer covered so much more ground in so little time. He made so many splendid and dramatic pictures as he stopped, crouched, rose, felt his way to his quarry. He added something worth while to a sport which needed the æsthetic badly. The setter seemed less clearly specialized for the sport. The pointer had almost no other uses. He was not a house-dog, knew nothing about retrieving, would not chase a pig, ate enormously, had dim eyes, and altogether was a machine constructed for certain uses, and when driving to his purpose was a glorious piece of mechanism — for the rest he either slept, or pleaded for food.

With all that could trim and decorate chicken shooting, Lincoln could not escape a feeling of remorse whenever he saw a young bird lying limp and bloody at his feet. They were so pretty and so helpless, and at last he came to Rance's conclusion, it was not sport, and he went no more to the killing.

He had less feeling about ducks and geese — perhaps because they were migratory and he did not see them nest and breed. The ducks came back each fall in enormous flocks, settling at night on the stubble-fields to feed, but they were wary — not so vigilant as the geese, but so difficult of approach that it was only at the expense of long, wearisome creepings through the dusk that the boys were able to get within shooting distance; and when they rose they were like a storm, a great, roaring, dark mass lit by sudden gleams of white as they turned. Occasionally in this way a brace or two were secured.

At other times, by hiding near a feeding-place, by

digging a pit and covering it with sheaves of grain or bundles of grass, Lincoln was able to carry home a greenhead or a teal or two. His mother had a prejudice against ducks and never liked to cook them, and, in truth, they never tasted very good, and for this reason, perhaps, the boys were less eager to kill a duck than a goose.

Geese and cranes appealed to them as worth killing because they were so big, so strong, and so wary. The wild goose is not a foolish bird. He is, on the contrary,

a wise and skilful and circumspect fowl. His voice, capable of enormous signalling power and subtle alarm, is a glorious addition to the sounds of the plain. In April he stirs the heart with thoughts of spring — in autumn he makes the settler shiver with sudden remembrance that winter is coming.

All wild geese are well led and well governed. They camp like the redmen, with sentries posted, and no alien sound escapes their notice. They know the difference between the movement of a browsing cow and the creeping approach of a hunter. The steps of the wolf and the fox are distinguished and announced. When on the wing they avoid all dwellings of men, or go by at a height which renders them safe. In all ways they seemed wise and watchful birds to Lincoln.

He never shot but one goose in all his life. Many times he crept through the wet stubble — crawling on his elbows and knees for a full half-mile, only to fail of even a shot at the flock as it rose.

He dug pits and laid in the muddy bottom thereof, till he was stiff with cold, all to no purpose. Their watchful eyes detected some movement, the gleam of a weapon or some sign of danger, — and the leader, uttering a loud honk, swerved suddenly aside, and they passed on.

Bryant's stately and imaginative poem on the wild goose was a great favorite with Lincoln. He loved the march of those lines —

> " Vainly the fowler's eye
> Doth mark thy distant flight to do thee wrong,
> As darkly painted on the crimson sky
> Thy figure floats along."

There was something grand in these great migrating birds. No one the boy had ever questioned had been far enough north to find their breeding-places by "the plashy brink or marge of river wide, or where the rocking billows rise and sink, on the chafed ocean's side." Their very flight was poetry, and the wild goose was never a jest among them.

The hired man one spring winged one with his rifle and gave him to Lincoln, who clipped his pinions and kept him alive, a sullen captive. With head held high, he moved slowly about his corral, his eyes forever on the sky, and when he saw a file of his people pushing to the north, he shook his mutilated wings and shouted like a captive chief. At such times Lincoln had a momentary wish to set him free — perhaps would have done so only for the bird's helplessness. After the geese had all passed north the captive sank into silent endurance of his lot, — uttering no sound except just before a storm, — then rising lightly on his feet and beating his great wings, he cried resoundingly to the heavens. Perhaps he was thinking of the splendid storms which used to sweep over his northern lake. Perhaps he acted instinctively as a foreboding seer.

One day in autumn when the wind was cold and swift from the north, a flock of returning geese came swinging aslant on the blast, hastening southward. As they came, "old Honk" became visibly excited. He fixed his eyes upon the far-off harrow in the clouds, and as its gabble reached his ear, he spread his wings and uttered a peculiar, vibrant note — a cry that was at once an alarum and a command.

The others answered, and the leader swerved a little in his course. Again the captive spoke, and the leader came round still more, making almost direct course over the barn-yard. Lincoln, seeing their coming, ran for his gun, but before he reached the house, the captive bird started upon a waddling run, beating the air with his wings. To his own surprise, he rose in the air and sailed over the fence. The wind got under him, he rose like a blown garment, uncertainly, and as he steadied himself, his voice rang exultantly. The flock, circling laboriously, seemed to wait for him; he took his place at the rear of the long arm of the harrow — the leader cried, "*On, on!*" and the captive was a free courser of the air once more.

The best hunters killed few of the geese. Sometimes with a rifle they picked one out of a flock in the fields. Sometimes by stalking behind a cow they came within gun-shot, and when the birds chanced to be sitting in the open, the hunters were able to dash up with a team within shooting distance before the lumbering fowls could get fairly on the wing.

Lincoln never killed a crane — in fact, he never tried to do so. They interested him profoundly. Their shadowy, awkward forms perched in a row beside some pool at dusk, their comical dances on a hillock in the morning, but especially their majestic flight, made them the most mysterious and splendid of all birds of the plain. They could be tamed, for Sam Hutchison had one nearly all summer. It stalked about, calmly inspecting all things with its round, expressionless eyes, as if to say, "This is a curious world — I'll stop for a while and look into it."

It had a dangerous habit of picking at shining things, — buttons, buckles, rings, and the baby's eyes, — and Sam killed it one day just after it had nearly blinded his little two-year-old girl. He tried to eat the dead bird, but confessed that he didn't like it worth a cent. "I'd as soon eat prairie hay," he said, when Lincoln inquired about it.

There were quails in the woodlands of the Maple and Cedar rivers, and partridges also, but the boys seldom secured more than one or two partridges — they were difficult to shoot on the wing, and without a dog it was nearly impossible to find them. Rabbits were thick, and Mrs. Stewart had occasion very often to make a pot-pie of these "jumping hens," as Uncle Billy Frazier called them. As he entered the maple woodlands, all the woodcraft he had unconsciously acquired as a child, came back to Lincoln. He could tell the difference between the tracks of various kinds of mice and moles and squirrels. He knew by the rabbit's footprints whether he had been feeding, or walking abroad, or fleeing in fear. He was able to distinguish the barking of the red squirrel from the gray, and knew the habits of the white owl and the partridge, as well as the quails — and yet, for all this, he was a poor hunter. Rance generally shot all the rabbits, while Lincoln talked with the blue jays, or walked around a tree to see a gray squirrel hide himself behind the trunk, or followed him as he traced out his aërial trail along the horizontal branches of the oaks. Neither of the boys were really dissatisfied to return without game; each considered the day in the woods profitable, even if no rabbit or partridge dangled at their belts.

Once they wandered all day in a November drizzle which froze on the trees till they were heavy with superb

armoring.   Toward night the sky cleared with a warm
western wind, and the heavily laden branches cracked
and groaned, shaking their glittering burden down on
the leafy ground, till the air was filled with a patter as
of flying fairy feet.   Not one creature did the boys kill
that day — they tramped on and on, feeling the charm
of nature in this singular mood, not talking much, content to mix and be a part of the universal mystery,
passing thoughtfully from the rustling ranks of the red
oaks to the silence of maple ridges, where only the voice
of some weary branch broke the silence.   Lincoln had
a delicious sense of being deep in the wilderness — like
" Leather Stocking," whose solitary life he loved.

Rance was an indefatigable listener, and Lincoln was
sometimes a voluble talker, though he could be silent
as a cat in the woods.   It made little difference to Rance
which mood his companion was in; he remained the
same unsmiling, almost taciturn youth.

They shot their rabbits on the run when they could,
because it was more sportsmanlike.   The clearings
where the heaped brush lay unburned and roofed with
snow was the best hunting-ground.   Softly approaching
these coverts, the boys leaped upon them suddenly, taking
the rabbits on foot as they fled to other shelter.   They
missed a great many, but succeeded from time to time in
bagging one, and this one was worth a dozen shot standing.   Squirrels they seldom cared to carry home, but
occasionally roasted them at a camp-fire in the woods at
noon.

As they grew older and wiser, they considered all the

game of the prairie too small, and they ceased to hunt. They talked of grizzly bears and buffaloes and panthers and cougars. One day in Lincoln's fourteenth year he reached a decision. "I kill no more hens and cats," he said, meaning prairie chickens and rabbits. "Anybody can go out and kill these things. When I go hunting now, it's got to be wolves or foxes or bears and buffaloes; now you hear me."

"Let's make a compact," said Rance. "Four years from now we meet on the plains."

"Done!" shouted Lincoln, in the terms of the pirate's usual oath.

But as they knitted their fingers together and swore, there was a smile in Rance's eyes. He had a suspicion then that neither of them would ever get out of Cedar County.

NOVEMBER

When the ground squirrel toils at gathering wheat,
And the wood-dove's sombre notes repeat
The story of autumn's passing feet;

When the cold, gray sky has a rushing breeze
Which hums in the grass like a hive of bees,
And scatters the leaves from the roaring trees;

When the corn is filled with a rising moon,
And the gray crane flies on his course alone,
Hastening south to the orange zone; —

Then the boy on the bare, brown prairie knows
That winter is coming with drifting snows
To cover the grave of the dry, dead rose.

CHAPTER XXIV

VISITING SCHOOLS

In some way, and for some educational purpose no doubt, there had grown up a custom of visiting schools. Whatever the obscure origin of this custom, the visits were considered red-letter days by the boys and the girls. The first invasion came as a complete surprise to Lincoln at least.

One beautiful warm sunny day in midwinter — a Friday it was — he sat humped over his spelling-book, with his thumb in his ears, oblivious to the outside world, and quite the last scholar to hear the sound of bells in furious clash, accompanied by the clamor of many voices in merry outcry, as two long bob-sleighs, packed to the brim with boys and girls, dashed round the corner, and drew up before the door with a royal flourish.

The room was instantly in disorder. Excitable girls began to giggle, shock-haired boys sprang to their feet in defiance of rule, and crowded around the windows. The teacher hurriedly smoothed his hair and dusted the dandruff from his coat-collar, while loud knocking on the door shook his nerves. At last he sternly said: " Be seated! Take your seats again!"

In silent, delicious excitement the scholars returned

to their places, and with eyes like onions waited the coming of the visitors.

"It's the Grove School," said Rance to Lincoln. The teacher, bowing and smiling his suavest, opened the door and invited his visitors to enter, with such show of hearty hospitality as a man in his situation could command. His collar was soiled, and he wore a long linen duster to keep the chalk of the blackboard from his black suit.

The visiting teacher led his tumultuous host with smiling dignity. The big girls came first, in knitted hoods and cloth cloaks, their cheeks red with the touch of the keen wind — their eyes shining with excitement. They took seats with the girls they knew, crowding three in a seat. The boys followed, awkward as colts, homely as shoats, snuffling, slyly crowding each other, and every one of them grinning constrainedly. They stood around the stove until the master pointed out seats for them. At last they were all settled, and nearly every seat held three explosive youngsters, ready for a guffaw or a trick of any kind.

The visiting master was well known as the music teacher of the township and a violinist. He was a small man, with a long beard and a pleasant hazel eye. His name was Robert Mason Jasper, but for some reason was always spoken of as "R. M. Jasper," not Mister or Robert or Bob, but "R. M." He beamed over the school with most genial good nature as he took a seat beside his host. It was plain he liked young people, and that they liked him.

To Lincoln the whole world had changed. The monotonous routine was broken up. The crowded seats, the lovely big girls from the Grove, the wiggling boys of his own age, the temporary relenting of rigid discipline, — all of these were inexpressibly potent and significant. He could not fix his thoughts upon his book though the master said, —

"Give attention to books now!" Nobody really studied for a moment. The big girls wrote notes, and the big boys slyly chewed tobacco and whispered openly, while Milton put his fingers to the tip of his nose till it turned up, and threw his handsome face into shape like Sim Bagley, whose eyes were crossed, and who had a habit of winking very fast. These performances threw Shep Warren and one or two other boys into paroxysms of laughter, which the master made perfunctory efforts to reprove. Hum Bunn had bored a hole through his desk, and by use of a pen-stock and a pen was able to startle one of the Angell boys.

There was very little reciting, for the teacher dared call only on his readiest and most self-contained pupils. The dullards had nothing to do but visit till the afternoon recess, which came early and lasted a long time. Then with a wild rush the boys broke into freedom. The two schools joined at once in friendly rivalry. The wrestlers grappled, the small boys fell into games of "stink gool," or "crack-the-whip," or divided into hostile legions, and snowballed each other with the fury of opposing tribes of savage men.

Some few of the big boys and girls remained in the

school-house and flirted openly with each other, which Lincoln considered rather soft, and Ben viciously said : " I'd like to soak Bill Hatfield with a hard snowball."

Rance shone gloriously in the games. His lithe, supple body, his swift limbs, his skill in dodging and wrestling, filled Lincoln's heart with admiration. He led the games round to those in which his chum excelled, such as " skinning the cat " and " chinning a pole," which tested the strength of the arms and shoulders. Rance could chin a pole nearly twice as many times as the strongest boy from Oak Grove. His muscles were like woven wire, and his skin as white as a girl's. The boys already man-grown found him so agile and so elusive that they were eager to grapple with him. They could crush him to the ground, but they could not put him on his back and hold him there. He shrewdly refused to wrestle " bear hug," or " side-holt," but was quite ready to meet any of them in " catch-as-catch-can."

Metellus Soper considered himself the " champion " of the Grove School. He was only eighteen, but stood five-feet-eleven in his stocking feet, and counted himself a man at every point. He could lift one wheel of a separator, and throw a sledge as far as any man in the township except Lime Gilman. At bear hug he could down any youth in his school, and none of the Sun Prairie boys cared to face him. They laughingly said, in answer to his invitation : " Go away. I don't want any truck with you."

At last Ben Hutchison consented to a " side holt,"

which was his choice. He flung Mett within the first minute, and the Sun Prairie boys howled with joy. They became silent again when Soper rose white with fury, but outwardly calm.

" We'll try that again," he said menacingly.

" Guess I'll stop while my credit's good," Ben laughingly replied.

" You try that again, or fight."

Ben was no coward. " Oh, all right — but play fair."

Soper was clearly the master, and as he put Ben on his back twice out of three times, his anger cooled. Looking round, he singled out Rance.

" I want to take a whirl with you," he said.

Lincoln cried out, "Oh, take some one of your size," and a number of the others supported him.

Rance stepped out. " I'll take you, rough and tumble," he said quietly.

" Any way 't all," replied Soper, complacently.

Lincoln was numb with excitement as he saw his hero facing his big and savage antagonist, but he knew the marvellous resources of that slender body, better than any one else in the world, and had no fear so long as Metellus wrestled.

With a confident rush Metellus opened the bout, but in the clinch found himself clawing Rance's humped shoulders, and hopping about on one foot, and an instant later was hurled into the air, to fall on his shoulder, with his cheek in the snow.

" Put him on his back ! " shouted Lincoln.

Rance himself had slipped, and could not follow up

2 B

his advantage. Soper turned his face to the earth, and was rising on his hands when Rance sprang upon him like a leopard. He was too light to hold the big fellow down. Soper rose, taking Rance with him, and reaching round, seized him by the leg, and little by little worked his long arms around his waist and flung him by main force. Rance landed on his hands and knees, with the big fellow on his back. Soper's face was sneering and confident. He had nothing else to do now but turn Rance on his breast. This was not so easy as he thought. Again and again he lifted the boy, but someway couldn't manage him. He could crush him flat against the ground, he could slide him and twist him and double him up, but he could not put both shoulders to the ground at the same time. His face grew set and ferocious again.

"Damn your slippery hide, I'll smash ye!"

"Go fair now," warned the boys.

Soper lay sprawling out to hold Rance down, while he devised some plan of action. Rance, looking up, saw Lincoln and smiled. For five minutes he had been worried by the big bully, but he was not merely unangered, he was laughing. Lincoln's heart leaped with pride in him. The crowd complained.

"Aw! Go ahead, Mett, don't lay there and tire him all out. That ain't rastlin'."

Rance, with a swift, sidewise movement, eluded the grip of his antagonist, and throwing his right arm around his neck, drew his head under till his bones cracked. Soper uttered a snarl and tried to rise. He tossed

Rance aside, but always the lad was on top. Now with both hands clasped around his middle and his belly bending Soper's neck to the ground, now swarming over his back, with legs stiffly resisting all efforts to draw him under. Soper rose twice, but Rance went with him with the under-hold, and threw him again on his hands, but could not turn him on his back, and Soper was equally unable to draw him under.

The wild yells of the boys brought everybody out of the school-house, and the teachers came over to see if the boys were fighting. Rance smiled at them to reassure them, and the struggle went on.

"Why Mett," said his teacher, "what are you doing there under this little boy?"

"Don't bother him," said Milton; "he's busy!"

Soper was ominously silent. With a last desperate effort he rose; Rance, swarming all over him, and winding his arms about him once more, threw him and fell upon him to crush his back to the ground. Rance twisted belly downward, and the frenzied Soper returned to his old methods to wear him out.

"Call it a draw, boys," said Jasper, and the rest took the cue. "Let him up, Mett. Call it a draw."

But not till the teachers pulled him off would Soper admit even so much as that. "This ain't ended," he said, menacingly, to Rance, as he put on his coat.

"I'm ready, any time," replied Rance. "But I want to tell you right now you've got to rastle fair, or I'll let the daylight into you. I won't be mauled around by a big bully like you."

And Metellus did not reply. There was a note in Rance's voice which he had never heard before.

Late in the afternoon the teacher said : " Lay aside books. We will now spell down. James Poindexter and Henry Coonrod may choose sides."

Jim and Henry stepped out into the middle of the floor and awkwardly received the broom from the master. Jim tossed it to Henry, who caught it in his right hand; Jim then placed his hand above Henry's. Henry put his left above Jim's, and so on until Jim's last hold covered the end of the stick, and Henry could not secure sufficient grip to sustain the broom. Jim chose first, and laughing, crowding, whispering, and grimacing, the two schools ranged along opposite walls of the room.

Lincoln's teacher pronounced the words, and the battle began. There were twenty on each side, and the few who remained in the seats quivered with excitement. One by one the bad spellers dropped away. Jim and Henry both went down early in the strife, but Lincoln stood side by side with Milton. " I can't wrestle for shucks," he sometimes said, " but I can spell with any of you." As each word was pronounced, Lincoln could see it as distinctly as if he were looking at the printed page, and he spelled unhesitatingly on and on, until Jim's battle line faded away, and only Ella Pierce, a slim, homely little girl, remained, and then the Oak Grove teacher took the book to see if his favorite scholar could not win the contest.

Lincoln was exalted by the honors he had won, and out of his mat of hair his brown eyes gleamed with resolution. The sun sank low in the west, filling the room with a light such as he had never seen before. He had heard of this girl's power and had no sentiment in the matter; he intended to win. The hour for closing was long past, but the interest in the contest continued unabated. The scholars in their seats cheered unreproved by the masters. At last Milton went down on " Cygnet, a young swan," and Lincoln stood alone on his side. Lincoln hoped to win — he felt sure of winning — till suddenly the teacher took up the dictionary and began to pronounce new and strange words. Then the light went out of the lad's eyes. He could not visualize these words — he was feeling his way in the dark. He stammered, hesitated, and went down, but Ella went down on the same word, and in that Lincoln found some comfort. The tension of the whole school found relief in stormy thumping of fists and stamping of feet. Technically the Grove won.

" School is dismissed," said the teacher, and bedlam broke loose. With wild cries the boys crowded into the entry way, and snatching caps and coats, escaped into the open air for a last rush of play, while the big boys brought the sleighs around, the Sun Prairie people shrieking and chattering. Those of the Sun Prairie boys who found sleighs going their way clung to the box-rim and the end-gate, while standing on the heel of the runners, and so stole a ride home. The bells clashed out, the drivers shouted to their teams, and away the great sleighs rushed, swarming with tittering girls and whooping boys.

Naturally this visit called for a polite return of the call, and the boys began to arrange about the teams at once, and would have gone to the Grove the following Friday, only for the restraining word of the teacher, who counselled a decent interval. But at last the great day came. Sun Prairie School District filled three sleighs and filled them full. Ben Hutchison furnished one team, Ed Blackler another, while Rance and Milton joined horses to make the third. Lincoln rode with them. Each one came to school that day dressed in his best, and there was a pretence of recitations in the early morning.

The day was cloudless, and the sun flamed in dazzling splendor from the unstained snows of the prairie. The boys raced horses, and the girls alternately shrieked with laughter and sang, "Lily Dale," "The One-horse Open Sleigh," and "The Mocking-bird." The small boys rode anywhere on the outside of the sleigh rather than on the inside where they belonged, and were constantly getting into trouble. At last the teams entered the woodland, which was always beautiful and mysterious to Lincoln, after the unshadowed sweep of the snow-crusted prairie, and a few moments later drew up before the door of the school-house, which was the largest and best furnished of all the schools of the township. It was used for church and for town-meetings, and Lincoln always entered it with a measure of abasement.

It had an organ in a battered box, and "boughten desks," and a sort of stage at one end. Altogether it seemed the next thing to the Rock River Court-house to Lincoln. It was the aristocratic district of the township. Its girls were prettier and its citizens more prominent in county politics. Sun Prairie stood next, but was handicapped by its lack of woods and streams, as well as by its comparative youth. To be invited to visit Grove School was considered an especially desirable favor.

Lincoln sat in the corner and dreamed, while his eyes explored every corner of the room, and noted the lines on every face, and followed the motions of every scholar. Under Jasper's direction they sang several choruses, which made a most poetic impression on Lincoln, arousing his ambition to distinguish himself. Rance, as usual, sat quietly in his seat, making no pretensions to be witty or wise.

Mett Soper was vastly excited and could hardly wait for recess to come before he challenged Rance to have it out.

"I don't care to rastle," said Rance.

"But you've got to," said Metellus, laying his hand on Rance's shoulder.

Rance leaped aside, and his face grew white, a dangersome signal, as Lincoln knew.

"Keep your dirty hands off me," he said. "When I say I don't want to rastle, I mean it."

Metellus followed him up. "I'll make you rastle or fight."

The other boys became silent with excitement, for Metellus was a boaster who carried out his threats.

Rance was prepared for this. He whipped out a knife and opened it.

"You big bully," he said. "If you touch me, I'll kill you." His eyes burned with a most intense light, and his face was set and old. "You're four years older than I am, and I won't be mauled by you. Now that's all. Leave me alone."

Metellus hesitated, and while he hesitated, the teachers both came hurrying out.

"What's all this? Rance, put up your knife," called his teacher, a tall, full-faced, gally young fellow.

"I will when Mett Soper promises to let me be — not till then," he replied doggedly.

"Shame on you, Metellus," said Jasper, "to persecute a boy."

Metellus turned on his heel, muttering a menace.

Frank Wilbur slipped forward, and said, "Rather than see Mett suffer for want of exercise, I'll try him a whack."

Metellus couldn't well refuse, and so sullenly said, "Name y'r holt."

"No holt at all is my holt," said Frank, who was a tall, broad-shouldered fellow with a smiling hazel-gray eye. He faced Mett, with his hands in his trousers pockets, his head bare, and his shirt-sleeved arms akimbo. "Put your hands in your pockets!"

Mett squared off, but reluctantly, for he knew Frank's skill. With right knees bent and toes tapping the ground the two stalwart young fellows circled around each other, feinting to draw a swing, swinging in the attempt to trip. All the scholars of both schools gathered around. Metellus was not without a following, and besides, he was the champion of the school. Therefore cheers went up for him as well as for Frank. There were few boys who cared to wrestle in this way, for when they fell they fell very hard. Metellus fought gamely, but Frank caught him behind the heel at just the right moment, and he fell with stunning force. He rose slowly, a rigid look of pain on his face. "Now try my holt," he said, but Jasper rang the bell, and the match was postponed.

The teacher called on some of his pupils to "speak pieces" after recess, and in return the teacher from Sun Prairie brought forward Lincoln and Milton to recite. Milton came first, and with calm and smiling face rattled off a part of "Webster's Speech at Bunker Hill," while Lincoln, with a great big chestnut burr in his throat, and his heart beating like a flail, waited in agony the teacher's call. Never before had such an audience faced him. These restless, derisive youngsters, and contemptuous big boys, and grown-up girls, might well have appalled an old and practised speaker.

When he faced them, his lips were twitching, and his tumbled brown hair seemed to lift in fright. His lips were dry, and his voice as weak as a kitten's. He was short, and his trousers were long, and rolled up at the bottoms. His feet were large, and his boots larger. His coat did not fit at any point, and altogether he was a comical figure; but he put his hands behind him and began to recite "Lochiel's Warning," which was one of his favorite selections. At first he could only speak a line at a time, so short was his breath, but at last he gained in confidence, his voice deepened, his head lifted, and he rolled out the bombastic thunder of Lochiel's scornful reply with such spirit that all listened. —

"False Wizard, avaunt !   I have marshalled my clan.
Their swords are a thousand, their bosoms are one.
They are true to the last of their blood and their breath,
And like reapers descend to the harvest of death."

And when he closed with the line, —

"Look proudly to heaven from the death-bed of fame,"

he broke all records by making a gesture with his right hand, while lifting his face in action suited to the words, and the scholars stamped and whistled, and the teacher said, " That boy is going to be senator some day."

It was a great triumph for him, and helped to establish his position among his fellows.   He was getting old enough also, at this time, to secretly desire the approbation of the girls, though a single word from one of them flooded him with bashful confusion.   It seemed especially worth while to distinguish himself before the girls of the Grove School-house.   He had the true male instinct — the daughters of alien tribes seemed lovelier than those who dwelt in the tents of his own people.

It was dark before they had distributed all the girls at their homes, and Rance went home with Lincoln to supper.   It had been a good day.

*   *   *   *   *   *

As the years passed, the homes of the prairie changed for the better.   Councill put on a lean-to, so did

Hutchison. Jennings added an ell, and Mr. Stewart put up a new kitchen with a half-story chamber above, which relieved the pressure a little. The garret above the sitting-room was lathed and plastered also, and the rooms below were papered. All of these improvements made vivid impression on Lincoln's mind. There was still no touch of grace, no gleam of beauty, about the house. The wall paper was cheap and flimsy, characters of pattern neutral if not positively harmful in color. A few chromos hung on the walls — wretched things even for chromos. These were the only adornments, and the homes around were not much different. Nature was grand and splendid — the works of man were pitiful.

The school-house changed only for the worse. Barns were built first, houses improved next, and school-houses last of all, though Sun Prairie was as public spirited as any of the districts.

The boys did not perceive the absence of beauty, but they were quick to note its presence. Nothing escaped them. One of the girls who taught the school in summer cut some newspapers into pretty patterns and put them over the windows, and when Lincoln entered the room next time, the softened light impressed him favorably. He took note also of every new touch of armament assumed by the girls — and this quite aside from any idea of courtship. He saw it as color, as being something pretty, and though he dared not use the word " beautiful," it was in his soul as it was in the soul of Rance and Owen.

The girls worked out a moiety of their craving for beauty on tidies and scarfs and wall-pockets, but these the boys seldom saw, for they were ill at ease in parlors. Lincoln only knew one, in fact, — the Knapp's, — and that he visited very seldom. It had a dim light, — like a sacred place, — but he had observed the " spatter-work " and the worsted sewn into perforated cardboard, and the faded carpet, and remembered them. The girls in their best dresses awed him, however, and he escaped to the barn as soon as possible.

His own mother was too hard-worked to do any " spatter-work " other than churning or dish-washing, and Mary was not yet old enough to begin; therefore, their home remained unadorned — except for the putting down of a new rag-carpet which he helped to make by tearing and tying old rags together during the long winter evenings. Once his mother had a " rag party," and the women came in to help on the carpet, and Lincoln was so averse to meeting them that he remained at the barn, and had Owen bring his supper to him. Later on in the evening he slipped into the kitchen and sat in the corner with Rance and popped corn for the others to eat.

This carpet glorified the sitting-room, when it came back from the old Norwegian woman who wove it, and once when the sun shone in upon it and a bird was singing outside, the boy thought, " Our home is beautiful, after all." But it was only the bird, and the sunshine on the floor!

As he grew older and the life of the prairie became

less free, Lincoln began to take a very vivid interest in the social affairs of the Grove School-house. He attended the meetings regularly and was to be found at all the Grange suppers, donation parties, and surprise parties. He often went to the dances, but did not share in them — though he longed to do so.

For several years the aspect of the neighborhood had been darkened and made austere by the work of an " evangelist," who came preaching the wickedness of the natural man and the imminence of death. Inevitably there was a rebound from this rigid discipline a couple of years later, and the people young and old met during the winter as often as any excuse offered. Nearly every week the Grange held an " open meeting and oyster supper," which packed the Grove School-house to the very doors. The boys seldom had a chance to eat oyster soup, and considered it a heaven-sent privilege. They gorged themselves upon it, and burnt little strips of skin off the roofs of their mouths in their haste to secure a second plate.

Oysters came from a far country, and could only be transported in cans or in " bulk," as they called it. "Oyster soup " was the only known way of using them, and an " oyster supper " meant bowls of thin stew with small crackers. The Grange suppers, however, consisted of fried chicken, biscuit, cake and coffee, and pie, always both mince and apple pie. The boys played " pom-pom pullaway " all the evening and came to the supper with the appetites of hired men. Lincoln at such times felt quite sure that he was having as much fun as any boy. Rock River was greater, but then no farmer boy could reasonably hope to live in such a large town.

The lyceum came on Saturday night generally, and the house was always crowded, no matter how cold the wind. The stove was a big square box into which some public-spirited soul rolled huge red oak "grubs," and the people entering hurried at once toward it and there stood scorching their outside garments, while shivering with the cold, which it seemed to drive in upon them. The men were big as bears in their huge buffalo overcoats, but the women were all badly dressed, and many of them were thin-blooded and weary with work and worry.

The girls wore hoods for the most part, and some of them began to look wondrously pretty to Lincoln and Rance, but neither of them had the courage to speak to one. Milton, however, was already a great beau and on familiar terms with all who came. They said, " Hello, Milt," and he replied, "Hello, Carrie," or "Hello, Bettie," in the same tone. The girls stood in awe of Rance, and though they seldom spoke to him, they were glad to be able to *happen* beside him as they stood by the stove to warm.

Rance was secretly desirous of their good-will, but his face was always dark and secretive in their presence, and they grew nervous and whispered elaborate nothings to each other in self-defence ; these dialogues he took to be derision of himself, and moved away. Metellus Soper, who also desired the good-will of the girls, while standing afar off, continued to seek a quarrel with Rance, and was always making coarse jokes in his presence. Lincoln often shook with fear when he saw Metellus edging toward Rance. Soper was always present at these lyceums and made himself conspicuous in foolish ways, whereas Rance was known to be a well-read boy and capable of taking part in the exercises if he would. Lincoln knew it would be a tragic battle if the two boys met in anger.

There was always a debate on some such question as this, "Was Napoleon a greater general than Cæsar?" or "Is gunpowder more useful than paper?" A great deal of hem-hawing accompanied the debates, and the judges solemnly voted at the end of the session, and one by one momentous questions of this character were settled. Before the debate it was usual to have some recitations and essays, and there Milton shone large and clear. He had a certain faculty in writing, and often presented himself with an oration on some political subject in harmony with his father's views — he had not yet reached the point of asserting himself. Lincoln also took part in the speaking, and occasionally made a pronounced hit with some comic recitation from Josh Billings or Mark Twain. He quite as often failed by being too ambitious and attempting some poem whose passion scared him and took his breath away just when he needed it most. Owen had developed a gift for singing, and with great calmness walked up to the platform and piped away at some ballad which he had derived from the hired hands or his Uncle David.

These evenings formed pleasant breaks in the monot-

ony of winter life, and the boys who were old enough
and brave enough to take the girls were well satisfied
with Sun Prairie.   The moon shone as brilliantly in its
season as anywhere in the world, and on moonless nights
the stars filled the heavens with innumerable dazzling
points of light, and the lovers, packed side by side in
long sleighs, sang cheerily on, unconscious of the cold.
At such times Rance and Lincoln, riding in silence behind some merry party, felt a singular twinge of pain.
They seemed left out of something very much worth
while — which was a sign and signal that they were
soon to leave boyhood behind.

It was at the lyceum that Lincoln acquired a definite
ambition.   The most conspicuous and successful partic-
ipants in the exercises were the young men and women
who were attending the Rock River Seminary at the
county town.   Their smooth hands and modish dress,
their ease of manner, the polish of their speech, made a
powerful impression on the other Sun Prairie boys.

Once or twice these "Seminary chaps" let fall a
contemptuous word about the lyceum debates which
opened the eyes of Lincoln to their absurdities.   He
perceived that in the eyes of cultured Rock River these
old farmers were laughable, and once as he rode away
in the cutter with Rance, he said : —

"I'm going to go to the Seminary myself when I'm
eighteen."

"I'm going to start in next year," said Rance, and
the quick resolution of his voice made Lincoln gasp.

"Oh, you're coddin'."

" Not much I ain't ; what's the use going on here ?
Our teacher can't carry us any further. I'm going to go
to college and I'm going to do something else besides
farm. You can't do anything worth while without an
education — I've found that out."

" Will your father let you go ? "

" He'll growl at the expense, but I can fix that.
The boys tell me they can live for about two dollars a
week down there by " baching it," and we could cut
that down if we had to. It's settled so far as I'm concerned. This is my last winter in Sun Prairie, now you
hear me ! "

Lincoln had never known Rance to be so emphatic
in the utterance of his ambition, and it stirred him very
deeply. It seemed that he was about to be deserted by
his hero comrade.

2 c

"POM–POM, PULL–AWAY"

OUT on the snow the boys are springing,
    Shouting blithely at their play;
Through the night their voices ringing,
    Sound the cry " *Pom, pull-away !* "
Up the sky the round moon stealing,
    Trails a robe of shimmering white;
While the Great Bear slowly wheeling
    Marks the pole-star's steady light.

The air with frost is keen and stinging,
    Spite of cap and muffler gay;
Big boys whistle, girls are singing —
    Loud rings out, " *Pom, pull-away !* "
Oh, the phrase has magic in it,
    Sounding through the moon-lit air!
And in about a half-a-minute
    I am part and parcel there.

'Cross the pond I once more scurry
    Through the thickest of the fray,
Sleeve ripped off by Andy Murray —
    " Let her rip — *Pom, pull-away !* "
Mother'll mend it in the morning
    (Dear old patient, smiling face !);
One more darn my sleeve adorning —
    " *Whoop her up !* " — is no disgrace.

Moonbeams on the snow-a-splinter,
   Air that stirred the blood like wine —
What cared we for cold of winter ?
   What for maidens' soft eyes' shine ?
Give us but a score of skaters
   And the cry, " *Pom, pull-away!* "
We were always girl-beraters —
   Forgot them wholly, sooth to say !

O voices through the night air ringing !
   O thoughtless, happy, boist'rous play !
O silver clouds the keen wind winging ;
   At the cry, " *Pom, pull-away !* "
I pause and dream with keenest longing
   For that starlit magic night,
For my noisy playmates thronging,
   And the slow moon's trailing light.

THE BLUE JAY

His eyes are bright as burnished steel,
   His note a quick, defiant cry ;
Harsh as a hinge his grating squeal
   Sounds from the keen wind sweeping by.
Rains never dim his smooth blue coat,
   The cold winds never trouble him,
No fog puts hoarseness in his throat,
   Or makes his merry eyes grow dim.

His call at dawning is a shout,
   His wing is subject to his heart ;
Of fear he knows not — doubt
   Did not draw his sailing-chart.

He is an universal emigré,
   His foot is set in every land ;
He greets me by gray Casco Bay
   And laughs across the Texas sand.
In heat or cold, in storm and sun,
   He lives undauntedly ; and when he dies,
He folds his feet up one by one
   And turns his last look on the skies.

He is the true American.   He fears
   No journey and no wood or wall —
And in the desert toiling voyagers
   Take heart of courage from his call.

CHAPTER XXV

A MOMENTOUS WOLF-HUNT

THE light from the faintly yellow east had begun to fill the room, when the sound of a galloping horse, rapidly approaching from the south, wakened Lincoln, and then a whistle mingled with the trample of the horse brought to a halt.

"That's Milt!" he cried, leaping from his bed into the frosty air, and hurriedly dressing.

He could hear some one stirring down below; Mrs. Stewart was on her feet. The smell and sizzle of sausages came up from the kitchen, and the sound of the coffee-mill informed him as to the exact stage of breakfast.

When Lincoln got outdoors, the horseman was at the gate, seated statuesquely on a restless gray colt.

"Hello, Link."

"Hello, Milt."

"Ain't you up awful early for a Seminary chap?"

"Oh, I guess I hain't lost all my staminy with one term o' school," laughed Milt. He looked very bright and handsome as he sat on his splendid young horse.

"Had breakfast?"

"Yup."

"Well, I ain't, so you put Mark in the barn an' wait a week or two, while I eat."

As he moved alongside, Lincoln looked at the gray colt admiringly.

"Ginger, but he's a jim dandy. I didn't think you'd ride him to-day. Rance better look out."

"I'm riding to win, this time," replied Milton, as he slipped from the colt, and led him into the warm, dark stable. "Steady, — Mark, old boy, — steady!"

"What horse you goin' to ride?" asked Milton.

"Well, I don't know. Rob, I guess. Cassius is too heavy for such work, don't you think?"

"No. Cassius is the best. You see the main thing to-day is, to have a horse that can hold out."

"What you got to shoot with?"

"A Colt's revolver that I borrowed from Lime Gilman."

"Well, I guess I'll have to confine my death-dealing weapons to my vocal organs," said Lincoln, dropping into long words, his favorite way of being jocose.

"Why so?"

"That is, if I ride Cassius. Look at the eyes of him," he exclaimed, pointing to a vicious sorrel, who showed the whites of his eyes when he saw the lifted hand of his master.

"Hoh!" shouted Lincoln, sharply, and the colt went all of a heap against the manger, his eyes staring, his body trembling, his wicked hind legs drawn under him.

"Look out, there," Milton yelled. Lincoln laughed and called, —

"Wo-up, old man — stiddy now!" and the horse untied himself and returned to his place. He quivered under the hand placed fearlessly upon him, though Lincoln seldom struck him — it was merely the wild nature of the brute. He had a strain of the bronco in his blood.

After a hasty breakfast, the boys went to the barn and brought out the colts. Mark came first, snuffling and alert, and Milton put one toe in the stirrup and swung gracefully into the saddle. Lincoln followed with Cassius, wild already, as if he smelled the game.

As Lincoln seized the pommel of his saddle, the horse plunged and reared and flew away sidewise, but the boy hung to the bridle and mane, and as he whirled, leaped into his seat and had the wild brute in hand before he could make a second rush. He was too good a horseman to be irritated by high spirits in a horse.

It was a glorious winter morning. The sun had made the sky red, but had not warmed the earth perceptibly, had not yet lifted its full face above the long, low bank of trees. A light snow was on the ground, and the prairie stretched away to an infinite distance — made more weirdly impressive by the clarity of the atmosphere, which lifted distant hidden barns and houses into view.

As they rode, the sun rose, and its rays, striking along the horizon, converted the level prairie into a flat basin, with the horsemen low in the centre. To the east the line of timber which marked the Maple River rose far out of its normal position. Ten miles to the left, the larger and deeper forest (where the Rock was sheathed like a sword in a scabbard) seemed only three or four miles away. Every house was doubled in height, and from each chimney a thin column of smoke rose straight into the air, like a slender elm tree.

"Will the boys be on hand?" asked Lincoln.

"Oh, yes! This snow'll bring 'em out. It was the signal. We'll find 'em at the school-house."

Some miles to the north, and just over the state line, a big square of wild land still lay. It was the property of an Eastern syndicate, and was not on the market. Upon it, as upon an island, the wolves and foxes and badgers had taken refuge, and the boys had made several more or less successful hunting trips "across the line," but Lincoln had never before taken part in them. Rance, who always had a hand in any expedition of this kind, had taken part in two wolf-hunts, and was the natural leader in the one on hand.

Milton and Lincoln rode steadily forward toward the school-house, the rendezvous of the band.

"There's smoke a-risin'!" cried Milton. "Somebody's on hand, anyway — and there comes the rest."

Three horsemen could be seen making easy way along a converging lane, and as his eye caught sight of them, Milton rose in his saddle and uttered a wild whoop, the sound, penetrating the still air, making a remarkable change in the pace of the other horsemen.

Answering yells rose, and a fine race took place. Lincoln let the rein loose on Cassius, and dug his heel into his flank, and was off before Milton's protest could reach him.

Milton held Mark down to an easy lope, and watched the race between Lincoln and the nearest horseman, mounted on a black horse. Lincoln was a little nearer to the goal, but had a ravine to cross; and though the iron-sided Cassius did his best, the black turned in just a neck ahead.

When Milton cantered calmly up to the crowd on the leeward side of the school-house, they all yelled derisively.

" He ain't any good, that gray horse ! "

" He's all show ! "

" Why didn't you let him out ? "

" You'll find out why, later in the day," responded Milton, coolly; "when the rest of your horses are all winded, Mark'll be fresh as a daisy."

" By jingo ! That's a fact. Didn't think of that," the rest replied.

Milton dismounted and found a place for his horse in the little shed, which had been built, after prodigious trouble, by the neighborhood. Inside he found the fellows sitting around the big box-stove, drinking coffee out of a big tin dipper, and eating hunks of sausages and bread, which they toasted in the open door of the stove, on their jack-knives.

The coffee being disposed of, the question of proceeding came up.

" Where's Rance ? "

" He's coming, I guess," said one of the boys at the window. " Yes, it's him coming licketty-split."

Rance turned up soon, riding Ladrone, no longer

young, but as swift as ever. The boys all swarmed out to meet him.

" Hello, cap ! We'd about give you up."

" Want some coffee, Rance ? "

"No, climb onto your horses."

A scurry to mount followed, and in half-a-jiffy a dozen boys were seated on their restless horses, impatient to be off.

" What you got to shoot with ? " asked Rance.

Frank Wilbur held up a shot-gun, Milton flourished his pistol, Cy Hurd had a rifle, and each of the others had a gun of some sort.

" All right. Now we must be off. Keep behind me and don't race and don't make too much noise. We strike for the big popple grove. Already — into line. March."

He wheeled his horse and rode away at an easy gallop, followed by his laughing, jostling troop, along the road, between fields, leading to the north. The day promised to be bright, the snow was just right, deep enough to aid in detecting the wolves, and not so deep as to interfere with the speed of the horses.

It was about ten o'clock Rance pulled up on the edge of the range. " Now, then, Lincoln, you take Milt and Cy, and strike into that patch of hazel bush to the right, and remember, if you start a wolf, don't try to run him down, unless you're close onto him. He'll run in a circle — and while you're after him, fire a shot to let us know, and we'll cut across lots. When we strike his trail you pull right off, and cut across behind us. If he turns to the right or left, let us know."

It was exhilarating to breathe the keen prairie air, to feel under one's thigh the powerful swing of muscles firm as iron, to know that at any moment a wolf might start up from the brush. The horses caught the excitement and champed their bits impatiently, and spurned the glittering snow high into the air. Soon a shot was heard, and wild yells from the right division. A moment later, out from behind a popple grove loped a wolf, followed by a squad of horsemen. Instantly all of the captain's commands were forgotten. *Everybody* joined pursuit, whooping, laughing, firing, without an idea of order.

The wolf was surprised, but seemed to grasp the situation. In less than ten seconds the whole troop were in a huddle and riding fast, except Rance, who was now on the extreme left, cutting diagonally across. He fired his gun to interrupt his mob of excited hunters, and rode right into their front and yelled.

" Halt! Hold on there! "

He was very angry, and they pulled up instantly. He waited till they all came back around him.

" Now, what kind of a way of doing business is that? How many wolves are you going to kill by winding every horse in the crowd the first jump? You'll kill more horses than wolves. Now listen to me: We don't want more than *three* horses after the wolf at the same time. The others must cut him off. Don't be in a hurry — wait and see where he's heading."

The boys were silent.

" Milt and Lincoln were all right. They started the

game. But the rest of you were all wrong. Now, the wolf is in that big tow-head there. Cy, you go to the right, and, Milt, you go to the left, and I'll take the centre, and we'll see if we can go at this man-fashion."

In a few minutes they had partially encircled the grove and were moving down on it. Again the wolf broke cover, and started to the left. He was not aware of Milton and Lincoln, because they were hidden by another bunch of aspen, and Lincoln gave a wild whoop as the yellow-brown grizzled creature darted around the grove, almost under his feet, and entered the brush before the boy could collect himself.

Cassius leading, the party of four rushed into the brown hazel patch, a rushing, snorting squadron. The brush impeded and bewildered the wolf, and he doubled on his track, bursting out on the prairie again, at an oblique angle to the course of the other horsemen.

The chase became magnificent. The wolf seemed to float along the ground, his long tail waving, his ears alert. Rance was riding like mad, to intercept him, and the wolf didn't seem to understand, — but he did : just as Ladrone seemed upon him, he disappeared. Rance reined sharply to the left, and waved his hat to Lincoln, who comprehended the situation. The wolf had entered a deep ravine, which ran to the southeast, and was doubling again, seeking his den.

"He's going back!" shouted Milton, letting Mark out for the first time. The grand brute, snorting with delight, slid over the ground, light as the wolf himself.

The rider sat him as if he were standing still, but exulting to feel the vast power and pride of his horse.

"See that horse run!" shouted Lincoln, in delight. The majestic colt swept down upon the wolf, as if all eyes were upon him, and his honor at stake. Milton could see the head of the wolf then. It seemed as if Mark must run him down, so certainly equal were the distances, but Mark thundered down the slope and into the swale a few rods in advance. The wolf whipped out behind, — Milton fired twice, — but the fugitive kept on. He reined Mark sharply to the right, with unabated speed, and rode back up the slope, on a wide curve, waving his hat to show the way the wolf had gone.

But the others had seen the change in course, and were driving down on the wily fugitive in a body. Ed Blackler was in the lead, his shot-gun ready, guiding his horse by the pressure of his knees. He was upon him with a rush, and fired. The wolf leaped into the air, rose, avoided the rush of the black, and started into the brush. Now was Lincoln's opportunity, and striking Cassius with the flat of his hand, he swept upon the wolf like a whirlwind. The wounded beast fell under the feet of the wild-eyed Cassius, who would have trampled fire in his excitement.

When Milton rode up to the circle of panting horses and excited boys, Lincoln was handing the tail to Ed Blackler, and Rance was saying : —

"The ears are yours, Link. That crazy old fool of yours did the business."

The boys were delighted with the result. Everybody praised the superb run made by Mark, the good shooting done by Ed Blackler, and the mad courage of Cassius, who bore the marks of the wolf's teeth on his legs.

"Now we'll strike for Rattlesnake Grove, and go through every patch of hazel brush on the way," commanded Rance. But it was high noon before they started another wolf, and he (or she) popped into a den just as Rance was drawing near enough to shoot. The ground was too hard to dig him out.

About this time they began to look for the commissary cutter, which they had left far behind, and forgotten until now. They were hungry. One of the riders was ordered to ride back to a swell, and signal the approach of the "supply train." In the meantime the others, after blanketing the horses, began to collect dry limbs, and to build a fire in the centre of one of the groves.

It was a fine moment as they grouped themselves around the smoking fire, toasting sausages on hazel twigs and drinking coffee. Nothing could be seen but trees, gray sky, and the blanketed horses. They resembled a camp of brigands. At last the captain said, —

"Fall in, everybody."

Lincoln saw the next wolf standing on the north side of a little round grove, listening intently, his head on one side, his steel-like muscles tense and quivering. He was looking away, and Lincoln whispered regretfully to Milton, "Oh, for a rifle!"

"Ride onto him with y'r pistol."

Milton was cautious: "No, wait; there's Cy Hurd, he's got a rifle. Why, he don't see him! the donkey! Hay! *there* he is!"

At Milton's shout the wolf gave a prodigious leap, and set off across the open plain, followed by Cyrus Hurd and his squad. Rance was far to the east.

Hurd fired his revolver as he rode, and soon the three divisions were riding furiously, side by side, nearly half a mile apart: Cy in the lead, but losing as the wolf laid himself to the work. It was a long chase, and one by one the fellows reined in, till only Rance and Blackler at the right, and Lincoln and Milton at the left, and Cy Hurd in the centre, were in the race.

Cy knew that the wolf would surely turn to the left, and pressed him hard, therefore, till he dropped into a deep ravine, running at right angles to the course. He pulled up short, unable to tell which way his game had gone, while both of the wing divisions pressed on at full speed, each expecting to intercept the cunning beast.

Milton was satisfied the wolf had not time to pass, so turned sharply as he entered the ravine, and thundered down to the right. He soon reined up, and was standing irresolute when the wolf came sailing around a bend in the gully. Milton will never forget the cool, cunning, yet astonished look in his eyes. He seemed a piece of faultless machinery doing its work without noise, friction, or waste of power.

Milton fired twice as the animal floated up the bank, Mark after him. On level ground above, the wolf was no match for the colt, and twice turned as his pursuer thundered upon his heels. The last time he gained time to cross the ravine again, and when Milton and Lincoln reached the level again, he was ten rods away, and running like the wind, apparently undisturbed.

" *Now*, Mark! " yelled Milton, and for the first time in his life Mark brought out all his powers. With nostrils expanded, and wide eyes full of fire, he spurned the loose snow, in a glittering shower, into the eyes of Cassius, close behind him, with Lincoln yelling like a Sioux. Now Cassius's reserve power began to tell. Slowly he drew ahead of Mark, who was worn with his previous race. With wild head gauming, Cassius tore down upon the now wholly desperate animal. Cassius, comparatively fresh, could overhaul the wolf, but Lincoln knew the wolf's tricks, and allowed the horse to gain but slowly, inch by inch. He was but a few rods in advance, and running silently and apparently easily, the play of his muscles concealed by his long hair. The pace was terrific, and Cassius tugged no more at the rein ; he was running his best, his breath roaring. The wolf, almost under his feet, had a curiously calm expression, not scared, not angry; then something happened. The earth shook, the sky turned black, and strange noises filled the air, faint and far away.

When he had time to think about these singular phenomena, Lincoln perceived that he was lying on the ground, and that the boys all in a group were shooting the wolf. He turned his head and saw Cassius galloping wildly in a circle, the stirrups pounding his ribs.

Then he thought he would get up, but one leg felt numb and heavy, and he sank back on the ground, just as the boys caught sight of him, and came riding up.

He waved his cap and gave a feeble shout, to show that he was not dead.

Milton reached him first, looking very queer.

"What's the matter? Hurt?"

"I guess my leg's banged up a little; it's numb. Where's my horse?"

"We'll take care of the horse," said Rance, as he dismounted. "Somebody get that cutter, quick. Catch the horse and take his blanket off. We'll need it to wrap Link up in. He's hurt pretty bad, I reckon."

There was a horrible limpness in one leg which Rance saw and shuddered at.

The leg began to pain him a good deal, but Lincoln said: "I guess I ain't hurt very much. The snow kind o' broke the force of the fall." But he groaned when they lifted him into the cutter, and the boys were badly scared. Rance got in with him, and the others fell in behind — a melancholy train. Rance wondered what Lincoln's mother would say when she saw Cassius being led riderless down the road. They were a long way from home, and when the road permitted it, Rance drove hard. He stopped at John Moss's house for some extra blankets, and Bettie came out to see the wounded boy.

"I'm all right," he said, though his chin trembled. "It don't hurt — much — now."

Bettie tucked him in nicely, but took the side of the wild animals, girl fashion: —

2 D

"It serves you right" (she didn't realize how badly he was hurt) "to go chasing those poor little wolves all over the prairie. How do you s'pose you'd feel to have a whole raft of Indians ridin' down on top of *you*, and shootin' pistols and yellin'?"

"Wouldn't feel much worse'n I do now," he said, with a wan smile.

One by one the hunters dropped off till only Rance and Milton and Cy were left to take the wounded comrade to his home.

"Milt, you ride — ahead — and tell mother — I'm all right," said Lincoln; and Milton spurred on, obediently.

It was long after dark when Milton knocked at the door and Mrs. Stewart came to the door. Something in his face alarmed her instantly. "Where is Lincoln? Is he hurt?"

"Not very bad, I guess. Cassius fell with him. He's comin' in the cutter."

"Tell Duncan, quick. He's in the barn. I've expected that colt would do something."

When Lincoln felt his mother's arm round his neck, his eyes were dim with tears. He had never seen her look like that, so white and drawn. Mr. Stewart was very grave, also, as he lifted his son out of the sleigh, for the limp leg was plainly broken.

"Saddle Rob," he said to Milton, "and get a doctor as quick as the Lord'll let you." Milton was in the saddle and clattering down the road before his chum was fairly in his bed. Rance stayed with him till the doctor came.

CHAPTER XXVI

LINCOLN GOES AWAY TO SCHOOL

LINCOLN had known little about sickness up to this time, and the sickness and confinement which followed produced a great change in him. To be stretched on a bed like a trussed turkey, helpless and drawn with pain, while Owen and Tommy, blowsy with health, were enjoying the sun and air, was very hard to bear. For many days he lay in his mother's dim little room, unable even to turn himself, his bones weary and sore with contact with the mattress, till his ruddy color faded out, his arms grew thin, and his hands almost translucent. The hearty, noisy boy became as weak and dependent and querulous as a teething child.

It was a wonderful trial to him. It taught him patience and self-reliance, for he was necessarily a great deal alone. His mother had her work to do, and so did Owen and his father, but Tommy, with his queer little ways, came to be a great solace to him. Rance and Milton and Shepard Warren, and others of his schoolmates came of a Saturday to see him, sliding into the room awkwardly to say, —

"Hello, Link, how are you?" but they only stayed a few minutes and vanished into the outer sunlit world from which he was barred. Their hearty dislike for sickness made his lot all the harder by contrast. Each day the outside world seemed farther away and more beautiful to him.

Sometimes lying alone, with all the family absent, he heard the jingle of sleigh-bells, and the singing of young girls, and his heart grew sore and he wept. In the sound of those young voices lay all the splendid winter life, from which he was shut out, and which it seemed he was never again to join. He sometimes reproached them in his heart for being so unmindful of his pain and weariness.

His brain was very active — too busy, in fact, for his good. Hopes, aspirations, plans, hardly articulate heretofore, now took shape in his mind. He was sixteen years of age, and in his own mind quite grown up, and the question of an education had come to dominate all others. He did not like farm work. The mud and grime and lonely toil connected with it made each year more irksome, while the town and other trades and professions grew correspondingly more alluring. Again and again, when they were alone, Rance and he had planned ways of escape together.

Captain Knapp was secretly pleased to have his boy ambitious, but hoped to keep him with him in spite of education. He had yielded the fall before, and Rance was attending school in Rock River Normal School, intending to fit himself to teach. Milton had also secured this privilege, but Mr. Stewart held out.

"You have all the education you need," he said, " if you're going to farm, and I don't intend to fit you to be a shyster lawyer in a small town."

All these things the helpless boy turned over in his thoughts as he lay stretched on his bed. The coming in of Rance or Milton added fuel to his fire, for they were full of talk concerning their school life. Their hands were growing soft and supple, their best coats being worn every day fitted better, for the boys accommodated themselves to the garments. They wore standing collars and fashionable ties, and their shoes were polished, and all these changes were eloquent of a world where hands were something more than hooks with which to steady a plough or push a currycomb. "I'll be with you next year, boys, or bust a tug," he said resolutely.

Mrs. Stewart sympathized with him in the way of mothers, but knew too little of the world to believe that her boys could earn a living in any other way than by farming. She counselled patience, saying, "Things'll come around by and by," which was a favorite phrase with her.

As soon as he was able to write, Lincoln composed a letter to his Uncle Robert, who was a carpenter and joiner in Ripon. To him Lincoln unconsciously appealed with boyish directness, telling of his hurt, and of his hope of being able to go to the Seminary the coming year. A few days later, he was surprised and deeply pleased to receive a letter in reply, in which his uncle said, "Times are slack just now, and I think I'll run out and see you."

The following Tuesday he came, a big, red-bearded man, like his brother Duncan in some ways, but gentler, more meditative. He was a good deal of a student, and had been a notable fiddler in his youth, but had given it up because it made him discontented with sawing and hammering. " My theory is, if you can't do the best thing in life, do the next best," he said once in speaking of life's problems.

He had visited his brother's family several times since their removal to the prairie, for he was very fond of children, and had none of his own. He often remarked of Lincoln, " He'll be an orator — this lad," and this time he came with a definite proposition to make concerning his favorite nephew.

" See here, Duncan," he said, almost at once, " you've a discontented, ambitious boy on your hands. He don't like farming, he's just at the age when a schooling is necessary. Why not let him come home with me? He can go to school in season, and help me at my trade during vacation. Mary and me have no children at all, and you have three and more a-comin'. You couldn't hold this boy more than five years more, anyway, and I can do for him at small expense what you don't feel able to do at all."

The good mother was at first profoundly saddened by this proposal, but Robert assured her that Lincoln could come home any time she sent for him, and gradually she came to the point of consenting. Duncan took a very practical view of it. He had held two very spirited arguments with Lincoln, wherein the boy declared with great emphasis: " I will not wear out my life milking cows. I hate it. Part of farming I like, but I am going to have an education in something else beside hauling out manure." Duncan knew that his boy was leaving him, anyway, and that Robert would be made happier by having Lincoln come into his lonely life. He had Owen and Tommy, and Owen, at least, had promised to follow in their father's footsteps.

It was an anxious moment when the result of their argument was communicated to Lincoln. He was sitting in an easy chair, with his school books beside him, as his father and mother came in from the kitchen. His mother had tears in her eyes, but his father merely blew his nose as he said, —

"Well, Lincoln, we've decided to let you go home with Robert as soon as you're able."

As he looked at them in stupefaction, his book slipped from his fingers, and his mother came over and, stooping down, kissed his hair, and put her arm about his neck. Tears were on his own cheeks as he said, —

"I won't go, mother, if you don't want me to."

Then Duncan said, "Come in, Rob; we've told him."

Robert Stewart came in briskly. "Well! Well!" he said loudly. "What's all this crying about? We're not going to put him in jail. Come now, if you're going to take it so hard as all that, I back out."

But this sadness was only momentary, after all. Mrs. Stewart resumed her serenity of manner, and nothing further was said about the matter, so far as the parents and the boys were concerned.

After a few days' visit Robert returned to Ripon, saying just as he was leaving, "Now take care of yourself, boy, and be ready to come on in April."

There was another moment of sadness when he told Rance and Milton about it. Rance looked very glum and said nothing, but Milton cried out : —

"Criminy! that's a deadner on us. I thought sure you'd be with us next spring. Well, it's a good chance for you. You can go to college now, sure."

"That's what I will," Lincoln stoutly replied.

He was able to read now, and life began to be less wearisome. He read — read anything — the *Toledo Blade*, *The Ledger*, *The Saturday Night*, "Ivanhoe," "The Farmer's Book," Milton — anything at all. As he began to grow stronger he set himself to study, going over his books in earnest, to keep fresh in them. He thought of nothing else but the new life opening up for him. Sometimes he was sad at the thought of leaving home, and there came moments when the great world outside seemed about to open up for him. He grew rapidly in intellectual grace during these months of confinement.

At last when the sun of March had melted the snow from the chip-pile, he crawled forth into the open air for the first time, the ghost of his old-time self, a pale, sad boy on crutches, with big, wistful brown eyes sweeping the horizon. The prairie chickens were whooping on the knolls, ducks were again streaming northward, and the hens in the chip-pile were caw-cawing as of old. On the south side of the house a little green grass

shone in the sun.   It was all so beautiful, so good to
see and hear and feel, that the boy was dumb with
ecstasy.   It was as if the world were new, as if no
spring had ever before passed over his head, so sweet
and awesome and thrillingly glorious was the good old
earth.   The boy lifted his thin face and big sombre
eyes to the sky, his nerves quivering beneath the touch
of the wind, the downpour of the sun, and the vibrant
voices of the flying fowl.   Life at that moment ceased
to be simple and confined — at that moment he entered
upon his young manhood.

The prairies allured him as never before, as the day
for leaving them drew near, but at the thought of parting from Rance and Owen and his mother, a big lump
filled his throat.   Why was it that an act so wise, so
beneficial as this one seemed, should now become so
filled with painful sacrifice ?   He puzzled and suffered
over this.   It lessened the pain only a hair's weight to
say, " I'll be back at Christmas."   The present sorrow
outweighted all future promise of joy.

Seeding was in full drive on the Saturday when he
went over to say good-by to Rance.   The sky was
softly, radiantly blue, and two cranes were weaving
wondrous patterns against a radiant cloud, wheeling
majestically, uttering their resounding notes — the walls
of heaven seemed to vibrate to their calls; frogs were
peeping in the marshes, the chickens were beginning
their evening chorus.   Robins were singing from the
tops of the Lombardy poplars which he had planted.
The boy's heart was big with emotion, and as he stood

waiting for his comrade, it seemed as if he could not say the cruel words, " good-by."

Rance saw him afar off and waved a hand, but he was driving the seeder and was obliged to watch his wheel-track closely. He wheeled his machine before he spoke.

" You don't look like a workingman. I didn't know it was Sunday," he said, with a smile.

Lincoln's eyes did not lighten. " I am going to-morrow," he said, looking away on the plain.

Rance made no reply till he had filled the seeder-box with wheat. " I thought it was next Monday."

" No, I'm going to-morrow."

" Well, I wish I was going, too."

" I wish you was," was all Lincoln could say, and then they were silent again.

" When you coming back ? "

" Oh, Christmas time, I guess."

There was another silence, then Rance said : " Well, this won't do for me." He took up the reins. " Write and let me know how you like it."

" You bet ! You must write, too."

" All right, I will. G'wan, Bill ! " and he was off for another round.

Lincoln walked away with the pain in his throat growing more intolerable each minute. It was as if he were about to die and leave the beautiful world and all his loved ones behind.

All wept when he said good-by next day. His mother clung to him as if she could not let him go, and at last fairly flung him away, and ran out of the room. The trip on the railway train, the return to his native State, helped him to take the obstruction out of his throat, but some subtle presence instructed him in these words : " *You are leaving the prairie forever.*"

LADRONE

And, " what of Ladrone " — do you ask ?
Oh ! friend, I am sad at the name.
My splendid fleet roan ! — The task
You require is a hard one at best.
Swift as the spectral coyote, as tame
To my voice as a sweetheart, an eye
Like a pool in the woodland asleep,
Brown, clear, and calm, with color down deep,
Where his brave, proud soul seemed to lie —

Ladrone !   There's a spell in the word.
The city walls fade on my eye — the roar
  Of its traffic grows dim
  As the sound of the wind in a dream.
My spirit takes wing like a bird.
Once more I'm asweep on the plain,
The summer wind sings in my hair ;
Once again I hear the wild crane
Crying out of the stemming air ;
White clouds are adrift on the breeze,
The flowers nod under my feet,
And under my thighs, 'twixt my knees,
Again as of old I can feel
The roll of Ladrone's firm muscles, the reel
Of his chest — see the thrust of fore-limb
And hear the dull trample of heel.

We thunder behind the mad herd.
My singing whip swirls like a snake.
Hurrah!   We swoop on like a bird,
With my pony's proud record at stake —
For the shaggy, swift leader has stride
Like the last of a long kingly line;
Her eyes flash fire through her hair;
She tosses her head in disdain;
Her mane streams wide on the air —
She leads the swift herd of the plain
As a wolf-leader leads his gaunt pack,
On the slot of the desperate deer —
Their exultant eyes savagely shine.

But down on her broad shining back
Stings my lash like a rill of red flame —
Huzzah, my wild beauty!   Your best;
Will you teach my Ladrone a new pace?
Will you break his proud heart in a shame
By spurning the dust in his face?
The herd falls behind and is lost,
As we race neck and neck, stride and stride.
Again the long lash hisses hot
Along the gray mare's glassy hide —
Aha, she is lost! she does not respond.
The storm of her speed's at its best —
Now I lean to the ear of my roan
And shout — letting fall the light rein.
Like a hound from the leash, my Ladrone

Swoops ahead —
We're alone on the plain!

*   *   *   *   *   *   *

Ah! how that wild living comes back!
Alone on the wide, solemn prairie
I ride with my rifle in hand,
My eyes on the watch for the wary
And beautiful antelope band.
Or sleeping at night in the grasses, I hear
Ladrone grazing near in the gloom.
His listening head on the sky
I see etched complete to the ear.
From the river below comes the boom
Of the bittern, the trill and the cry
Of frogs in the pool, and shrill crickets' chime,
Making ceaseless and marvellous rhyme.

But what of his fate? Did he die
When that terrible tempest was done?
When he staggered with you to the light,
And your fight with the Norther was won,
Did he live like a guest ever more?

No, friend, not so. I sold him — outright.

What! sold your preserver, your mate, he who
Through wind and wild snow and deep night
Brought you safe to a shelter at last?
Did you, when the danger had end,
Forget your dumb hero — your friend?

Forget! no, nor can I.   Why, man,
It's little you know of such love
As I felt for him!   You think that you feel
The same deep regard for your span,
Blanketed, shining, and clipped to the heel.
But my horse was companion and guard —
My playmate, my ship on the sea
Of dun grasses — in all kinds of weather,
Unhoused and hungry sometimes, he
Served me for love and needed no tether.

No, I do not forget; but who
Is the master of fortune and fate?
Who does as he wishes and not as he must?
When I sold my preserver, my mate,
My faithfullest friend — man, I wept.
Yes, I own it!   His beautiful eyes
Seemed to ask what it meant.
And he kept them fixed on me in startled surprise,
As another hand led him away.
And the last that I heard of my roan,
Was the sound of his shrill, pleading neigh!

O magic west wind of the mountain,
O steed with the stinging mane,
In sleep I draw rein at the fountain,
And wake with a shiver of pain;
For the heart and the heat of the city
Are walls and prison and chain.
Lost my Ladrone — gone the wild living —
I dream, but my dreaming is vain.

CONCLUSION

WHEN he next saw Sun Prairie, Lincoln was twenty-four years of age, a full-grown man, with a big mustache. Shortly after he went to Ripon his father's younger brother died, and Duncan returned to the homestead in Wisconsin, and Lincoln had never made his promised visit to his friends on Sun Prairie.

It was a changed world, a land of lanes and fields and houses hid in groves of trees which he had seen set out. No one rode horseback any more. Where the cattle had roamed and the boys had raced the prairie wolves, fields of corn and oats waved. No open prairie could be found. Every quarter-section, every acre, was ploughed. The wild flowers were gone. Tumbleweed, smartweed, pigweed, mayflower, and all the other plants of semi-civilization had taken the place of the wild asters, pea-vines, crow's-foot, sunflowers, snakeweed, sweet-williams, and tiger-lilies. The very air seemed tamed and set to work at the windmills which rose high above every barn, like great sunflowers.

Rance met him at the station, and together the two young men rode up the lanes which they had known so well. It was mid June, and the corn was deep green and knee high. The cattle in the pasture, sleek and heavy, did not look up as the teams rolled by. "They are not much like the cattle of the range," said Lincoln. "It seems a long time ago, don't it?"

Rance smiled in his old-time fashion, and slowly said, "Seems longer to me than to you. I've spent all my vacations at home."

Lincoln sighed a little. "I wish I had taken Madison instead of Ripon, but it was a ground-hog case. How do you like teaching?"

"First rate. It gives me time to read, and pays as well as anything I can get into."

"Do you go back to Cedarville next year?"

"No; since I wrote you I've got a better thing. I go as assistant principal of the Winnesheik High School."

"That's good. I hate teaching. It looks now as though I'd have to be a shyster lawyer, as father says; but I'm going into politics a little. They're going to run father for county treasurer, and that will put me in line for promotion. That's Old Man Bacon's place. Old man must be dead. He never would fix up like that."

"Oh, Lime Gilman did that. He's moved in on the old man. Old Bill fell and hurt his back, and can't do anything but just hobble around."

"That's hard lines for him; what a worker he was! I'd like to see Marietta. Is she as handsome as ever?"

"Pretty near. Lime takes care of her. They have the best furniture in the township. Lime is the same easy-going chap that he used to be."

As they approached the old place, Lincoln's heart beat distinctly faster. It was like rediscovering a part of himself to retrace his steps. He could shut his eyes and see every slope, every ravine, every sink-hole; but when he came opposite the house, it was less familiar than he had hoped. The trees had grown prodigiously. The Lombardys towered far over the house and barn. The wall was shaded by the maples he had planted, and the wind-break had become a grove. Something mystical had gone out of it all. It was not so important as his imagination had made it. It was simpler, thinner of texture some way, and he drove on with a feeling of disappointment.

The great change of all lay in the predominance of the dairy interest. The wheat-fields were few and small, the pastures many. Lincoln spoke of this.

"Yes," replied Rance, "when the wheat crops began to fail, all these changes came with a rush. The country went from grain to cows in a couple of years. I used to notice a difference every year when I came home. Less wheat, more cows."

"That's Hutchison's place; looks very much the same. Ben at home?"

"No, Ben went to Dakota. There's a big exodus just now for the Green River valley. Hum Bunn — you remember Hum and our fight? — well, he's out there, and Doudney and the Dixons and Peases. Milt thought of going, but he married Eileen Deering and got a county office, and that settled him."

"I heard about that. Milt will take care of himself. He'll joke his way into Congress sure as eggs raise chickens, as Old Man Doudney used to say."

The country looked rich and tame. Every acre was cultivated, — all loaded with hay or corn or timothy; no sign of the prairie grass existed. Along the lanes clover had taken root, the hazel bushes had been cut down by the grading-machine.

" I'd like to see a strip of wild meadow. Is it all gone? " asked Lincoln.

" I don't know of any — not a rod. There may be some off to the north where we used to hunt wolves. We might go and see."

" Let's do it. It would do me a heap o' good to see some of the good old weeds and grasses. I suppose a fellow'd have to go clear to the Missouri River to see a vacant quarter-section."

" I don't believe there is any vacant land in the state — there may be some in the extreme northwest, over beyond the Coon Fork. Last year brought a tremendous rush of settlement, and I hear everything was taken clear through to the line. Norwegians came in swarms. Well, there's the Knapp place — not so much changed ; trees have grown up, that's all."

Lincoln began to smile. " I used to stand very much in awe of your sisters. Is Agnes at home? "

" Yes. Bess is in Dakota. She married Ed Bartle."

" I remember your writing to me about it. I used to think they were the handsomest women in the world."

" Owen, I hear, is a great sprinter," said Rance, after a little pause.

" Owen is all right," said Lincoln. " He's 'short stop' in the college nine, and has held first place on the two hundred and twenty yards course for three years. He's actually had his name in the Chicago papers and is quite set up about it. He's a good all-round athlete, but not a bit ambitious otherwise."

" I'd like to see the boy. He was a queer little josy when we all rode horses on the prairie. By the way, do you ride ? "

" Haven't been on a horse since I left here."

" Neither have I. It might be a curious job to dig up some saddles and ride out to-morrow."

" Good ! I'm with you."

As they drove into the yard, Captain Knapp came out to see them. He looked much older than Lincoln had expected, but he held his place much better than most of his old acquaintances. Lincoln had grown to him, but not beyond him. He was very cordial in his quiet way, and led his guest to the house, where Agnes, a pale, thin girl of twenty-eight or thirty, stood to meet them.

She was very pretty in spite of her pallor, and met Lincoln with outstretched hands.

" We had almost given up expecting you," she said.

As they sat talking that evening, Lincoln was aware of curious changes in his own mind. The familiar voices of these friends sank deep into his old self. Agnes seemed two persons. At one moment he saw her with the eyes of his awestruck boyhood, and the next she was a pale young woman, almost painfully shy in his presence. Captain Knapp was as aloof as ever. He, too, had grown. His deep black eyes, his slow, thoughtful voice, his well-chosen words, kept him in his place — a man of really deep thought and serene outlook on the world.

The parlor was unchanged except that mixed with the spatter-work were some engravings which Rance had sent home from time to time. Rance slept in the same room on the east side of the house, and when Lincoln looked in, he had a return to his old boyish timidity before his hero.

He lay awake till late, musing over the many changes eight years had brought to Sun Prairie. Change was going on just as fast during the six years he had lived here, but he had not observed it. Coming back in this way, all the deaths, births, marriages, and departures made up a long list which saddened and bewildered him. It was as if some supporting, steadying hand had been withdrawn, and the wheels of life had hurried suddenly in their courses. This was an illusion, but he could not brush the thought aside.

In the talk that followed next day, he learned that many of the younger sons were away at school or had become successful professional men. The prairie had seemingly turned out a large number of bright minds. The Grove district had done as well.

In the afternoon Rance took Lincoln out to the barn, and after some search dug a couple of rusty saddles out of a barrel, and with a look of mingled sadness and amusement said : —

"From the looks of these saddles the rats thought we were done with them. I guess they're right. It would lame us, anyhow, to ride these big horses; if we had Ladrone and Ivanhoe, the case would be different. I guess we'll have to drive."

Ladrone and Ivanhoe! As he spoke these words, Lincoln's heart leaped and his throat swelled. The plain with all its herds, grasses, wild-fowl, and fruits, were associated with those words. Both those beautiful creatures were dead and their saddles covered with rust. Nothing else could have spoken as those dusty, rusty, rat-eaten pieces of leather.

Both boys were silent as they rode away on their search for a little piece of the vanishing prairie. They drove along dusty, weedy lanes, out of which the grass-hoppers rose in clouds. Big hay-barns and painted houses stood where the shacks of early settlers once cowered in the winds of winter. Pastures were where the strawberries grew, and fields of barley rippled where the wild oats once waved. The ponds were dried up; the hazel bushes cut down; not even a single tree of the tow-heads existed, except along somebody's line fence.

The king-bird was still on the wing, haughty as ever, and a few gophers whistled. All else of the prairie had vanished as if it had all been dreamed. The pigeons, the plover, the chickens, the vultures, the cranes, the wolves — all gone — all gone!

At last, along a railway track that gashed the hill and spewed gravel along the bottom of what had been a beautiful green dip in the plain, the two friends came upon a slip of prairie sod.

Lincoln leaped from the carriage with a whoop of delight and flung himself into the grass.

"Here it is! Here they are — the buffalo berries, the rose bushes, the rattlesnake weed, wild barley, plums — all of it."

Carefully, minutely, the prairie boys studied the flowers and grasses of the sloping banks, as they recalled the days of cattle-herding, berrying, hazel-nutting, and all the other now vanished pleasures of boy life on the prairies, and on them both fell a sudden realization of the inexorable march of civilization. They shivered under the passing of the wind, as though it were the stream of time, bearing them swiftly away ever farther from their life on the flowering prairies. Then softly Rance quoted : —

> "We'll meet them yet, they are not lost forever ;
> They lie somewhere, those splendid prairie lands,
> Far in the West, untouched of plough and harrow,
> Unmarked by man's all-desolating hands."

TO MY YOUNG READERS:

When I began to write the pages which make up this volume, I had no expectation that they would be published in book form; in truth I had no great faith that they would ever assume the dignity of print. This was in 1885 and I, a youth of twenty-five, was living in an attic room—almost the traditional garret —in Jamaica Plain, a lovely suburb of Boston. I had been a year in that storied city, and I was just beginning to earn a very meager wage by teaching literature to the pupils of a school of oratory on Beacon Hill.

My father and mother and my sister Jessie were far away in Dakota, while I in some illogical way had taken the backtrail, for it was from Boston that my father, a native of Maine, had started on his western exploration. He had been a shipping clerk for a dry goods firm on Tremont street when in the spring of 1850 he decided to set out for Milwaukee, Wisconsin. He never retraced his steps; on the contrary he had kept moving, moving, always toward "the sunset regions," until at last he had found a more or less permanent camping-place in Brown County, South Dakota.

I tell you this in order that you may see me as I was, a lonely western youth, longing for familiar things while at the same time I was happy in my opportunity to share the history, the books, the music, and the drama of Boston. I began to write *The Prairie Corn Husking* in a mood of homesickness, but there was more than homesickness in my impulse, for I had be-

---

This is the Introduction written by Hamlin Garland for the 1926 Allyn and Bacon edition, which was used as a school text.

gun to hope that I might be, in some small way, the historian
of homely Middle Border family life. All my life I had read of
New England husking bees, apple parings, barn-raisings, and
the like, finding in them the charm of my ancestral life; but no
writer, so far as I knew, had ever put the farm life of the West
into literature, either as poem, essay, or novel. With no confidence in my ability to write a story, I believed I could set down
in plain words the life I had known and shared. With a resolution to maintain the proper balance of rain and sun, dust and
mud, toil and play, I began an article descriptive of an Iowa
corn husking, faintly hoping it might please some editor.

You see I had the advantage of having spent many days in
husking corn. Indeed I knew every detail of each season's work
on a Middle Border farm. My experiences were still fresh in
my mind and writing was made easy for me by the magic of
distance, and also by the contrast between my deeply exciting
city life and the life I was about to describe. As I went on with
my composition, my design broadened. From a resolution to
write of my personal boy-life experiences, I began to dream of
depicting the habits and customs of my elders. I became a short-
story writer and later a novelist and chronicler of the region I
like to call the Middle Border. For forty years I have kept to
this field.

My plan, my critics say, was nobler than my product, and
with this I must agree; but at its lowest you will find, in
Boy Life on the Prairie, an honest and careful attempt to delineate a border community building and planting from 1870 to
1880—a settlement as seen and shared by a boy from ten to
twenty.

You may, if you wish, substitute Richard Garland for "Duncan Stewart," Hamlin for "Lincoln," and Frank for "Owen," for
this book is substantially made up of the doings of my own fam-

ily. "Rance Knapp" is Burton Babcock, who in 1898 went into the Yukon with me, a trip which I have described in a book called *The Long Trail*. "The McTurgs" are in truth my mother's family, the McClintocks, who figure so largely in *A Son of the Middle Border* and *A Daughter of the Middle Border*. David McClintock was my boyhood hero, a handsome, dark-eyed giant of a man who played the violin with a skill which enraptured me. Most of the other characters have actual proto-types, and the scene of this volume is mainly that of Dry Run Prairie, about six miles north and east of Osage, the county seat of Mitchell County, Iowa, which was at that time on the line of the Middle Border. It was a level country, with long, low swells like waves of a quiet ocean, and Osage was but a village with a new railway "spur" running up from the south. All of the events, even those in fictional form, are actual, although in some cases I have combined experiences of other boys with my own.

It is a vanished world now—that of the prairie—much more deeply buried than my words at the ending of this book would indicate; and many of the customs and characters herein re-corded have no other place, save in the memories of men and women of my own age. I take it as a high compliment that you and your teachers have found in this homely chronicle some-thing worthy of use in your classroom. Perhaps at some time I may be able to read some of it for you.

It remains to say that I wrote this book while still a young man. It is therefore not an old man's dream of the past; it is the recorded recollection of a writer of thirty years of age.

With best wishes to you all,

I am faithfully your historian of the homely things of the Middle Border,

Hamlin Garland

AUTHOR'S NOTES

Page   1—*hickory shirt*: a blue and white checked shirt. Hickory was perhaps the name of the brand.

Page   2—*coolly* [*coolee*]: the French word *coulée* means a little valley, scooped out by running water. At the bottom of every coulee is a little trout stream. The word is used throughout the Northwest, in all the region explored by the French.

Page   9—*crow's-foot*: a tall grass similar to bluejoint (see note on *bluejoint*) with three stalks at the top like the toes of a crow. The *wild oat* is a similar grass but its berry has a barb. The three grasses, bluejoint, crow's-foot, and wild oat, were often intermingled, growing tall and rank in the upland meadows.

Page   10—*share*: a broad, horizontal blade on a plough which runs below the ground and divides the upper soil from the lower. The *standard* is a steel support which extends down to hold the share underneath the ground.

Page   11—*prairie chickens*: the prairie chicken is the pinnate grouse. The *partridge* is the ruffed wood grouse of the north, the one that drums on a log. The *quail* is a much smaller bird and usually lives all winter in flocks.

Page   13—*coulter*: a knife which stands upright in front of the standard of the plough and cuts the soil into strips about fourteen inches wide.

These notes were prepared by Hamlin Garland for the 1926 Allyn and Bacon edition, which was used as a school text.

Page   19—*popple trees*: a native poplar with a round, trembling leaf and a trunk perfectly white like the birch. Groves of these were commonly called "tow-heads." The poplar tree belongs to the cottonwood family.

Page   20—*burr oaks*: smallish sturdy oak trees, somewhat similar in shape to an apple tree, growing a burr acorn.

Page   25—*dare-goal*: the games of goal or "gool" were all similar in that the object of the game was to avoid being the last man touched. The goals were generally established a certain distance apart, sides chosen, and the men at each goal would dare the other side. In some cases the man touched became a prisoner and could be rescued when a man from his own side touched him. In other cases, when touched he became a partisan of the other side. Other games of goal were "stink gool" and simply "gool."

Page   27—*linkum vity*: a phrase taken from an expression meaning very hard wood.

Page   48—*open days of winter*: warm thawing days,—warm enough to work without an overcoat.

Page   50—*counters*: the hard upper part of the heel of a boot.

Page   63—*drags*: the prairie farmers used the word "drag" to mean a harrow. The drag was made in two ways: first, two large pieces of wood were studded with iron teeth and fastened together somewhat like the letter A. This was called the "A-drag," or "A-harrow." Second, the hinged drag consisted of two square sections of criss-cross framework set with square-pointed iron teeth and hinged together. The drag was drawn diagonally so that the teeth would not track closely but cut individual paths and so pulverize the soil more thoroughly.

Page   64—*south forty*: a section consisted of 640 acres. The section was divided into quarters of 160 acres each, which in turn were divided into halves or quarters, and a farmer usually spoke of these divisions according to their position as the "east eighty," or the "northwest forty."

Page   68—*sink-hole*: this was a wonderful feature of the prairie —to the boys. It was a circular depression in the soil from six to thirty feet deep with a hole in the bottom through which the water disappeared. These holes were found only where limestone lay underneath the soil and where there were underground caverns into which the water ran. When the Stewarts first went to the prairie, some of these sink-holes during certain parts of the year were inhabited by wild animals. The basins filled up and almost entirely disappeared as thrifty farmers ploughed around or through them.

Page   70—*lapped half*: when the horses pulling the drag were driven across the field, they were turned and driven back with one horse on the mark made by the harrow and the other horse on the unharrowed land. In this way the drag lapped half over the ground already harrowed. Lincoln's job was to keep the horses exactly astride the outer mark of the harrow.

Page   95—*bluejoint*: a tall beautiful grass, growing often as high as a man's shoulder. Apparently it is green, but close study shows that the joints, which are six or eight inches apart, are really dark blue or purple, the color shading off above and below the joints. The boys chewed the joints for the sweet juice. In the autumn before withering and becoming sear, the grass turns a reddish purple.

Page 107—*doodles*: conical piles of hay about shoulderhigh, so built as to shed the rain. Owen enjoyed sliding down these piles.

Page 123—*thunder-pumpers*: this bird, which makes a queer noise like a suction pump, is a kind of heron, grayish in color with long wings, a long neck, and almost no body. It is a solitary bird, inhabiting lonely bends in the river, and standing for hours on one foot in the water. *chokeberries*: these are really wild cherries. They grow in beautiful ruby clusters, and are very ornamental but very astringent, puckering the mouth and throat. As the season advances, they turn almost black, and are quite delicious. *sheep-sorrel*: a low, green, and very sour plant. *Indian tobacco*: a little fuzzy, green plant that has a soft, white, velvety flower, in a cluster at the top. The juice of the plant resembles that of tobacco. *kerosene torches*: these were made by fastening small tin cans on the ends of poles, filling the cans with oil, and using rags for wicks. A rude, flaring light was produced. These torches were made in imitation of the torches which political parties used at that time in celebrating elections.

Page 125—*Lombardy poplars*: this tree was imported from Lombardy in Italy and was very generally planted on the prairie in the early days because it grew so rapidly, often reaching a height of ten feet in a single year. The little stick or cutting from the parent branch was planted early in June by ramming it into prepared soil. When planted in long rows, these groves formed valuable windbreaks to the north and west of the homesteads.

Page 129—*Wapseypinnicon*: [Wapsypinnicon] a small river or creek fifteen or twenty miles to the east of the Stewarts' farm.

Page 215—*Boscobel*: this town is in a rather pretty region in Wisconsin not far from Madison on the Wisconsin River. The author uses it as typifying the more charming and sheltered life of the coulee country.

Page 216—*hi spy*: the players began each game by standing in a circle while some one counted out, pointing at each player and pronouncing a word of the following ancient rime simultaneously:

> Intra, mentra, cutra corn;
> Apple seed and apple thorn;
> Wire, brier, limber, lock,
> Three geese in a flock;
> One flew east and one flew west,
> And one flew over the cuckoo's nest.

In some cases this ended the count, and the person marked by the last word was "it." Sometimes the following line was added:

> O-u-t out!

Page 262—*skimmer-bugs*: on all quiet water in midsummer these marvellous little bugs may be seen skimming about exactly like miniature six-oar row boats.

Page 266—*two-masters*: small boats with two masts.

Page 277—*old fashioned cradle*: this tool was a modification
of the scythe. Five or six long curved "fingers"
made of hickory wood set above the blade caught
and held the grain when the cradle was swung,
enabling the reaper to lay the grain in an orderly
swath.

Page 278—*gavel*: the loose mound of grain left by the cradle or
the reaper, lying in an oblong heap with the heads
all one way and the butts all another. A continuous line of gavels was called a *swath*.

Page 288—*apron*: an endless broad belt three feet or more wide
and eight or ten feet long, made of canvas and
two-inch slats set on edge. It revolved on two rol-
lers. The straw rode on top of the slats while the
chaff and wheat were carried in the crevices between the slats. The straw was delivered to the
carrier, which elevated it to the stack, while the
wheat and chaff dropped into a fanning mill, where
the chaff was cleaned from the wheat.

Page 291—*down-power*: the original horse power was a "tread"
power. The horse stood in a box and trod a moving platform. Later the "tread" power changed to
a "down" power, which permitted the use of ten
horses moving in a circle. "Mounted" power was
the same power mounted on wheels for transpor-
tation.

Page 332—*Poland-China pigs*: very large, white gentle hogs.

Page 332—*Norman horses*: about 1876 or 1877 the farmers
changed from the small, beautiful, alert Morgan
horses to the great draft horses which came from
Normandy and England.

Page 340—*gauming*: making awkward movements, such as writhing of the neck, twisting of the head, and opening of the mouth.

Page 343—*bud*: local word for a short switch.

Page 354—*liver-and-white*: every bird hunter on the Border owned a liver-and-white pointer. This kind of dog had large spots of reddish brown on a white body, the spots often very grotesquely covering part of the face, one ear, or a side of the back.

Page 357—*greenhead*: a wild duck commonly called the mallard.

Page 359—*harrow in the clouds*: the wild geese generally fly in a formation similar to the "A-harrow," with the point of the A in front, each goose breaking the force of the wind from the one behind.

Page 380—*wall-pockets*: these receptacles for newspapers and magazines, open at the top, hung on the wall. They were made of pasteboard and were usually covered with fancy cloth. *spatter-work*: a pattern or design of some object was cut out and placed on a sheet of white cardboard which was spattered with ink. When the pattern was removed, there was a design in white on a black background.

A NOTE ABOUT B. R. McELDERRY, JR.

Professor McElderry comes by his interest in Midwestern life naturally enough: he is a native Iowan with an A. B. from Grinnell College and a Ph. D. from the University of Iowa. He taught English and American literature at Wisconsin, Western Reserve, and the State College of Washington before going to Southern California in 1946. His major areas of interest are the Romantic and Victorian periods in English literature and American literature generally.